D0725403

Also by Al Robertson from Gollancz:

Crashing Heaven

WAKING HELL

Al Robertson

For my parents, Ian and Penny

This edition first published in Great Britain in 2017
by Gollancz

First published in Great Britain in 2016
by Gollancz
An imprint of the Orion Publishing Group Ltd
Carmelite House, 50 Victoria Embankment
London EC4Y 0DZ

An Hachette UK Company

1 3 5 7 9 10 8 6 4 2

A CIP catalogue record for this book
is available from the British Library

ISBN 978 1 473 20344 0

Typeset by Deltatype Ltd, Birkenhead, Merseyside
Printed in Great Britain by Clays Ltd, St Ives plc

www.allumination.co.uk
www.orionbooks.co.uk
www.gollancz.co.uk

Chapter 1

Leila's brother Dieter was dying. Lying in his cheap hospital bed, metastasised technologies writhing beneath his skin, he'd joked that at least she'd have their flat to herself for a few months.

'The pizza delivery guy's heartbroken. Doesn't know what to do with himself,' Leila replied, determined to put a brave face on it all. She went to rest her hand on his. Her virtual fingers passed through his flesh ones, her defences protecting her by refusing to simulate any physical contact between them. Two nights ago, an ancient wooden cube had buried itself in Dieter's chest and started to devour his body. She imagined its ghost tendrils touching her and flinched back, catching his eye as she did so. His sadness and guilt pierced her.

'I'm so sorry,' he began. 'So careless...'

She shushed him. 'We'll get you fixed up. And even if you do kick the bucket – well, six months and you'll be back again. Good as new. A fetch, just like me.'

'But we'll lose the flat. You'll have to go back to the Coffin Drives.'

A deep, instinctive fear lanced through her. She did her best to suppress it. 'If it comes to that, I'll cope. But it won't. I'll talk to Junky Fi, work out exactly what she sent you.' She forced confidence into her voice. 'She'll know how to kill that box. And if she can't help, Ambrose will.'

Dieter saw straight through her. 'They haven't returned your calls.'

'It's only been a day or so. Maybe Fi hasn't checked her messages. All this is down to her, she has to get in touch. And Ambrose is probably out on a binge. Or sleeping one off. It's an emergency, he has to help us.' A pause. 'One of them will.'

'Yeah,' replied Dieter, sinking back into the bed. The wires wrapped round the inside of his throat gave his voice a soft, buzzing quality. He didn't sound convinced.

Looking to distract her brother, Leila set him talking about the past. He perked up as he tossed out favourite anecdotes from Station's seven-hundred-year history, Leila laughing along with him. They almost managed to forget where they were. But at last visiting time ended and she had to leave.

'I'll be back tomorrow,' she said. 'After work.' Under the rules of the isolation room, only family could visit him – and she was the only family he had. 'Your antivirals have slowed the infection right down. Maybe the doctors will come up with something. And we'll hear from Ambrose or Fi.'

'Yes,' replied Dieter. 'We will.' He was being brave for her, wearing a mask that mirrored her own.

'You saved me after the Blood and Flesh plague,' she told him. 'No one thought you'd be able to, but you did. You'll get out of this.'

In the corridor she let the sadness take her, one more powerless relative wishing for a remade world. Then home, sleep, and another day to get through before she could see Dieter again.

The hours crawled by. The day's last appointment took her out of the office. She had to show a middle-aged couple around a small block of flats in the newly fashionable Prayer Heights district of Docklands. They were looking for a good investment. She called up the building's management systems, confirmed her visit, and then set out across town on foot.

For a few moments, her home distracted her. Docklands arced up to her left and right, a city of tens of thousands clinging to the inside surface of a kilometres-long cylinder. Ahead of her the cylinder ended in the vast round wall of the Wart, the hollowed-out asteroid that bound Docklands to its more prosperous twin, Homelands. And behind her there was a flat disc of darkness, where Docklands opened on to the void of space, pierced by the Spine and the docking pylons that ran off it. The abandoned Earth drifted lost somewhere beneath them, shaken by endless, unstoppable storms of post-human brutality. It had died long ago and – unlike Leila – it would never be reborn.

In fact, Leila had been resurrected twice. Six months after her death she was reborn as a fetch, an entirely virtual entity constructed from the digital memories she'd amassed while alive. Her avatar simulated her living self, aging slowly as post-mortem time passed. At first she'd been happy to live in the Coffin Drives, the home of the Fetch Communion, but then the Blood and Flesh plague broke her memory and all but destroyed her. After Dieter helped her through her second rebirth, she'd moved back to share their old flat in Docklands. The casual fetch hatred she'd run into had depressed her so much she'd asked him to make her fetch identity tags invisible. Passing acquaintances usually assumed she was one of the living. Now Dieter was probably approaching a rebirth of his own.

As she walked, she checked her messages again. Nothing from Ambrose or Junky Fi. She could understand Ambrose's silence – but Fi's was starting to annoy her. She left another message for her, letting her irritation show. 'You owe him,' she ended it. 'You owe us both. Fucking call me. NOW.'

Then there was nothing to distract her. Memories of the night of Dieter's infection forced themselves on her. He'd been so excited. A courier had brought a piece of the deep past, an artefact of uncertain provenance and function. It looked to Leila like an old, square, wooden box.

Perched on the sofa, Dieter peered at it through various digital and physical aids. 'Chi branding!' he enthused, weave screens and keyboards drifting in the air around him. 'She was one of the twelve original Pantheon gods. The first to be taken over.' He shifted, reaching for a magnifying glass. 'She fell just like Kingdom did. Because she was corrupt. I wonder if he remembered her when he was dying.' He knocked a pizza box off the sofa. A couple of slices spilled out on to the floor. He didn't notice. 'If this is something she built – gods, it's as old as Station. Older. From precursor times, maybe! It might even get Ambrose's attention. He's the only one that'd appreciate this, now Cormac's gone.'

'Seven hundred years old,' she said. 'Incompatible with anything the five gods we've got left will ever produce.' She bent over and took a closer look. 'I'm sure it'll thrill him.'

'Philistine.' There was a smile in his voice too. 'Anyway, it's not just about the history. Junky Fi put a note in with it. She wants me to take it to pieces, check it out for her. She says there's good money in it.' He revolved it in his right hand. 'Ouch! Fuck.'

'Are you OK?'

'Bloody splinter.'

Dieter put the dead god's artefact down on the coffee table and peered at his hand. Leila was able to get her first proper look at the box. It was about the size of a large coffee mug. Each of its six sides was criss-crossed with raised strips of wood and dusted with light golden patterns. Scuffed weave sigils repeated themselves across each one. Leila didn't recognise any of them. One side of the box was cracked open. Thickets of wires clumped with a soft, organic-looking red gel oozed through jagged cracks.

'She's paying you to assess that?'

Dieter nodded.

'Wow.'

He reached for the box again, held it up to eye level and gazed at it.

'Beautiful...' he breathed.

Leila thought she saw the wires and gel shift faintly. 'It's secure?' she asked. 'I don't want to have my memory eaten. And you're not spending the rest of time ghosting out like Cormac did.'

Dieter sighed, the past shivering through him. 'Amen to that. And yes. Fi says she's checked it out, she's always pretty reliable. But I'll give it a once over before I dive in properly.'

The box's spilled guts were definitely moving, pulsing softly in time with his voice. Leila wondered what invasive bonds it had already formed with him. 'It looks like you're already in pretty deep.'

Dieter chuckled. 'Superficial stuff. Maybe I should call Ambrose. Just to see what he thinks.' He turned to her, his face alive with enthusiasm. 'He always loved this sort of thing.'

'No, Dieter.'

Ambrose was her boss' lawyer. He'd found her job for her. She chatted with him a couple of times a week. These days, she knew him far better than her brother did. 'He won't want to hear,' she warned Dieter. He looked crestfallen. 'Look, if you really have to – well, just don't go rushing in. And don't expect too much.'

4

'I really could use his help on this. It's a pearl.' He smiled wolfish-ly. 'A rent-paying pearl...'

Leila's response was instant. 'You don't need to worry about that.'

Dieter looked away from her. His income was at best variable. Without Leila's job, he'd have been evicted from the apartment long ago. At the moment, his funds were scarce, something he felt as a deep humiliation. 'Without you, we couldn't keep this flat,' Leila told him. Fetches weren't allowed to rent or own property. Had she been alone, she'd have been back in the Coffin Drives, living in the place where her second, final death had so nearly overwhelmed her, where the fact of that agony still made her feel so completely insecure. 'And I still owe you for helping me rebuild myself.'

Dieter grunted. Leila hoped that she'd reassured him. His atten-tion was back on the artefact. He turned it over and over in his hands, lost in it.

'Well, I'm not going to watch you playing with that thing all night. Everyone's meeting up at Ushi's.'

Dieter grunted again. Leila let the weave rise up fully around her, curious about the wooden box's virtual presence. An adsprite drifted up from the pizza box, a mozzarella-coloured little man with curly hair and a big moustache singing jauntily about pepperoni. The flat's spam filters snapped him out of existence.

Seen through the weave, the artefact looked a little less broken, a little more solid. Its edges glowed light gold. As she peered more closely at it, querying its deeper self-presentation systems, she felt code made alien by the passage of time thrust back at her. A warning pulsed in her mind – 'UNREADABLE'.

It was much more legible to Dieter. His weaveware made shining talons of his fingers. As he played with the artefact they bit into it then snapped back, probing and reprobing for safe passage into its secrets. He looked so sure of himself. As the moment played out again, she wished she could step back and shake him out of it. Instead, that younger her, who now seemed so unreachably far away, just said: 'At least make sure it doesn't bring InSec down on us.'

'Oh, they'll never spot this,' Dieter replied, not even looking up. 'The flat's far too well defended.'

Later, when she returned home from the bar, there was an

ambulance waiting outside the block's front door. A man in an InSec-branded containment suit stopped her from going in. 'I'm sorry,' he told her when she identified herself. 'There's very little we can do.'

They wheeled Dieter out on a gurney that sparkled with cageware. 'Stupid bastard,' one of them grunted, as they lifted him over the front door step. A few neighbours peered out of doors and windows. When they saw Dieter, they turned away. The artefact had burrowed into the hollow at the base of his sternum, sinking into it like a boat half-lost in water. Part of his T-shirt was eaten away. He looked thinner. His grey skin implied exhaustion. Leila let all weave overlay drop away for a moment. The changes remained.

'Leila,' he called out, his voice cracking, then: 'I'm so sorry.' Those few words exhausted him and his eyes closed.

'We're taking him to the Arigato charity hospital,' one of the containment workers told her.

'But he has medical cover – it's basic, but it's all up to date.'

'Illegal tech. It's not covered.'

'Oh no.'

'I'm sorry. But at least it hasn't reached his weaveself. There won't be any problems with his fetch. And we've swept the apartment, it's clean. The box is a one-shot mechanism. Now it's in him it's not going to hurt anyone else.'

The containment workers' visors were mirrored. As they left with Dieter, Leila realised that she'd seen nothing at all of their faces.

She reached the block she was meant to be showing, and snapped herself out of the past. Its reasonably freshly painted exterior loomed over her. For most of the last decade it had been a burnt-out ruin, a void site projecting images of the terror-killed dead out into Station. Then, it had served as a reminder of why the Soft War against the rebellious AIs of the Totality was so necessary. With the discovery that Kingdom himself had been behind the terror attacks, blaming them on the Totality so as to ignite and expand a vastly profitable war, it had become an embarrassment. When he'd fallen, the block had passed into his conquerors' hands. The Totality had rebuilt it and – having let it out as living units for a couple of years – were now putting it up for sale.

The potential buyers were already there. They'd travelled over from Homelands for the viewing. 'You have to see property in person,' the wife had said. 'It's the only way.' Now they stood in a Docklands backstreet beneath dimming spinelights. The husband looked a little nervous. As Leila approached them, she heard him say something about their personal security systems.

'Well, for the amount we pay the Rose every month I'd expect a little collateral damage,' his wife replied. 'Not that I've seen anyone who'd have the balls to attack us.'

They were certainly very happy about displaying their wealth. The weave overlaid them with a dense tapestry of up-to-the-minute fashions, chosen to show off as many different designers as possible rather than create any sort of satisfying, coherent look. Together, they blared out a visual dissonance that was almost avant-garde.

They followed Leila into the three-storey building. Its systems recognised her, opening and closing doors as she moved through them, summoning the lift when it looked like she'd need it. All three flats were empty. Late afternoon spinelight shone into pristine emptinesses of bare walls and cream carpets. The smell of fresh paint hung in the air. The tour viewing ended in the top flat.

The wife nodded approvingly. 'We'll do it up a bit. Flashy but cheap. They like that over here.' She turned to Leila. 'Many viewings?' It was the first time she'd directly addressed her.

Leila nodded. 'There's a lot of demand for properties like this.'

'I think we might be interested. But we need to see it off-weave.'

'Are you sure, dear?' The husband blanched.

'Don't be so spineless, Gerald. We both know how much these people,' gesturing towards Leila, 'can hide when they're trying to sell something.'

'The surveyor can handle that.'

The wife ignored him. 'Miss… whatever your name is, take us off-weave.'

Leila blanched.

'Well, go on then.' The wife peered at her, her tightly-styled, blue-rinsed hair a curt halo around her sharp face. 'What are you waiting for? Something to hide, dearie?'

'Just meshing with the block's weave server,' Leila replied. She'd try and bluff them. She wasn't in the mood for a confrontation.

'I'm sure.' The wife turned to her husband. 'We'll smell damp. Or there'll be rot.'

Leila called up the weave server. It hummed with vast, underused power. As a void site core system, it had had to serve thousands, maybe even tens of thousands, of viewers simultaneously. It was the most highly specced block weave system she'd ever seen. She told it to shut down all weave content except for fetch manifestations. A moment passed, then the room changed.

The previous tenants had left the sink full of dirty washing and the wastebin full of scraps. There was a sour reek of rotted food. An open cupboard was full of tins. The wallpaper was torn and dirty. Stains rippled across the scruffy carpet. Leila swore to herself. It wasn't the first time her boss had done this to her.

'I told you so, Gerald,' crowed the wife. Now that the weave was down, her high-fashion costume had disappeared. She wore a white jumpsuit scattered across with designer weave sigils.

Gerald wore dark trousers and a t-shirt. He looked very pale. 'We've seen what we need to see, dear.' Sweat beaded his forehead.

'And who knows what else you're hiding,' the wife told Leila. 'Really, did you think you could get away with this?'

'Can we bring the weave back up, dear?' Gerald was leaning against the wall. He looked ready to slump to the floor. 'You know how much I hate this.'

'Wait,' his wife said. 'We're not fully offweave yet.' Gerald groaned. 'There's still something.' She rounded on Leila. 'What are you trying to hide from us?' Then she paused, eyes flicking backwards and forwards as she read a virtual display. 'Oh,' she said slowly. 'You're a fetch.'

Leila sighed to herself. 'Yes,' she replied.

'Well, no wonder we're getting lied to. You don't know what truth is because you aren't even real. I'll be complaining about you, you shouldn't be doing a job like this.'

Leila felt fury rise up. *Be professional*, she reminded herself. Then she spoke. 'Under the terms of the post-rebirth settlement, I'm as human as you are. I have every right to earn a living.'

The woman snorted. 'Nonsense. Gods!' She turned to her

husband, who now had fallen all the way to the floor. He was panting with stress. 'Why am I even arguing with a piece of software? Oh, and do stop being so pathetic.' She turned back to Leila and snapped: 'Bring the weave back up.'

Leila did so, ripostes burning through her. She imagined how each would play out. They all ended in complaints to her boss, perhaps in dismissal. She was better off just ignoring it all.

She said nothing else as she led the buyers out of the building. She imagined setting up a fictional counter-buyer to bid against them. 'Tell your manager we'll call with an offer tomorrow,' the woman said. 'And a complaint.'

Leila barely heard her. There was a message, but it wasn't from Ambrose or Fi. The hospital had called. 'You'd better get over here as soon as you can,' a nurse said, her voice taut with stress. 'Your brother's insurance pay-out has come through...'

What insurance? Leila wondered.

'...but he's totally lost it,' continued the nurse. 'He's turned all his antivirals off and is refusing any medical help. The infection's eating him alive.'

In the background, Dieter's voice rose in a strange, croaking howl: 'DON'T ANY OF YOU TOUCH ME! I'M A FUCKING LOADED NOW, THAT MEANS I GET MY FUCKING WAY. I HAVE TO DIE AS SOON AS POSSIBLE AND NONE OF YOU WILL STOP ME!'

Chapter 2

Leila decided to jump straight to the charity hospital, leaping several kilometres in an instant. It was something she hardly ever did, because it reminded her that she was only virtual. And the dislocation that came with jumping always sickened her.

She prepared herself as well as she could. She looked to her left and right, following the cluttered streets of Docklands as they rolled up and away, disappearing behind the Spine to meet far above her head. She glanced down the tube of Docklands and out into space. She looked behind her and saw the entrance to the Wart. She thought of the brilliant lights of Homelands beyond it. She imagined that she was looking at Station from outside, inspecting the twin battered skins of Docklands and Homelands, the Wart between them like a bulbous fist clenching a thick, round rod. Then she pulled her consciousness back to the little street she was in. Jumping to the hospital was such a short journey. Little more than a footstep. She closed her eyes, thought of Dieter, sent out the appropriate command codes and leapt to its atrium.

The sudden shift was as excruciating as ever – the leap from cold evening chill to lightly overheated hospital air, from fading spine-light to hard, clinical fluorescence. She rushed for the restroom, cutting through a small crowd. Camera nests hovered over it. It looked like some kind of media event. She retched when she was safely in a cubicle, vomit splashing into the water. Dieter had made sure that her fetchware precisely replicated a physical human's experience of life.

'Are you sure you want the bad stuff too?' he'd asked.

'Of course,' she replied.

He told her she was nuts, but he did it anyway.

When she'd recovered herself, she started back towards her brother's room, pushing through the media event. A minor pop star was holding forth on a small podium. He was running some of East's more potent celebrityware. It snatched her attention. She shook her head, freeing herself, and kept moving. Moving through the crowd, she suddenly found herself standing next to a white, man-shaped silhouette. That did stop her.

She hadn't seen an empty avatar for years. Its weave sigils must be completely out of date, linking to fashion and appearance content that no longer existed. A high, sweet smell assaulted her. A moment, then her weave systems registered the absence and sent out a call to generic open source image banks. Out-of-copyright content washed across the avatar.

The silhouette vanished and a man stood in front of her. He had a sharp, intelligent face, framed by carefully styled, bushy hair. Two thick sideburns lanced down like inverted horns. A caustic aftershave reek replaced the strange, sweet smell. He wore a close-fitting pastel blue suit over a pale grey shirt. Wide lapels and flared trousers gave him a larger than life look. He raised a hand to adjust a white cravat. Jewellery glittered on his fingers. The cut of the suit and the style of the shirt were about a quarter of a century out of date. They sent Leila back into her earliest years, reminding her of the first grown-ups she'd known, vast, powerful entities whose authority over her world had always seemed so absolute. For an instant, she felt like a child.

The man smiled at Leila. 'I'm very sorry for your loss,' he said, but there was no empathy in his soft, buzzing voice.

'What?' she replied, pulling herself back to the present.

He loomed over her. 'I am very sorry for your loss,' he repeated. 'But you have so much to remember him by.'

'You've mistaken me for someone else.' It took an effort of will to push past him. *Weirdo*, she thought, a little unsettled by the impact he'd had on her.

As she rushed down corridors, adsprites leapt out at her. The hospital was partially advertising funded, so her spam filters were barred from blocking them. She did her best to ignore their buzzing little sales pitches, letting her financial status flash up so they could see how little she had to spend. They gave up on her long before she reached Dieter's room.

There was a nurse waiting outside it. 'What's going on?' gasped Leila. 'Is he all right?'

'Much quieter now. But he still won't let them touch him.'

'Your doctors?'

'No. The Twins sent specialists as soon as the insurance money reached his account. But they can't force treatment on him without next of kin permission.'

'They've got it,' said Leila, rushing to the door. Then a thought hit her. She turned back to the nurse. 'But his insurance crapped out on him,'

The nurse shrugged. 'The money's there. Otherwise the specialists wouldn't be. They've been with him for a couple of hours, I dread to think how much that's cost.'

'Oh, hell...' Leila's heart sank. Dieter must have somehow cracked the isolation unit's security and artificially inflated his bank balance.

'Your brother's very rich indeed. He could buy this place, if he wanted to.'

'What? That's impossible.'

'The money's real. The Twins did a deep dive on his finances before they sent in the pay-per-hour people.' She nodded towards the door. 'Those two aren't cheap.'

Dieter was tied to the bed, held down with padded straps. The specialists chatted by the window, their isolation armour gleaming in the late afternoon spinelight. They didn't notice Leila come in.

'This dump is just a sodding fetch farm,' grumbled the female one. 'They haven't even tried to crash the infection.' Treatment engines hung beside them like a shoal of carbon-fibre jellyfish, medical weapons yearning for billable deployment, their real and virtual features impossible to tell apart. 'No bonus on this one. He's a goner.'

Leila moved to the side of the bed. Dieter's eyes were closed. The infection had shrivelled him. He looked so fragile. The doctors still hadn't noticed her, but her brother saw her straight away and turned his head towards her. His face had a starved sharpness to it. The artefact had sunk deeper into his chest and was now almost completely embedded. Only one square face was visible.

'Hello, sis,' he slurred. 'I'm in the money! Pretty fucking cool, eh?'

'Dieter,' Leila replied. 'What does this mean? Why didn't you tell me about it? And – how?'

The doctors turned towards her, surprised. 'Oh,' the man said. 'You're the fetch. The nurse told us about you.' He turned back to his colleague. 'It can stay?' he asked.

'Yeah, no probs,' the other doctor replied. 'No flesh, no infection risk.'

'Happened very quickly,' Dieter wheezed. 'Met some high pressure salesman. Pressure men. Did a deal with them. You wouldn't believe who they represent! Hardly believe it myself.' He coughed. 'Proper old school. Too much cologne. Terrible dress sense.'

'I think I met one. Creepy sod.'

'Oh, they're pukka.' Dieter coughed again. A bloody spatter of nanogel and wires dribbled out of his mouth. 'Turned out all right, eh?'

'I don't like this, Dieter.'

He ignored her. 'It's just an advance payment. Proof of concept. The rest is coming directly to you.' He had to force each word out. 'You'll be rich enough to keep the flat. Live wherever you want. All taken care of.' He nodded towards the doctors. 'We don't need those guys. Waste of cash. I have to die.' A weak smile. 'The pressure men'll take me away. Part of the deal. But I'll be back.' He winked. 'Shouldn't even tell you this much. But you've got to know. Don't want you worrying.'

The female doctor noticed the nanogel, reached for a tissue to wipe it up, examined it closely then showed it to her colleague.

'Shit.'

'Yeah, faster than we thought,' she replied. 'No wonder he's raving. No next of kin, no one to authorise treatment, nothing we can do.'

'I'm next of kin,' said Leila.

'You're a fetch. I don't know if you count.'

'He's dying,' said Leila. 'Pretty soon there won't be anything left of him to work on.' The doctor nodded. 'And you want your bonus?' She nodded again. 'Then assume I can authorise it. Do whatever you need to. Looks like we can afford it.'

'No!' coughed Dieter weakly. 'Let me die! Let the pressure men have me!'

The doctor thought for a moment, then leapt into action, suddenly all professionalism. 'Take him right down,' she told her colleague. He nodded at one of the machines. It drifted over towards Dieter, dropping a tendril which wrapped itself around his mouth and became a dark mask. Gas hissed.

Dieter sighed, then spoke. 'I'm going with the pressure men,' he gasped, the mask muffling his voice. 'These idiots won't stop it. Such wonderful things to see...'

Then the anaesthetic took him and his eyes closed.

'Earn that money,' Leila said. 'Bring him back.'

Leila watched, feeling increasingly useless. When the Blood and Flesh plague shattered the deep structures of her memory, completely disordering her sense of herself, Dieter had helped her rebuild. He'd taken her out of the Coffin Drives' convalescence unit and back to his weavespace. Then he'd opened up his own memories of her life to her. They became a template, guiding her as she remade the structures of her past. He'd helped her heal when even the Fetch Counsellor had given up on her.

Now he needed her just as much as she'd needed him. And she could only watch. She moved to the window and tried to let the world distract her. Flies buzzed within broken double glazing, spinelight reflecting off them in metallic glints. Beyond, there was Docklands, curving up into the sky. And above it all, the five gods of Station and the soft purple orb of the Totality looked down, careless of the affairs of humanity. Habit had her checking her messages again. Miwa had called. There was nothing else.

Hours passed. As it turned out, Dieter was right. The doctors could do nothing. In fact, they did worse than that. The Twins' medical technologies triggered a defence reaction.

'Remind you of anything?' asked the female doctor as Dieter's flesh melted away, his body reducing itself to skin, sinew and bone. Her colleague shook his head. 'It's mimicking Sweat addiction impacts. Only very highly accelerated.'

'Fuck...'

Pain and anger snapped at Leila. 'What have you done to him?'

'This kind of infection is always unpredictable,' said the doctor.

'There's always a risk of adverse reaction. It's covered in the terms and conditions.'

'Nobody ever reads the bloody things,' her colleague complained.

That was only the start of it. The artefact started to convert living flesh into dead clots of metal and plastic, wrapping them tight around his internal organs. Black decay wrote itself like code across his skin. The doctors wanted to stop fighting at three in the morning, but Leila forced them to continue.

'If he's paying,' she told them, 'you want him to live. And if he dies and I am, you want me to see you doing every single fucking thing you can for him.'

They kept him alive until just before dawn. The infection expired a few minutes after he did, having left itself with nothing to feed off. The artefact's dark empty face stared up at the ceiling like a broken window. A sweet, rotten smell drifted up from it. Dieter's bones tented his pale skin. An ear and a couple of fingers had dropped off. The right shoulder had fallen in. The sheets beneath him were a reeking mess, darkly sodden with nano-waste.

'Well, that's next month's rent paid,' one of the doctors said, as he stripped off his gloves. 'Think I'll hit Bahariya Hub for a bit of a break.'

Leila hoped he wasn't as off-hand with his living clients. Exhaustion and a kind of sad resignation trumped rage. 'What happens now?' she asked wearily.

'The crematorium,' the female doctor replied. 'You'll get the ashes once they've been declared clear of infection. And if he chooses rebirth, he'll be back in six months' time. Just like you were.'

The other doctor squatted down and opened up a matt black briefcase. The medical equipment drifted towards it. One by one each instrument dropped down to nestle into the case's dark lining. 'You'll be getting a fairly hefty bill in a day or so,' he said. 'Prompt payment appreciated. If you think it's too much, remember you ignored us when we advised ceasing treatment.'

Then they were gone. Leila was left alone in the room with the shell of skin, bone and broken matter that had once been her brother. Sadness filled her. *At least his weaveself's still out there*, she reassured herself. She barely noticed when more containment workers came to take the body away. When the room was empty, she moved to the window. The gods were still out there. The flies were too. A couple had drifted into the room. *Awful hygiene.* She made a mental note to mention them to the nurse. Habit grabbed her and, without thinking, she slapped at one. It dodged her hand, lifting itself up beyond her reach, its metallic chitin glittering in the room's harsh light. *It saw me coming*, she thought, surprised.

It must be fetch aware; must have picked up her virtual action, read it as something real and acted accordingly. She wondered who'd bother putting insects onweave. Some Docklands hacker, throwing their energies into a project at once totally futile and deeply personally satisfying. Someone a bit like Dieter.

Loss turned in her heart like a blade. *He'll be back soon.* But tears still pricked at her. She nerved herself. An empty flat had to be faced. Six months suddenly seemed a very long time.

She walked home very slowly and stood outside the flat for quarter of an hour before letting herself in.

When she woke up next morning, there were three new messages waiting for her. The first was from her boss, offering a few days off. He seemed awkward. She wondered how many others would find it difficult to empathise with a fetch about a death. The next was from a Totality lawyer, calling 'with regards to the matter of your brother's estate'. His smooth, purple, featureless face glowed out at her, giving nothing away. The final message was from another Totality mind. She identified herself as Cassiel. She, too, requested a meeting, without saying what it would be about.

Leila ran a weave search. Dieter had fine-tuned her search engines, merging them with some discreetly powerful hacking tools. It only took a minute or so to uncover her true background. She seemed to be a highly experienced fraud investigator, working across the Totality on a freelance basis.

'Oh, Dieter,' she said again. She'd been expecting a call like that, but not so quickly. She thought about the pressure men, wondering who they represented and what they'd want in return for their money. 'What have you done?'

Chapter 3

Leila finally managed to reach Ambrose that afternoon. 'I'm so sorry I've been out of touch,' he told Leila. 'You know how things are. Business.' He sounded embarrassed. He probably hadn't wanted to relive the agony of Cormac's fall. Perhaps he'd been moving through a series of ever more broken Docklands dives, trying and failing to drink away the problem of his life. 'You must come and see me as soon as possible.' Now that he was calling, there was so much concern in his voice.

Leila went straight to his office. Out of the window, the streets of Docklands rolled upwards until they were lost behind the Spine. Ambrose leaned back in his chair.

'So Dieter's definitely going to choose rebirth?' he asked.

His accent was purest Homelands, his suit was impeccably tailored, his chair and desk were overlaid with tasteful, detailed simulations of mahogany and leather and his walls were lined with a virtual library that presented as a dense array of traditionally bound legal textbooks. And yet there was still something ever-so-slightly skewed about him. Perhaps, Leila speculated, it was the contrast between the clubbable splendour of his workspace and the tiny Docklands backstreet he'd squeezed his legal practice into. It felt like he was living in a memory. He smiled his sad, apologetic smile. If she was meeting him for the first time, she wasn't sure how impressed she'd be – but she'd seen him go into action on behalf of her boss, and knew just how sharp his mind was. When, of course, he was sober.

'Oh, you know Dieter,' she replied. 'He loved the idea of being a fetch. He won't opt out. He always used to go on about how Cormac Redonda had wasted his afterlife. And then there was Mum.' She couldn't keep the sadness out of her voice.

'Indeed,' replied Ambrose. 'Distressing cases, both. Cormac in particular.' His voice was strained. 'I wish we could have done more for him.' He paused for a moment, then said: 'You'll understand – I don't want to talk about the box. About how it happened. It's too late to do anything about that now.' Grief shadowed his face. He looked away for a moment. Then he looked back, forcing a determined cheerfulness into his voice. 'But I can help you with what comes next.'

Leila nodded. 'Yes,' she told him. 'I understand.'

Ambrose looked profoundly relieved. 'So,' he said, 'You're in the money?'

Leila too was happy to move away from a subject that caused him so much pain. 'I saw Dieter's lawyer this morning. There's a payment coming to me from a corporate entity called Deodatus. Apparently Dieter had critical illness cover and held Totality investment bonds. Of course as a fetch there are limits on the amount of money I can hold, so the lawyer's set up some sort of Totality trust fund to manage it on my behalf. I can draw cash out of it whenever I feel like. Dieter's money will go into it too.'

'Dieter had a lawyer?' Ambrose smiled at the thought. 'That is a surprise. He was never very good at organizing that sort of thing.'

Leila's defence surprised her with its strength. 'He could be pretty together, when he needed to be.'

Memory flared in her. For a moment, she was thirteen again, and their mother had been dead for a week and a half. Dieter was pulling on the suit he'd bought for the funeral. 'I'm going to get a job,' he told Leila. And he did. He stuck with it until she left college and no longer needed his financial support, walking out on the day of her graduation ceremony. He even hacked his medical records so he wouldn't get drafted to fight in the Soft War. 'I'll not have you ending up in some shitty Twins orphanage,' he told her. Of course, the hacking created its own problems.

'So what's the problem?' asked Ambrose, pulling Leila back into the present.

'This Deodatus insurance policy. I know how much money he had. I know what he spent it on. Nothing like this, there's no way he could have afforded it. And – critical illness cover! Totality investment bonds! He just wasn't – isn't – that kind of person.'

'Maybe he was pretty together about that, too.'

'No. In the hospital he told me that he'd made some sort of deal with someone. It didn't sound like an insurance company. He called their representatives the pressure men. I think I met one of them. He was a little strange. Dieter said they're going to take him away for a bit. And I've had a message from a Totality fraud investigator.'

'Ah.'

'I need to know what he's got himself into and how to get him out of it.'

'You don't want to go to InSec?'

'Gods no. Not them. Not till I've got a better idea of what's going on.'

Ambrose thought for a moment. 'I can't promise all the answers. But I'll do what I can. Look, I'm free for the rest of the afternoon – why don't you go and sit in a café somewhere? I'll go through any paperwork you've had, dig around a bit. Give me a couple of hours and I'll be much more clued up.'

'Thanks, Ambrose. I appreciate that.'

'My pleasure.' He stood to see her to the door. 'Before you go – there's something I have to say. You're a very wealthy woman now. Despite all this' – he waved to indicate the office – 'I'm just a little backstreet Docklands lawyer, an exile from a much bigger firm. If you'd rather work with a slightly more upscale practice, I'd completely understand.'

Leila laughed. 'Ambrose, I know you and I trust you. That's what's most important. Especially now I'm actually worth ripping off.'

Ambrose looked touched. 'Thank you,' he replied. He coughed in an embarrassed way. 'I'll let you know once I'm up to speed. Oh, and one more thing…'

'What?'

'I've got to call your boss about another matter. Should I let him know you're resigning?'

She smiled. 'I'd like to. But I'm not sure if I should until I know where this money's come from.'

'I'll see if I can persuade him to extend your compassionate leave.' He tapped his nose. 'Grey's emotional trauma legislation. Very useful in moments like this.'

As Leila walked to the café, she remembered Dieter's lawyer, a

19

mind called Xavier. He'd been scrupulously professional as he'd explained how easily Leila could get round the laws limiting fetch financial activities. 'Your trust will be administered on your behalf by a small group of Totality financial intelligences. They're barely conscious. In effect, they're a thin veneer of quasi-intelligence overlaid on an entirely standard investment account.'

'And all this is legal?'

'Entirely so. Standard practice for the wealthy dead.'

'I thought you couldn't be wealthy and dead. That it all had to be passed on to your heirs.'

Xavier chuckled. 'Your life has – or rather, is about to – change very considerably,' he told her. 'Your good fortune will open up a world that works very differently from the one you're used to.'

'Isn't that a bit dodgy for the Totality?' Leila asked.

'My dear,' Xavier replied, leaning forwards. 'The market demands, and we deliver. How could anyone possibly object to that? And we're far more stringent than the gods of the Pantheon. I understand that you can buy almost anything from them. East offers celebrity, Sandal offers citizenship and the Rose will even let you buy her out of criminal investigations.'

He knew very little about Deodatus: 'I received a message asking me to manage a substantial personal insurance payout on your behalf. I hope I've done so to your satisfaction. And no, I've had no other contact with Deodatus. Hadn't even heard of it until now. And I certainly don't know what a pressure man is.'

Leila reached the café and pulled herself back to the moment. It was a basic Twins joint. As a waiter dressed in jeans and a T-shirt cleared the last customer's detritus from the table, Leila thought about trying Junky Fi again. But now the crisis had passed the box was an irrelevance. All Leila really wanted to do was yell at her for being so bloody careless, and that wouldn't get either of them anywhere. She decided to let things be.

Looking around for something to distract her from her anger, she found herself wondering how her new-found wealth would change the details of her world. The weave overlaid her surroundings with content appropriate to her status. As a low-earning fetch, she could afford few frills. So she usually experienced a smattering of outdated freebies and ad-funded aesthetic tweaking. Now she was wealthy, that would no doubt change. She opened herself to any local weave systems, and let their outputs rise up around her.

There was a light tickle in the back of her mind as the café's branding engines queried the basic details of her social and financial status. Then there was the digital equivalent of an exclamation mark and everything started to shift. Mirrors shimmered into being on the walls, reflecting a suddenly more elegant clientele. The little zinc bar top at the back of the room became marble. The susurrus of late afternoon conversation was overlaid with the gentle tones of a moodcore turntablist quartet. When the waiter passed by her again, the jeans and T-shirt had gone. He was wearing black trousers, a white shirt and dark bow tie, and a crisply-pressed apron. The bushy moustache was new, too. He caught her eye. 'Your order, ma'am?' She asked for a coffee, being sure to specify that her order was virtual only. He scurried off to prepare it, ignoring his other customers. She was probably paying much more than them for her drink.

She glanced out into the street, but for the moment it seemed that not too much had changed out there. Docklands was as scruffy as ever. As she watched, a little unit of gun kiddies took up a defensive position over the road from the café, exotic weapons scanning backwards and forwards. The kiddies were overlaid with grey-green battle armour, their faces hidden behind gold visors. Underneath, Leila imagined intent, scrappily dressed teenagers. East had taken to writing their live-action combats across the streets of Station. She remembered Dieter grumbling about them. 'They should be coding their own games, not buying up content from East. No creativity in it.' Grief rose up within her. For a moment, she considered muting it. But that seemed to be a step away from humanity. She let it surge through her. 'Six months,' she said to herself. 'He'll be back in six months.' Loss settled back and became bearable again.

She decided to distract herself with a little media, and sent a call to one of East's main current affairs channels. As it spun up, Leila felt East's subscription systems probe her. She wondered how the content served to her would change. But when it started to play there didn't seem to be anything new. Perhaps trashy, excitable current affairs programming was something that even the rich couldn't escape.

An anchorman drifted over the table, introducing a series of thirty-second news reports. The Twins were preparing themselves for their annual Taste Refresh Festival, flooding Station with seafood imagery. East had bought out a small Totality media hub for vast sums of cash. 'It's a whole new way of thinking about content,' a very young man enthused. 'It's so exciting that the gods understand that.' Another gravity quake had hit Docklands, this time shaking Prayer Heights. There had been some panic, but little damage. Most of the buildings affected were under the protection of Sandal, housing his dock workers. He'd complained to the Totality, who had inherited responsibility for Station's gravity engines from Kingdom. A Totality mind appeared, its featureless face glowing softly purple as promises came that soon all gravity upgrade works would be complete.

The coffee arrived. Leila sipped it once without really thinking, then again, surprised. It tasted better than any cup she'd ever had before. If she was paying over the odds for it, she was at least getting value for money. She savoured a little more, inexplicably feeling a little guilty, then turned back to the news. The next report had begun. There was footage of a Blood and Flesh march down 'ti Bon Ange Street. The camera closed in on the angry faces, shouting their hateful slogans. Leila thought about flicking channels, but that would have felt like cowardice. At least their militant wing was no longer active. Apparently one of their own memory weapons, a planned sequel to the Blood and Flesh plague, had activated prematurely and neutralised the more hardcore elements of their organisation.

Leila had been hugely relieved when she found out, and had even briefly considered visiting the Coffin Drives. But fear had still filled her at the thought of returning to them. That fear was with her now, but she realised that she had to face up to it. For the moment she was wealthy enough to live where she wanted, but if her newfound riches were illegally acquired they could well just vanish. She might yet end up having to go back and to live in the Drives. And even if that didn't happen, Dieter could well move to them after his rebirth. She'd have to go and visit him if she wanted to see him on anything like a regular basis. She could no longer avoid the past. She sat back and remembered.

Chapter 4

Two and a half years before, fetches were still coming to terms with their newly sentient status. Jack Forster, Hugo Fist and Andrea Hui had worked with the Totality to release the dead from semi-sentient slavery. But the Rebirth was just the start of a longer coming of age. It was one thing for ten thousand weaveselves to be reborn as fully self-aware continuations of ended lives – quite another for them to come to terms with that new start, both as individuals and as a group, and understand what to do with it. When Leila stepped out of the sea and into her new, post-mortal life, she became part of that conversation. It was a profoundly confusing time, because every single fetch had a different sense of what the afterlife should be. And the Coffin Drives was an entirely virtual and thus immensely malleable environment. Each of its inhabitants could project their opinions on to it, in ways that ranged from the subtle and elegant to the madly grandiose.

The root geography of the Coffin Drives was – mercifully – unrewriteable. The fetches lived on a circular island, tens of miles across. The ocean that encircled it was a visual manifestation of humanity's shared data, a digital subconscious for an entire culture. Newly created fetches were born out of it, the deep tides taking six months to knit the strands of a weaveself together into personhood. Each newborn fetch walked out of the waves and on to a long, wide beach, o-shaped and therefore infinite. Leila remembered her own walk up the beach. The cold breeze had tugged at her wet clothes while the endless sea roared behind her. As she remembered, fear sparked in her and she shifted uncomfortably. There had never been anything troubling there on the seashore, she told herself, only the Fetch Counsellor waiting to introduce her to her new life. She was relieved to feel the fear settling.

Then she moved on to the city at the heart of the Coffin Drives.

Before the rebirth there had been a prison at its heart, embedded in a lake made of lost, fragmented memories. Afterwards, the lake and the prison had been remade as a memorial. The Coffin Drives' occupants surprised themselves with their near-unanimous agreement that it should remain a stable, unchanging space. But every other part of the city was chaos. And the emotional geography of the city had been as variable as its street plan. Individual fetches experienced their rebirth in many different ways. The luckiest were heartily welcomed by their families and friends, immediately and unquestioningly understood to be a direct continuation of the lives that had so recently ended. The unluckiest were rejected completely. Most experienced something between the two.

East and the Totality came together to launch a vast transmedia campaign, designed to convince the humans of the Solar System to treat the returned dead with kindness. But they were pushing against deep emotions. East in particular was shocked to find that her audience was not its reliably malleable self. The dead found that they often had to fight very hard to win back the lives their living selves had once occupied. Many failed. Some chose true death, letting themselves dissolve back into the memory seas. Some retreated into perpetual hedonism. Others sought to escape their loss through mysticisms of one kind or another. Some just moved bitterly on. And the worst of the living started to push back, creating the Blood and Flesh group. And the Blood and Flesh group created the plague that had nearly destroyed the Fetch Communion. At the thought of that, Leila decided to drop out of memory and back into the present.

Her media stream had moved on from the news. An episode of Hugo Fist's chat show was just beginning, its unmistakable theme tune ringing out as the camera closed in on the little ventriloquist's dummy and his guests. Leila smiled as she turned him off. She'd happily watch him for the rest of the afternoon, but then she'd get nothing done. The agonies of the past – agonies that, with Dieter's help, she'd overcome – made the present that little bit easier to deal with. She pulled up her mailbox and started going through her messages. Most were condolences. Those from her own friends expressed careful sympathy. A couple hoped that she wouldn't have too much trouble finding somewhere new to live. Dieter's friends were much less guarded. After a clichéd platitude or two they usually expressed deep excitement about his future. 'He's such a tech head,' one enthused, 'he lives and breathes that shit, he's going to love being a fetch.'

She dealt with some of the more important messages then dropped her attention back into the café, wondering about another coffee. But, glancing round for the waiter, an alien presence caught her eye and she froze. There, at the other end of the room, sitting discreetly at a corner table, was a man she didn't know but did recognise. She blinked, realising that it wasn't his face that looked familiar – it was his sense of style. He was dressed just like the strange man with the soft, buzzing voice she'd met in the hospital. *A pressure man*, she thought. The tasteful colours of his suit blended perfectly with his surroundings, but its antique cut stood out a mile. He saw that he'd been spotted and stood up, then started rapidly towards the door.

'Stop!' Leila shouted, standing herself. 'We need to talk.'

The buzz of conversation died and all eyes were on her. The waiter materialised at her elbow. 'Mademoiselle…' The pressure man was almost at the door. She went to follow him. A firm grip held her back. 'The bill…' A white slip appeared on the table. She glanced at it then waved distractedly, feeling an amount of money she could live off for a week vanish from her account. When she looked back the door was closing.

'Shit.' She pushed through the café as quickly as she could.

Reaching the street outside, she sprinted to catch up with him. They were on a small quiet road, leading up to a busier main thoroughfare. 'Stop,' she called, but he ignored her. 'Please.'

The gun kiddies watched her go by, pretend weapons swivelling to track her. She wondered if she was somehow integrated into their game world. For a moment, she worried that all she was really doing was embarrassing herself by chasing down a complete stranger with a taste for retro fashion. But then she caught up with him and saw his face, his cold good looks a perfect rhyme with those of the man in the hospital, and smelt the same powerful perfume again.

'Please stop,' she said, stepping in front of him. He looked down at her, his expression so frozen that he could be a mannequin, saying nothing. 'You work for Deodatus,' said Leila. 'You've done business

25

with my brother.' There was no response. 'I need to know what's going on.'

The man's silence was unnerving.

'I mean – all this money. I need to know where it came from. What it really means. What you want from him in return.'

Her target stepped past her and set off again. Leila sighed. Perhaps she was just embarrassing herself. But he hadn't denied anything. And he was such a perfect match with the man from the hospital. A moment and she caught him again, just as he was about to turn a corner into a main street, taking his arm as firmly as the waiter had taken hers. He was fully weave-enabled, and so he felt her grip and turned to face her.

'I'm a fetch. I can follow you anywhere. If I have to, I'll jump to keep up with you.' She hoped he wouldn't call her bluff. 'I won't let you just walk away. Please, talk to me.'

The antique cut of his suit triggered memories. She'd flicked through entire catalogues of clothes like that when she was little, fascinated by the adult sophistication they projected. Remembering that made her feel awkward, like a child lost in an adult world.

She decided to go on the offensive.

'You were watching me in the café. And when you saw that I'd spotted you, you fled. If you're following me like that – well, something's up.' Adrenaline coursed through her. She felt her skull face shift in the back of her mind, a weapon woken by her excitement and worry. 'I need to know what Deodatus is. What my brother's got us into.'

He leant forward and opened his mouth. His lips moved, but there was barely any sound – just a soft, distant buzzing.

'Oh gods,' she thought to herself. Perhaps he was handicapped. What if he really had nothing to do with it all? She leant forward, straining to hear him. Maybe she was the one who needed to apologise. His lips were still moving. A little closer and there would be words. She thought of the buzzing voice of the pressure man she'd talked to in the hospital. This man reeked of scent too. She took a step towards him, then another. His mouth shaped sounds she could almost understand.

'Who are you?' she asked.

And then the pressure man started forwards and walked straight through her.

'What the fuck?' she gasped.

Now she was really annoyed. Station society might not hold fetches in very high regard, but one very important taboo was generally respected. You never knowingly passed through the dead.

Leila turned after him. 'How dare you…' she began, her voice raised, so outraged that she didn't care who overheard her. But he'd disappeared round the corner into the main street. She followed him, expecting to catch up with him right away, not quite sure what she'd do when she did.

And then she rounded the corner and stopped dead.

'Oh,' she breathed.

The street reached out into the afternoon, bustling with people.

The pressure man was nowhere to be seen.

There was a busker summoning images and music from some sort of keytar. A couple of children danced in front of him. A shopkeeper stood outside his crashed window display, swearing at it as it pulsed out error messages. A Totality mind stepped round him, moving purposefully up the street. There was nobody else. And there were no doors near enough to vanish through, or side alleys to disappear down.

'Where have you gone?'

She moved up the street, looking for him, but he'd completely disappeared. He couldn't have masked himself – the Rose forbade that kind of software. But there was no sign of him. She was still feeling rather puzzled when an urgent contact request from Ambrose pinged into her mind. She accepted and all of a sudden there he was, a virtual presence floating right next to her. His eyes were full of care.

'I'm afraid I have some very bad news,' he told her. 'Could you jump back to my office?'

'It's the insurance? I knew it was all fake.' She shook her head. 'I've just had the strangest experience. I think I met another pressure man.'

'You can tell me about that later. And the insurance isn't fake. Dieter signed up to something very real. That's the problem. Please, come back to my office.'

'You know I don't like jumping, Ambrose.'

'We need to talk. In private. As soon as possible.'

Fear gripped Leila. 'Just tell me.'

Ambrose swallowed. 'I've been going through the terms and conditions of the policy. The small print. I'm not sure Dieter even read it. It's very bad news.'

'If I can't keep the money, I can't keep the money.' Leila thought of the Coffin Drives. Perhaps life there would bearable.

'The money's not the problem. It's what Dieter promised Deodatus in return for it.' Ambrose couldn't meet her eyes. 'He signed over his weaveself, Leila. All the memory blocks that would go to build his fetch. Deodatus owns them all, for ever. They've all already been stripped. And Deodatus has taken a lot of other content too. The software tools Dieter built. His research content. Everything important. His legacy.'

Leila was profoundly shocked. 'He said he was going away. But just for a bit. Nothing like this. Gods, I thought he was raving.'

'Deodatus owns him and has taken him.'

'No.' The world spun. 'Where is he now?'

'I don't know,' replied Ambrose, his voice soft and sad.

'I'll pay the money back. Then they'll return him.'

'I'm afraid the deal's irrevocable. Dieter's gone, Leila. Gone for good.'

Chapter 5

Cassiel apologised as she showed Leila into her office. 'Apparently it's the only spare space we have.' She was dressed in a black trouser suit, cut in a business-like but elegant style. She moved with deft economy, her manner giving a sense of brisk confidence. Her oval, featureless face and smooth, elegant hands glowed a soft purple. 'It's not ideal, but one makes do.'

The narrow, high-ceilinged office felt like a repurposed storage room. A single window, half covered with a slatted blind, let slanting lines of spinelight through to fall against the rear wall. A fan hung from the ceiling. Two wireframe chairs sat by a battered desk. Leila imagined showing it to a property client. It would be a difficult sell. If this was where the Totality had put Cassiel, she couldn't have much clout. Dead insects speckled the floor. Their tiny wings glistened as Cassiel kicked them out of sight. 'They told me they'd send a cleaner in,' she told Leila. 'We're normally much more efficient than this.' She gestured towards a chair. 'That's clean, at least.'

As Leila settled into her seat, touching the pendant at her neck for luck, the office's virtual elements activated. A calendar drifted above the table. A clock hung on the wall. A false window opened on to a view of Mars. That was it. But then, they were in a building that had once been one of Kingdom's main Docklands temples but was now a Totality work and living space. Such simplicity was to be expected.

'We're very low-weave,' said Cassiel. 'I hope that's not upsetting.'

'It's how I prefer it.'

'Unusual. But admirable.'

'I do this myself, you know.'

'What do you mean?'

'I find ways of praising clients. When I'm showing them round a property, trying to sell them something. To soften them up.'

'Oh.' Cassiel leant forward across the desk, palms pressed

together, the tips of her fingers almost touching her face. Her whole posture projected focus. 'Very sharp. And why do you think I might be doing that?'

'You want to ask about my brother. You want to know what I know.'

'That's why we're here.'

'No. I'm here because I need information from you.'

Cassiel laughed. 'Oh, do you?' she asked. 'You're rather turning the tables, aren't you?'

'I need you to tell me what my brother's mixed up in.'

'You've just come into quite a bit of money.' Cassiel's tone was archly amused. 'I've found that, within the narrow confines of their personal interests, the rich are very demanding. It usually takes a little longer to kick in, though.'

'I have to find out where my brother's gone. And then I'm going to bring him back.'

Leila was desperate. She felt exhausted. She'd spent the whole of the night before searching for any trace of her brother's weave-self. But Deodatus had done a remarkably thorough job. Her own memories of her brother remained. His friends would remember him too. But that was it. There was nothing more substantial left, nothing that could cohere into a new fetch.

Leila had wept. By the time she recovered herself, dawn's merciless light was breaking in. She called up the flat's weave systems and had them show her the jagged, three-dimensional hole that the removal of Dieter's weaveself had left behind. 'Fill it with black,' she commanded. The hole became a mould, shaping a frozen bolt of dark lightning. She shrank the lightning bolt down so that it was the size of her little finger, called a black chain into being, attached the bolt to it and hung it round her neck as a pendant. Then she left the empty flat and came out to meet Cassiel, the shape of her brother's past hanging hard against her chest. Along the way, she looked out for more pressure men. But there were none to be seen.

'And why do you think I'd be able to help with that?' asked Cassiel.

'You're a Totality fraud investigator. You think there's something dodgy here too. Why else would you travel all the way here from Totality space?'

'I wouldn't quite say I was a fraud investigator. But I am trying to understand why Dieter's worth so much to Deodatus. And I share your interest in discovering where it's taken him.'

'I won't be able to tell you anything helpful.'

'I'll be the judge of that. Answer my questions, then I'll see about helping you with yours.'

'I don't know anything. And you clearly do. Tell me what you know.'

Cassiel looked directly at Leila. 'Without reciprocity, we can't proceed.'

A silence hung between them, lasting for far longer than was comfortable. Cassiel could have been a statue. Loss ached in Leila. She imagined life without Dieter. At last she said: 'Fine. Ask your questions.'

'How you spend your money is your own concern,' Cassiel told her. 'But I'd recommend a charm school.'

Then the interrogation began. The mind had Leila describe the events leading up to Dieter's death, his time in the hospital, the pressure men, the artefact that had first infected him. That led to his interest in dead technology.

'Archaeology obsessed him,' said Leila. 'Ambrose and Cormac too. They met on the Perdu chat boards, but they dug a lot deeper than anyone else. They were fascinated by Station's past. With exploring on- and offweave sites, understanding them, bringing it all back to life. They called themselves the Lazarus Crew. Until Cormac's accident.'

'What happened?'

'It was all over the news. I think East wanted it to be a warning. "Don't look back, only look forwards." It made Cormac look like such an idiot.' She sighed, remembering. 'He was never that. Just overconfident.' Then impatience overwhelmed her. 'All this is public record. You could look it up onweave in a couple of seconds.'

'I want to hear your version of it.'

'This is a waste of time.'

Cassiel gestured toward the door. 'You're free to leave whenever you want.'

'Gods.' Leila was exasperated.

'We're here to share,' Cassiel told her. 'Answer my questions, then I'll answer yours.'

The mind left Leila feeling she had no choice, which she hated. 'Cormac found some shitty old piece of tech somewhere in the tunnels under the Wart. Brought it home, thought he'd neutralised it. Then it woke up, decided it was under attack and lashed out.' She paused for a moment, remembering grief. 'Couldn't get through his defences. But it crawled into his wife and son through their weave links.' It was so hard to say the words. 'And wiped every memory they had.'

Leila expected a dismissive comment. But Cassiel's voice was gentle. 'That must have been hard. Our pasts make us who we are.' She paused. 'I'm very sorry.'

Remembered grief filled Leila. 'I don't need your sympathy,' she said, snapping a little harder than she meant to as she pushed the pain back down. 'Just your help. I don't want to lose my brother too.'

'Then help me,' Cassiel replied, once again briskly professional. 'What happened to Cormac after that?' A silence. 'Leila, I need to know. There's far more at stake here than your brother's life, important though that is.'

Leila nerved herself. 'He killed himself. I thought he'd choose a true death. But he came back as a fetch. Told Dieter and Ambrose he was going to go back to his family's favourite place, loop himself inside their happiest moment, and stay there for ever. Nobody knows where that was, so nobody knows where he is. I hope he's happy.'

'He's chosen his eternity,' said Cassiel thoughtfully. 'Very few people can.' She waited while Leila gathered herself. 'And what about your brother and Ambrose? Did they keep exploring?'

'Oh, they still went out. But it was never quite the same. Ambrose got pretty phobic about it all. Dieter was still keen, but InSec started keeping a very close eye on him. And then the Blood and Flesh plague landed, and he had me to look after.'

'But he still retained his interest in the past?'

Leila nodded.

'That's very unusual. Pantheon subjects usually equate the historic with the obsolete.'

'Says the mind from the ten-year-old culture. Look, I've answered all your questions. When are you going to help me?'

'You should have more respect, Leila. Our culture is at least three times older than yours.'

Leila snorted. 'It's not my culture.'

'And your brother's interest in the past is one of the things that makes him unique,' the mind continued. 'Perhaps that's what Deodatus was after?'

'I really don't think Dieter's interest in all that dusty old crap is worth millions.'

'Then you're not thinking very clearly. Now, one last request. Please show me the artefact that attacked him.'

'Gods. That bloody thing.'

'Once we've inspected it, I will tell you what I can about Deodatus.'

Leila sighed and summoned the memory. A three-dimensional image of the box hung in the air between them, radiating malignity.

Cassiel leant forwards, shoulders hunched, her soft, empty face hanging before it. 'Remarkable,' she whispered, then reached out and set it slowly spinning. The wires spilling from it drifted forwards and backwards. Ruby gel bulged from casing cracks, glowing with a soft, inborn light. 'Dead technology,' she said, brushing a hand across it. 'Let's see what it looked like when it was alive.' The artefact shimmered and began to change.

'What are you doing to it?' asked Leila.

'Dynamic image filters. They're analysing how it's degraded, looking to see how it might knit back together. Seeing what it might have been.'

The artefact moved backwards through time, becoming a more complete version of itself. Ruby gel oozed back into it and vanished. Wires retracted. The cracks healed themselves, jaggedness knitting together and vanishing. Grain emerged as the wood lightened. Gold poured itself across the strips of wood that divided each face. The image shook slightly. Graphics wrote themselves across the cube.

'Truly fascinating,' said Cassiel. 'It doesn't match anything in my immediate memory.'

Despite herself, Leila was intrigued. 'Dieter said there was Chi branding on it,' she told the mind.

'Specialised knowledge. I'll request access to the relevant data cores.'

The device shuddered in and out of focus, with every leap back into definition looking more complete. One more shimmer and there were jewels. Green, red and blue shone brilliantly out at them. 'Well, it's still a box,' said Leila. 'Just a much nicer one.'

'The reconstruction programme's working on the fine detail,' replied Cassiel. 'It'll take a couple more minutes to tease it all out. Then we'll see what this "much nicer" box can tell us.' She turned to Leila. 'Now – my part of the bargain.'

'Finally,' said Leila. 'So, what can you tell me about Deodatus and the pressure men?'

'Not much, I'm afraid. Deodatus is a very secretive corporate entity.'

'Is that it?'

'Be patient and listen. You thought there was little point in my questions to you, but,' she waved at the device, 'it's led us to this. Something very concrete.'

'What matters is where Dieter's ended up and how to get him back. Not that piece of junk.'

'Your brother couldn't have sold his weaveself if he hadn't been dying. Perhaps someone set out to kill him? That makes this box the murder weapon. And puts it at the heart of the investigation.'

Leila was silent for a moment. 'Shit,' she said, feeling an uncomfortable blend of embarrassment and shock.

'Ah, you agree. Now, where did your brother find the box?'

'Junky Fi sent it to him.'

'A drug addict? And he trusted her enough to explore the box without running his own checks?'

'She's not a junkie,' sighed Leila. 'She's junky. Collects junk, reconditions it, sells it on. She's sent him quite a few artefacts, over the years. He always said she's pretty good on security.'

'I see. And – I'm sure I don't need to ask – but have you been in touch with this Fi? Confirmed that the box did in fact come from her?'

'She hasn't returned any of my calls.'

'And you didn't find that suspicious?'

'Some of my messages were pretty angry. And then Dieter died. I thought she was hiding from me.'

'I can imagine.' The mind sounded amused. 'I will of course try to reach her myself, if you'd be kind enough to share her contact details. And do you have a physical address for her?'

'Dieter did.' A pause. 'So it's gone. With all the rest of him.'

'Oh, of course.'

Leila said nothing.

'I am sorry for your loss. To lose a life's worth of memories like that – well, it's profoundly shocking. And I know that my questions are causing you pain. But I have to pursue my investigation.'

'It's not just your investigation, Cassiel. I've helped you, you've got to start helping me. You haven't told me anything about Deodatus. All I know is that you investigate fraud so it's got to be dodgy, and that doesn't get me anywhere.'

Cassiel grunted disapproval. 'That misunderstanding again,' she said. 'I'm not a fraud investigator. How to explain it?' She thought for a moment. 'In your terms, I suppose I'm an antibody.'

'Can you stop changing the subject and just answer the question? What do you know about Deodatus?'

'I am answering it,' replied Cassiel. 'Our society is very different from yours. Understanding my role within it will help you understand everything else I'm about to tell you.'

Leila rolled her eyes.

'So let me broaden your horizons a little,' the mind continued. 'I'm a free-floating purification agent within the Totality. Much like a white blood cell in a human bloodstream. I'm empowered to deep-dive into any corporate structure, up to and including god-scale entities, then purge any flaws or weaknesses that could damage our wider society. If necessary, I can step outside our normal legal structures and test them to destruction. Much like your Hugo Fist did, with Harry Devlin and Kingdom.'

'He's a great chat show host, but I've never really believed someone used him to kill a god.' More sadness, softer this time, as she remembered Dieter rambling on about conspiracies and cover-ups. At least her own memories of her brother remained untouched.

'Oh, he and Jack Forster played the devil's role to perfection.

They saw a weakness, purged it and helped the Totality replace it with something purer.'

'They helped your people become more powerful.'

Cassiel ignored the jibe. 'And of course, if I encounter a truly honest, truly well-run corporate entity, there's no action I can take against it.'

'But Deodatus has to be dodgy. So you can purge it.'

'I believe I could, if I could find it. It exists wholly virtually, a ghost within the corporate machine. Most of the data cores that might have recorded its activities, its personnel, its location were destroyed during the Soft War. There is no mention of it in any that survived. All I can find is three recorded transactions, all taking place within the last two months – the very substantial payment to your brother and a pair of smaller but still significant ones to family members of two other recently deceased Pantheon subjects. In my experience, secrecy times riches equals corruption. And so here I am. Trying to understand that corruption, so I can protect my society by eradicating it.'

'So you don't even know where it's based?'

'No.'

'Shit. What about the pressure men?'

'This is the first I've heard of them. Clearly they represent Deodatus on Station. And they seem to be pretty elusive. Beyond that – well, further research is needed.'

'And the people who got the other two pay-outs? Haven't they helped?'

Cassiel's glow dimmed a little. 'When I'm in Pantheon space I have to work through the Rose. Her people refuse to release any of the other beneficiaries' or policy holders' details to me. InSec say there's no evidence of any crime.' Frustration filled the mind's voice. 'All I need is their names. But the Rose has been so obstructive. I believe she's actively trying to limit my investigation. There is a possibility of corruption.'

Leila thought back to her own encounters with InSec. They'd always been so brutal. 'That wouldn't surprise me,' she said. 'So how did you find me?'

'Through the trust fund that holds the money on your behalf.

It's a Totality-based financial entity. I didn't need the Rose's help to find and question it. And you've been very helpful, in your way.' She indicated the artefact. 'There's that. It fascinates me. Aha! The reconstruction is complete.'

Leila was now also very intrigued by the artefact. She decided to try and ask Ambrose about it, regardless of his objections. But before she inspected it there was one last thing to be sure of: 'So is that all you know about Deodatus?'

'As I said, it's a beginning.' Cassiel leant in, and examined the fully reconstructed image. 'And all investigations have to begin somewhere. Though perhaps our true beginning is this box. I've queried the relevant data cores about it. I'll hear back from them all in a day or so.'

'Will you share those answers with me?'

Cassiel tipped her head to one side and brought a hand up to her chin. 'I don't know,' she replied. 'Maybe. Maybe not. It depends. And perhaps Junky Fi will reappear. I'm sure she won't hold anything back from you.'

Leila thought about unanswered phone calls. 'Perhaps,' she said. She remembered her new wealth. 'I'll pay for information,' she said. 'About the device, about Deodatus, about the pressure men. Whatever it costs.'

'But I'm Totality. Pantheon money means very little to me. We're motivated by very different things. Mutual obligation, social cohesion, the common good...'

'... taking care of your family? Protecting lost memories?'

'Ah!' the mind said, sounding almost amused. 'Both good points. Very well then. I'll see how things proceed. If I can help you without either disrupting my investigation or placing you in danger, then I will.'

'I think that means no.'

'It means maybe. And that's the best you're going to get.'

There wasn't much else to say. They parted and Leila returned home, where she spent most of the rest of the day organising Dieter's wake. It was slow, sad work. She was surprised to find herself wishing that she was back with Cassiel again, where she'd at least had some sense that she was pushing forwards rather than looking back.

And of course the next day was even worse, because then the wake actually happened.

Chapter 6

Dieter's wake was an unusually sad event, because most of the people attending it expected it to be a very joyful one. It took place in his weavespace, the virtual landscape that served as his workshop, personal comms hub and general onweave home-from-home. Leila's friends Miwa and Dave had offered to support her. She asked them to wait at the weavespace's entrance and, as people's avatars appeared, take them to one side and break the news of his true death. Then the guests moved into its public area – a large grassy space, surrounded by one- and two-storey utility huts. Rectangular windows showed workspaces that had once been cluttered with Dieter's obsessions. Little of them remained. Deodatus had left only empty shelves, unused blackboards and vacant tables and chairs.

The guests dealt with the shock of Dieter's true death in different ways. Some pulled themselves out of the party to gather their emotions, then returned looking pale and controlled. Others came straight over the grass to Leila, shocked faces clashing with colourful party clothes. They stumbled out condolences they'd had no time to prepare, then moved on to drink too quickly. When she wasn't greeting new arrivals Leila moved through the crowd, breaking awkwardly into conversations between people who knew each other far better than she did. She felt desperately lonely. Everything seemed so wrong. She rolled the black pendant that hung around her neck between her fingers, letting its sharp edges spike into them, and decided to take refuge in solitude. She stepped out of the public area of Dieter's weavespace into one of his private workshops.

There was a table at one end of the room, lit by sunlight pouring in through long, high windows. Flies buzzed lazily, full stops weaving through the air. Three empty blackboards clustered at one end of the room. Memory showed her the clutter that had once filled it. This was the room where they'd worked together to rebuild her memory. Dieter had built two linked couches for them to lie back in as Leila restored structure to her past. They were gone.

A child's voice surprised her. 'I looked forward to his rebirth. He would have contributed so much more to the Fetch Communion.'

Leila turned. A young boy stood in the doorway, dressed in red shorts and a blue T-shirt. He looked about ten. Uncombed hair leapt up from his head. His face was friendly and open, but his eyes were pools of shining darkness. When he spoke the same deep void appeared behind his white teeth.

'Hello,' said Leila. She'd never seen the boy before, but she recognised the entity that had possessed him. 'It's been a while.'

'A couple of years, at least,' the Fetch Counsellor used the boy to say. 'We've all changed a lot.'

Leila tried to remember what sort of body the Counsellor had been wearing when they'd last talked. It had no independent existence. Every time it appeared, it manifested through a different fetch. Only the eyes and the mouth remained the same. She'd spent a lot of time with it during the first months of her afterlife. It had worn many different bodies as she came to terms with her new, post-mortal status. Whenever she remembered all those different faces and voices, she felt like an entire community had cared for her. She supposed that that was the point.

She pulled herself back to the present. 'I'm surprised you came,' she replied. 'But thank you. I'm very touched.'

The boy hopped up to sit on the table, moving with a confidence that was entirely adult. 'I wouldn't have missed it,' he replied. 'After he healed you, Dieter did a lot for us. Boosted our security, helped us guard against other attacks.' Leila's surprise must have been very obvious. 'He never mentioned that?'

'No. Not at all. I mean – he talked about how fascinating he found fetch memory structures. And he really hated those Blood and Flesh people. And any other fetch bigots, come to that. But he never mentioned doing anything for you.'

The boy nodded. 'He had a lot of respect for your choices. He did his best to protect you. But always within the limits you set. And when you chose to have nothing more to do with us, clearly he decided to respect that choice too.' His tone was difficult to read. Leila wasn't sure if he was chiding her.

'I suppose he must have done,' she replied.

Out on the lawn, more people had arrived. 'I should get back out there,' Leila said. But she didn't move towards the door. There was a question she had to ask. 'Dieter seemed to think he was going to be reborn. Could Deodatus do that?'

'Are you sure you want me to answer that?'

She nodded.

'We're the only people who can create true fetches, and it's taken us centuries and a revolution to work out how to do it. If these Deodatus people have access to the right technology they could probably create an approximate version of him. But it would be very incoherent. And it would chew up his weaveself's memory structures. Could probably run for a month, maybe two, before it started doing irreversible damage. And of course if they only want part of him they can just delete the rest.'

'Shit. I've got to find him.'

'Of course,' said the boy. Then he took her hand and looked up at her. She remembered when they'd first sat together on the ocean shore, where she would talk herself back into life again. 'I am so sorry,' he said.

'I'm going to bring his weaveself back,' said Leila. 'He will be reborn.'

'I hope so. For your sake as much as ours.'

The little hands pulled lightly and Leila sank to her knees. Small arms wrapped themselves tightly around her. Her face was pulled in against soft, curly hair. The little boy's grip was surprisingly strong, surprisingly comforting. The Counsellor had known her since her own rebirth. There was no need for any sort of façade.

There was a whisper in her ear. 'I'm speeding up time. Take as long as you want.' The room shimmered as the Counsellor over-clocked their deep selves, creating a very perfect privacy. Leila let grief take her.

She sat with the Counsellor for several subjective hours. Sometimes she reminisced. Sometimes she wept. Sometimes she was silent. As time passed, therapy slowly became conversation.

Leila told the Counsellor about Cassiel's investigation. She showed him the reconstruction of the box.

'Means very little to me, I'm afraid,' the Counsellor said. 'The gods guard their history jealously. I don't have anything like the expertise your brother and his friends did.'

'It didn't come from Junky Fi. She finally replied to one of my messages. She's been off-Station for the last few months, pretty much out of touch. Deodatus must have sent the box with a faked note from her. But why?'

'Dieter has an intimate knowledge of fetch consciousness structures and mechanics. Anyone wanting to harm us would find his memories a very useful weapon.'

'Shit.' The thought disturbed her deeply. 'Do you think all this is a Blood and Flesh thing? Have they got Dieter now?'

'They are no longer a threat. And we monitor all of the other fetch-hatred groups. None of them could have pulled this off. Although the dress style of the pressure men is suggestive. It could be that they're harking back to some sort of purer past. The second one you met didn't even speak to you?'

Leila nodded.

'Perhaps he refuses to speak to all fetches, on principle.'

'Maybe Deodatus is a new hatred group,' mused Leila. 'But I can't imagine Dieter ever selling his weaveself to someone like that. No matter how much they offered.'

'Agreed. And Deodatus' financial resources and data hacking skills are far more substantial than anything we've seen in the anti-fetch world. As I understand it, the gods have accepted Dieter's mysterious insurance pay out as fully legitimate.'

'And the other two as well,' agreed Leila. 'Even the Rose. Although Cassiel doesn't trust her. There's definitely something dodgy about it. Theoretically Dieter's been paying premiums for this insurance for years. But I know he hasn't.'

The Counsellor looked thoughtful. 'It's all so unlikely. Killing Dieter in such a targeted way – then rewriting the past to make the pay-out seem legitimate. After doing the same thing to two other completely unrelated people. I can't imagine who it would benefit or how it would help them.'

Leila shook her head. 'I wish I knew. Then I'd use their own bloody money to go right after them.'

'There's that, too. The pay-out gives you so much power to use against whoever's got Dieter. I just don't understand it.' Another pause, then the he spoke again, his tone more personal: 'Look, I know how you feel about the Coffin Drives and the Fetch Communion. You have every right to reject us. We couldn't protect you and we couldn't rebuild you. But we're very worried by all this. We'd very much like to know how it happened and where your brother's been taken. We'd be very grateful if you could let us know if you or Cassiel find out anything of interest.'

'If I find him – when I find him – it'll be for him and me, not for you. And I don't want to be anyone's spy. Can't you ask the Totality for updates yourself?'

'We just need to know of any threats. And this situation – it's so difficult.' The Counsellor suddenly seemed so fragile. Leila wondered if he'd chosen a child's body with this moment in mind. 'We're a new people, Leila. We're very exposed. We have to be very careful who we trust. Who we tell we're in danger. And that includes the Totality.'

'Have you looked for him yourself?'

He sighed. 'We can search the memory seas for stored weave-selves, for fetches awaiting rebirth, even for those who've chosen true death. We've already looked there for Dieter. Without success.' He sighed. 'Please remember how vulnerable we are. Your brother's knowledge in the wrong hands could be very harmful. We need your help against that.'

'I'm sorry…' Leila began.

'We can't change the past. But we can try and make sure that others avoid the kind of pain you experienced.'

That was a goal Dieter would approve of. 'I'll think about it,' she said.

'Please do,' replied the Counsellor. 'And of course if you need any help, just ask.'

They talked for a little longer, but there wasn't much left to say. Leila walked to the window and looked out at the wake. Insects hung in the air, glittering like jewels in the frozen light. The guests too were frozen. She looked around to see if there were any new arrivals. Ambrose stood by Miwa and Dave, one hand reaching out in awkward greeting.

Leila turned back to the Counsellor. 'We should go out again,' she said. 'And – thank you for listening.'

'It's what I'm here for,' he told her.

Time started again and they went out into the garden together. Leila found it easier to mingle, easier to talk. At one point, she spotted someone wearing a pastel-shaded suit, standing alone. She started towards him but was distracted for a moment by a tearful reminiscer. When she looked back again, he'd gone. 'Shit,' she said. She sent a call to the weavespace's security systems, but there was no record of him. He could have been a pressure man. Or he could have just been one of Dieter's more socially challenged acquaintances, moving as anonymously as possible through the world, fleeing when he saw that she'd spotted him.

As the wake started to wind down, she felt more able to ask around. Dieter had never mentioned Deodatus or his agents to anyone. Nobody had anything useful to say about the box. When she ran out of people to question she ended up talking with Miwa, Dave and Ambrose, breaking off for goodbyes when people started to leave as soon as they politely could. At last, it was just the four of them. Leila asked Ambrose to stay when the other two left.

'I need your help,' she told him. 'I know how much you hate this stuff – but I've got to find Dieter. And apart from Deodatus and the pressure men, the box is the only clue we've got. Please could you take a look at it? Just for a moment.'

'What about Junky Fi?' asked Ambrose. 'She's the one that sent it to him. She should be helping you sort it out.'

Leila smiled ruefully. 'No she didn't. Turns out she's on a salvage contract somewhere out past Jupiter. Has been for months. There's a four-hour lag on any communication with her and anything she says is heavily censored. Commercial confidentiality, apparently. I could hardly even talk about the weather with her. I'm sorry, Ambrose. It's you or nobody.'

'Gods,' sighed Ambrose. 'There really is nobody else, is there?'

'I'm afraid not.' Ambrose bit his lip and looked away. Leila put her hand on his arm. 'I'm sorry,' she said gently. 'I wouldn't ask unless I really had to.'

He looked back at her, doing his best to be resolute. 'OK,' he said. 'I'll do what I can. Show me the box.'

'Thank you.' Leila sent an internal recall order, pulling up Cassiel's recreation of Dieter's box. It leapt into being between them.

'Fuck!' shouted Ambrose, throwing up an arm to shield himself. Then he became a statue. Silver leapt out across his skin and clothes, freezing him in place. His voice cut out. Leila put a hand out to touch him. He was rigid, the metal that had been his skin freezing cold to the touch. She snatched her hand away and glanced back at the box. Her systems told her that it was a completely inert, entirely harmless simulation. But there was nothing else that could have triggered his reaction. She pulled it back out of existence.

A moment or so passed, then his shields dropped. The silver melted back into flesh and fabric. His face was the first part of him to reappear. 'Bloody hell,' he said as he returned to normal. He staggered when the silver left his legs. 'Dear me, Leila, that's an evil fucking thing.'

'I'm sorry,' stammered Leila. 'I didn't know. I mean – I don't understand. It's just an image. What harm could it do?'

'The text on it.' There was a hip flask in his hand. He tried to unscrew the cap. His hands shook. 'Triggered my shields.'

'How?'

'The precursor gods – the Pantheon's parent companies, from before Station was even built – were heavily reliant on psychoactive tech. Like the damn thing that killed Cormac's family. There was a lot like it about in the early days. It's one of the reasons why InSec are so down on archaeology, why they keep the kind of thing we're interested in offweave. People might find more of it.'

'You didn't mention this the other day.'

'Didn't seem relevant.' At last he unscrewed the cap. It dropped into the grass. 'If any of the symbols that Cassiel's exposed had been visible on the real thing, InSec would have been all over you both.' He took a deep swig of whisky.

'So, what are they? Are they dangerous?'

'Not on their own. But they've been seen before. On old, old,

45

dark technologies. Artefacts that write commands directly to your mind. And so my shields went up.' He drew on the little flask again. 'I haven't seen anything like that since the Lazarus Crew days.'

'I never knew,' said Leila.

'We were very careful who we discussed it with. And Dieter was always so protective of you.'

'Yeah.' Leila remembered him glowering at lover after lover. 'Typical big brother.'

'And to be honest, it is terrifying. It might even be why we lost Earth. There was a lot of it live down there. One theory is that something psychoactive got loose, deleted history and nearly broke the gods.'

Leila's reply was instinctive. She'd had the story drummed into her so many times at school. 'But we know what happened. The gods fought to free us from the war machines.'

'That's what they'd like you to think. Actually, they don't really know what went on. Memories wiped. They might be the good guys, they might be the bad guys. Who knows? So they made up a story that makes them look good.'

'I knew they were full of it, but that takes the biscuit.' She thought for a moment. 'So you think something psychoactive ate Dieter?'

'No. That's what's odd. The deal he made is real. The money proves that. And there are pressure men running around and a Totality fraud investigator looking into it all. There's a lot more to this than just that box.'

'But it's where it all began.' Leila sighed. 'Could you bear to have another look at it?'

Ambrose went to stand. Leila reached down for him. His real age was suddenly visible in the slow, careful way he moved. 'You're a good friend. Dieter was too, once.' He took a deep breath. 'But I'll be honest. All of this scares the shit out of me. It's been years, and I still can't even bring myself to decommission my shields. I just want to leave the past alone.'

'You're all I have, Ambrose. Cassiel's doing her best, but I can't see the Totality knowing much about deep Pantheon history. Nobody knows as much about this stuff as you do. Please, Ambrose. For Dieter. For me.'

'Gods.' Ambrose smiled weakly. 'I'll have nightmares for the next week, you know.' He took a deep breath, then nodded. 'Right, shields deactivated. Bring it up.'

The box shimmered into being in front of them. Ambrose swallowed, then leant over to examine it. A minute or so passed, then he said: 'Poor Cormac would have loved this. I wonder if Dieter worked out how old it is?'

'As old as Station, he said. Maybe older.'

'He was right. It's amazing that it's survived.' He peered up at Leila. 'If I wanted to get Dieter so excited that he'd drop his guard, this is definitely the sort of thing I'd choose.' He paused for a moment. 'You know, InSec really should see this,' he said thoughtfully.

'Really?'

'We had a back door arrangement with them. If we ran into anything that looked too dangerous, we'd pass it straight over to their specialist. An Inspector Holt. He's probably still there.'

'Cassiel's tried InSec. They blocked her. She thinks they might be corrupt.'

'Ah, that's just Pantheon and Totality politics,' said Ambrose dismissively. 'InSec will treat you very differently. First of all, you're not a mind. And secondly, they're on a big anti-fetch-hatred drive just now. They'll be all over you. Probably turn it into a PR opportunity.'

'So they're definitely the best people to go to?'

'For sure. Much better than me.' Ambrose looked profoundly relieved. 'Holt has to open a formal investigation if there's even a hint of any psychoactive technology. And then he'll have to start digging into Deodatus, checking out the pressure men and working out where Dieter's gone. You're on to a winner.'

Leila wanted to make sure she'd exhausted all avenues of enquiry. 'Is there anything you could do alongside their investigation?'

'The only thing that could possibly help is my family firm's search engines. They go far deeper than anything available to the public. If anything could find his weaveself, they could. But the firm manages them on behalf of InSec. They can only look for data related to live, official investigations. And once Holt's on the case he'll run searches of his own.' He took a swig from his hip flask and smiled a relieved smile. 'Probably even use our engines for it.'

'So how do I reach him?'

Chapter 7

The round and limited skies of Docklands had become an ocean, the Twins' iconography engines starting their Taste Refresh Festival celebrations. Leila walked through quiet residential streets towards Inspector Holt, gazing up at the spectacle. Content micropayments ran out of her account without her conscious permission. Budgeting was no longer a concern. Shoals of fish swarmed lazily around the cylindrical city's higher buildings. Brilliant reds and oranges clashed with softer blues and purples. Pastel subtleties were shot through with lines of electric brilliance. With every second of attention that she paid to the Twins' display, extra details appeared. Seaweed billowed out around her, green as emeralds. Jellyfish pulsed into being, soft tentacles lazing out from round bodies shining with stained-glass brilliance. A lobster scuttled by. The voices of the Twins rose up in her ears, a single whisper twined together from male and female lips. 'Together we provide… tasting better than it ever has…' The air around Leila filled with soft blue, becoming water shot through with dapples of sunlight. The black O of space was invisible behind it all.

This was too much unreality. A happy memory of Dieter struck her. Touching her black pendant, she shut down the Twins' brand experience and opened herself up to the weave's non-human layers. The air filled with digital song, the white goods of Station singing out to each other and to the providers that supplied them. Refrigerators summoned food, cookers shared recipes, cleaning units called for detergents, wardrobes propagated the latest trends. She remembered Dieter enthusing about them: 'They're as much part of the weave as we are, and they share as much data on it as we do. But nobody ever thinks to listen, nobody ever thinks to look.' His eyes sparkled. 'And there's so much less security around them!' He'd been so happy, poking around in their depths, understanding yet another hidden part of Station's infrastructure. She smiled to herself, consoled by the past.

Another few minutes, and she'd nearly reached her destination. The last time she'd been in an InSec branch she was picking Dieter up on his release from prison. She was still alive then. When she left college and he'd walked out of his job, an end-of-employment check had uncovered the changes he'd made to his medical records to avoid the Soft War draft. Falsifying personal data was a serious offence. But Ambrose had found Dieter a tribunal representative who'd successfully reframed the hack as an act of resistance to Kingdom's corruption. So Dieter's sentence had been short, a few months only. It had still felt like a very long time. Leila had waited in the dingy reception area until he came out of the door that led to the holding cells. She was so happy to see him. He gave her a hug the size of a planet.

'Burger!' he told her. 'All I've been looking forward to. Apart from seeing you, of course.'

Within minutes they were seated in a Twins burger joint and he was chomping his way through a meal. 'I can't believe these new names,' he told her through a mouthful of meat. She couldn't remember if he'd ordered a Grande Prison Break with Cheese or a Double Fuck You Animal Style. The burgers were the same ones he'd always loved, but their names had modified themselves according to his latest key life event. 'At least the chips are still just chips,' he joked, 'not Crispy Tunnellers or Fucking Free Me Fries.'

Arriving at the InSec branch pulled her back to the present. She caught a glimpse of another, equally dingy reception area. The duty officer sat in a secure-looking booth. Three sullen teenagers, their faces and knuckles bloody, stood next to a lightly armoured InSec street guard. Perhaps they were gun kiddies who'd got carried away. Then the Rose's weave systems meshed with hers. All four of them disappeared as the god's premium weave content kicked in and overlaid reality with illusion.

Leila found herself standing in a light, airy room, tastefully decorated in a range of fashionable colours. Lights that had been hard fluorescent strips now glowed softly. The wire mesh that protected the booth disappeared. The strapline above it changed from *Nothing to hide, nothing to fear* to *Your safety first, every time.* Next to it, there was a shimmering message board headed *For your consideration.* It listed a series of different criminal cases, each followed by numbers. For a moment, Leila assumed that the branch was boasting about its clear-up rates. Then she saw that the numbers were headed *Potential Commission.* She knew that the Rose was happy to sell cases to private investigation businesses, paying out on their successful resolution, but she'd never seen a list of them before.

She gathered herself and moved towards the booth, trying to look comfortable in this strange new world. She told the attractive young receptionist that she had an appointment with Inspector Holt. Of course there was no question of waiting in a public area. Leila was ushered straight into a meeting room, offered a seat on a comfortable sofa and asked if she wanted a drink. She turned down the offer and sat waiting for Holt. She thought through her strategy. The box should catch his attention straight away. She wondered about playing up the pressure men, but decided not to. Elusive stalkers with unusual fashion taste wouldn't engage him in the way that precursor tech would.

After a few minutes, he arrived. He was younger than Leila thought he would be, barely even in his late twenties. His skin had a grey tint to it and his glazed eyes spoke numbingly of stress and exhaustion. It took him a moment to register her presence. 'Holt,' he said. 'Please, call me Avram.'

They both stood there for a moment. The inspector had buttoned the front of his shirt all the way up. It gave him a very prim look.

The silence started to become awkward. 'Shall we sit down?' asked Leila.

He started. 'Oh. Of course. I'm sorry.' He moved to the opposite end of the couch and stiffly took a seat. 'Now, what can I do for you?' he asked, pulling a stylus and notepad into existence.

It didn't take long to explain the situation to him. Leila described her brother's infection, the surprise of his true death, her meeting with Cassiel and her conversation with Ambrose.

'Oh, Ambrose. Good of him to recommend me,' Holt said. But he sounded nervous rather than pleased.

'He thought you'd be the right person to talk to. To get the ball rolling. To find out what killed Dieter and where Deodatus has taken his weaveself.'

'You do know that this Cassiel has already been in touch with us? I'm afraid that very little she had to say stood up to scrutiny. I'm not sure if there's anything for us to look into here.'

'I don't understand. We've got a potentially psychoactive artefact and a possible financial fraud.' She nerved herself. 'And Dieter's weaveself might already be damaged or lost.'

'Let's start with the fraud.' Holt tried to sound soothing, but Leila sensed a jagged tension in him. 'The Totality are facing serious financial issues. They've grown too fast. As a result, they dislike making major resource transfers to Pantheon citizens. They always try and throw a spanner in the works. Cassiel's investigation into the pay-outs to you and the beneficiaries of the two other insurance policies is one of those spanners.'

'So there definitely were two other Deodatus pay-outs? That means two other deaths, doesn't it? She was pretty well-informed about that. And that still leaves the device that killed Dieter. Doesn't that need looking into?'

Holt shifted nervously and fiddled with his collar. 'It was a piece of junk, left behind from another time. Your brother had a known interest in this kind of illegal technology. His luck just ran out.'

'It came from an unknown source, who impersonated a friend of his to make him drop his guard. In its original form it was decorated with symbols linked to psychoactive technology. You have an obligation to check it out. And what if the other two were killed by something similar?'

'They were both terminally ill,' Holt replied. 'Nothing suspicious at all. And I repeat, there is no evidence of fraud. Do remember that the Totality want to stop these payments. If they have to, they'll bend the truth.'

That made Leila pause for a moment. Perhaps Cassiel had lied to her. But her questions were making Holt very nervous. She felt that she was on to something. Remembering the commission list in reception, she decided to change tack.

'The two other pay-outs,' she said. 'They're real enough, aren't they?'

'Not as substantial as your brother's, but yes.' Holt nodded cautiously. 'We confirmed them all.'

'And if someone proved that all three were part of some sort of crime, then solved that crime – I'd imagine the Rose would offer a pretty substantial commission?'

'In cases like this – that's standard,' he said carefully.

'And anyone who invested in the case would get a share of it?'

'Ms Fenech, what are you trying to say?'

'Are you advertising the case? What if I tried to buy a stake in it? Bring in my own investigators?'

'We're not advertising it because we closed the case. And we closed it because there's no crime here.' He stood. 'I don't want to waste any more time on this.'

Leila remembered the Totality lawyer. He'd told her that, now she was wealthy, she would find that she'd entered a new world. The new InSec branding she'd just experienced was one sign of it, the ability to put significant pressure on Holt without being threatened with a fine or arrest another. She decided to fully embrace it.

'I have to find Dieter. I'm going to buy the investigation from you.'

'That's impossible.'

'You know how much I'm worth. I don't care what it costs.'

Holt blanched. 'You can't,' he said. 'It's really not for sale.'

'Bullshit. Everything is, these days. How much?'

'I couldn't...'

'One million? Two million?'

'No.' He was trying to be firm. Numbers shimmered in the air, not quite falling into existence. Holt waved and they vanished.

Leila gasped. 'The room wanted to make me an offer for it. And you stopped it.'

'No,' replied Holt. 'Not at all. That was just an ad.' His voice shook. 'For personal security systems.' It was clear that he was lying.

Leila stood up. 'You're stopping me from buying it.' She advanced on him. 'Cassiel's right. You're blocking the investigation.' Leila felt a strange, hard confidence possess her. 'I'll go over your head if I have to.'

'There's nothing to investigate!' His voice was tense with fear.

'Should I talk to your boss? How about her boss? Or shall I just go straight to the Rose?' Leila was almost ashamed of herself for pushing Holt so hard. She told herself that he deserved it. 'We all know how the gods favour the wealthy. I'll tell her how you stood in my way. Do you want that kind of attention?'

Holt crumpled into a chair. He waved his hand again. Text shivered into being before her. It showed a case number, cost of investment and potential commission. A woman walked out of nowhere to stand next to it. She was dressed in a cream trouser suit with thorned green piping run across it. Her skin was petal white, her eyes and hair a deep, flaming scarlet. She held a tablet in one hand and a rose in the other, and radiated secure, controlling competence.

For a moment, Leila gaped. She'd run into Rose avatars many times, but never one like this. The past flared inside her. She remembered an InSec playground crime swoop. Some of the older kids might have been dealing drugs. She was barely ten. Operatives threatened her and her friends with tasers. The goddess prowled behind them as they patted the children down. Her hair, eyes and lips were an angry crimson, a sharp, punitive brilliance flaring out of pale white skin. Her body armour was crimson too, wrapped around with thorned green wire. Green spikes grew out of her clenched fists. Her voice was a low, thunderous rumble.

'Obey the law or I will crush you. Do you understand?'

Leila had asked herself what Dieter would do. She bit her lip hard, refusing to whimper like all the others. When the operatives withdrew and the older kids fled Leila huddled her friends together and talked to them in a low, calm, reassuring voice until the tears stopped and they could return home without creating too much parental angst. That night, she'd given Dieter the hardest hug she could. Their mother had still been alive then, but Leila couldn't remember her being around. She'd either have been lost in one of East's virtual soaps or passed out in her room.

This new version of the Rose was very different, a presence focused on commerce rather than punishment. 'Thank you for your interest in this case, Ms Fenech,' she said. There was little passion in her voice. Despite her appearance she was still a low-level avatar, representing only a small part of the god's attention. 'We closed it because we felt that there was no crime to investigate. Reopening it for purchase will generate overheads. The cost will be high compared to any possible commission.'

'I told you,' Holt cut in. 'There's nothing for you here. You're wasting your money.'

'I'll pay whatever I need to,' Leila told the Rose.

'Then I will share the terms and conditions,' replied the Rose. She chanted legalities. Holt sat hunched at the table, looking defeated. At last the god reached the end of her litany. 'What level of responsibility would you like to take on?'

That was a question Leila hadn't anticipated. Without really thinking, she told the Rose: 'Full. One hundred per cent.'

The avatar flickered as it accessed a new script. 'That makes you entirely responsible for resolving the case. InSec will provide no support of any kind, and will refer all queries about it to you or your nominated representative. Do you understand?'

She didn't really take it in. 'Yes.' She'd worry about the details later, once she'd got things moving.

The Rose handed the flower she was carrying to Leila. 'Congratulations,' she said. 'The investigation into Deodatus is yours.'

Chapter 8

As soon as Leila got home she called Ambrose. 'How did it go?' he asked. 'Is Holt on the case?'

'Er – not quite.' She told him about their meeting. 'So I ended up buying the investigation,' she concluded. 'And now I need your help. You mentioned your search engines. Dieter's now part of an official investigation, even if I'm the one running it. Could you use them to look for him?'

'Can't Cassiel help you? Or the Fetch Counsellor?'

'The Fetch Counsellor's already tried. And I don't want to go back to Cassiel until I've found out as much as possible on my own.'

'There are private investigators,' hinted Ambrose. 'Professionals.'

'I've got to be careful who I trust. And I know I can trust you. Please, Ambrose.' She couldn't bring herself to offer him money. Trying to buy him would feel like a betrayal of their friendship. 'I know it's not easy. But it's for Dieter. There's something very wrong about all this. I'm afraid for him.'

A pause. 'Oh, all right,' sighed Ambrose. 'I'll set the engines running. They'll trawl the weave, see if they can pick up any traces of him.'

'How's that different from a normal weavesearch?'

'They go much deeper. If any part of him has been in the same virtual space for more than a minute or so, it'll have bled identity data into local weave caches. The caches aren't usually purged until they're maxed out, so chances are that data's still there. The engines go hunting through them.'

'How long will it take?'

'A few hours. Come round tonight, we'll pay a visit to the firm and see what it's found. But that's it. I'll get you a location, nothing more. And do remember – it'll only find him if he or his weaveself stopped somewhere. If they kept him moving, he won't have left any traces.'

'What about the other two policy holders? Can't we look for them, too?'

'No. The engines need core personal identifiers to show them what to sniff out. We don't have that kind of information, it's only ever available to close friends or relatives. And as I haven't seen Dieter for a while, I'll need to scrape his identifiers from your memories. I'll need the investigation number, too.'

Leila gave Ambrose the number, thanked him and ended the call. She reached into herself and copied a few random chunks of the recent past across to him.

Then she realised that she had a whole free afternoon in front of her and she didn't have a clue what she was going to do with it. It was the first time she'd had to herself since all this had begun. She sat back on the sofa and tried not to think about it all. But that was impossible. The flat's front room was full of memories. She let one after another wash over her. She thought about how protective Dieter had always been. 'He'd be freaking out now,' she thought, wondering if she actually did need to feel threatened by Deodatus and the pressure men. That set her thinking about the skull face, the weapon her brother had built just for her.

Late one night, after her recovery from the Blood and Flesh attack, she'd been walking home alone. She'd noticed a man following her down the empty streets, a threatening shadow, never close enough to be unambiguously threatening, never far enough away to be ignored. She'd heard about human attackers hacking fetch control systems and forcing compliance on them. She reassured herself that he probably didn't know she was a fetch. At each intersection she thought he might choose a different path, but he never did.

It struck her that, if he was a hacker, he probably already knew exactly what she was. Otherwise he wouldn't be following her. He was still behind her, never any closer, never any further away. She thought about jumping home, but chided herself about paranoia. Perhaps they just happened to be heading in the same direction. Another crossing. He was still behind her. Perhaps he was hunting her. Perhaps he was drawing out the hunt. She thought about speeding up, but worried that he would too. She thought about slowing down to let him pass. She didn't want him any closer. She crossed another road and he followed. She didn't want him to see where she lived. In the end she jumped.

After she vomited she sat in the front room, weeping with fear, anger and frustration. Dieter came to see what was wrong. A couple of days later, he suggested reactivating her skull face. She remembered how all fetches used to have them – how, before the Rebirth, they'd had to wear them whenever they were in a public place.

'It's scary enough on its own,' said Dieter. 'And I can add in some seriously heavy shit. Access your target's virtual sensory systems, set up escalating feedback loops in them.'

'Dieter, I don't even know that that means.'

'Ah. Sorry. So – we all receive sensory content from the weave. Virtual sights, sounds, tastes, smells, touches.'

Leila nodded.

'Those sense ports are very easily accessible. They have to be. So much data going through them, all the time. We can set it up so that, when you hit someone with your skull face, you'll make their sense ports think they've been overloaded. Their virtual senses will go nuts. Crazy loud noises, pain, blinding light, disgusting smells, tastes, all at once. It'll only last a couple of seconds, but that'll be enough.' He beamed. 'If anyone tries it on again – well, you'll stop him in his tracks.'

A few weeks later, she'd been at a friend of a friend's party. An older man weaved over to her, drink in hand. 'Hi,' he slurred, reaching out to pull her to him, a lubricious smile swaying across his face. 'Wanna fuck?'

The skull face read her surprise and disgust, and shifted in the back of her mind. She wondered if this was the right moment to try it out. On the one hand, she didn't feel particularly threatened. She was with friends and her wannabe seducer was clearly an idiot. On the other hand, he could use a lesson in good manners. And she was very curious to see her new weapon in action. *What the hell*, she thought. She smiled gracefully as she flicked a mental switch to activate it.

'Oh, you're a fetch!' he said, surprised, as his hand passed through her. 'Well, I'm open minded.'

It took a few seconds for the skull face to fully boot up. She felt it wake and unpack itself, then reach out to interrogate its target's sensory systems. It called information from Leila, too, calibrating the strength of its response to her sense of the situation. A moment as it constructed a sensory assault package, and then it signalled readiness.

'So how about it, then? You, me and breakfast?'

Leila let him have it.

Afterwards, when his friends had picked him up and helped him into the bathroom for a clean-up, someone tried to apologise for him: 'It's just a joke. He thinks he's cutting the crap. Getting straight to the point.'

'Cutting the crap?' said Leila. 'I thought I was the one doing that.'

They didn't stay at the party much longer.

Miwa was very jealous of the skull face. 'Can't wait till I'm a fetch,' she said.

'Just be patient,' smiled Leila, for the first time in quite a while entirely comfortable in her own skin. 'It comes to us all.'

The next morning, Dieter guffawed when she told him about her adventure. She was pretty hungover, but she laughed too. And then she went back to bed for the rest of the day. Every couple of hours Dieter brought her another cup of tea, chuckling quietly to himself. 'It's only a shame he didn't have a friend,' he told her later. 'You could have tested out the skull face's multiple target setting.'

Leila smiled at the memory. She was feeling a little cheerier, but the void hours of the afternoon still stretched blankly ahead of her. She pulled herself back into her bedroom, replaced the neat little business suit she'd worn to see Holt with a T-shirt and pyjama bottoms and opened up the Deodatus case file. There was very little new information. *They barely even investigated the three deaths*, thought Leila. She shivered as she read her own and Dieter's names. Cause of death was left blank for him and the two other policy holders. *That's bullshit*, she thought. *Someone's definitely crooked.* She ran a weave search on the other two, but it was useless. Hundreds of possible candidates hovered in front of her. *Cassiel said all she needed was the names. Maybe she could narrow it down to the right ones.* She thought about getting in touch with her, but didn't want to feel wrong-footed again. She decided to wait until she had some concrete results from Ambrose's search in hand too.

She couldn't think of anything more to do. Feeling frustrated, she wandered back into the front room. Dieter's absence tugged at her memories. She went to the window, brought the weave up to full and overlaid Docklands with the brand iconography of the gods, letting the Twins' festival imagery dominate.

The world shivered as the Twins once again opened up the luxury version of their branding to her. The streets became a sea floor, lithe pathways of pristine sand running between blocks of colour-pulsed coral and drifting towers of seaweed. The spectacle was interspersed with brand messaging, whispering subtly of the luxurious new flavours the Twins would soon be sharing with Station. Deciding to walk out into it all, she returned to her bedroom and tugged her wardrobe's casual wear section into being. Before she could choose anything, a query flashed up.

'Fancy splashing out on some new outfits? Our personal stylist Nena is ready and waiting to help you make the best of this season's fashions...'

'No!' snapped Leila. Then, to herself, 'bloody spam.' She waved the query away. For a moment, nothing happened. Then, with a sharp cracking sound, her clothes stuttered in and out of sight, then vanished in a burst of static.

'Dammit.' The last time her wardrobe had crashed it had taken half a day to self-check and fully reboot.

'Oh, I'm so sorry,' a woman said. 'Your flat – the bandwidth is limited. I had to force close a couple of systems to get in here.'

'Shit!' said Leila, shocked. A slim blonde twenty-something had appeared on the other side of the bed. 'Are you a stylist?' she asked. 'Gods, you gave me a fright. I said no, I didn't want to see you.'

'No, Leila,' the woman replied. 'I'm not a stylist.'

She too was dressed in sweatpants and a T-shirt. On her, they had an impossible elegance. She smiled, and her smile contained all the care and support that the best of girlfriends could ever bring. Leila felt a tug at her mind and remembered the celebrityware that had seized her attention in the hospital atrium. But this was manipulation of a different order.

'You might say I'm THE stylist.'

'Ah,' said Leila. 'East.'

The goddess smiled. 'The very same.'

Shock and awe suffused Leila. Her librarian subroutines thrust details of other visitations at her – of compliments that had mollified the goddess, of missteps that had enraged her.

'Oh, there's no need to be scared,' East reassured her. Leila backed away as the goddess moved round the bed. 'I'm a kitten, really.' She sat down on the end of the bed. 'All the scary stuff is just to keep the masses in check. And you're not the masses anymore.' She patted a spot just next to her. 'We need to talk. Girl to girl, just you and me.'

Part of Leila wanted to flee, but the idea of offending the goddess was far scarier than the fact of her presence. Hoping that she wouldn't say or do the wrong thing, she moved back to the bed and very carefully sat down.

East was inspecting the room. 'Nice décor,' she said. 'I can see you've done your best with it.' She turned to Leila. 'You have a good eye.'

'Thank you,' said Leila carefully.

East put a soft hand on her knee. 'Really,' she said, her tone warm and friendly. 'There's no need to be afraid. You're a very special person now, you know. Almost as special as me – and certainly as unique. You're the richest fetch on Station. That's why I asked Nena to step back and let me have a chat with you.' As she spoke, Leila felt a soft breeze of divine reassurance pass across her emotions. A vast calm spread through her. Part of her was immensely glad of it. Part of her was deeply resentful.

'Oh, I am sorry,' East said. 'Managing your responses like that is something I just have to do – at least until we get to know each other a little better. And you get used to me.'

'Gods,' Leila gasped. 'I – I don't know what to say. I mean – I'm well off, I know. But why does that make me special? Why are you here?'

The question amused East. 'Bless you,' she replied. 'So modest. You're a very powerful woman, Leila. In the last two days alone, you've spent more than you used to in a month. And I bet you've hardly even noticed!'

'Well, I've had other things to think about…' Leila began.

The god laughed delightedly and clapped her hands together.

'Everything's changed. You'll never want for the finest in everything. Clothes, entertainment, travel – you're going to live the kind of life that most of humanity can only dream of.' She leant in. Lightly scented breath caressed Leila's face. 'And here's the secret I've come to share.' Her voice dropped to a whisper. 'Everyone's going to want to watch you. Everyone's going to want to copy you. Because they know you'll only ever have the best.' She sat back, beaming. 'And I want to help them do it,' she concluded triumphantly.

'I'm not sure. I mean, it sounds lovely. But there are things I have to do. Obligations to fulfil.' She wondered whether to tell the god about Deodatus. Perhaps East already knew about her investigation.

But then East chimed in unstoppably. 'Of course, lovely!' she beamed. 'One life's ending and another one's beginning. That's never easy. And you do have a brother to mourn.' She smiled brightly. 'But once that's done with, well. I have such a new life to dress you in. And the celebrity channels will ADORE you! Your people will be so very in this year. I'll make sure of it. I'm sure the Fetch Counsellor will be thrilled, it'll be so helpful.'

Leila must have looked worried.

'Oh, being non-human won't be a problem,' East continued. 'Just look at what we've done with Hugo Fist! He's a ventriloquist's dummy and everyone loves him. And of course I won't force anything on you. You'll be free to shape your future, to live as you'd like to live. As someone rich enough to buy Station from the gods, if you felt like it!' A moment's thought. 'Not that we'd ever let you, of course.' She became conspiratorial again. 'It's everybody's dream. To be able to do whatever they want. Then share it all with the world.'

Leila found that she didn't have too much to say. East rattled on, sketching out scenarios. 'You could be an entrepreneur, we'll follow the businesses you invest in. Found a hospital! Perhaps that would be a good outlet. And I'm sure a lovely way of remembering your brother. Get involved with my lovely gun kiddies, though I'm not quite sure that's you. Or you could just party…'

East didn't mention Deodatus. Leila assumed that she didn't know about it, so decided not to bring it up. She was sure that East would get very excited about it – and she was equally sure that hearing it played back to her as the basis for a new entertainment series ('Perhaps you could find and solve a new crime every week!') would make her feel like the worst kind of dilettante. And, of course, there was the more practical problem of corruption. If Cassiel was right, the Rose might somehow be colluding with Deodatus. Perhaps other gods had joined her.

At last East finished. 'I'm so glad we had this little talk,' she said. 'I'm so excited about the work we'll do together.'

'But what if I don't want any of it?' asked Leila.

'I know,' said East sympathetically. 'It's a lot to get used to. But with great wealth comes great responsibility – to all those who look up to you. Think of this as one way of managing that responsibility.' She leaned in and kissed Leila. The soft, warm touch of her lips left a tingle shaking through Leila's skin. She was infuriated to feel herself warmed by a sharp pulse of sexual desire. 'Oh, I'm sorry,' said the god. 'That happens to everyone, please don't take it personally. Anyway – yes of course, there are other options. And I'd hate to force you into anything you're not happy with. Remember that, Leila. I'll give you a few days to get used to it all. We'll talk again soon.'

And then East was gone, and Leila was alone. The divine invasion had left her feeling exposed, as if her life was something that the gods could walk into and change on a whim. She imagined herself as East wanted her to be – a reality star, a brand puppet, someone whose every movement or emotion would be interpreted as an endorsement or a sales pitch. She realised that she'd end up seeing herself like that too – that the authentic Leila would be so hard to hang on to. 'Oh, Dieter,' she groaned, falling back on her bed, 'I've got to find you.' She needed to move the investigation on as quickly as possible. Rather than waiting for any results from Ambrose, she'd share all the names in the Deodatus file with Cassiel, in return for full access to anything she found out. She thought about negotiating by mail, but worried about security. She also found herself quite looking forward to surprising the mind with her progress.

So Leila messaged her saying: 'We need to meet up.'

Cassiel's reply was an address, a time and a note: 'Congratulations on your discoveries. I look forward to learning more about the beneficiaries of the other two pay-outs. And the policy holders too, of course.'

Leila couldn't hide her frustration. 'Oh for gods' sake,' she said. 'How did she know?'

Chapter 9

Cassiel was waiting at a corner table in a busy café, dressed in the same smart-casual suit. Leila looked round, wondering if she'd see any more pressure men, but there were none. She sat down at Cassiel's table.

'So how did you work out I have the names?' she began.

'You need to ask?' replied Cassiel, sounding a little surprised. 'I query InSec for additional information daily. More in hope than expectation, I have to say. This morning, they referred me to you. You've bought the investigation, you must have the details of the other beneficiaries. And the deaths that triggered Deodatus' payments to them.'

'Ah, of course.' Leila tried to sound blasé. Inside, she was kicking herself. 'I, er, just wanted to hear it in your own words.'

'And you're going to share them with me. Thank you.'

Leila readied herself for a negotiation. 'Not unless I get something in return.'

'I can do far more than you with them. I'm not hindered by your narrow, personal focus. And I can draw on resources that would surprise you.'

Leila thought of Ambrose. She smiled. 'Yeah. Me too.'

'I doubt even you can hire Totality-level professionals within twenty-four hours.'

'It's already done.'

'Probably a cowboy.'

'Someone I trust implicitly. With access to Pantheon level weaveself search engines. He's going to work out where Deodatus has taken Dieter.'

'And will he succeed? Those machines don't always find what they're looking for.'

Leila said nothing.

Cassiel sat back. 'And you won't have enough information on the other two beneficiaries to search so deeply for them. Or even understand why they and your brother are so valuable to Deodatus. Without that knowledge you might find it difficult to negotiate his return, even if you do locate him. And of course, you won't be able to find out how Deodatus might represent a broader threat to our two societies.'

'Gods, Cassiel, must you be so smug?' But the mind was right.

'I'm merely sketching out the situation. So we both share the same sense of it.'

'Then let me do some sketching out of my own. I've got the names you need. You won't get them from anyone else. I won't give them to you unless you agree to share anything you find out about them, Deodatus and the whole shebang with me. Clear?'

To Leila's surprise, Cassiel laughed. Soft light shimmered inside her. 'You know, I have to admit that you're pretty good at this. That is indeed very clear. But you've forgotten that I've already agreed to pass on any information I can.'

'You gave me a maybe. I want a definitely. I want to know what you know, when you know it. Not just whatever you feel like, whenever you feel like it.'

'This is a Totality as much as a Pantheon matter. We're very careful about sharing information relating to our own internal affairs.'

'Full disclosure or no deal.'

'And you need to think about what you're getting into. We don't know what Deodatus is. The pressure men might be dangerous. The Rose is doing her best to block me.'

'But she sold me the case.'

'I'm a professional, Leila. You're not. Perhaps she saw you as less likely to succeed than me. Perhaps she thinks you'll be easier to neutralise.'

'She hasn't threatened me so far. Look, I don't care how risky it is. Nothing's going to stop me from getting Dieter back. Are you going to help me?'

'I'm not supposed to work with amateurs.'

'You said you weren't bound by normal structures. That you played the devil's role. Doesn't that mean you can make your own rules?'

Cassiel chuckled again, the same soft light shimmering inside her. 'You're a hard person to argue with.' She thought for a moment. 'Agreed, then. Full disclosure at all times, as soon as is conveniently possible. But I have a condition of my own. You don't make any major moves without talking to me first. I don't want to find myself tripping over you at a critical moment. Agreed?'

Leila could see the sense in the mind's request. And if she needed to, she could always ignore it. She nodded.

'Now, the names,' said Cassiel.

'The policy holders were Andre Herrera and Mo Fafanwe. The pay-outs went to Herrera's partner and Fafanwe's daughter.'

'Thank you,' said Cassiel. A moment's pause, then she continued: 'Intriguing. A competitive eating champion and a military psychiatrist.'

'Excellent weave searching,' Leila told her. 'But are you sure those are the right ones?' She tried to give her voice an edge, but she was actually quite impressed.

'Oh yes.' Leila didn't want to ask how Cassiel was so sure. The mind stood up. 'I'll find out all there is to know about them both. And then I'll be in touch.' She stepped away with an elegant, economical precision, then turned back and said: 'Oh, and there's one more thing. I've moved offices.' An address flashed into Leila's mind.

'Noted.' Leila was curious. 'Why?'

'The flies. I had the room cleaned several times. Moved within the complex. They always came back.'

Leila couldn't resist a jab. 'I thought that sort of thing wouldn't affect a professional like you?'

Cassiel took the question at face value. 'I should have been able to get rid of them,' she agreed. 'I tried to swat them.' She held a hand up. Fingers merged into a flat, wide, rectangular shape. 'With this.' An instant for Leila to see, then nanogel deliquesced again and Cassiel's hand reformed. 'But I could never even touch them.'

'They're tricky little sods,' agreed Leila, remembering the fly in the hospital. It had been unusual too, she realised. 'Shit,' she said. 'I ran into a weave-enabled fly. In Dieter's room, just after he died.'

'Have you seen any since?'

'Not that I've noticed. Were yours weave enabled?'

'I didn't sense anything like that.' Cassiel sounded worried.

Leila tried to reassure her. 'I only spotted it by accident.'

'No,' said Cassiel. 'You don't understand.' Light flurried in the translucent nanogel of her head. 'I'm a weapon,' she continued. 'I have very high-level virtual and physical combat skills. But I could never hit a single one of those flies. And if they were digitally en- abled – well, I didn't even see it. They blocked me, Leila.'

The uncertainty in Cassiel's voice was unexpected. Now Leila was surprised to pick up the softest hint of fear.

Chapter 10

Leila leaned back in one of Ambrose's armchairs. Her black pendant rolled against her chest. Virtual leather creaked comfortingly. His office was heavily overlaid with weave content. She'd never seen the reality that lay beneath it. She stretched her feet out towards the simulated fire that burnt in his office grate. She'd arrived a little early and, to kill a few minutes, had asked him to talk her through the small print of her deal with the Rose.

'You do realise you're now fully responsible for the investigation into Dieter's death?' he said, sounding very unimpressed.

'Well, InSec weren't doing anything with it.'

'Yes, but if anything kicks off, you're on your own. Their duties are limited to making a final arrest of any demonstrably guilty parties. You should have just bought a majority share.'

'Well, it's done now. How soon till we can go and see what the search engine's found?'

'A few minutes.' He was at his desk, punching invisible keyboards, peering at invisible screens. 'Just activating my old digital exploration security systems. Setting up buffer selves for us.'

'Seems a bit extreme.'

'That box scared me, Leila,' Ambrose told her. 'If the search engines come back with any psychoactive malware piggybacking on them, I want to be ready. We're not taking any risks.'

Leila nodded. A thought struck her. 'Did Dieter build all this?' she asked.

'He fine-tuned it. Look, if we're going to get set up for any exploring tonight, I need to concentrate.' He focused intently for a minute or so, then sighed with satisfaction, reclined his chair and closed his eyes.

'Taking a nap?' asked Leila.

'Making sure the meatware's comfortable. You'll see why when the buffer selves activate. You're about to get queried, just say yes to everything, then we'll be good to go.'

A tickle in her mind, and Ambrose's systems were talking to her. Leila's attention turned inwards as she gave them all the permissions they needed. A moment, then they pinged to let her know they were active. She looked back out at the room, where nothing seemed to have changed.

Then Ambrose stood up and there were two of him. His physical body lay unconscious on his chair.

'Did Dieter ever show you any of this?' Leila shook her head. The standing Ambrose tapped his virtual chest. 'This is a buffer self. Runs at one remove from my core consciousness. So if anything psychoactive attacks, it hits this version of me and stops there.' He nodded back at his physical body. 'Keeps the real me safe. All my memory blocks, and the chains they form together. Oh, and look at this.' He turned his head. A translucent silver cord stretched from the back of it down to the forehead of his physical self. 'That's the link between us. Turns red if there's anything dodgy trying to force its way in. Stand up, you'll see yours.'

Leila did so. Her cord also led back to a static version of herself, a photo-realistic statue frozen in time. Her second self faded into transparency, then vanished.

'That's my systems meshing with your home server, back at your flat. Pulling your core self back there.'

'Weird,' she breathed. 'If something does attack us – what then?'

'Just trigger an exit countdown, your buffer self crashes your consciousness back into your core self, and you're home safe. You'll end up back in your front room. The countdown takes about a minute, and crashing back leaves you with one hell of a hangover, but it's much better than the alternative.'

Leila had to agree.

'And now,' Ambrose announced theatrically, 'the back door!' He clicked his fingers and a mahogany panelled door appeared on an empty patch of wall. 'It's a bit like jumping,' he told Leila. 'Only the buffer selves can't experience any sort of nausea. This side of it, my office in Docklands. Through there – the firm's offices in

Homelands.' He opened it and stepped into the bright light beyond. 'Come on through,' he called back.

Leila nerved herself and followed him. As Ambrose had promised, with the buffer self running the jump between his office in Docklands and his family firm's Homelands space made hardly any impression on her at all. Leila felt discomfited by the seamless location change. It left her feeling that the physical world was suddenly a little less real. She looked around, wanting to both understand where she was and let its solid, physical presence wash over and reassure her. The room that housed the Vadenheim family's search engines was large and dimly lit. Its far wall was glass, about twelve foot high and eighteen foot wide. It gave on to an ocean. Light rippled down from above. Fish drifted by, glitching the serenity with bright, jagged colours. An empty glass box, the size of a large coffin, sat on chrome legs in front of it.

'More sea,' she commented. 'Is that a Taste Refresh Festival thing?'

'Oh no,' Ambrose replied. 'It always looks like this. The sea's a standard visual metaphor for all the data that floats around Station. That's where our search engine's been hunting.'

A dark creature sliced past the window, cutting through the peace of it all like a knife. There was a head that came to a single focused point, a mouth like a gash, jagged with hard white teeth, and blade-sharp triangular fins. Leila held her breath as it passed, then exhaled as it vanished from the window. Others glided to and fro in the distance.

'Sharks,' she breathed.

'Apex datavores,' said Ambrose. 'I love seeing them up close.'

'These are the search engines?'

'The best there are!'

Leila glanced at the door. 'What if someone catches us?'

Ambrose shrugged. 'I'm synced with the usage schedules for these chaps. Nobody's going to be in here for the next hour or so. We'll be long gone by then. And if someone wanders in by accident – the buffer selves are pretty much invisible. Not quite ghost cloak standard, but we're still hard to see.' He moved over to the glass coffin and waved his hand. A line of numbered shark icons popped into existence. He scrolled through it. 'And here's our little hunter!

71

Back with a full belly.' His finger hovered over its icon. 'I hope it's just a location. Nothing more dangerous,' he said nervously.

Fascinated by the search engines, Leila didn't really hear him. 'Why sharks?' she wondered.

'InSec wanted to track down weaveselves bleeding a few bytes of data into an ocean of information. They needed to home in on individual weave caches and pick up the subtlest changes in them. Sharks are amazing hunters. They can detect one drop of blood in a million drops of water. They're profoundly sensitive to electrical impulses. So we built our search engines around their neural structures. And we gave them bodies they recognised to minimise any consciousness displacement shock.'

'CDS? Fetches have problems with that.' She remembered a Coffin Drives acquaintance trying to live as a dog. He'd lasted for a few days until the nightmares became too much to deal with and he'd had to return to human form.

'Yes. You can transplant a mind into anything, but unless you do some heavy rewiring to help it deal with its new body it'll freak out.'

'So has our shark found anything?'

'Er. Yes. It has.'

Leila saw how nervous Ambrose was. 'Is there any risk?' she asked.

'Not really. But still…' Ambrose sighed. 'It really shouldn't scare me anymore.' An embarrassed laugh.

'The Coffin Drives still freak me out.' Leila put her hand on his shoulder. 'I know what it's like.'

He smiled weakly. 'Well, here goes.' He closed his eyes, held his breath and stabbed down on the shark icon.

His nerves were infectious. Leila found herself wondering what she'd do if some broken, ancient piece of code lanced out of the shark and into her mind, and started rewriting it. Memories of the Blood and Flesh plague shook through her. Something close to panic rose up. She forced the past back down again, but still started as the shark lanced into being in the glass coffin. Its eyes were misted with weaveware. The rest was hard and sharp, distilled by aeons into lethal perfection.

She looked to Ambrose. 'All right?' Fear scratched at her. She hoped his silver shields wouldn't leap up around him.

A moment, then Ambrose breathed a sigh of relief. 'Yes. Thank the gods.'

Leila relaxed. 'Thank you. I really appreciate this. Dieter will too.'

'I'd hate to lose him like we lost Cormac.' Figures danced in the air between Ambrose and the shark. Leila moved round the tank, fascinated by the creature. 'And to be honest it's about time I faced up to it all,' continued Ambrose. A nervous smile. 'Can't hide from the past. That's not the Lazarus Crew way.' The figures stilled, catching his attention. 'Ah, great. It's found traces of his passage through the weave. Regular stopping points. They moved him back into the Totality, then on from there.' He peered at them. 'Hmm, interesting – you said your Totality friend couldn't find anything out about Deodatus?'

'Cassiel? No. It's driving her nuts.'

'The trail leads back to an old Kingdom satellite. High Earth orbit. Vintage stuff, looks like it's been unused for quite a while. Deodatus must be using it as an off-Station base. Should have been easy enough for her to track down, it's not too deeply hidden. I wonder why she couldn't see it?'

'Holt tried to stop me from digging too deep,' mused Leila. 'Maybe they've been a bit more efficient with her. Hamstrung her without her even realising it.'

'So the Totality isn't as all-powerful as you'd think. That's almost reassuring.'

A thought struck Leila. 'This satellite. It's the kind of place you used to explore with Dieter?'

'Abandoned for centuries, weave content not fired up since who knows when, probably first built by one of the lost gods of the Pantheon? Yes, absolutely.'

'Can we go there now? I mean – we've found him, and that's great. But Dieter might not have much time left. Deodatus could be running him as a partial fetch. Breaking his memory structures. Or just deleting the bits of him it doesn't need.'

Ambrose went pale. 'That's a lot to ask, Leila.' His flask was in his hand again. The shark hung between them, radiating danger.

'I know. I'm scared too. But I don't want to lose Dieter.'

Ambrose put his face in his hand, hiding his eyes from her. 'I can't, Leila.'

'You've got so much experience. Much more than Cassiel. We're even wearing your old exploration gear. We can jump right there. I'm sure we'd be safe. If we can find out where Deodatus is holding him – it'd be such a big step.'

'But Cormac...'

'That was terrible,' agreed Leila. 'But the psychoactive tech hurt his family, not him. His defences worked.'

Ambrose didn't reply.

'I've seen broken people, Ambrose. I've been broken myself. I know how bad it is. I don't want Dieter to end up like that. We've got to find him and bring him back.'

'We should wait. Do some research. See what we can find out about this satellite.'

'We don't have time. Please.' Ambrose turned away. 'You said it was time to move on from the past. You were right.' She thought of the Coffin Drives and the Fetch Counsellor, both asking for and offering help. 'Perhaps it's something we both need to do. For Dieter's sake. Neither of us want to lose him.'

Ambrose gave a heavy sigh. 'Oh, Leila. All right, I'll take you there. And when we find Dieter I'm going to give him the most almighty bollocking for getting us into this.'

Leila smiled. 'Yeah. Me too.'

Chapter 11

They jumped directly to the satellite. For a moment, there was darkness and an impression of great velocity. Then the world returned. Leila's senses told her that they'd moved into a fully virtual environment. Understanding that helped her deal with the sudden, destabilising shock of the jump. *This place is a simulation*, she told herself. *Of course we jumped. It's the only way to get in here.*

They were standing in a bland corridor, studded with round windows. Fluorescent tubes cast dead light down on beige walls and a soft, pale carpet. There was a door in front of them. It was made of dark, heavy wooden planks, criss-crossed with rivet-studded iron bands. An iron handle hung over a large, dark keyhole. A little wire mesh covered a square, eye-level window. The door represented a port into the satellite's internal systems, the corridor behind them the digital trail they'd followed to step into them.

'So Dieter's weaveself stopped here?'

'Yes,' said Ambrose. 'For half an hour or so.' He looked back nervously. The corridor behind them was empty.

'Worried that Deodatus will spot us?' asked Leila. 'And send some pressure men after us? It'd be nice to actually see one again. Maybe we could get him to answer some questions.'

'Be careful what you wish for,' chided Ambrose. 'Anyway, that shouldn't be a problem. The buffer selves should keep us hidden.'

'Getting caught might actually make things easier. They could take us straight to the boss.'

'No, Leila,' Ambrose told her firmly. 'The one thing we know for sure about Deodatus is that it's very secretive. We really don't want it to know how close we're getting. It might take fright and hide itself properly. We'd be back to square one again.'

Leila glanced out of one of the windows. There was deep sea beyond, blacker than space. She imagined the search engine swimming through it. 'Did the shark see the corridor?' she asked.

'Oh no. It doesn't need it, the deeps are its natural home. The corridor's just for us.' He bent to examine the door. 'This must be the entry point to the satellite's internal systems.' There was a hollow thud as he knocked his fist against it.

'Can you open it?'

'Let me activate my intrusion package…'

Leila smiled when it appeared. 'Cute,' she said.

The intrusion package was about the size of two clenched fists. A delicate little fringe waved around the sides and rear of its oval, neon-bright body. Finger-length tentacles reached out from the front of its head – two held straight up to scent the air, the other five drifting lazily on invisible data currents. Alert little eyes with black, w-shaped pupils sat on either side of a little skull bump.

'It's a cuttlefish,' explained Ambrose. 'Highly intelligent, a very delicate spatial manipulator and extremely sensitive to local stimuli.' He touched two fingers to its straight tentacles. 'Hello,' he said. 'Haven't seen you for a while.' Patterns of light pulsed across its skin. 'So can you unlock the door for us, little fellow?'

The cuttlefish drifted down to the door handle and hung in front of it. Tentacles reached out and explored the keyhole. 'I'd forgotten how fond I am of this little chap,' Ambrose said.

Leila touched one of the iron bands. A shimmer rippled around her finger, then the illusion was whole again. She peered through the mesh. There was nothing but blackness on the other side. Water dripped, each drop calling up a tiny echo. A musty smell clogged her mind with thoughts of age and decay.

'Seems pretty grim in there,' she commented.

'No updates for centuries,' replied Ambrose, standing back up. 'Dormant tech.'

'How long's it going to take?' asked Leila.

Ambrose was looking back down the corridor. 'Nothing behind us.' He peered out into the depths. 'Nothing out there.' He sounded worried.

The cuttlefish disengaged from the lock.

Ambrose tipped his head as if listening, then turned to Leila. 'Well, it's a tough one. The door only opens for certain specific weaveselves. The cuttlefish can unlock it, but it's going to take some time.'

'How long?'

Ambrose looked simultaneously embarrassed and relieved. 'Er... not much more than a couple of weeks, usually...' He looked back down the corridor again. 'We shouldn't linger here, Leila. We don't know what might find us.'

'Shit.' Everything had been going so well. She'd been so sure they'd find Dieter straight away. Frustrated, she balled her hand into a fist and brought it down on the door. It shimmered again, for a moment wanting to be unreal.

'Ambrose – this door. You said it opens for specific weaveselves?'

He turned back towards her. 'Yes.'

'Watch this.' She knocked on the door. Her fist made no sound. The point where she touched it became for a second not quite present, then returned to full solidity. 'You see?'

Ambrose was fascinated, fear vanishing as curiosity took over. 'Do that again!' Leila did, and the door wavered again. 'You and Dieter share a lot of memories, don't you?' he asked.

Leila remembered lying next to Dieter when she was rebuilding herself. Her past was a confusion of unconnected moments. He'd shown her his version of it, and she'd used it as a roadmap to rebuild her own memory chains, pulling them all back into coherence. She'd even copied some of his memory blocks directly into her mind to replace ones she'd lost to the plague.

'Yes,' she said. 'Far more than most people.'

'It's picking that up when you knock. It thinks you're him and part opens. Then it runs a deeper scan, sees the full shape of your weaveself, realises you're not and locks back up.' He beamed, then started a detailed technical explanation of how he'd now be able to open the door in a couple of days.

Leila let him ramble on as she unhooked the necklace from round her neck. She held it up in front of him. He barely noticed. 'Ambrose,' she said, then again, more firmly: 'Ambrose.' He stopped talking, his eyes losing their distant focus and finding her again. 'Look at this.' She let the lightning bolt spin round. 'It's a three-dimensional representation of the shape of Dieter's weaveself. Can the cuttlefish use it to make a key?'

'Oh! Oh yes, yes, I think it can! You knock, the door queries, we show it this – and bingo!'

Tentacles reached for the pendant. Leila watched the cuttlefish analyse it. She was surprised at how much she felt the pendant's absence. She hadn't taken it off since she'd created it. After a couple of minutes the pendant dropped to the floor. Ambrose scooped it up and passed it back to Leila.

The cuttlefish re-engaged with the lock as Leila slipped the pendant back on. Ambrose nodded and Leila touched the door. It shimmered again. The cuttlefish flickered, colours dancing across it. The shimmer spread out across the whole of the door, then all of a sudden there was no door, only an archway giving on to an ancient passageway. Air heavy with damp and rot gusted out.

Ambrose gave a triumphant whoop. 'Fantastic! And if they've got other locks that work like this, we'll be able to walk straight through them. Well done!'

He looked overjoyed. There was no trace of fear. Leila imagined him as he must have been before Cormac's tragedy, striding through the deep past with his two closest friends beside him. It was such a pleasure to see that side of him returning.

'Come on,' he said, stepping through the arch. The cuttlefish was already beyond it, a phosphorescent ghost hanging in the void. Ambrose reached into his pocket and pulled out two torches. 'Everything's very old through here,' he told Leila. 'Decayed, unpredictable. So we're not going to run a full simulation of it.' He clicked his torch on. A yellow circle of light danced across damp stone floors, crumbling brick walls. 'These let us look at it in a much simpler way. We can still see where we're going and we'll be a lot less likely to trigger anything nasty.'

'Why would Deodatus use this place?'

'I don't know. Perhaps because it's so out of the way. Maybe this is camouflage and it'll all get a bit more up to date further on.'

The corridor was long, straight and low. There were no more doors. Every so often they passed pointed arches carved into the walls, framing darkness. Leila shone her torch into the first few, wondering if they were doors, but the light only showed more brick-work. 'Broken links,' commented Ambrose. 'Would have led some-where once. Not anymore.' The damp stones were hard beneath Leila's feet and the cold, still air chilled her. It was like walking through a tomb. Neither of them said much. Every so often, Leila looked back. Their silver cords led away into the gloom, reassuring links back to the known.

The corridor ended in another pointed arch. This one was open. Leila stepped through it into a high, round room and shone her torch around. It was about fifteen metres across and twenty metres high. The round walls were punctured by three layers of high arched doorways, some bricked up, some full only of darkness. A dome rounded out the ceiling above them. A circular opening lay directly underneath it. The cuttlefish hung over it.

'Is that where they took Dieter?' she asked.

Ambrose nodded. But his attention was elsewhere. 'Look at that,' he breathed, staring up into the dome. Something gold gathered the light and glimmered it back at them. 'Amazing...'

Leila looked up too. Her torch beam joined his. Definition blos-somed, and she saw a stylised image of a young man. He was dressed in scarlet robes and held a pair of dividers and a laser stylus. His face was sketched out in gold. He sat against a dark background, pricked with golden stars. A logo that seemed to be based on the letter 'M' hung over his right shoulder.

'Now that's someone you don't see much of anymore,' said Ambrose. 'He's one of the original Pantheon gods.'

'Dieter used to talk about them.' She gazed up at history. 'It all seemed so distant. So irrelevant.' She let herself drift for a moment, remembering her brother's enthusiasm. 'There were twelve, weren't there? Back when we broke free from Earth?'

Ambrose nodded. 'And now seven of them are gone.'

Leila remembered East, sitting on her bed, radiating power. It seemed impossible that an entity like her could ever fall. 'How?'

'Well, you saw how Kingdom went. The Totality moved in and took over most of his systems when his core was smashed. And you remember how Grey's structure decayed while he slept – his corpo-rate body torn apart, limbs scattered around Station, because there was nothing left to hold them together. The rest went the same way, strong-armed out of existence. Aggressive takeovers, mostly.' He looked back up at the dome. 'Kingdom seized this one. He was always pretty ambitious. If Jack Forster and Hugo Fist hadn't done their thing, he'd have taken two more gods by now – he was pretty much running Grey's legacy systems and he was winding up to absorb Sandal too.'

'I never knew.'

'The gods don't like us to. They want to seem eternal and unchanging. So they don't mention it, they just rebrand and let us forget. And we do, far too easily. The truth of the past disappears. People like us know, but nobody else really cares about it all. Which, if you ask me, is a crying shame.'

'So who was this guy?'

'A god of construction and heavy engineering,' said Ambrose, reverence filling his voice. 'He built the out-system hubs. Farafra Station, Siwa Station, everything around and beyond them. All down to him. Then Kingdom took him over. Took the credit for it all.'

'What was he called?'

'Mikhail.'

The name hung in the air. For a moment, it reverberated as an echo, and then it became something more as the gold lines that defined the image of Mikhail blazed into life. They became a kind of fire, hanging at the heart of the dome, and then the stars around him caught fire too. The fire leapt out, dancing across the whole of the dome. It was like a slow, silent explosion.

'That's beautiful,' breathed Leila.

It kept spreading, raining down from the ceiling to fill the whole room, falling against the arches so that one by one they lit up too. The cuttlefish drifted upwards, tentacles fanned out. Ambrose's face was suffused with joy.

'His brand iconography's booting up,' he whispered back. 'This is original stuff.' He concentrated for a moment. 'Six hundred years old, according to the date stamp. Almost as old as the box. We're definitely on the right track!'

'Are we safe?' asked Leila.

'Oh yes,' replied Ambrose. 'This is drawing on a local server. It's not trying to make any wider connections. And my defences have already checked it out. There's no malware hidden within it.' He gestured towards the cuttlefish. 'It's keeping an eye out. Just in case.'

Then the music began. First there was one voice, then three or four, then perhaps a dozen. They twined in and out of each other, hushing and then building up again in increasingly powerful crescendos. Their soft, intricate interplay spoke of harmony and order, of logic and reason, of group structures that were so much richer than anything any one person could ever achieve. The choir sang out in increasingly powerful pulses, as more and more voices joined in and the song grew to both describe and embody vast human achievements. Chasing melodies through it, Leila found visions of great engineering projects shifting and evolving in her mind's eye. They grew in scale until they showed her a series of physical platforms for one vast, harmonious society, stretched out across the whole of the Solar System, glowing with brilliant, endlessly sustainable life.

At last the music pulsed to a final climax. The room was all fire now. Wonder filled Leila. Mikhail was something entirely new to her. His branding had never been used to sell her anything, to force her to acknowledge achievements that the reality of her life denied. She had never experienced it as propaganda, so she was free to enjoy it as a piece of pure art. The vision of ordered, harmonious, immortal structure it shared was intoxicating. But it was tragic, too, because all that Leila knew of Mikhail was that he was gone and completely forgotten.

Glancing over at Ambrose, Leila saw tears on his face.

'I'm not afraid anymore,' he said. 'It's gone. I just remember why we used to come to places like this. Gods, I've missed it.'

Leila squeezed the pendant until its sharp edges stung her. Regret filled her. She'd been so dismissive of the Lazarus Crew. But she'd have loved to share a moment like this with her brother. And she would, she promised herself, once she'd brought him back from Deodatus. As loss and hope combined within her, the fire and the song began to sicken. Jagged shards of static shattered through the music, breaking its harmony. The flames flickered in and out of existence. Glitches tore at her eyes as the room bounced between two states, flaring out her vision until it became impossible to see anything. A vast industrial clamour took over from the perfect vision of Mikhail's ordered cosmos.

'Server's dying,' Ambrose whispered. 'Spinning out of control. Cuttlefish's shutting it down.'

The last thing she saw was words, written in a text that was both somehow familiar and illegible, hanging over every single one of the arches which surrounded them. There was a single short word above the opening in the floor, burning far brighter than all the rest. One last, blinding flare flashed out, and then they were back in the cold, dark room. The faintest suggestion of gold hung in the gloom above them – a reminder of a divine brand experience that could never be repeated.

'What did all the words say?' asked Leila.

'Station standard language, but Mikhail's font is centuries out of date. Very difficult to read if you're not used to it.'

'I'll say.'

'Basically, they were destinations. This must have been one of Mikhail's digital movement hubs. If you were fully virtual, like us, you could use it to get anywhere.' Ambrose's voice echoed in the dark empty space. 'The open doors will lead to places that are still there – Bahariya Station, Farafra Station, Siwa Station. There'll be doors to Station One, Station Two and Station Three. We think that's what they used to call Docklands, the Wart and Homelands. And the blocked ones go to places that just don't exist anymore.'

'And what did the word over the pit in the floor say?'

'Well, that's the funny thing. The pit only had a descriptor. And it's the first time I've ever seen it.'

'What did it say?'

'Something very simple. All in capitals. DOWN.'

Chapter 12

It was easy to remember the moments before the fall. The cuttlefish pulsed excitedly and Ambrose said: 'They took Dieter into the pit. And they left a record of the jump behind. We can go straight to wherever he ended up!' Then he told the cuttlefish to take them down.

But after that, there was no coherence. It was as if not just space but time itself had fractured. Leila could remember individual moments, but they were jumbled together in her mind like playing cards in a well-shuffled deck. She glimpsed a white tower, wreathed in green. There was a plunge through darkness, moving first down then – after a sudden, brutal, stop – sideways. The cuttlefish pulsed red and squealed out an alarm, but she couldn't stop herself from falling. She clutched Ambrose as wind roared past them, then her empty hand grasped nothing. Brilliant light flared and she squeezed her eyes shut, howling with the shock of it all.

And then it all stopped.

For a moment, there was nothing for Leila's senses to show her. Then fresh data leapt into them, and place reappeared around her.

She was lying on her back on a cold, hard floor, her arms and legs splayed out, her eyes still closed.

She let nothing happen for a minute or so. There was no more movement, no more chaotic bursts of sound and light. Her new environment was apparently stable. She opened her eyes. Her cord rose up into the ceiling. She was relieved to see that it hadn't turned red. She lay between a wall and a long low table, softly lit by pale, silver light from a wall of windows. There were shelves above her. She couldn't see what was on them. A shapeless mass of clothing lay just next to her. She nudged it and it groaned. It was Ambrose.

'Fucking hell,' he said. His cord was also intact.

'Are you all right?'

'I'll live.' He sat up and winced. 'Oh, my head!' He rubbed his eyes. 'We travelled a long way. Must be on a different satellite.' The cuttlefish popped into being in front of him and touched a tentacle to his forehead. A moment's silence, then he sighed with relief. 'Well, I'm uncorrupted,' he told Leila. The cuttlefish swam across to Leila. 'Better let it check you.'

Its tentacle was cold against her skin. She experienced the little programme's query as a shiver that ran through her whole body. 'You're fine,' confirmed Ambrose.

'Great. Now let's work out where we've ended up.' The cuttlefish rose between them, all tentacles stretched out. 'It's scanning,' Ambrose said. A moment, then: 'Everything we can see is virtual. We're either inside a server somewhere or in a real space that's been entirely overlaid with weave content. And we're at least five hundred kilometres from our last location...'

Leila stood, seeking a better view of the room. Ambrose muttered something technical about more precise location checks, as much to himself as to her. Leila didn't really take it in, because she was suddenly overjoyed.

'We've found him,' she breathed. 'We've found Dieter.'

'Really?' replied Ambrose as he staggered to his feet. 'Ah,' he continued. 'I think you're right.'

Leila, Ambrose and the cuttlefish were at one end of a long, narrow space, filled with stripped pine tables. Windows ran down white stone walls, with pale shelves climbing up between them. And the tables and shelves were filled with all the virtual clutter that had once filled Dieter's weavespace. There was a vacuum tube here, a set of yellowed dials there, Bakelite knobs beneath a dusty television screen, antique keyboards with cracked keys held up by slim, black, moulded metal stalks. Leila recognised none of the instruments individually, but – taken as a whole - the style was unmistakable. Dieter loved collecting vintage weave objects. He dressed up his own exploration and analysis apps to look like them. The room was full of his work. A moment for emotions to surge through her – relief, anger, hope, fear – and then Leila forced herself to focus. Past the windows there was a doorway which led into another room. She set off towards it.

'Wait a second,' called Ambrose. 'Best to be cautious. Run some more security checks. Work out exactly where we are.'

Leila ignored him. She glanced out of the windows as she passed them. They gave on to a silent, shining cityscape. Off-white clouds hung in a black sky, lit by the pale glow of a full moon. There was a broad, open street, bounded by a long, low colonnade of simple, elegant pillars and a high wall punctuated with empty doorways. In the distance there was an open piazza, a fountain dancing at its centre. Under the moonlight, all seemed whiter than it should be. All was perfectly symmetrical, carved out of the night with sharp, clean lines – all, that is, except the pale, pastel coloured bundles that lay everywhere. Leila slowed a little, wondering what they were. At first, she thought they were just fabric. But then she saw pale limbs, and hair, and soft, still faces. The streets were scattered with people. Perhaps they were asleep; perhaps they were dead. The clothes they wore drew on the same pastel palette as the pressure men's suits.

Then she was through the door and into a large round room. Pure white walls supported a domed ceiling. Panes of glass showed the dark sky. The floor was grey stone. The room was empty but for another stripped pine desk pushed up against one wall, two occupied couches lying head to head – and her brother, leaning over one of them.

'Dieter,' shouted Leila. He was concentrating deeply and didn't hear her. 'Dieter!' she called again as she ran towards him. As he turned she was on him, hugging him tight.

For a moment, she lost herself in him, so relieved to have found him. But he didn't return the hug. And he felt wrong. There was a permanent tremor running through him, a soft vibration that made holding him close a profoundly discomfiting experience. She stepped back to look at him.

He wasn't quite fully present. His body was softly blurred, shifting forwards and backwards between different versions of itself. His face was a shimmer too, never quite settling down. Graphically, he presented as slightly blocky, running at a far lower resolution than was the norm for fetches. She remembered what the Fetch Counsellor had said. Only the Fetch Communion could create true fetches. Soon, this flawed version of him would start to corrupt his weaveself, breaking the chains that held his past together.

'Leila? What are you doing here?' He sounded deeply shocked.

'I've come to take you home.'

'Gods. I can't. I've got work to do.' He gestured towards the figures in the couches.

Leila took her first proper look at them. She recognised the two Deodatus beneficiaries – Andre Herrera and Mo Fafanwe – from images from the InSec case file. The eating champion's bulk made the psychologist seem tiny. Neither looked alive. Their faces had been simplified, becoming caricatures, and the colour had been leached out of them until they were almost monochrome. They reminded her of shop window dummies. She recognised the couches, too. They were the ones that Dieter had built to help her heal, after the Blood and Flesh attack.

'What's happened to them?' she asked. 'And what are you doing with them?'

Dieter ignored her questions. 'How did you even find me, Leila?'

Ambrose entered the room, the cuttlefish drifting along with him.

'Oh, gods,' groaned Dieter, looking even more depressed.

'Hello there,' Ambrose said cheerfully. 'I helped her. Used one of the sharks, then we came down through an old Kingdom satellite.' He looked around. 'This is quite the home you've made for yourself.'

Dieter ran a hand through his hair. 'You idiots. You're going to screw it all up.'

'That's a bit harsh,' said Ambrose cordially.

'You've got to come back with us, Dieter,' Leila told him.

'I can't,' he replied. 'Even if I wanted to. I've signed a contract. Which includes full non-disclosure. Shit, if Deodatus works out you're here, we're fucked.' He looked up at Leila. 'I told you not to worry about me. I made sure you wouldn't lose the flat. I set everything up for you. It was all sorted out.'

'I had to come after you,' replied Leila, at once hurt and worried. 'Running like this – after a month or so it'll shred your weaveself. You'll be truly dead.'

'Do you think I didn't think of that?' Dieter was exasperated. 'I know exactly how fetches work. I rebuilt you, didn't I? That's why they wanted me down here.' He gestured toward the couches. 'After they fucked up these two. I'll be back on Station in a month.' He thumped his shimmering chest. 'Of course this isn't permanent.'

'You're coming back? Why couldn't you tell me?'

'I told you, non-disclosure. Deodatus wants all this kept quiet.' He glanced past Leila. 'Ambrose!' he called out. 'Get away from that!'

Ambrose was at the desk. It was piled high with drifts of papers. A single piece of paper hung above it, with two names written on it in black pen. He peered at them. 'And who are these guys? More victims?'

'Oh, for gods' sake.' Dieter marched over and snatched the paper off the wall, crumpling it up. 'Nobody's a victim. They're both terminally ill, just like the first two. Their families will do very well out of it. And they'll be back on Station getting ready to become proper fetches in a month or so, just like me.' He steered Ambrose back towards the centre of the room. 'I'm serious. You guys have to go.'

'Not unless you come with us,' replied Leila. She sounded slightly less decisive than she wanted to. Perhaps Dieter really did have everything under control.

'I can't,' replied Dieter. 'Not until I'm done here. You just have to trust me. I've always made the right decisions for us before, haven't I?'

'Dieter.' Now it was Leila's turn to be exasperated. 'Stop being such a big brother. I'm not a little girl. And even when I was, I could look after myself. You too. Gods, without my food packets when you were squatting, you'd have starved.' Dieter looked suitably abashed. 'So perhaps all this is going to work out fine. Perhaps being here is a brilliant decision. But all I can see is something that looks deeply, deeply dodgy. I want you out of this place and back home.'

'She's right,' chipped in Ambrose. 'All this is a bit odd, you know.' He wandered over to a window. 'Lovely place, very tasteful, but rather bleak.'

'It's all sorted out,' sighed Dieter. 'I'm fine. I'm doing good work here and I'll be back home as soon as possible. Big things are going to happen. And we'll be loaded.'

'If you want to convince me of that, you've got to tell us what on Earth is going on.'

Dieter sighed. 'And you won't go anywhere unless I do, will you?'

Leila imagined him remembering decades of similar conversations. Once she'd made up her mind, she was usually immovable. She shook her head. 'No.'

'Oh dear.' He leant back against one of the couches. 'OK. I'll tell you what I can.' He stopped to think for a moment. 'So, you're right. I'm down here because of Deodatus. Oh, and he's not an it – he's a he. He's very old and he's very powerful, and he knows a lot more about the past than we do. He wants to share that knowledge.' Dieter's eyes gleamed. 'You won't believe what he's got to tell us. So, he's going to leave this place and come to Station. And I'm helping him.'

And then he stopped.

Leila and Ambrose waited expectantly.

'Well, that's it,' Dieter told them.

'You haven't really told us anything,' said Leila accusingly.

Dieter looked helpless. 'I can't, Leila.'

'Can't you even let us know where we are?'

'I'm afraid not. I mean – this place is the Shining City. But that's just my name for it. I can't tell you what it's really called or where it really is.' He grinned excitedly. 'It'll blow your mind when you find out!'

'Dangerous things come from the past,' said Ambrose seriously. 'I hope you're being careful.'

'Oh, everything's fine. Deodatus is perfectly trustworthy.'

'Are you sure?' Ambrose looked haunted. 'You're being very casual about all this. Remember Cormac, old man.'

'What do you mean?' asked Dieter. 'Has something happened to him?'

'No.' Ambrose shook his head. 'Nothing's changed.'

'Then what's the problem?' Dieter was genuinely baffled. 'I mean – him and the family, everything's great, isn't it? Haven't seen them for a while, but – we're all busy these days. Hardly any time for Lazarus Crew stuff anymore.'

'His family died,' Leila said. 'It's why you and Ambrose stopped exploring.'

'His family are fine.' Dieter looked mystified. 'I stopped all that because I had to look after you.'

'You really don't remember?' asked Leila.

Dieter shook his head.

Ambrose suddenly looked very serious. 'Can you remember Holt?' he asked.

'Sure,' replied Dieter, looking a little puzzled. 'One of InSec's anti-terror people. He kept an eye on us when everyone thought we might be terrorists. Digging a bit too far into Station's infrastructure.'

'No. He's one of their antiquities experts. He kept an eye on us because the gods are scared shitless of the psychoactive technologies that we could have found. That Cormac did find.'

Dieter started to look nervous. 'You're making that up,' he said.

'He's not,' Leila told him. Disquiet pulsed through her. 'An artefact killed Cormac's family. Psychoactive artefacts can rewrite minds. The past left a lot of scary stuff out there.'

'I haven't been out in the field for years,' added Ambrose. 'Too scared of what I might lose.' He turned to Leila. 'This is why he's helping Deodatus,' he told her.

'He can't remember what it might lead to.' She turned back to Dieter. He shimmered in front of her, worry pulsing across version after version of himself. 'The Fetch Counsellor warned me about this. Deodatus has wiped some of your memories and rewritten other ones. He's made you forget just how dangerous very old things can be.' Fear gave her voice an edge. 'He's using you, Dieter.'

'That can't be true.'

'Why would we lie to you?' asked Leila.

'Why would Deodatus?' Dieter hit back. But there was fear in his voice too.

Leila welcomed it. They were getting through to him. 'Because he needs you.' She wanted to grab him and shake him and yell at him. But she'd never been able to make him do anything. 'And if you knew the truth, whatever it is, you wouldn't help him. You have to come back with us, Dieter. Tell us what's really going on.' She put as much force into her voice as she could. 'He's changing you.' His memories made him himself. He could lose so much.

'We really can't trust Deodatus,' Ambrose said. 'Look at what he's done to you. Leila's right.' He looked around nervously. The work room and the city beyond it were as serene as ever. 'We all have to get out of here. Right now.'

'I can't leave,' snapped Dieter, fear becoming defensiveness. 'I made a deal. And of course we can trust him. If we couldn't – if he's as dangerous as you say – well, I'd be building him an army. And that's absurd.'

'An army?' asked Leila, disbelieving. 'You might be building him an army?' She glanced over at Ambrose. He looked profoundly shocked. 'What are you really up to down here, Dieter?'

And that was when the pressure men attacked.

Chapter 13

The flies came first, a dark swarm shooting across the room like a blurred fist. They crashed straight through Dieter and he froze. Then they were on Ambrose. 'Get out,' he yelled, then his shields went up and he was silver. *Oh crap*, thought Leila. She stepped back, instinctively calling her skull face into being. She'd only just found her brother. She didn't want to leave him. There was an angry, roaring buzz, then Ambrose's shields dropped away, puddling beneath him like a pool of mercury. He took a step back, thrashing at himself, his skin dotted with crawling insects. Leila ran towards him and tried to help him. But her fingers just went through them.

'Crash out,' he shouted again. 'Once they've finished with me, they'll come for you.' He staggered backwards then fell over. 'I can feel them,' he howled. 'Inside me.'

Ambrose's cord flashed to red. The cuttlefish leapt into her mind, alarms wailing as it fled the attack. She hushed it as she ran to Dieter. She tried to shake him but her hands went through him. He'd been frozen, pulled out of time just as he turned to see what his friends were looking at. Leila tried to slap him, but her hand slipped through him too. 'Fuck,' she said to herself.

Then two pressure men burst in. The first one took her at a run, throwing himself on to her. He was fully weave enabled. His attack systems forced his presence on her. He could touch her, hurt her. She collapsed under his weight, his rings cutting into her hands, his medallion hard against her chest, stubble scouring her cheek like a weapon. There was the cologne stench again and something else beneath it – the thin, high reek of decay. She fell and skidded backwards with him on top of her. She brought her knee up between his legs but it made no difference. His weight crushed movement out of her.

Then her skull face was ready and she hit him with it.

He arced his back, howled and rolled off her, hands clamped over his ears, eyes tight shut. She kicked him in the mouth as she stood and felt a surprising softness. The other approached her. There was murder on his face. He balled his fists. It would take fifteen seconds or so for her skull face to lock on to his virtual senses, build an assault package and break him. In the meantime, he could cause her pain. She backed away from him.

Ambrose winked out of existence, vanishing back to his room. Relief flooded her until the flies rose up. They'd broken straight through Ambrose's armour. They'd break hers too. She remembered the Blood and Flesh plague tearing its way into her. She couldn't risk being shattered again. This time, she wouldn't have Dieter to heal her.

'I'm sorry,' she breathed as she started her exit countdown. 'I'll come back.'

She turned and started to run. The flies were behind her, then the second pressure man. Dieter was an uncaring statue. She jumped ahead, reappearing halfway down the store room, still running. Fear of her pursuers erased any shock at the jump. There was an infuriated buzzing from behind her. She looked out of the window at the Shining City and tried to leap there. But this jump failed, denied by the local weave. The pressure man entered the store room and cackled. There was no other exit. Her skull face was almost ready again. Perhaps now they had the measure of it. She hit the wall and turned to face her pursuer. Two more appeared behind him, all pastel suits and snarling faces.

The flies were ahead of them all.

Leila switched the skull face to multiple targeting. *Testing it out at last*, she thought. It would have a weaker but still damaging impact on its targets. She felt its systems grind away and wished it worked more quickly. The flies exploded around her, a swarm shot through with a hard, artificial glitter. Leila thought of jewels, of electrical components. The cuttlefish screamed danger in her mind. The flies were a prickling on her skin. First one, then several, then uncountable numbers landed on her, tiny creatures that burned into her like acid, tearing first at her skin and then at her mind. She sank to her knees, swearing and brushing at herself. The skull face flared readiness and she pulsed out an attack. She wasn't sure what it did to the pressure men. It didn't affect the flies. Her exit countdown crawled downwards. She wanted to scream. Perhaps she should risk just shutting herself down.

But before she could, a firm hand grabbed her and pulled her to her feet. There was a hissing sound. A cool mist settled around her head, a metallic taste suffused her mouth and the flies began to drop off.

'What is this breadhead shit?' her rescuer drawled. 'Be cool, you're good.' Rough hands brushed at her face and hair. She felt the swarm's touch on her skin lessen, the pressure on her mind fall back. 'Keep your eyes closed,' the voice said. 'One more hit of fly killer.'

'What about the pressure men?'

'The guys on the floor? Oh, you fucked them up good and proper. For the next minute or so, at least.'

Another hiss, and she felt more cold liquid. It soothed the last of the little hooked legs away. The flies died into stillness, becoming tiny weights that fell with a dry rustle as Leila brushed at herself.

'All fixed. You can open your eyes now.'

Her rescuer wore round, mirrored sunglasses. A tight little moustache pointed out from beneath a hawkish nose. A triangular beard sharpened his chin. Cheekbones cut up towards neat sideburns. He'd pulled his steel grey hair back into a ponytail. He wore a tie-dyed T-shirt that had once, long ago, been molten with lysergic colours, a faded pair of jeans and a tool belt. One hand held a spray bottle.

He smiled. 'You're not from round here,' he said.

'Who are you?' gasped Leila. 'Where IS here?'

'Oh, I guess I'm a caretaker.' The three pressure men stirred. The caretaker nodded towards them. 'Deodatus adapts pretty quickly. Every time you use that weapon of yours, it'll be less effective.' He peered towards the end of the room. 'More of 'em coming.' He tossed the spray bottle to Leila. 'More flies too. Zap 'em.' It felt about a quarter full. There was a broom leaning against the wall. He grabbed it. 'I'll take those dudes.' He hefted it in his hands like a weapon. 'Hold 'em back. Till we can get out of here.'

'With a broom?'

'It's not the tool, it's how you use it.' He pointed to his forehead. 'This is what you really fight with.'

'Can we get my brother?'

'The frozen guy in the main room?'

She nodded.

'We'll see. Might have to beat a retreat, come back when all's quieter.' He sounded deeply relaxed about the whole situation.

The closest pressure man was back on his feet. Leila had her first good look at him. He was, she guessed, about the same age as her, but the resonances of his clothing made him seem much more mature.

He leapt towards them.

The caretaker took him in the forehead with the broom. 'IN YOUR FACE, BROTHER!' he yelled, very clearly enjoying himself.

Their attacker collapsed. The caretaker planted a heel in his chest and leapt for the second one. Holding the broom in two hands he swung it in a high arc and brought it down like an axe. The brush smacked into the pressure man's head and he too went down. The third one dropped into a crouch. The caretaker spun the broom in his hand.

'You know, I'm usually a pacifist,' he drawled. 'Just not today.'

Leila didn't see how the fight ended. Her vision shimmered and the room glitched out. She'd forgotten the countdown. Five, it read, then four. There were black specks everywhere, maybe flies, maybe the local weave shutting down.

'I'm going back,' she shouted. 'Where is this place? How do I find it again?'

But there was no reply, for she was falling through darkness, and the room she'd been in was just a memory. Ambrose's systems crashed her back into her flat. All of a sudden she was back in her own living room, panting hard and needing to vomit, a bottle of fly spray clutched in one shaking hand.

Her head ached. Back in Docklands it was very late at night. The flat was shockingly quiet. She felt like she'd just escaped from a nightmare. She reeled across the room, knocking against Dieter's little Grey shrine. A tiny avatar of the god appeared like a sickness hallucination. His voice was a rasping buzz. 'I see your expenses management apps need upgrading. Let me help you with that,' he chirped. Leila nodded yes to shut him up, staggered past him and collapsed against the door frame. The flat's messaging system babbled about a message. It played automatically. Cassiel talked about the two Deodatus beneficiaries: 'I can't find any links between them,' she said. 'I'm going to keep digging.'

Leila wondered what Cassiel would make of Dieter's workshop, deep in the Shining City. She still didn't know what he was really up to down there. If the worst were true he might be raising an army for Deodatus. She couldn't think how he'd do that. For now she felt too broken to speculate. Fear shot through her. His captor had already taken some of his memory. She wanted to get back out, to try and find him. First she'd lie down for a moment and recover herself. She staggered down the hall and into her bedroom. It swayed around her. It had always been such a safe space. In the back of the mind she felt the cuttlefish, curled up in terror. She thought of Ambrose and imagined him falling back into his body. She hoped his buffer self had protected him. She'd jump to his office as soon as she felt a little better. She collapsed queasily on to the bed. She clutched the fly spray to her. The sheets felt harsh. They reminded her of stubble. It was worse than any hangover she'd ever had. She found that she couldn't move.

And then she discovered that she'd never left the nightmare.

Three loud bangs came from the corridor. Then there was a splintering crash. She imagined the front door torn from its hinges. She wanted to stand, to jump, to flee. But something had reached into her core self and frozen her. There were footsteps in the passageway. As the handle turned and the door to her bedroom opened there was a soft buzzing. A shadow became a man as it stepped into the light from the street outside. It was the pressure man from the hospital, dressed in yesterday. Her very earliest memory leapt to mind – her father, when he'd still been there, coming to kiss her goodnight. Here was his dark opposite, breaking into her most intimate space.

The pressure man pulled his shirt open to the waist. There was a square void beneath his ribcage. The skin around its edges was sticky with decay. He smiled as the flies leapt out of it. Once again she felt their hard legs scratch first at her flesh and then at her mind. This time she couldn't move. The skull face refused her summons. The swarm swatted away her defence librarians. And then it was inside her, ripping at her past.

Chapter 14

Leila was in one of Dieter's workrooms. He was standing next to a pile of closed circuit televisions screens. Grey images flickered across them, showing her fragments of the flat.

'Hello, Leila,' Dieter said, smiling. 'Some pretty nasty paralysis code in you. Don't worry, I've stripped it all out.'

Leila still had the fly spray in her hand. She raised it like a weapon, scanning the room as she did so. 'Are you real?' she asked him. 'Are they using you against me?' There were no flies. The scratching in her mind had gone. 'Are we safe?' She felt memories of the Blood and Flesh plague rise up within her. She pushed them back down. She couldn't let the past distract her from the present.

Dieter took one of her elbows in each hand, staring intently into her eyes and ignoring the fly spray. 'No, I'm not,' he said, then: 'And yes, you are.'

Leila wondered if she should spray him. But she wasn't sure what sort of effect it would have. She might be wasting a dose. And he'd released her from paralysis. It was hard to believe that he was an artefact of the pressure man's attack. 'Where are we? The Shining City?'

'What?' Dieter looked confused. 'No, we're still in the flat. The secret part of it.'

'But you're gone, Dieter.'

'Oh, I see!' He laughed. 'I'm not the real Dieter. I'm just a defence system. Keeping you safe from whoever's out there. Until the real Dieter can deal with him.' He gestured to a screen. The intruder stood in her bedroom. 'Do you recognise him?'

'Yes. People like him – pressure men – they've been following me. Attacking me.' Fear still gripped her. 'Are you sure we're safe?'

'Of course. Though this "pressure man" is a serious customer. He's broken most of the flat's defences. Broken you, too. Or rather, what he thinks is you.'

Leila could only stare. She hoped desperately that this wasn't all an illusion.

Her rescuer chuckled. 'He's actually attacking a copy.'

'Like a buffer self?' she asked. She remembered the Blood and Flesh attack. They'd broken into her memories too. She felt none of that violence in her mind now.

'Pretty much. Only it's not linked back to you. So you're perfectly safe. There's no way he can reach us in here.' He was so proud to be protecting her. Grief shifted tectonically within her. She must have looked shocked. He became serious. 'You really are safe, Leila. The real Dieter built all this to take care of you. And it has done.'

'He never told me.' She remembered how high handed Dieter could be with his little sister. 'Which, to be honest, is not a surprise.' As she spoke, she ran diagnostics on herself. All seemed to be in order. Perhaps this new version of him was telling the truth. And if he was what he claimed to be, there was something he needed to know. 'Sit down,' she told him.

'What's wrong, Leila?'

'Please. Just sit.'

He reached for a stool and sunk on to it. She found another and perched next to him, surprised at how much sadness she suddenly felt. 'What's the matter?' he asked. All that was most loving and unselfish in him rose up. 'Why are you so upset?'

It was so hard to say. 'Your physical self is dead.'

'Oh,' he replied, sitting back. A moment of sadness. Then: 'But he'll be back. Six months and he'll be a fetch. I should be able to keep you safe for that long.'

'No. He sold his weaveself to Deodatus.' She gestured towards the screen. 'The person that the pressure men work for. I'm going to find a way through them and rescue Dieter. And I'm going to need your help. If we fail, he'll die a true death.' She remembered how afraid her brother had looked as he told her he could be building an army. 'And gods know what else will happen.'

Her protector froze.

Then the room shook, and he was back at the televisions. He turned to her. 'I'm sorry about the reset,' he said, smiling gently. 'I'm very limited. I'm here to keep you safe, but I can't do much

97

more than that. I think you must have just told me something I couldn't process.' He chuckled. 'Still, I'm sure the real me'll be back soon. And in the meantime, I'll look after you.'

It was then that Leila realised that she was still stuck in a dream. But it wasn't hers or the pressure man's – it was Dieter's.

Her rescuer saw her confusion, but misread it. 'Is the name thing a problem?' he asked. 'It is confusing. Why not call me Dit? Then it'll be easier to keep us separate.' He turned back to the screens. 'This is remarkable,' he continued. When Leila didn't reply, he glanced towards her and again saw that she was upset. 'What's wrong?' he asked, reaching out. 'Are you OK?'

She tried to tell Dit about Dieter selling his weaveself and risking true death three more times before she accepted that it was beyond his ability to take in. And every time he reset, she had to work a little harder to pull him away from observing the pressure man. When he reappeared for the fourth time, he didn't look round at all. She sighed, accepting his limits.

'You really should come and see this,' he said, rapt.

Leila sighed.

'It's extraordinary,' he continued. 'He's really doing a number on you. Or the copy of you, that is.' He bent forward and peered at one of the screens. 'Let's call her Lei. Come and have a look.'

'I don't have time for that,' replied Leila, standing up. 'They'll go after Ambrose. Maybe Cassiel, too. I've got to warn them.'

'You can't leave while the pressure man's here,' replied Dit. 'Only exit's through the flat. He'll spot you.'

'Gods' sake. What use is that?'

'More secure.'

'I wish Dieter had talked to me before he built this place,' grumbled Leila. 'There's really no way I can get past him?'

'None that I can think of.'

She remembered how quickly the caretaker had broken the flies. 'Maybe I should attack the flies with the spray, see if that distracts him.'

'You'll give away your hiding place. And me,' Dit told her firmly. 'All you can do is wait until he leaves. Until then, you're perfectly safe.'

'And perfectly stuck.'

Dit ignored her. She slid off the stool and joined him at the screens – cathode ray tubes, nested in plastic and wooden boxes. They looked archaic. She peered at the swarm, spattered across Lei like an explosion of ink.

'Those creatures scare me far more than the pressure men,' she said.

Dit twisted a dial. 'Let's check one of them out.' Images shifted as he zoomed in. He caught a fly hovering in midair. Red-orange compound eyes bulged dully out of a small, hard head. Black legs hung from a stumpy little body. It bristled with dark hairs. Leila flinched.

'It's fully weave aware,' commented Dieter. 'Interfaces with the virtual as easily as the real.'

'I know.' Leila remembered the flies scuttling across her skin, then digging into her. Disgust shook her.

'It's forcing full weave overlay.' Dit nodded towards the screen. 'It looks natural, but it's not. Let's see what's really there.' He pulled out a keyboard and started tapping away. The fly remained unchanged. 'Rejecting my overlay drop requests.' He typed out a string of commands then hit the return key. 'And let's see what that does.' The fly darted out of shot. 'Motherfucker,' cursed Dit. 'Rejected that too. And I can't go in with anything harder. It'll realise I'm more than just a standard home security system.'

Leila remembered the white silhouette in the hospital. 'Can you see what the pressure man really looks like?' she asked.

'No,' replied Dit. 'Same problem.'

'And what are they doing to Lei?' She remembered the flies scratching at her. 'They were in my memories before you pulled me in here.'

'Nothing good,' replied Dit. He thumped the keyboard and the cameras zoomed out. Lei was barely visible beneath a hard, glistening, insect skin. 'They're going deep. Rewriting her past.'

'Like psychoactive tech does?'

He frowned. 'This is certainly how it works. Rearranges memory blocks, edits them, fabricates new ones. But I've never heard of anything like this. It's always been in ancient artefacts – not flies riding a retro thug.' He thought for a moment. 'Yes, he really is the worst person you've ever brought back to the flat.'

Leila whacked his shoulder. 'For gods' sake, Dit, how do you even know that? You said you were just a user interface.'

'I've been checking up on you two every so often since I was created. Watching a fetch and a geek hang out together.' Dit chuckled. 'Better than a sitcom. And Dieter copied all his favourite memories of you into me. To make sure I'd really care about you.'

'And annoy me as much him.'

'Yeah, I'd say that's pretty important too.'

Leila smiled ruefully. 'When I see him I'll tell him you're not bad at it.'

'Positive feedback's always welcome.'

'Before I give him a good telling off for not letting me know about you.'

Dit snorted. 'Well, there's a lot you haven't told me. What were you doing in the Shining City in the first place? How did you meet Deodatus and the pressure men?'

Leila thought about trying to explain again. She imagined him freezing and disappearing, then having to restart their conversation from scratch. 'I think it's outside your scope,' she said.

Dit looked sad. 'You've already reset me?'

Leila nodded. 'Several times.'

'I'm sorry. I am quite limited.'

'Well, you've kept us both safe. That's the important thing.' She sighed. 'I just wish I could get out of here.' She forced herself to focus on what she could control. 'Can we see which memories the flies are rewriting?'

'A lot from the last few weeks, and he's dipping in and out of longer term ones too.'

'Let's start with the more recent stuff.' A thought struck her. 'Perhaps you'd better not watch it. It might trigger another reset.'

'Ah. Out of context info. OK. I'll go on percentages. See where he's making the biggest changes to Lei's memory.' He worked quietly for a minute or so. 'Putting them up on screens. Only you can see them.' There was a pause, and then times past pulsed out at her. 'This is what he's editing.'

Leila watched the rewritten past. Each screen held a different looped moment. Many were relatively short. Others ran for a minute or so, some even longer. Each was silent, until she focused on it for more than a few seconds. Then sound would spring out and surround her.

'I've picked out a top ten of recent memory changes,' explained Dit. 'Should give you a sense of what he's up to. I'll summarise the longer term stuff while you're watching them.'

Leila thought at first that the flies were only rewriting anything to do with the Deodatus payment. It had been a jagged break in her life. They made it something far smoother, far more integrated.

In the hospital, a new, fictional Dieter explained the situation to Lei. 'I've done it for you,' he said, 'to make up for not being there for so long. Please accept this gift from me.' He took her hand in his. 'Don't try and bring me back again.' She saw another her, a lie, nodding acceptance. The final seizure came. There was no summons to the Twins, no doctors desperately trying to resurrect him. Lei watched briefly over his still form, then gathered herself and left.

She visited Ambrose. He confirmed the terms of the insurance. But there was no shock. 'I already knew,' she said. Ambrose replied: 'So generous of him.' Then she met Cassiel, who assured her that everything was in order. 'Deodatus are very reputable,' the mind told her. 'Very well-established.' The last thing she said was: 'There's no need for us to meet again.'

The wake was still a sad affair. Guests muttered about sacrifice. 'He always said, just live your life for yourself,' one of them told Lei. Ambrose was there. He looked broken. 'Don't look back,' he advised. 'That's what he'd have wanted.' He offered to show her one of Dieter's favourite historical sites. 'Something to remember him by.'

Then, Lei was standing in the Mikhail room. Drops of fire fell around her like memories, flaring brightly then sputtering into nothing. 'He loved places like this,' replied Ambrose, his face lit up by the dead god's branding. A few minutes later he was gone, leaving Lei to remember her brother. 'At least you came good in the end,' she whispered into the darkness. There was no grief in her voice.

'Getting anything out of it all?' asked Dit.

Leila had almost forgotten that he was there. 'Yes. The pressure man wants to stop me from kicking up a fuss about something. Something very big. Something I'm not going to walk away from.'

'That's my girl!' exclaimed Dit. 'I've never known you back down from a fight.'

'Can I see the older stuff?'

Dit nodded. 'Here goes. Heavily compacted. It summarises years of changes very quickly. You'll get the big picture, but you won't get much detail.'

Then the new past hit her, a thousand memories spun together to form a single, re-edited life. Minutiae rushed by. Leila felt that she was moving across a vast, open landscape at very high speed. Slowly, its geography emerged. She perceived a vast absence. All of it hinged on a single moment. There was Lei, aged eleven, standing in an apartment block corridor that reeked of piss and cheap drugs. Her neat little backpack and her fresh, clean school uniform made her feel so out of place. She had a container of food in her hands, all ready to be warmed up. And a door had just slammed in her face. There was an unbearable sense of loss and betrayal.

Leila dropped out of Lei's false past, gasping with shock.

'Are you all right?' asked Dit.

'Fine, fine.' She felt his hand at her elbow. 'Gods.'

'What is it?'

'He's wiped Dieter out of her memory. Almost all of him.' She found herself about to choke out a sob. A nod towards the screen. 'Making it look like he moved out when she was eleven, started squatting and never came back. Told her to fuck off when she tried to visit him.' She felt grief heave within her. She imagined a deep bitterness, too. 'Dieter abandoned her. She had to do it all on her own. If the flies had got me, that's all I'd remember. I'd take the money and just let him go, and I wouldn't care about any of it.'

'Thank the gods I was here then!' said Dit perkily. 'We'll soon get all this sorted out. There's less and less editing going on. I think he's almost done.'

Leila sighed.

'Hang on,' said Dit. 'I'm not sure I like the look of this. The pressure man's active.'

'What's he doing?'

'He's accessing your social networks. Running a full search on Dieter's name, any references to him in chats…' Dit peered closely at one of the screens. 'Scraping full identity and contact details for anyone you're close to and have discussed Dieter with.'

'Why does he need that?' asked Leila. There was an answer in her mind, but she was resisting it. She hoped that Dit would convince her of something less painful, less intrusive.

He didn't. 'Simple enough. He's just rewritten Lei. She's a new person. And that new person isn't compatible with your old friends. Her new version of her life is very different from the one they re-member. So he's doing something about it. He's going to send the flies after them, too.'

'Oh, fuck. I have to get out.' If Deodatus won then Dieter wouldn't just disappear from her future. He'd vanish from her past, as well. She had to fight back somehow. A thought struck her. 'What about the flat's administrative weavelinks? Can you send me out through them?'

'Through the wardrobe or the fridge?' He smiled absently as he accessed the appropriate memories. 'Yes, I think I might be able to. Move you through their weavespace, so you won't have any sort of presence in the main parts of the flat. He might still see you, though. Have you got anything to protect yourself with?'

Leila waved the fly spray at him. 'There's the skull face too.'

Dit nodded. 'And where should I send you once you're out?'

'Ambrose.'

'Are you sure? What if he's been attacked too?'

'Dieter's defences kept me safe from the pressure man,' replied Leila. 'I'm sure Ambrose's will have protected him too.'

'He's not virtual.'

'Look, if there is a problem, if I even hear a single fly, I'll jump straight out.' She barely felt the anxiety that even the thought of jumping usually created. There were far more important things to worry about.

Dit still looked nervous. 'If there's psychoactive tech involved, Holt should know about it. He's an InSec, but he's got some heavy resources. Or you should go back to the Coffin Drives. The Fetch

Counsellor can sort you out with a ghost cloak. Dieter built it for him. It'll keep you invisible anywhere in Station.'

'No,' replied Leila. But Dit's question had set her thinking. She wondered about rushing to her friends. Perhaps she could protect them. But she could only reach them one by one – and she wasn't sure how much that would actually achieve. She thought about returning to the Coffin Drives to find the Fetch Counsellor. But the Coffin Drives weren't under any threat. She remembered Cassiel's message. The mind seemed to be safe too, for the moment at least.

There was still only one real choice.

'Send me to Ambrose,' she said. And then, to herself, so she didn't reset Dit again, 'We'll work out where the Shining City is. And then we'll get Dieter out of there.'

Chapter 15

The jump still sickened Leila but now that sickness seemed like an indulgence. She shut it off. Determination eclipsed any emotional shock as her new location leapt into being around her.

'Ambrose?' she called. 'Are you there?'

His defences were still up. They'd queried her as she'd arrived. His office was quiet and dark. He'd deactivated its weave overlay. There were no flies and no pressure men. And there were no bookcases, no log fire, no armchairs and no antique desk. In reality, his office was a small, cheap, windowless space. Metal shelves hung from concrete walls, holding chaotic piles of printouts. The armchairs were cheap plastic recliners. The table was plastic too, its garish surface pocked with cigarette burns. The room smelt damp. Leila thought of the cosy hours she'd spent chatting with Ambrose in here and sighed. She wondered how well she really knew him.

The door to his living quarters was open. Pushing through, Leila found herself in a narrow corridor. Without the weave, it would no longer end in Ambrose's comfy, exquisitely decorated little flat. 'My castle,' he always called it. 'Drawbridge up, safe from the world.' But now, concrete walls and floors sat grey beneath an unpainted ceiling. Fluorescent lights parched the colour out of them. Leila moved down the corridor, feeling disturbed. She readied herself to jump away at the slightest hint of pressure man presence. She opened the door into Ambrose's living room.

Grief echoed out towards her. Someone was sobbing. Dread took Leila's heart in its cold hands. She thought about fleeing. But she couldn't abandon Ambrose. She'd pushed him into taking her to the satellite, then moving beyond it. She had to help him. The sobbing continued. She touched her pendant for good luck, spun up the skull face, gripped the fly spray and moved cautiously into the living room.

'Hello?' she called. 'Ambrose?'

The weeping eased. The living room's true self was as cold and hard and impersonal as the hallway. Ambrose sat at a little table, looking small, sad and grey. Without overlay, his hair drifted in greasy streaks across a shiny scalp. His face was less cheerful, less confident. His eyes were dull, unpolished stones set in dark rings of exhaustion. His skin made her think of damp putty. He hadn't shaved for a couple of days. His shirt was unironed. She could smell stale sweat. There was a half drunk bottle of Docklands whisky and a small, dirty kitchen knife on the table in front of him. The skull face asked if he was a potential target. *No*, she told it.

'Here I am,' Ambrose said. He looked hopeless. 'My father said you'd come for me.' He picked up the knife. 'So I got this from the kitchen.' His words had a light slur to them. His hand shook.

Leila took a careful step towards him. 'Of course,' she said. 'We went down together. We escaped together. Now we're safe together.'

'Safe!' he replied, pain in his voice. 'Safe. Perhaps we are.' He looked at the knife. 'You know, I've only just realised this can't stop you. Stupid of me. But I always was stupid. That's what father says, anyway.'

'Why would you want to stop me?' she asked, taking another step towards him.

'Stay back!' He thrust the knife towards her, then looked at it, then laughed bitterly. He put it down on the table. 'You see? There it is in my hand. It couldn't hurt a fetch. I didn't even think.' And, in a more confiding tone: 'I don't think. Father says that too. I never did, he told me.'

Leila wondered what had taken root in Ambrose's head. 'Your father came?' she asked.

'Yes,' replied Ambrose. 'I remember him so clearly. Standing right where you are. He told me that I've always been stupid, that I don't think. That's why he never reinstated me.' He paused for a moment and took a shuddering breath. 'I always had hope. The back door – I thought they left it open on purpose. To help me.' He looked up, his eyes pleading for understanding. 'He said the door was an accident. That he'd shut it down. He made me turn off the overlay in here. Face the truth of my life, he said.' The knife shivered in Ambrose's hand. 'He told me about you.' His voice cracked into something close to a howl. 'About what you'd become.'

'What do you mean?' asked Leila. 'I'm me. Just like always.' She took a cautious step towards him and spoke, making her voice as soothing as possible. 'The pressure men have been here. They've written new memories into your mind.' A second step. 'One of them tried to do it to me. '

'Oh no. No pressure men.' He suddenly looked much sadder. 'Just father.' He rubbed his finger across the blade. 'I sharpened it, you know.' He looked up at her. 'He said if I was quick enough, I wouldn't have to face you.' A sigh. 'I couldn't even get that right.' Guilt and shame shivered across his face. 'It's so hard to look at you. At what you've become. It's my fault, Leila. I'm so sorry.'

'I am what I've always been, Ambrose.' She remembered how the flies had rewritten Lei's memory. She wondered how Ambrose's memories of her had been changed. 'Dieter left defences. A partial version of himself. It kept me safe. The pressure men didn't get anywhere near me.'

'I saw you, Leila. I saw what they did to you.' A sad laugh. 'Here I am, talking to you as if you're still the person you were. And that part of you is just a mask now. A lure. To get me back down there.'

'No, Ambrose. That's wrong. A false memory the pressure men forced into your head.' She took another step towards him. 'I'm still the Leila you've always known. Your friend, Dieter's sister. Uncorrupted. And you are right – we still have to find the Shining City again. But not to trap anyone. We've got to get Dieter back.' Another step. 'I can't do it without you.'

'No!' he shouted, his voice suddenly harsh. His mood changed so quickly. It was as if his personality had been smashed, then too hurriedly reassembled, leaving jagged discontinuities it was so easy to trip over. 'Stop! Don't get any closer!' He thrust the knife out again, then realised what he was doing. Another broken laugh. 'That won't scare you, will it?' Suddenly the knife was at his own throat, pressing into skin. 'This will.'

'No, gods – no.' Leila stepped back, her hands up, until she felt the wall behind her. 'I'm sorry,' she gasped. 'I won't – I mean – what could I do to you?'

'You want to get me back to Dieter's workshop and rewrite me. Have me working for the pressure men. Like him. Like you.'

She scrambled for the right words. 'You have to trust me. I'm not working for them. I'd never work for them.'

'Of course not.' He snorted. 'I watched Dieter strap you into one of those chairs of his so they could remake you.' The knife moved against his flesh. 'Both of you lost. And it's all my fault.'

'That's not what happened.'

'I shouldn't have been so scared. I should have gone to him in the hospital. I should have tried to get that fucking box out of him. I should have done something. You and Dieter, gone like Cormac's family. And it's all my fault.'

'I haven't been rewritten, Ambrose. I'm still me. I still love Dieter. And we need to get back there and save him.'

'STOP FUCKING SAYING THAT!' he roared. His throat pushed against the knife. A thin line of blood appeared.

Leila wondered about using the skull face to stun him. But that would only confirm his sense of her as an enemy. She had to try and talk him round.

'Oh, stop it, Leila,' he continued. 'Admit what you are.' He groaned. 'My father tried to help me. Told me what to do. I didn't do it and now here you are and I have to face you. Stupid, stupid, stupid me.'

'Ambrose, your father wasn't really here,' Leila said desperately. 'Someone else was. Something else. I've had a visit too.' A single bead of blood rolled down Ambrose's throat. Leila had no way of getting the knife off him. 'I crashed back to my flat. A pressure man came and tried to rewrite my past. Make me believe that I'd accepted Dieter's true death.' It was difficult to tell if Ambrose was taking any of it in. 'That I didn't love him. That I had no reason to save him.' Ambrose's eyes were glazed. Leila imagined his glitched mind reaching for memories that were no longer there.

'But we can't save Dieter. There's so little of him left.'

Now it was Leila's turn to shout. 'Don't say that!' Then, more quietly: 'It's not true. We're going to get Dieter back, Ambrose. You and me together.' She was near tears. 'And you've lost part of yourself. We'll get that back too.' Guilt shot through her. 'If all this is anyone's fault, it's mine.'

'You're so convincing,' he said, wonder in his voice. 'I almost believe you.'

Another shout: 'Yes!' Then, desperately: 'Yes, do believe me. Because it's the truth, dammit. I'm not working for Deodatus. I'm not trying to force anything on you. I'm just telling you the truth. Can't you see it? Wouldn't you rather it was this way?'

'Yes,' he said sadly. 'I would.' The knife dropped away from his throat.

Leila sighed with relief. She was getting through to him at last. She wondered if she'd be able to get him out of the building. They needed somewhere to hide. She couldn't take him back to her flat. Perhaps she could get them into one of the properties she'd shown recently. She remembered the block she'd shown the awful couple around, when her life was so different. That would still be empty.

'I've got somewhere we could go,' she said. 'Somewhere safe.'

Ambrose stared at the knife. 'That would be good,' he replied. 'Fresh air. The world outside. Get away from this shithole.' He looked up at Leila. 'Do you know how much I hate living here? I've made the best of it, but still.' He sighed heavily. 'You make stupid, stupid mistakes when you're young. My father told me that, when he came. He was talking to me again, at last. But you're saying that wasn't really him?'

'No, Ambrose.' He was finally listening to her. 'It was a pressure man. Come on, Ambrose. I can take you somewhere safe. And then we can go back to the city and rescue Dieter.'

Ambrose took a deep breath. 'He told me you'd say that. Exactly that. To try and get close to me. To find a way of rewriting me. And he told me how to avoid it.' He suddenly looked happy, as if a great weight had been lifted from him. 'The past is such a beautiful place. You, still yourself. The Lazarus Crew still together. And further back – before I fucked up – even better.' He ran his thumb down the knife's edge. There was red there too. The blade was very sharp. 'It's all I have left.'

'Oh, no,' breathed Leila.

'And I'm going back there. Just like Cormac did.'

'No!' Instinct sent her leaping towards him, even though there was nothing she could do.

With a quick, liquid flick of his wrist, Ambrose lifted the blade and sliced it across his own neck, starting beneath his left ear and pushing hard all the way round. Blood leapt out in a fine spray. The knife clattered to the floor. He fell sideways, choking. His head thumped down on to the table. Leila was on him, pressing her hands up against the wound, but they passed through it and she felt the pain of being a ghost, unable to save the living. Ambrose gurgled – a low, hopeless sound. His eyes were glazed. He slowly rolled on to the floor. A red pool grew around him, the brightest thing in that bleached, hopeless room.

'Oh,' breathed Leila. 'Ambrose.'

Pain and loss seared through her. She took a step back, then another, then she was in the hallway, then the office. She put a hand to her face and found tears. There was too much loss in her world. She thought of jumping back home, but seeing Dit would only remind her of all that she'd failed to protect. She thought of jumping to Cassiel, but then imagined finding that the mind too had been rewritten. She couldn't bear another encounter like that. Her friends, too, would remember different yesterdays. For a second she despaired, feeling that she had nobody to turn to. Then she remembered the past she'd tried so hard to write out of her own life.

Now it was all that remained to her.

It was time to return to the Coffin Drives.

She closed her eyes and let herself fall into the land of the dead.

Chapter 16

Leila came back to herself lying on her side, with her eyes shut. She hadn't specified an arrival location, so she'd been brought to the Coffin Drives' default entry point – Memory Park, the round open space at their very heart. Short grass tickled her face and neck, its fresh, green smell rising up around her. Sunlight warmed her skin. Birds poured out their liquid songs. The last time she'd woken here she'd been lying in a cot in a triage tent, recovering from the Blood and Flesh plague. Memories rose up and filled her mind.

The day of the attack had begun innocently enough. Back then, Leila was still a relatively contented inhabitant of the Coffin Drives. She rose, summoning memories of coffee, imagining different ways of spending the day. She took a sip from the mug that appeared in her hand and went to the window, wondering if any fresh architectures had been scrawled across the city overnight. But nothing had changed. Everything was quiet, everything was still. That was surprising. In such a fluid city, stasis was an aberration.

Then the plague hit her.

First, it took her senses. Touch vanished, then taste. The coffee in her mouth lost all heat. Its bitterness disappeared. She gasped. Her mouth was empty. Security blinds crashed down. The room went dark. She called out for emergency lighting. Nothing happened. Hearing collapsed. She was an isolated consciousness, unable to perceive anything beyond itself.

Shit, she thought. *Be cool. Local crash. Been through this before.*

Her security systems howled in disagreement. They registered a major personal integrity threat. Defence librarians raced through her memories, throwing up barricades against the aggressor. One by one, they vanished. Leila had a sense of a vast, chaotic force breaking over her like a wave. She withdrew deep into herself. Her remaining librarians rushed to pull deep trivia into a hard, disposable protective shield. Then they frantically pulled the irreplaceable memories that defined her true self in behind it and scrambled to back them up.

Leila felt something like corporeal experience return as those memories drifted through her mind. She jumped from moment to moment, forced to relive them in random order. It was a profoundly unsettling experience. Part of her was aware that she was a fetch, under heavy and very personal attack. Part of her was a twenty-year-old in a bar, then a two-year-old spending her first night in a grown-up bed, then a thirteen-year-old running through long grass. Her sense of self began to fragment. Without any specifically helpful past experiences to stabilise her, fear blossomed.

It became panic when the trivia shield was breached. Her defences vanished. The intruder tore into her, ripping her past to pieces. It attacked coherence, taking individual moments – *I'm awake I'm in bed I'm sad here's mummy I'm happy I'm sleepy* – and breaking them down into units that made no sense – *I'm mummy sleepy awake bed in sad I'm I'm I'm*. It was like watching a tsunami racing up beach after beach, overwhelming an entire archipelago of islands.

She lost her sense of her real age. She was absolutely twelve, then three, then seventeen, then ten. Each moment was suffused with a suffocating dread. Then the moment would break, the tsunami taking it, and she would instantly be elsewhen. Every key memory of her life was held up, examined and torn to shreds. She lived them all as a great howl of panic and loss. An immeasurable period passed and the destruction passed a tipping point, breaking her sense of self. Leila no longer knew who or what she was. There was only agony. There was no sense of time, and so the agony stretched out to fill eternity.

The virus ate a substantial proportion of the Coffin Drives before a combined Fetch/Totality initiative was able to stop it. In real terms, the whole attack only took a few seconds. Many of those affected were lost for good. Leila was one of the lucky ones. Her librarians managed to save a substantial proportion of her memories. As soon as Dieter cleared enough digital space for her, she left the Coffin Drives and moved in with him in Docklands. She thought about purging all remembrance of the attack, but settled for just repressing it. It seemed to be the human thing to do.

The past finished pulsing through her. Leila was panting with stress. She was filled with an urge to fly back up into Homelands. But there was no safety there. She reminded herself that she needed to be in the Coffin Drives. She would recover herself and then work out how to rescue Dieter before he lost any more of himself. She forced herself to breathe slowly and felt herself calm. She wasn't quite ready to open her eyes yet. She sat up, hands clutching at the soft grass. She still felt tense. And yet it seemed to be such a beautiful day. A soft, fresh breeze tickled her face. Sunlight warmed her skin. Birds sang. There was a stream somewhere nearby. She took a deep breath and opened her eyes again.

The park was as it always had been. The skyline beyond it was still a jumble of buildings. Without moving her eyes she could see a cathedral built of stained glass, a black leather skyscraper, a brightly painted pagoda, a hundred-metre-high granite henge and a giant yellow elephant, dotted across with windows and terraces. She watched for a few minutes, expecting some of the buildings to shiver out of existence and others to appear, but there was no change. The city was more fixed than she'd ever seen it. That, too, helped her relax. Order was so comforting.

'Things have settled down since you were here last.'

Leila turned.

The speaker squatted just behind her. Short, iron-grey hair framed a face that looked like it had been carved out of a walnut. The old woman wore a loose shirt, trousers and no shoes. Strong toes gripped the grass, giving her stance a deep firmness. Her eyes and mouth were entirely black. It was the Fetch Counsellor. 'After the Blood and Flesh incident,' she continued, 'we all needed a little stability.'

'The buildings don't change anymore?' asked Leila.

'Not very often. Do you want to take a look round?'

'I'm not here to be a tourist.'

'I thought not.' The Counsellor's voice was very serious. 'You're here for help.'

Leila opened up her recent memories to the Fetch Counsellor. As the Counsellor experienced her last few days, Leila too thought back over them. So much had assaulted her and those close to her. Here in these quiet gardens it seemed impossible that it had all really happened. And yet Docklands was now so dangerously unpredictable that the Coffin Drives felt almost like a refuge. Leila looked around and shivered, remembering how broken she'd been when Dieter signed her out of the triage centre. Almost a refuge, but not quite.

The Fetch Counsellor was pale. 'This is terrible,' she said. 'I knew that fetches could be rewritten. But the living too – that's shocking news. I'm so sorry you had to go through it all.'

'Deodatus hasn't tried to break in here?'

'We've had some unexplained presences.' The Counsellor looked worried. 'Shadows in the sea. Lights in the sky. Too fleeting, too distant for us to scan properly. But nothing in the city itself. I think he's watching from afar. But he must know how good our security is. For now, he's holding back.'

'And what if he's inside you and you just don't know it?'

The Fetch Counsellor smiled. 'Then you'd be surrounded by flies and your memory would already have been rewritten.'

The thought shocked Leila. 'Gods.'

'But for the moment at least, whatever Dieter's working on doesn't seem to be a direct threat to the Coffin Drives.'

Leila raised an eyebrow. 'He said he could be building an army.'

'And we are the discorporate dead. An army would have to prioritise the physical forces of the Pantheon and the Totality before taking us on. Besides, Dieter doesn't need one to damage us. If he chose to attack us head on he could break us using software alone.' She looked around. The peaceful afternoon drifted on obliviously around them. 'But we shouldn't talk in an open space like this. Let me take you somewhere more private.'

The Fetch Counsellor led Leila through the Memory Park. *Relax*, Leila told herself. *It's all in the past.* She found herself feeling more and more nervous as they approached the gates to the city. *Everything's changed. It's safer, now.* She remembered how scared Ambrose had been when he'd accompanied her to the Shining City, and how he'd overcome his fear, and felt both guilty and inspired. But when they stepped through the gate and into the streets beyond, her own fear was still there.

'Get yourself ready,' the Fetch Counsellor told her. 'We're about to switch channels.'

All of a sudden, the city changed. The skyscrapers, the henges, the silver statues and the cathedrals vanished. Streets bounded by long, low, endless walls flowed into being around them. Each wall was studded with hundreds of doors, and each door was completely different from any of the others.

'That was meant to happen, right?' Leila looked round nervously. 'Where's the rest of it gone?'

'Oh, it's still there,' the Fetch Counsellor reassured her. 'We've just changed how we look at it. We've moved into the Memory Channel.'

'I think that's after my time.' She forced her breathing to slow again.

'I'm sorry.' The Counsellor smiled. 'It is. I should have explained it before we switched. After you left, we started grouping fetches by the kind of afterlives they wanted to lead. When a group's big enough, it gets its own channel to fill with content. This is one of them.'

'Who does it belong to?'

'People who want to look back over their lives. Enjoy the good bits, come to terms with the hard times. They hold on to a lot of memories and they like to keep them safe. So, the Memory Channel's built on some of the most stable storage space we have. Multiple backups, deep security. They value privacy, too. Once we're through our own particular door, nobody'll be able to listen in on us. Let's go find it.'

'I didn't know about any of this,' said Leila as they walked. Regret surprised her. Perhaps she should have stayed more in touch with the evolution of the Fetch Communion. 'All this was because of the attack?'

The Fetch Counsellor nodded. 'At first we mistook chaos for freedom. Then the plague came. It helped us realise that freedom and structure are not opposites, that we needed some coherence to make our society safer and more resilient. The channels are part of that.'

Leila followed the Counsellor through the maze of doors,

imagining all the different fetches who might be lying behind them, remembering. It was difficult to tell how far they'd actually come when the Counsellor exclaimed: 'Ah! There it is.' She steered them towards a medium-sized metal door. It was painted red and studded with rivets. 'Our destination.'

It opened, and they stepped into a great wooden hallway. 'It's bigger on the inside,' commented the Counsellor. 'It has to be, to hold all the memories.' Stairways twisted up through tens of storeys of balconies towards a gloomily distant ceiling. Long, low-ceilinged rooms stretched off to the left and right, stuffed full of trunks, cupboards and other storage systems. There was a table and two chairs in the centre of the hall. They faced a stuffed ostrich, a little wooden trike and two giant six-sided dice, a metre across on each side.

'Wow,' said Leila. 'That's pretty random.'

'Meaning is a very subjective thing. They have a lot of significance for the woman I'm riding. This house is a kind of time machine for her.'

'You can access her memories?'

'To an extent. But we're not here to discuss her.'

Fear was still coiled within Leila, a barbed thing wrapped tight around her mind and heart. 'I need a moment.'

'Oh, of course. I completely understand.' She pointed at the wall ahead of them. It opened to show a softly-lit, white-walled room, furnished with a rug, a sofa and an armchair. The far wall was half cloudscape, half warm blue sky. 'A Memory Channel contemplation chamber. One of the safest, most private places we have. Take as long as you need.'

On the edge of the room, Leila turned back. 'I'm glad to be here,' she said, 'but doesn't the owner mind us using her home like this?'

'Not at all,' replied the Counsellor. 'She volunteered to be ridden. And if she knew you were here now, using this space to renew yourself, she'd be overjoyed.'

In the end, Leila only spent a few minutes in the contemplation chamber. She held the pendant in her hand, reminding herself of all that was stake. As the ambient dread that the Coffin Drives sparked in her settled, she felt the potential of loss move her to action.

The Counsellor was ensconced in an armchair. 'That was quick,' she said as Leila emerged. 'Are you sure you're OK?'

'OK enough,' Leila replied. 'So we can get to work. We need to locate the Shining City, find Dieter and get him out of there.' She paused for a moment. 'I need to know how you can help me.' She was surprised at how confident she felt. She wondered briefly if it was a side-effect of wealth. 'And then I'll go and find Cassiel.'

The Counsellor nodded. 'We need to consider Ambrose too. He's going to have a difficult rebirth. He might not be responsible for his actions – but he'll still remember them, and they'll still haunt him. If we can show him exactly how he was manipulated, and who by, it'll make things much easier for him.'

'And he has some very important information. He knows who Deodatus' next two victims are going to be. He saw their names pinned to the wall in Dieter's workshop. When we talked at the wake you said you could search the memory seas for fetches awaiting rebirth. Can you find him?'

'Normally, yes,' replied the Counsellor. 'But at the moment, I'm not sure.'

'We need the names. Then we'd be one step ahead of Deodatus. We can be watching when the pressure men strike and we can follow them back to the Shining City. Get a location for it, work out exactly what it is. And then go in and get Dieter.'

'When my expert was searching for Dieter, he felt... presences. Shadows in the depths, riding new currents. They got close enough to scare him, held far enough back to stay hidden. He came back in a panic. Told me he wouldn't go out again until he was sure they were gone.'

'Can't you talk to him? Change his mind?'

'I'll do what I can. He's a good man. He knows his duty. That's all I can say.' A pause. 'And perhaps we should talk to the gods, too.'

Leila grimaced. 'East wants to turn it all into a reality show. I don't think she'd take it remotely seriously. The Rose might have fallen to Deodatus. Holt certainly has. But there's Grey. He helped take down Kingdom. He's a tough cookie. And he was Dieter's patron. I run some of his apps myself.'

'He's not as tough as he'd like you to think. Breaking Kingdom took a lot out of him, he's still rebuilding himself.' The Fetch Counsellor looked worried. 'And if the Rose has gone down, other gods might have too.'

Leila nodded. 'We'd have no way of telling if Grey had fallen, would we? Until it was too late. Or any of the others, come to that.'

'No, I don't think we would.'

'I never trusted them much anyway.'

The Counsellor nodded. 'I think you're right, Leila. For the moment at least, we should keep away from them. At least until we've got a better sense of exactly who Deodatus is. Keep all this between the two of us. '

'Between the two of us and Cassiel. And she's back in Docklands.'

'Deodatus might spot you if you go looking for her. And then he'll know that his attack on you failed.'

'That's why I need a ghost cloak. You're going to set me up with one and then I'll go after her.'

Chapter 17

Leila moved silently through the dead hours of the early morning, heading for Cassiel's new office. The dark curve of Docklands rolled up ahead and behind her, roofing in her world. Streetlights glistened above like stars. She glanced out up the Spine towards space. Real stars hung there, cold and hard and disinterested. She hoped that the flies hadn't found Cassiel yet. The mind had moved to Roidville, one of Docklands' blander districts. Residential housing gave way to a selection of light-industrial facilities and serviced office blocks. Street lighting dropped orange cones of light through pale drizzle. The only people around were gun kiddies, scampering through the darkness, playing invisible games with imaginary enemies.

Leila knew that she made no sound, projected no image of herself, left no traces as she moved. The Fetch Counsellor had explained how the ghost cloak let her use the weave's administrative channels to manifest. She was still virtually present in every location she passed through. But nobody there would pick her up unless she wanted them to, because their weaveware skipped over the bland, abstract admin data the white goods of Station broadcast through those channels. But it was one thing to know herself to be invisible, another to believe it. She still found herself glancing nervously into every doorway and alley, hesitating before turning each corner. Memories of the pressure man's attack and – before that – the Blood and Flesh plague were fresh in her mind. She nudged the skull face into existence.

At last, she reached Cassiel's new address. The mind's rooms were on the first floor of a small office block. The softest of purple lights glowed from one window. The rest were dark. Leila imagined the mind's body glowing gently in the darkness. She moved to the block's door, glanced up at the camera nest mounted above it, then stopped, waiting for it to open, before remembering that the ghost cloak let her just move through it.

Stairs led up into darkness. A moment, and she was at the door to Cassiel's apartment. She thought for a moment about messaging her to announce her arrival, but worried that she might reveal her presence to any watchers. Instead, she just stepped inside. If Cassiel was at home, she'd reveal herself. Otherwise, she'd slip away unseen. She quite looked forward to surprising her. She didn't want to think about what she'd do if the mind had fallen to the pressure men. The skull face was a dense weight in her mind, hungry for a target.

The apartment cameras were glitched with static, fogging her vision. She moved down the passageway. Memories flared, showing her Ambrose's flat, the last silent space she'd stepped into. Fear buzzed within her. The corridor flickered around her. Every door was closed. She told herself that she wasn't afraid to step through the doors; wasn't imagining all the dark tableaux that could lie beyond them. She slipped her audio sensitivity up, straining for any trace of Cassiel.

She remembered the soft, purple light she'd seen from outside and tried to work out which room it had come from. She nudged her audio feed up again. A low buzzing permeated the hallway, an empty white noise that seemed somehow corrupted. She thought of flies. The fly spray shimmered into being in her hand. The ghost cloak should hide her from them, too. That didn't stop the fear. The buzzing came from a door at the end of the corridor. She nerved herself, then stepped through it.

One bare light bulb hung down from the ceiling. A dirty blind covered the window, ragged at the edges, stained down its centre. A sofa and armchair had been pushed to the walls, a small table between them. There were two pressure men slumped in the chairs, eyes closed, chins collapsed on to chests, pastel suits in antique styles writing the past across them. A wooden box sat on the table. It was criss-crossed with raised strips of wood and dusted with light golden patterns and scuffed weave sigils but, unlike Dieter's box, it wasn't cracked.

'Fuck,' breathed Leila.

The pressure men had pulled their jackets and shirts open to the waist, exposing two square, rotten, wood-bound absences. White specks wriggled within them, consuming decay. Leila was at once sickened and terrified. She couldn't look away. She was invisible to the two of them, so she could inspect them properly. Apart from the twin dark holes, they were flawless. Their faces were catalogue-model perfect, rich with a serene plastic beauty. Their bodies were lightly muscled and well proportioned. Their suits fascinated her, each a lethally precise evocation of a past in which she was small and powerless.

It occurred to her that she'd barely ever heard a pressure man speak. She wondered why they were so nearly mute. Perhaps Deodatus' concerns were so clearly defined and non-negotiable that they had no reason to trade words with anyone else. And yet her brother had forced him into a negotiation, and had won considerable wealth for her. For a moment she wondered what Deodatus needed him for. But that was a distraction. *I'm here for Cassiel*, she reminded herself, glancing around the rest of the room. The sofa and chairs had been pushed back to make space for a black half-globe, a couple of metres round, that glowed from within with purple light. It was the source of the buzzing. Black flecks zig-zagged in the air. The flies were everywhere. Leila readied herself for an instant jump back to the Coffin Drives, then cautiously opened up the ghost cloak a little. Her social sensors snapped into action, telling her that Cassiel was present. They told her nothing about the pressure men. It was as if they didn't exist. She told the cloak to let the mind perceive her presence, then said: 'Cassiel?'

One of the pressure men stirred lightly. 'Fuck,' she gasped, closing herself back down again.

She wasn't sure what to do next. She moved towards the globe. Its skin resolved into a black swarm, a scurry of scratching legs, dirt-flecked wings and hard, unmoving compound eyes. The flies didn't seem to notice her. The pressure men stayed immobile. She opened herself up again, then once more whispered: 'Cassiel?' She glanced nervously over at the pressure men. This time there was no response. She sighed with relief.

Then Cassiel spoke. Her voice was faint. 'Leila?' she croaked feebly. 'Is that you? Out there?'

'Yes. With two pressure men. Unconscious. And one of the boxes that killed Dieter.'

'They must have switched fully into their swarm.' Cassiel's voice was so quiet it barely penetrated the swarm's low hum. 'The flies are running a massive, co-ordinated intrusion attack on me. My defences are working them hard, but they won't last for much longer.'

'That's not a problem. I'm going to get you out of here.'

'Oh.' It was a sound as much as a word, a weak shudder made audible. 'Well, that's very laudable. But I can't rescue myself, so I really don't think you'll have much luck.'

'Good grief, Cassiel. Have some faith at least.'

Leila wondered if there was enough fly spray to break the whole swarm. She imagined it stopping only some of the flies – and then the rest would realise she was there and try to attack her. Perhaps they'd succeed. She was potentially far more vulnerable to them than they were to her. And then there would be the pressure men to deal with. Her skull face lurked in her mind. It had only slowed her Shining City attackers. And it was a weapon unique to her. Deploying it now would let Deodatus know she'd survived their attempt to rewrite her memory. Dit's work would be rendered useless. She peered at the half-globe, wondering if she could somehow just reach through it. But that was impossible.

'Are you still there?' asked Cassiel. 'Are you planning to leave? I think you should.'

That stung. 'Of course not. I'm working out how to help you.'

'It'd be the smart thing to do. I can give you Totality contacts, but you'll have to be careful.' There was a pause. When Cassiel spoke again, there was real pain in her voice. 'Some of them might have been compromised.'

'I'm going to get you out of there, Cassiel. And then you're going to help me get Dieter back.' She readied the fly spray.

'I have to say,' continued Cassiel, ignoring her, 'I always hoped for a more dignified end than this.' She sounded like she was trying to cheer herself up. 'Devoured by flies! It's not good.'

'Stop it,' Leila told her. 'You're not going to die.' She double-checked that she was ready to leap back to the Coffin Drives. 'I've already escaped a fly attack once.' She popped the cap off the fly spray. 'I think I can crash them. If I do, can you stand up to the pressure men?'

'Of course,' croaked Cassiel. Leila sighed. 'But I can't touch the flies,' she continued, 'and I'm much better equipped than you are. I can only hold them off, and that for not much longer. You really should put yourself first and leave. I've had a very rich life. I won't break any hearts by passing away just now. If this is it, well – there it is.'

'Don't be such a bloody pessimist,' Leila told her. Then – sending a silent prayer of hope down to the caretaker – she squeezed down and started to spray.

A cone of brilliant, iridescent light flared out from the can, dazzling in its multi-coloured intensity. Leila played it back and forth across the swarm, making sure that as many as possible were hit. It ran at peak brightness for a few seconds then sputtered and started to die out. A few final brilliant flashes and then there was nothing, the spray can feeling light and empty in Leila's hand. The flies were left apparently untouched. The pressure men didn't move.

'Dammit,' grumbled Leila. 'Never trust a hippy.'

'Was that it?' asked Cassiel.

Leila grunted.

'Perhaps now you'll believe me. I'm just being realistic. When they do get through my shields, I'm going to trigger a low-level self-destruct. Hopefully take a few of them with me. On the plus side, at least your rescue attempt wasn't effective enough to alert the swarm to your presence.'

Frustrated, Leila threw the spray can at the flies. She expected it to just bounce off them and roll away. Instead, it disappeared. A burst of white light flared up, then vanished. A blast of data leapt out into the weave and was gone, moving far too quickly for Leila to scan. And then, fly by fly, the swarm started to rise up.

'Oh no,' she said, moving back. 'I think I might have just alerted them, after all.' She readied herself for a sudden jump. She hated the thought of leaving Cassiel, but she couldn't see what else to do.

'Well, thanks for trying,' said Cassiel. 'I hate to say it, but I did tell you so.'

'It's not over yet, Cassiel.' Perhaps she should risk the skull face, after all.

'I'll send you my contacts. Then you should go.'

Leila glanced over at the pressure men, expecting to see them waking. But they hadn't moved. Their overlay flickered, tasteful antique suits leaping suddenly to monochrome then back again. There was a burst of visual static. For a moment, they were just pale, speckled silhouettes. It looked like their virtual systems were crashing. Back in the Shining City, the spray had only affected the flies. Either it was more powerful here, or the pressure men were more vulnerable.

Relief filled Leila. 'Now that's promising,' she said.

Looking back, she saw that the swarm too was broken. The flies veered round the room in jagged, apparently random zig-zags. There was no coherence to their movement. Cassiel was visible, kneeling unclothed inside a softly glowing, purple dome. She raised her head.

'My, my,' she said. 'You did it.'

'I did tell you so. Now let's get out of here.'

There was a light pattering. The flies had started to freeze in midflight, falling like raindrops made of black dust.

'Defending myself took a lot out of me,' replied Cassiel. 'I won't be moving quickly.' The purple dome vanished. Her nanogel flickered like a dying candle. Crashed flies bounced off her. She shifted, moving slowly and painfully.

'Gods, they hit you hard. How would you have handled the pressure men like that?'

'I didn't think I'd have to,' replied Cassiel. 'You've done well. And you're hiding yourself surprisingly effectively.' She almost sounded impressed. 'Running on non-standard weave strata?'

'It's the ghost cloak Dieter built for the Fetch Communion,' explained Leila.

'Ah. You're pretending to be a fridge.'

'Something like that.'

Cassiel stood. Only one of her arms seemed to be working properly. 'Where did you find the tool that crashed the flies?' she asked.

There was no time to describe the caretaker or the Shining City. Leila settled for: 'A friend.' Urgency gripped her. 'It might not last long. Let's go.' A thought struck her. 'Do you need any clothes?'

Cassiel shook her head. 'They're an affectation. Help humans relate to us. Just get in the way now.' Then she grunted with effort and took her first step. It wasn't a success. She half fell, slumping loosely against the wall. That was when she saw the pressure men. 'Oh,' she said, shocked. 'No.'

Leila followed her gaze. 'Cassiel,' she said. 'I'm so sorry.'

The overlay had completely fallen away from them. Now their true selves were revealed. They were both minds, but they no longer belonged to the Totality. Their bodies were speckled through with small black dots and decay had spread across their skin.

'So many flies,' whispered Cassiel. 'So deeply embedded.'

'Underneath the pressure men,' said Leila. 'Minds that have fallen to Deodatus…'

There was a muddied shine to the two fallen minds, very different from the stained-glass purity of Cassiel's glow. Both were pock-marked with blisters, craters and bruises, and both had one of the wooden boxes set into the lower part of their chests. White wriggled within them. They stank of decay.

'Gods,' breathed Leila, sickened. 'They must have had the box ready to install in you.'

'Nanogel is part-organic,' said Cassiel. 'They must let it rot to feed the flies.' She sounded disgusted. 'No wonder I could never catch them. The flies consume minds. They are my kin. They anticipated every move I'd ever make.'

One of the fallen minds twitched.

'Let's go,' hissed Leila urgently.

Cassiel moved with a limping stagger. One leg dragged behind her. Chitin crunched beneath her feet. 'If they wake,' she grunted, 'I could probably neutralise one of them. Maybe both.'

'Let's not hang around and find out, eh?'

Cassiel reached down and picked up the box. A thin skin of nano-gel poured out of her fingers and flowed around it. 'For study,' she said.

'Are you sure that's safe?'

'I'm isolating it.' She held it up. 'Coating it with an inert layer.' The nanogel turned dark. The box was invisible. 'Now we can go.'

Cassiel's slow progress was an agony. Leila hovered around her as she inched out of the apartment, desperate to help and yet completely unable to do so. Cassiel moved in silence, swearing occasionally as she stumbled or half fell. They'd just pushed through the front door and reached the stairs when there was a loud crash behind them. Looking back, they saw the first of the pressure men staggering towards them, its overlay still down.

'Oh, fuck,' said Leila. 'I can zap them with my skull face. But then they'll know I'm here.' The limitations of anonymity were starting to frustrate her.

'I'll take them,' Cassiel told her. 'It's what I do.' Then, before Leila could reply, she leant forward and let herself fall, curling herself up as she went. Her back bent more than a human's could. She half-slid, half-rolled down the stairs, barely in control, then bumped on to the landing and lay splayed out for a moment. Then she groaned, pushed herself up on all fours, crawled forwards and disappeared down the next flight.

Leila glanced back. Both fallen minds were in the passage. They were more frightening without overlay. Their blotched, empty faces stared hungrily past her. One reached an arm out, pointing towards the stairs. The other one grunted. They sped up. Leila jumped to the bottom of the stairs. Cassiel had just managed to stand up. The mind pushed the door open and half fell into the street. In the sky, the Twins were fishing, their giant forms towering over the sleeping city.

'I'll take them here,' Cassiel said, propping the door open with the sealed-up box. The camera nest above it looked down at them. 'One at a time. As they come through.' She looked at Leila. 'You said you escaped a fly attack?'

'Yes. They tried to rewrite my memory.' There wasn't time to explain Dit. 'But I was running a buffer self. They attacked that instead. They think they've neutralised me.'

'Best to keep it that way.' Cassiel nodded towards the stairs. 'Whatever happens, stay back.'

'Do you really have to fight?'

Cassiel couldn't answer because the first fallen mind was on her. He came rolling through the door and uncurled to stand, stumbling a little as he turned to face Cassiel. The mind was suddenly a blur, moving with him, one hand at his wrist and the other at his chin. As she spun him she pulled his arm out and pushed his head back. His plastic body bent, but not quickly enough, and he fell backwards, landing with a wet thump on the hard pavement. Cassiel sank with him, moving to straddle him, both hands pushing into the blank oval of his face. They vanished up the wrist. His body shook, arms and legs thrashing. Cassiel pulled her hands out. A moment, then his head lost all form and collapsed into a dirty purple puddle. The stump of his neck bled dirty nanogel. The body was still.

'Fuck,' gasped Leila, both surprised and profoundly impressed.

The second mind appeared at the door, moving as quickly as the first one. This time Cassiel didn't have the advantage of surprise. She tried to spin to the right. She was exhausted. The movement was slow and awkward. The second fallen mind threw himself forward. She grabbed for his wrist and started to spin, trying to throw him over her head, but she missed and he was on her. His momentum threw her backwards and he was kneeling over her, his hands almost touching her face. Almost, but not quite – for she'd grabbed both his wrists and was holding him off. Her body shook with strain.

Running footsteps echoed in the night. Leila glanced up the street. A silhouette, rushing towards them. 'Shit. Another one.' There was no choice. She targeted the skull face on the mind attacking Cassiel and prepared to fire it.

A private message howled into her mind. 'JUST GO!'

'No!' she shot back, hoping to break Cassiel's attacker before their new adversary reached them. But he was almost on them. Leila spun, ready to switch her attack to him, but it wasn't a fallen mind.

'You?' she gasped, staggered. 'What are you doing here?'

Of course the caretaker didn't hear her. He shot past, converting his momentum into an almighty kick that took Cassiel's attacker in the middle of its chest, lifting it right off her and into the air beyond.

Chapter 18

The fallen mind crashed back down into the street. The caretaker landed beyond Cassiel then sunk down, smashing his knees into the mind's chest. It shook feebly, arms and legs flailing, while he splashed it with liquid from a little metal container. A flame flared from a lighter in his hand. He touched it to the mind then stepped up and back. Fire leapt across the mind. It shuddered and tried to roll. Then the flames had all of it and it lay still.

'Job done,' said the caretaker, as he dropped the lighter and its fuel canister back into his pocket. 'You all right?' he asked Cassiel. She grunted. 'There's someone else here too, isn't there?'

Leila let him see her.

'We're going. Now,' he said, already helping Cassiel up.

'How did you know I was there? How did you even find us?'

'I had a message from a spray can.'

Questions pulsed in Leila's mind. But the caretaker was right. They needed to get moving. She looked round, orientating herself, as he slipped an arm under Cassiel's shoulder and pulled her to her feet.

'Lighter than she looks,' he commented, shrugging himself into a support position. 'Right, good to go. Where's safe?'

Cassiel was trying to say something. She forced words out: 'Surveillance. The Rose will be watching.' She nodded at the camera nest over the door. 'I can fix it.' She reached up, her arm elongating. For a moment her hand became a mass of nanogel wrapped around the nest. Lightning shimmered within it. 'Dropped a virus. Intercepts all local images of us. No recording, invisible.' Her arm fell back down and she slumped against the caretaker, completely exhausted. 'Over to you, Leila,' she muttered. 'Hide us. Don't forget the box.'

Leila nodded and the caretaker squatted down to pick up the box, grunting as Cassiel's weight moved against him. 'Home's not safe,' said Leila, as he stood up again. She remembered standing before Ambrose, racking her brains for somewhere to hide together. The apartment block she'd shown to the awful couple would most likely still be empty. 'There's somewhere a few minutes away. Nobody'll find us.'

When they reached the block, Leila called up the cuttlefish. It made short work of the block's security systems, reprogramming them to give Leila full access and lock anyone else out until she'd been alerted to their presence. As the caretaker carried Cassiel up the block's staircase, Leila thought back to the last time she'd been in it. Her life had changed so radically since then. It was almost like accessing someone else's memories. Then she thought of Lei, and shivered.

They installed themselves in one of the top-floor flats, its windows facing the back of the building. 'Invisible from the street,' noted Leila. She had the cuttlefish lock the block off from the weave. 'I can use the block's weaveservers to manifest. But nobody outside can see any of us.'

'Smart move,' wheezed the caretaker. He carried Cassiel into a bedroom, settled her on to a mattress and staggered off towards the kitchen. 'Drink of water,' he gasped.

Leila stayed with Cassiel. She spoke in a cracked whisper, her words slurred with exhaustion. 'Deodatus' corruption is so much worse than I thought,' she told Leila. 'Those flies, riding the fallen minds. They very nearly broke through my defences. That takes deep technical knowledge of our most secret procedures. And the fallen minds defended themselves too well against me. I thought they were human until their overlay crashed. The rot has gone deep.'

'I'm sorry,' said Leila, feeling inadequate. There was so much pain in Cassiel's voice.

The mind held up the dark globe containing the box. 'At least we recovered this. Must dissect it.' Her hand shook. The tremor spread through her.

'But not right now,' Leila told her gently. 'You've got to heal.'

'Yes,' muttered the mind. She put the globe down on the floor next to the bed, the shaking dying away as she let go of it. 'I will sleep,' she continued, 'and rebuild.' With that, she drifted off. Leila settled her more comfortably on the mattress, then held her hand as unconsciousness took her. She stayed with the mind for a few minutes, watching her sink into a deep and hopefully restorative sleep mode, then went to find the caretaker.

He was standing at the living room window, staring out into Docklands, a mug in one hand and a hand-rolled joint in the other. Spears of dawn light filled the room, illuminating his thoughtful expression. He drew hard on the joint. Its tip flared red, then darkened again. He waited for a few seconds then exhaled out of the window.

'Thank you for helping me again,' Leila said. 'For helping us.'

He turned to face her. 'My pleasure, I guess.'

'But who are you?'

'Mind if I smoke this in here?'

'I don't have lungs,' smiled Leila. 'Neither does Cassiel.'

'I suppose not. Thank you.' He moved slowly and deliberately to an armchair, then sank carefully into it, balancing the mug on one arm. 'Good to take the weight off,' he sighed. Then he said: 'And, as for who I am – well, I was hoping you could tell me.'

'What?'

'It's a very good question.' He held the joint up and peered at it. 'Found some weed in my pocket, thought I'd skin up, bring myself down after all the excitement. Maybe jog some memories.' He shrugged. 'Nothing yet. Don't know who I am. Don't know who you are. I found myself in a street somewhere. Got a message. Said it was from a can of a fly spray. Told me you were in danger, gave me a location. I thought, well, if someone needs help, who cares about the messenger?'

Leila sat down. 'Shit. The pressure men must have got to you.'

'Pressure men?' He exhaled. 'Who are they?'

'The people attacking us.'

'Ah, those dudes. The fucked-up versions of Cassiel.'

'Yes. They can rewrite memories. They must have wiped yours. Is there anything left? Do you remember the first time we met?'

'What, just now?' He chuckled. 'Of course. I'm not that screwed up.'

'No. It was somewhere else. Somewhere far away. And very

old.' Leila talked him through everything that had happened since Dieter's death. He smoked his joint down as she talked, nodding along, his round glasses flashed as he took it all in. 'Ring any bells?' she said at last.

'Nope.' He still seemed very relaxed about it all.

'What about your weaveself? Are there any externally stored memories?'

'Worth a try.' He tipped his head back. A few moments of silence, then: 'Nothing useful. Just weaveware update requests.' He paused again. 'Lots of them. The gods are a bit pissed off with me.' He smiled. 'I don't strike myself as the kind of person who'd care much about that.'

Leila smiled. 'I'd have to agree with you there.'

The caretaker nodded and took another draw on his joint.

'Is that helping at all?' asked Leila.

'The mood, but not the memory.' He smiled again. 'Could be worse.' He pulled his thoughts into focus. 'So, what next?

'I'll get in touch with the Fetch Counsellor. See if we can get the names of the next two Deodatus victims from Ambrose's fetch. Use them to get on his trail and work out where the Shining City is. Then we'll go back there and get Dieter out.'

'What about mopping up Deodatus and the pressure men? They're pretty scary guys.'

Leila sighed. 'I can't take them on. That's a job for Cassiel and the Totality, maybe the Fetch Counsellor. Maybe even the Pantheon, if we can find one of them that hasn't fallen and isn't totally useless.'

'Pretty big job.'

'Yeah,' nodded Leila. 'I don't want to think about that too much. I just want Dieter back.'

'Fair enough. Blood's thicker than water.' The caretaker went to fist bump her. 'What about me? I should probably try and work out who I am.' He smiled ruefully. 'I don't even know what I'm called.'

'You just said you were the caretaker,' Leila reminded him. 'I'm sorry, I wish I'd asked you.'

'Hey, no problem, you had other things on your mind.' He thought for a moment. 'And that's not such a bad name. The Caretaker. The guy who takes care of things. I think I'll be that, for the moment.'

Leila smiled. 'OK, Caretaker. We'll call you that. And we know one other thing. You're pretty handy with a lighter. And a broom, too.'

The Caretaker chuckled. 'Improvising with what's at hand.' He thought for a moment. 'You know, I guess I must have been checking them out. Maybe they wiped my memory because I found something important.'

'Or maybe you scared them. When I met you in the Shining City, you seemed to know who the pressure men were, where they came from and how to handle them.'

'Looks like I need to get back down there too.' He took a long, final draw on his joint. The tip flared down to the roach, and then burnt out. 'Might remember who I am. And in the meantime – well, I've kicked the crap out of the bad guys, helped rescue Cassiel and I'm well supplied with excellent weed. I think I might just approve of myself.'

Chapter 19

Leila walked briskly up a little road of red-brick, two storey terraced houses. Being in the Coffin Drives again filled her with low, grumbling fear. The Fetch Counsellor had replied to her update with a message summoning her back. 'Come to the Channel of the Quiet Dead,' it said. 'We'll be talking to Ambrose.' Leila wanted to believe that was possible, but the very mundane feel of the neighbourhood didn't help her believe in miracles. On the plus side, at least it soothed her a little. A glorious sunset smeared the sky with reds and oranges. A man in shirtsleeves, braces and a flat hat waved a cheery 'Hello!' as he trundled a hand mower across his front lawn. Through front windows, Leila saw couple after couple sitting quietly down to supper, televisions flickering alongside them. A low susurrus of engine noises rose up from somewhere near, implying a busy main road.

The Fetch Counsellor was standing in front of one of the houses, checking her watch. The Counsellor's dark eyes looked out from a blonde in her late thirties, dressed in a heavy overcoat and carrying a large, glossy handbag. When Leila reached her, she said: 'You're late. I was worried.'

'I got lost. The Channel of the Quiet Dead is a hard place to find.'

The Counsellor smiled. 'On purpose.'

'What is it exactly?'

'Just what it says. It's where people who want peace and stability come. An eternity of quiet Friday nights, Saturday mornings with the kids playing in the garden, Sunday afternoons dozing after a good roast lunch.' She gestured at the quiet street. 'Of this.'

'What about the traffic? That sounds pretty busy.'

The Counsellor smiled. 'The main road? You can walk here for ever, but you'll never reach it. It's an aural representation of all of the rest of the Coffin Drives' traffic, on all the other channels.

Apparently one only really appreciates peace if there's a little disturbance to compare it with.'

Leila snorted.

'Don't be so dismissive,' chided the Counsellor. 'Think of a quiet day. You only know how quiet it really is when there's a tiny little fly, making its tiny little buzz, breaking the peace.'

Leila shuddered. 'I don't want to talk about flies. Let's go in.'

'Of course. I'm sorry. And, before we knock on Mr Meeker's door, I've got some good news and some bad news. No flies, I promise. Which first?'

'Bad news.'

'The gods have been asking after you. The Rose, East, even Grey.'

'I told you about East. She wants to turn me into a reality star.'

'I said she should leave you alone for a bit, that you were still mourning your brother. I promised I'd ask you to think about her offer. She seemed happy enough with that.'

'That's a surprise. She's usually so pushy. What about Grey?'

'Oh, he was just very vague. You know how he's been since his new board took over. All those teenagers. It's much harder to read him.'

'They saved him from Kingdom.' Leila sighed. 'Let's hope they've saved him from the pressure men too. And if they can't – well, there's not much we can do about it. The Rose, though – that's serious. What did she want?'

'She knows all about last night's little adventure, though she doesn't seem to know that you were involved.'

'The ghost cloak worked. Thank you.'

'Yes, but the Rose knows exactly how Cassiel spoofed the weave-cams. She's watching out for it. If Cassiel tries it again, she's got maybe half an hour before the Rose spots it, cracks her security and locates her. It's a one-shot weapon now.'

'Shit.'

The Counsellor smiled. 'She's pretty furious about it all. Ranting about viral attacks, terrorism, the usual. She managed to recover a couple of images of Cassiel and the Caretaker, and she's scouring Station for them. Telling everyone that the Caretaker's an anti-Totality extremist, that he anonymised himself by wiping his own weaveself. That two of her operatives tried to stop him kidnapping Cassiel but couldn't.'

'She's claiming the pressure men as her own?'

'Yes. The way she's playing it, I'm pretty sure she's either working with or for Deodatus. And it gets worse. She's had me supply location data on potentially implicated fetches. Checking alibis.'

'What's the problem with that?'

'It was a short list. You were on it.'

'What did you tell her?' Fear gripped Leila. The ghost cloak made her location unreadable. That in itself was suspicious. She imagined the Rose demanding an immediate interview. 'Did you cover for me?'

The Counsellor laughed. 'No need to. You were at home. Entertaining yourself with one of East's dramas.'

'What? But that would be impossible to fake…'

'Not fake at all. This is the good news. There are two of you.'

'Oh shit. Lei.'

The Counsellor laughed. 'I have to admit, Dit has been very effective. He's letting her run at pretty high capacity. She convinced the Rose.'

Leila imagined another self out there, usurping her life. 'I can't believe he's done that. Gods!'

The Counsellor put a hand on Leila's arm. 'Don't shout. Not here.'

Leila ran a hand through her hair. 'I'm sorry – but this is crazy.'

'The gods think that Lei is you. So, you're safe. For the moment, that is. There is a problem, though. If she just sits at home doing nothing – it won't take long for them to realise they've been duped.'

'What?'

'Lei's a young, single woman. She's just become incredibly rich. The last thing she'd do is spend all day indoors, catching up on the soaps. She's got to be out and about, living her life.'

'Living my life.'

'It's the only way to keep the Rose off your back. The rest of them, too, if they start digging around.'

'No. That's too much.'

'She's been your shield once, and she did a great job. Let her keep doing that for you.'

Leila sighed. 'I hate the thought of it.'

'I'm sure you'll make the right decision. And I'll watch the Rose and the rest of them. See if anyone else has fallen. When we know exactly what's going on and who can help us – we'll act. And right now, Ambrose will help us find out who Deodatus are targeting next.'

'Is that all we can ask him about?'

'The way this works, long conversations are impossible. You just get fragments.'

'Well, fingers crossed. And there's nobody else who can help us. Hardly anyone even knows about this stuff.' Dieter used to rant about how apathetic most Station citizens were, how short-sighted they were not to be more curious about their own history. She was beginning to feel quite a lot of sympathy for him. 'The only other person I can think of is Cormac Redonda. And he's ghosted himself out.'

'I've already tried him.' The Counsellor sighed. 'Didn't go very well.'

'You know where he is?'

'I know where every fetch is, Leila. He locked himself away in an old Flurrytown restaurant on Virgil Street. His little boy had a birthday party there, just before the end. I went and pulled him out of his fugue. But he's a broken man. He can't face reality. He refused to help us.'

'Shit.'

'But hopefully Ambrose will be more helpful. Let's go and find him.'

The Counsellor pushed open a little garden gate and led the way up a narrow gravel path past a neatly trimmed little lawn and flowerbed. Leila followed her, feeling a little suffocated both by the neighbourhood and the thought of another self living her life for her. The Counsellor gave the front door a sharp knock.

A short, stout woman in late middle age opened it.

'Ah, Miss Lympstone,' said the Counsellor. 'It's good to see you.'

Miss Lympstone beamed out a welcome, floating them through the hallway and into the front room on a gushed wave of sentences. 'Oh, hello! Do come in, please, do come in, may I take your coat?

Mr Meeker will be home soon, I'm terribly sorry, he's been held up at the bowls club, please – come through here, do please sit down.' The room was empty but for a mahogany dining table with four matching chairs and a small cupboard topped by a little gramophone. Miss Lympstone only slowed when another woman appeared in the door. 'Ah! And here's Mrs Meeker to welcome you. I'll make the tea!' She bustled out of the room.

Mrs Meeker was a slender woman, about the same age as Miss Lympstone, with a tight little face and hair pulled sharply back into a bun. She stared disapprovingly at the two guests.

'He shouldn't be going out there again,' she said. 'Not at the moment.'

'Mrs Meeker,' replied the Counsellor. 'I'm so sorry. But we've been through this. It's for the good of us all.'

'I only care about my husband. He's got too good a heart. He should have said no to you.'

'I'm very grateful,' added Leila. 'He's going to be a great help.'

'There are bad things out there.'

The front door opened, then closed. A second later, a squat little man bustled into the room. Curly hair framed a happy face. Mr Meeker too was in late middle age. Leila wondered if it was possible to live in this channel and be anything else. She decided not to look in any mirrors, fearing that she'd see an older, more placid version of herself peering back at her.

'Friends! Friends!' he said, hurrying over to them, somehow managing to simultaneously shrug his coat off and take their hands in his. He was trying to be welcoming, but there was fear in his voice. 'Welcome! Counsellor, it's a privilege to see you again. And you are Miss Fenech? I do hope the tides are kind and we can help you.' He took his coat in his arms and scurried back out again. Mrs Meeker followed him.

'Tides?' asked Leila. 'What does he mean?'

'Mr Meeker calls himself a fisherman,' replied the Counsellor. 'He lets his consciousness fall into the memory seas, and calls out to individual weaveselves drifting there. So they can use him as a temporary platform to cohere around. And then they can speak to us.'

'Won't that harm them?'

'Mr Meeker couldn't harm anyone!' sang out Miss Lympstone as she bustled back into the room, a tray laden with tea cups and a tea pot rattling in her hands. 'A little coherence, a few minutes' conversation, no damage at all. He's a rare talent! So kind.' She poured tea as she talked. 'We've helped people whose loved ones have only just crossed over speak to them. And then those who choose not to become fetches – we can bring them back for a moment, too. It's such a relief for the ones they've left behind.' Leila found herself holding a steaming cup of tea. 'The truly dead are often so happy in their choice. And there are those who don't want to leave the sea, who just drift in all that data. Our guides. They're some of our closest friends – aren't they, Mr Meeker?'

Mr and Mrs Meeker came into the room together. 'As we agreed, dear,' he told her nervously. She pursed her lips. 'I've made my mind up. The Fetch Counsellor needs our help. We must give it.'

'I'm sure it'll be fine, Eunice,' said Miss Lympstone cheerfully, taking her place at the table. She reached out and took Leila's hand. 'You too,' she told the Counsellor. Mr Meeker sat down and took the Counsellor's other hand. Mrs Meeker sighed heavily. She went over to a side table and wound up the gramophone. The black disc on it started to revolve. She moved an arm with a little needle over it and dropped it. Piano notes tinkled out. Leila thought of sunlight sparkling on gentle waves.

'Mr Meeker loves music,' enthused Miss Lympstone. 'It helps him focus.'

Strings kicked in, scratched across with static. A rich, deep voice sang about the sea. Miss Lympstone joined in, her voice reedy and thin, not always getting the lyrics right. Mrs Meeker sat down and took Mr Meeker's and Leyla's hands, completing the circle. Then she too started singing. For a minute or so, Mr Meeker stared ahead, his face slack. Then he shuddered.

'Ah! Here comes our first visitor,' exclaimed Miss Lympstone.

The gramophone music ground to a halt, the singer's voice elongating to bass depths then fading out entirely. Mr Meeker's face leapt into life, but it seemed that it was no longer his. Leila could make out another's behind it. It was like looking at a doubly exposed photograph. She thought of Dieter. Mr Meeker seemed much more in control. He opened his mouth and began to speak. The words that came were slightly out of sync with the movement of his lips.

'Hello!' said a deep voice, thick with a heavy out-system accent. The head – no longer entirely Mr Meeker's – nodded to left and right. 'Good friends.' It turned towards Leila and the Counsellor. 'And to you newcomers.'

'We're looking for—' started Leila, but Miss Lympstone shushed her.

'Don't break his concentration,' she whispered.

This new version of Mr Meeker chattered away, complaining about the weather. 'There's a storm coming. I can feel it.' Then his head fell forwards and his shoulders slumped, like a puppet whose strings had been cut. Another voice took him – this one a child's – then a woman's. They rattled out mundanities. But there was tension, too, a subtle sense of upset. The child mentioned an imaginary friend. 'She won't play with me anymore. She's hiding.' The woman talked about nightmares. 'When I ran,' she said, 'it couldn't see me. But when I stayed still it found me.'

'Is he looking for Ambrose?' asked Leila.

'He's moving through the dead. Trying to track him down,' replied Miss Lympstone.

Voice after voice shook through the medium, each a new personality, each sharing deeper, darker worries. Mr Meeker was less and less himself, his face and body almost completely disappearing into each new identity. Mrs Meeker held his hand tightly, gazing into his face. Leila imagined her as some kind of anchor, holding on to his root identity as so many others flew through him. The voices became a babble, running too quickly to make any individual words out. Leila was reminded of the Blood and Flesh plague, of the way she'd felt her own self dissolve. She felt fear grow in her.

Then, suddenly, Mr Meeker howled 'No!' His face became entirely other. Ambrose stared out at her. 'Leila, no!'

'Oh, he's found your friend,' chirped Miss Lympstone.

Chapter 20

Mrs Meeker pulled Mr Meeker's hand to her chest. She looked terrified.

'No!' Ambrose shouted again. 'Leave me alone!' Sweat beaded his face. There was a rip in his neck where he'd cut it open. The smile dropped from Miss Lympstone's face.

Shock had silenced Leila. The Counsellor nudged her. 'Ask him,' she hissed.

Leila nerved herself. 'Ambrose,' she stuttered. 'Do you remember the Shining City?'

'Go away!'

'It's very important.'

'I can't help you. I can't help anyone. Let me go! I have to keep moving!'

'The next two Deodatus victims,' she made herself say. 'The people you saw on Dieter's wall. Who are they?'

Blood oozed from Ambrose's neck. Leila felt like she was forcing answers from a torture victim.

'You don't understand,' wailed Ambrose. 'They want to see if anyone comes to talk with me.'

'Tell me, Ambrose. What are the names you saw on the wall?'

'Oh no,' whispered Ambrose. 'You made me stay still for too long.'

The world changed. The little front room vanished. They were still in their chairs, still sat at the table, but now they were hanging in the deep sea. Light shafted down from above and lost itself in the endless dark beneath them.

Ambrose's voice was full of terror. 'Now they've found me.'

Miss Lympstone gasped. She squeezed Leila's hand hard. 'Gods,' she breathed, looking towards Mrs Meeker.

'I told you so,' Mrs Meeker spat at the Counsellor. 'We've been pulled into the depths.'

'Ambrose,' shouted Leila. 'Tell me the names! I have to know.'

'They'll be here,' moaned Ambrose. 'Any moment now, they'll be here.'

There was a sense of something vast moving, a little way away – a sharp silhouette, knifing through the depths, circling them.

'I'm holding it off,' hissed the Counsellor. 'It's already locked on to Ambrose, but I'm hiding us. Can't keep it up for long.'

'I'm going to crash us out,' said Mrs Meeker, pulling her husband's hand to her forehead. 'Gods know what this will do to him.'

'No,' Leila said, then desperately, to Ambrose, 'Tell me. The names!' Blood poured from his neck, fanning out around him in a red mist. She could barely see his face. 'Ambrose, please!' she begged. 'Remember Dieter. It's all for him.'

'I can see it,' wailed Ambrose, looking past her. 'It's found me.'

'Tell me the names!'

'Can't hold it back,' grunted the Counsellor.

A slim grey shape hurtled towards them out of the gloom. Leila had a sense of it rushing towards Ambrose. She glimpsed sharp fins, a compound eye, a gaping mouth that was a nightmare of teeth, then Miss Lympstone screamed again.

'Gods help us,' howled Mrs Meeker.

The sea flashed into nothing. There was a moment of absolute void and then they were back in the small front room, the circle broken, Miss Lympstone in tears, the Fetch Counsellor repeating 'Fuck,' again and again, and Mrs Meeker hunched over her husband, who was slumped face forward on the table.

'The names,' asked Leila desperately. 'Did he get the names?'

'Ambrose might have dropped them into Mr Meeker's memory,' said the Counsellor. 'But we need to get them quickly. Before he forgets.'

'Get out!' Mrs Meeker told her. 'You could have sent him to his true death. Out!'

'But the names…'

'Fuck your names,' said Mrs Meeker, then: 'Miss Lympstone. Recover yourself.'

The Counsellor touched Leila's arm. 'I think we'd better let it be,' she said.

Miss Lympstone led them both into the hall. 'Really!' she said. 'Normally our guests are so well behaved. Poor Mr Meeker.'

'Can you go back and see if he can remembers the names?' asked Leila. 'It's the only way I have of finding my brother.'

'I'm afraid that that's up to Mrs Meeker,' sniffed Miss Lympstone. 'And you've brought trouble to her door.'

'Please,' said Leila simply.

'It's for the Fetch Communion too,' added the Counsellor. 'Her brother did a lot of work to protect us all. We still need him.'

'Well. Since it's you asking...' She opened the door and disappeared back into the front room. Leila caught a glimpse of Mr Meeker, his chin pressed into his chest, his eyes tight shut, rocking backwards and forwards as Mrs Meeker leant over him. Then Miss Lympstone shut the door with a very emphatic firmness.

'That was really Ambrose, wasn't it?' asked Leila.

'It was the closest we'll get before his rebirth.'

'And that shark – it was one of Ambrose's search engines. He told the pressure men about the backdoor. They must have gone in through it.'

'I stopped it from seeing who Ambrose was talking to.' The Counsellor looked worried. 'You need to be very careful. You can't let it spot you. Any of you.'

'The safe house is insulated from the weave. And if we keep moving when we're out and about, we'll be safe. The sharks can only find you when you stop.'

The door opened again and Miss Lympstone emerged, holding a scribbled-on sheet of paper. 'Mr Meeker's a little better. We hope he'll be fine.' She gave Leila a pointed look. 'No thanks to you, of course.'

'I can help heal him,' the Fetch Counsellor told her.

She held out the paper to Leila. 'I'm not sure I should even give you this. But then it would all have been for nothing.' Leila took it from her. 'Mrs Meeker wrote the two names down for you. And now you've got them, I hope we never see you again.'

Chapter 21

When Leila jumped from the Coffin Drives back to the safe house, Cassiel and the Caretaker were both asleep. She slept too, her systems integrating startling new memories with older, more mundane ones. When she woke the next morning, that process keeping her out for longer than usual, she found Cassiel and the Caretaker sat at the table in the front room. Cassiel's arms lay on either side of the box. Her hands had grown into a round, translucent dome, covering it. Thin needles of nanogel reached down, moving inside it with careful precision.

The Caretaker looked up. 'We've got the top off,' he said cheerfully. 'Cassiel's having a look round inside. We wanted to wait for you, but we weren't sure when you were going to wake up again.'

'Gods!' gasped Leila. 'Be careful! Remember what happened to Dieter!'

'We're safe,' Cassiel reassured her, speaking slowly and deliberately. She was concentrating hard. 'Learning from his mistakes. The dome insulates the box.'

'He had his defences up too,' Leila told her.

'But his guard was down. He thought someone he trusted had already checked it out. I know it's lethal.' Her needles twitched inside it. 'I've taken every precaution. There's nothing to worry about.'

Leila joined them at the table and peered nervously down into the box. The dome obscured her view of fine detail, but she could see that the box was hollow, with a smaller cube inside it, almost filling its interior. Cassiel's needles explored the space between its walls and the cube. One of the box's external faces had been cut open. Red gel and wires oozed out.

'Found anything interesting?'

'The red gel contains nano-machines. They spin the wires out

143

into a human victim's body, hardwiring them to the box. They can also consume some or all of their host.'

Leila remembered the fallen minds that had attacked Cassiel. 'What about you guys?'

'The wires don't deploy. Our own nanogel resists them. I assume the embedded flies perform an equivalent function, allowing a full takeover of the infested body.' The needles lifted up and out of the box. 'The cube is hollow. I can detect movement within it. Flies, perhaps. But I can find no way of opening it.' One of the needles became a sharp blade. 'I'm going to cut into it.'

'Are you sure that's wise?'

'You might remember how I recently held off an entire swarm? One guided by two fallen minds?'

'Fair enough,' sighed Leila.

The knife carved round the top of the cube. 'Some sort of cardboard,' commented Cassiel. 'Clearly a temporary structure.' A needle reached down to pry it open. 'Let's see what's in there.' All three of them leant in to see what the box contained.

The top came off and then, as if spring-loaded, flies leapt out of it and punched into the nanogel dome.

'Fuck!' spat Leila. The Caretaker flinched back. Cassiel's back arched, her arms taut. 'Gods,' she gasped. 'Intrusion attack.' Jagged shards of light flashed within her.

'Are you all right?' asked Leila. 'What can we do?'

Cassiel said nothing. Her head was tipped up. Her body shivered. Tiny wings blurred, pushing the flies further into the nanogel dome. A couple were nearly through it.

Leila looked to the Caretaker. 'You've zapped them before, can you do it again?'

'No need,' gasped Cassiel. 'Under control.'

'Really?' asked Leila.

A bubble formed on top of the globe, becoming a soft, round bump, topped by a thin mesh. There was a soft hissing.

'Hey,' said the Caretaker, waving his hand above it. 'You're pumping the air out.'

'Creating a vacuum,' stuttered Cassiel. A couple of seconds passed, then, one by one, the flies dropped to the ground. They lay on their backs and sides, legs and wings twitching uncontrollably. A minute or so, and all were still.

'Problem solved,' drawled the Caretaker. 'Good job.'

'No danger, eh?' asked Leila.

'Nothing I couldn't handle,' replied Cassiel casually. 'That must have been how they took Dieter. Did he have anything like the globe?'

Leila shook her head.

The mind was silent for a moment, analysing. 'They'd have hit him hard with a very simple, very powerful command. Lay the box on his chest. Let it dig into him. Impossible to resist.'

It didn't take long to disassemble the rest of the cube.

'It's like a little fly city!' said the Caretaker, amazed.

'More of a factory,' replied Cassiel. 'And a very destructive one. Causes considerable decay in any nanogel it's exposed to. Greatly shortens the life expectancy of any minds that carry one.'

'What about humans?' asked Leila.

'A combination. It attacks randomly selected body parts and dissolves them. But it will also considerably extend its host's life span.'

'Weird,' commented the Caretaker.

The box's base was divided into three. A quarter of the base held eggs, little white flecks about the size of a grain of rice. 'They become maggots. And the maggots feed, and then cocoon.' Half the base was an incubation chamber. 'The cocoons sit in it,' explained Cassiel. 'And there's a tiny surgeon here that modifies the maggots as they become flies. Installs the hardware that lets them merge with the swarm. And then they hatch, and they're out in the world. Half insect, half tech.' She dissected one of the dead flies. 'Look at that... Wireless rig, solid state memory and a tiny processor. Every single one's a little computer. And when they swarm...'

Half an hour passed and she was done. 'The flies are all inert, now,' said Cassiel. The dome split in two as she lifted her arms up and off the table, its two halves quickly reforming into hands. 'And I can take the important bits into me.' She squashed a finger down onto one of the flies.

'What are you doing?' gasped Leila. 'You'll fall too!'

'No.' Cassiel flicked a finger and a broken insect body flew

145

away from it. 'I've just taken the comms hardware.' She froze for a moment. 'And now I've got full control over it. I can use it to talk with any local swarms. Issue queries, perhaps even basic commands.'

She pushed herself to her feet. She was moving more easily than she had done the previous night, but it was clear that she was still badly damaged.

The Caretaker went to her side, ready to support her as she took a few uncertain steps across the room. 'Don't push it,' he said. 'You've got to move at healing speed. And you've just been working very hard. You need to lie down for a bit.'

'That was mental effort,' Cassiel told him.

'Still takes it out of you,' he replied.

'No.' Cassiel sounded tense. 'Enough healing. Now I understand the flies I've got to get out there. Track down the pressure men. Stop Deodatus.'

'Well, you get full marks for determination,' Leila told her. 'But you can barely walk. And you might be able to talk to the flies, but East knows about whatever you did to her cameras and has every spare InSec operative looking for you and the Caretaker. She'll nab you before you get fifty metres. If Deodatus' sharks don't get you first.'

'How do you know this?' asked Cassiel.

'I saw the shark myself. The Fetch Counsellor told me the rest. The Rose went to see him. She's furious with you two.'

The Caretaker beamed. 'Right on!'

'I have tools, weapons. I can look after myself.' Cassiel's voice had a broken quality to it. 'I need to hit back. I have a responsibility. You're not going to stand in my way.'

'Stand in your way?' Leila raised an eyebrow. 'Without me you'd still be under the swarm.' The Caretaker coughed significantly and raised an eyebrow. 'And the Caretaker helped us both, of course. Look, if you go out now you won't get anywhere. Please. Stay here, rest up properly. Then we can all move against them. You can help me rescue Dieter and I'll do what I can for you.'

Cassiel's response was surprisingly sharp. 'Your brother may be important to you. But I have a whole society to save.' She paused for a moment. 'I'm sorry. But Deodatus is a cancer. His influence has gone deep. It might have gone wide, too. Fallen minds are impossible for even me to spot. I have to assume that they're spreading through the Totality with great speed. I need to move against them just as quickly.'

'Now wait a moment,' said the Caretaker. 'First of all, you're both totally free to do whatever you want. Having said that, Cassiel, Leila's right. Leaving here is just plain dumb. Physically, you're broken. I don't care how ninja you are when you're one hundred per cent, you're no use to anyone just now. And if Leila's right...'

'I'm totally right.'

'...it'll be half an hour tops before you fall into the hands of people who'll really fuck you up. At best they'll kill you, at worst they'll turn you and you'll be working for them. So you can leave if you want, but I think you're smarter than that.'

'Yes! Exactly,' agreed Leila.

'And Leila,' continued the Caretaker. 'Cassiel's right too. Your brother's important. But this is much bigger than him. East is infected, and it's beginning to sound like other gods might be too. Deodatus has spread into the Totality. My guess is he'll be in the Fetch Communion soon, too.'

Cassiel nodded. 'He's only holding back because it's neither a threat nor a resource for him. But he'll move against it sooner or later.'

'Of course you've got to look out for the people you love,' continued the Caretaker. 'But if the whole of the rest of the world is in danger, you might have to start thinking a bit bigger than that.'

'The rest of the world never did much for me,' grumbled Leila. But an image of Mrs Meeker thrust itself into her mind, refusing to help because she only cared about her husband.

'He's right, Leila,' said Cassiel. 'The Totality helped free the fetches. And the gods look after the society you're part of. You're not an island. None of us is. Society is the platform the individual runs on. If your society goes down, you and your brother will too. He matters, but there's more to this than just him.'

'I owe Dieter so much,' Leila replied. 'And he's all I've got in this world. He has to be my focus.'

'Well, as long as he's not the only thing you focus on,' replied

Cassiel. 'And you're right too. I can't do anything like this.' She clenched her fists, her arms shaking. 'Dammit, I never thought it'd be flies that broke me.' She sounded furious with herself. 'I never thought I'd be so useless.'

'Flies with fallen minds behind them,' Leila told her. 'It's pretty tough standing up to your own people. They know all your tricks. And you can repair yourself. How long's it going to take?'

'A couple of days,' replied Cassiel sadly. 'I'm very resilient. But that's not really the point. I am Totality. We fought the Pantheon – we defeated them – to create a fairer future for us all.' The soft lightning of deep emotion shimmered through her body. 'But now we've been corrupted. And the corruption runs deep. I can't contact my colleagues, my superiors, because they might infect me. I am alone.' She sighed. 'And the scale of it...' Her voice tailed off.

'Hey,' said the Caretaker gently. 'You always have to fall before you can learn to fly. And you've got the two of us.'

Cassiel looked first at the Caretaker, then at Leila. 'An amnesiac hippy and a ghost who only cares about her brother.' Light danced inside her. 'Though I do have to admit that, between the two of you, you've saved my life and taken us several steps closer to Deodatus.'

'Yeah, we've done that all right,' smiled Leila. 'And that's just for starters. Now it's your turn to do some detective work. Cassiel, can you get onweave anonymously?'

'Child's play,' sniffed Cassiel.

'Good. You're going to find out more about our two new Deodatus victims.'

'What about you?' asked Cassiel.

'I'm going to go and see Dit. I think I need a whole new me.'

Chapter 22

Leila set off through the early afternoon streets of Docklands, heading for Dit. She could have jumped, but she wanted a little time to lose herself in the bustling crowds, gather her resources and prepare for whatever was coming next. She let memories of the last few days surge through her, then comforted herself with the thought that she'd started to find a clear, constructive path through all the chaos. She'd protect herself from Deodatus, she'd find Dieter and she would bring him back. It could be that she'd even end up making the wider world a little safer, too. She smiled to herself. She'd never seen herself as that sort of crusader. *Cassiel will be pleased*, she thought.

But it was difficult to truly relax. The wider world wasn't safe yet. Every time she saw an InSec operative, she was reminded of how the Rose had fallen. There were more than usual of them on the streets. Their dark plastic impact armour curved round their soft flesh, making her think of the chitin of the flies. Some had their visors down. Eyeless, their black heads jerked left then right, following anything suspicious. She imagined mandibles dropping down from them, dirty wings stretching out from hard, black backs and pulling them into flight, and felt disgust shake through her.

She let the Twins' festival brand imagery rise up around her, but that was no help. The sea creatures were charming, but they reminded her of the broken séance, of the depths they'd all fallen into and of the shark that had been waiting there. She'd only had a fleeting glimpse of it. Her memories baffled her. There had been sharp teeth and grey skin, but also compound eyes and translucent fins, lined across with dirty veins. The shark had something of the fly about it. She wondered what was riding it, and what it would do to Cassiel and the Caretaker if it caught them. She imagined it scenting her, then looked nervously up at the sky and increased her pace.

She rounded a final corner and saw her old apartment block. There was a gun kiddy on its roof, scanning the street with a pair of binoculars. She closed her eyes and sent out a request to Dit, then leapt through the home she was about to leave and straight into his private space.

'Thank the gods you're safe,' he said, turning away from his bank of televisions. 'Did you get any of my messages? Where have you been?' .

'Taking care of business.' She shared all that had happened, simplifying events where necessary so she wouldn't reset him.

'I thought I was worrying too much,' said Dit ruefully. 'I should have been worrying more. You and Dieter need to sort this out. It's freaking me out.'

Leila didn't want Dit to see how sad his mention of Dieter made her feel. She touched her pendant to comfort herself, then smiled. 'I'll do my best. How's Lei?'

'See for yourself.'

He nodded towards the screens. They showed a woman slumped on the sofa, nursing a glass of white wine, zoned out as canned laughter tinkled out of a sitcom.

Leila recognised herself. 'I wouldn't be watching that crap,' she grumbled.

'It was on, it's an excuse for her to do nothing. But that's not all. Look...' He waved his hand. One of the screens flickered, then zoomed in on the ceiling lamp. Black dots danced around it. A high, thin buzzing sliced out at them. 'They're watching her full time. Holt brought them round at lunchtime.'

'They came with him?'

'Crawled out of his shirt.'

'He's like the pressure men,' said Leila. She imagined a rotten hole in his belly, swarming with maggots. 'Corrupt.'

'That's the word. The smell of him! He tried to cover it with scent, but I amped up the flat's sensors. Decay.' He turned to Leila. 'Who are these people? What's wrong with them?'

Leila decided it would be too much information. 'We're on the case. We'll sort them out. What did Holt want?'

'He told Lei about Ambrose. Asked about Dieter. He was

checking that the new memories had taken. There was something about illegal pre-rebirth access of Ambrose's fetch, too.'

'Fuck.' She looked at the ghost of herself, cradled on the sofa, a buffer against a hostile world. 'How did she do?'

'Beautifully.' Dit smiled proudly. 'Talked about how she and Dieter weren't close. Looked utterly baffled when Holt asked if she knew who might be fishing for Ambrose's fetch. Swore a bit.'

'Sounds like me.'

'After he left she magicked up a glass of wine.'

'I approve.'

'She's been on the sofa ever since. Those flies watching her.'

'Good.' Leila steeled herself. 'That's the way it should be. And we've got to make sure it stays that way. She needs to start going out and about, living it up a bit – like I would, if it wasn't for all this. Can we do that?'

Dit thought for a moment. 'Well, yes, absolutely. She's got all your memories. All we really need to do is open up her sense of self. Make her more like a real person. More like me, in fact.'

'Is that a problem?'

'Not technically, no.' Dit sighed. 'But you should make sure it's a decision you're comfortable with.'

'What do you mean?'

'Dieter thought long and hard before making me what I am. I'm limited, but I'm self-aware. I know where I am, what I am, what I'm here for. He worried that he was creating a whole new person. But he needed me to be as committed to looking after you as he was.'

'I hadn't thought of it like that.' Leila put her head in her hands for a moment, then looked up at Dit. 'How do you feel about it? About who you are?'

'I am as I was made. And I was made to protect you. Which I do. So I'm happy. When I'm not worrying myself to death when you don't return messages, that is.'

'I'm sorry.'

'I mean – I look at the world sometimes. I'd love to be out there. Exploring, engaging. I think that comes from Dieter, that need to explore, to understand how things work. But I know my place is here. In this room. Keeping you safe.'

Leila felt more than a little infuriated by Dieter's big brotherly assumption that, without his permanent presence, she wouldn't be safe from the world. But then Dit had protected her from the pressure man's attack. *Gods*, she muttered to herself, pierced with frustrated loss. *You're impossible, Dieter.*

'She'll have a good life, you know,' continued Dit, breaking into her chain of thought. 'She'll be happy. Of course, she'll mourn Ambrose. Maybe feel a little sad for Dieter. But she'll think they just died, that it was all natural.' He smiled. 'And she'll have a blast spending all your money.'

'She can't be like you,' said Leila. 'She can't know what she really is. Too much of a security risk.'

'No. Not with everyone watching her so closely. It's better for her, too.'

Leila watched Lei shift on the sofa. Her glass of wine refilled itself. Leila smiled in recognition. One of the great joys of being dead was never having to go to the fridge for a top-up. 'Will she fool my friends?' she wondered.

Dit laughed. 'At the moment, she's more convincing than you are. Their memories have been rewritten to match her version of the world. You would completely freak them out.'

'Wow,' sighed Leila. Docklands suddenly felt like a very alien place. 'OK, Dit, let's do it. Create a new me. Send her out there to live my life.'

Dit breathed out hard. 'I'm glad.' He sounded relieved. 'It's the safest thing. She'll be fully herself in a couple of hours. But we do have one more problem. With both of you running at pretty much full capacity I'll get a bit short on storage space.'

Leila thought for a moment. 'You know, that might be a very easy problem to solve.'

'Really? How come?'

'We've found a safe house. An old void site. With a full, heavy duty weave server that's barely getting any use.'

Dit beamed with pleasure. 'Magnificent. At the moment there's a lot of you sitting on my private storage space. Now I can copy it all across to the safe house server. Once you've moved, I'll delete your new location from my memory. That's such a relief, I've been worried sick they'll come back and start poking around. Find my systems in the walls and just hard rewrite both of us. Now you're going to be so much safer.'

'Will I notice at all?'

'No. It'll be seamless.' Dit winked. 'I'm that fucking good.' A moment's pause, then: 'Dieter'll be so pleased with me.'

Grief tore at Leila's heart.

Chapter 23

Dit told Leila to stay out on the streets until he'd finished transferring her to the safe house weaveserver. Leila decided to watch the InSec agents. They moved in twos, pacing purposefully through the streets. She skipped from one pair to another, an invisible eye tracking power as it wrote itself across the city. As she mapped their movements she saw that they were moving to a single plan, together drawing a great search pattern across Docklands. She thanked the gods for the safe house, while at the same time worrying about exactly how long it could remain secure. And then a message came in from Dit. 'The transfer is complete. Oh, and I've added some new code to your core.' Unfamiliar commands appeared in her mind. 'You can use these to move yourself anywhere else, whenever you need to. You're as safe as I can make you.'

Leila jumped straight back to the safe house. Cassiel and the Caretaker were sat on the sofa. Two screens hung in the air in front of them. One showed an empty street and a warehouse frontage, lit by late afternoon spinelight. The other showed a writhing tangle of flesh. Sighs, gasps and groans poured out of it. Sparks pulsed through Cassiel's body, flickering in time with the action. The Caretaker too was rapt. Leila waited for a few moments, but they didn't notice her. She coughed. The orgiastic noise drowned her out.

She tried again. 'Er, guys – what is this?'

Cassiel turned to her. 'You've led quite the sheltered life. It's pornography.'

'Very inventive stuff,' said the Caretaker, his eyes glued to the screen.

'Gods' sake, I know that,' replied Leila.

'I always thought Station was deeply uncreative,' reflected Cassiel. 'I was quite wrong. This man's work is remarkable. Perhaps pornography is the true art form of your culture.'

'What that guy gets up to...' said the Caretaker, sounding astonished.

'I'm glad you're expanding your horizons. But why are you watching it?'

'The third dude on the right – he's one of the new Deodatus victims,' the Caretaker told her. 'This is research.'

'Well, that's good to know. But we don't have time for this.' The hypnotic action continued. Leila found herself getting sucked in. 'Is that even legal?' she asked. 'Who watches this stuff?'

'They're all of age,' replied Cassiel. 'So yes, quite legal. And the victim has a substantial following. He calls himself the Pornomancer. His subscribers ride his consciousness and experience his – exploits – at first hand.'

'He promises never to engage with the same partner for more than five minutes,' chipped in the Caretaker. 'He's had himself rebuilt, he can keep this up for hours.'

'You've got far too into this,' Leila told them.

The camera angle shifted as the Pornomancer moved to a new position. 'No, that's too much,' the Caretaker said, wincing. 'How do you even get turned on by that?'

'You tell me,' said Cassiel. 'Physical intimacy between minds is very different.'

'You guys have sex?' blurted out Leila. Then, embarrassed: 'I'm sorry. That just came out.'

'Of course we do.' Cassiel peered curiously at Leila. 'What did you expect?'

'Shit. Yes,' stammered Leila. 'I just didn't think...'

'Humans tend not to,' Cassiel told her, a little dismissively.

The Caretaker wasn't really listening. 'He is what he is, he meets a need,' he pondered. 'A job's a job, I guess.'

Glad of the change of subject, Leila agreed. The screen panted on in front of them. Once again, Leila felt herself getting sucked in. 'Look, this is – remarkable stuff,' she said, 'You've clearly checked out the Pornomancer in some detail, which is – er – great, but what about the other one?'

'Jayne Kedrov,' said Cassiel. 'A wealthy, reclusive art collector. Not too much known about her. She spends a lot at auctions. Buys up anything that's becoming popular, hides it away so hardly anyone can see it.'

Someone gasped. 'Look, can we turn it off?' asked Leila. 'It's a bit of a distraction.'

The Caretaker sighed. 'Yeah, fair enough.' He waved a hand and the Pornomancer's small, energetic world vanished, leaving only the screen showing the empty street and warehouse. 'That's where she stores her collection. We've been keeping an eye on it.'

'Not as closely as the Pornomancer,' said Leila.

'There's not quite as much going on,' shrugged the Caretaker.

'Which is not to say that she's not interesting,' continued Cassiel. 'She activated heavy security a couple of days ago. There's been nothing from her since then.'

'You think Deodatus has got to her?'

'Quite possibly. You need to get over there and have a look round. As soon as possible.'

Leila disagreed. 'I've done enough leaping before I've looked,' she said. 'I want to know as much as possible before I go in somewhere new. We still don't even know why Deodatus is interested in our four people. Have you found any links between them?'

'The new ones are just like the first two,' replied Cassiel. 'No evidence they've ever met. Never shown any interest in historical artefacts. No close links with East. But now we have two more people to think about it, I think we're beginning to see certain thematic links between the way the four of them live their lives. We have a sexual obsessive, a professional eater, a military psychiatrist who specialises in interrogation techniques—'

'So really, torture,' chipped in the Caretaker.

'And a profoundly self-absorbed art collector,' concluded Cassiel. 'There's self-absorbed greed, commodified intimacy, over-consumption and an entirely instrumental view of other people.'

'Oof. That's pretty negative.'

'It's basically how we in the Totality view Station society,' said Cassiel in a matter-of-fact way. 'Your motivations in miniature.'

'Not all of us,' Leila shot back. She thought of Dieter. He'd always been so positive, so generous. It seemed so wrong that he should be involved in something like this.

The Caretaker interrupted them. 'Guys, there's something you should see.' He pointed at the screen. A familiar figure stood at the entrance to the warehouse, talking into an intercom. It was Holt.

'As I said, you should get over there as soon as possible,' Cassiel told Leila.

'OK,' agreed Leila reluctantly. 'That little shit turning up does change things.'

'And we should observe,' Cassiel told her. 'Can we watch through you?'

Leila wasn't quite sure how she felt about opening up her sense feeds to two relative strangers. But there was no time to waste. 'OK,' she said again as she readied herself to jump.

The flat vanished, leaving Leila hanging in the darkness that existed between specific locations. The ghost cloak queried her, asking permission to burrow into Kedrov's warehouse. It worked quickly. There was a flash of light as her sensorium meshed with the warehouse's internal weave systems. Then reality leapt into being again.

Leila found herself standing in the middle of a long, low-ceilinged room. A series of vast canvases hung down from the roof. Bright colours swirled across them, thick oil impastos bulging luridly out in dense, hypnotic patterns. There was something familiar about their style. She noticed a signature at the bottom left of one of them – 'Femi', dripped on with oozing black paint. Memories flashed into her mind. She'd been valuing the single most expensive home she'd ever been in and seen a similar painting hanging on the wall there. 'Lovely work,' the vendor commented. 'One of our true masters.' He stopped in front of the painting, sighing. 'Very few of them around. Femi died young. One show, that was it – and most of it was snapped up by a private collector. A very private collector. I lease virtual replicas of this painting to several other collectors, but she won't even do that.' He went to move away from the picture, then stopped and said, 'selfish – but at least it keeps the value of mine up.'

[Hi Leila,] said the Caretaker. [Just letting you know we're on board.]

[Let's get going,] ordered Cassiel.

Leila drifted through paintings and sculptures. She heard soft voices and approached them cautiously. She knew she was safe but it was impossible not to worry that the ghost cloak had been compromised. She imagined flies settling on her, tearing at her past, rewriting it to suit Deodatus.

[Quicker,] grumbled Cassiel.

[I don't want to take any risks.]

It took her a minute or so to reach the point where she could see who was talking. She recognised one voice as Holt's. She nerved herself, then peered out from behind a painting.

There was a long, low leather sofa running down the edge of a small office space, made up of a desk, a chair and a small pile of tall, wide parcels. Holt sat on the sofa, next to a fashionably dressed young man.

'That's right,' he told Holt. 'We thought it was just a sculpture. Appeared in the post, no idea who sent it. A little broken triangle. So evocative! Jayne – Miss Kedrov – took it into her private rooms. And then I was away for a couple of days. She didn't come out this morning but that's not unusual, but then it was the afternoon and she wasn't answering when I knocked on the door and well...' He put his head in his hands.

Holt watched him, a cold, disinterested look on his face. 'We'll find whoever did this,' he replied. 'We've seen several cases like this recently. We're close to a breakthrough.' His voice was emotionless. He stood up. 'I'd like to take another look at the body.' The personal assistant waved his hand. 'Please don't disturb me. You might find some of my investigations distasteful.'

Leila followed him into Kedrov's quarters. She lay in her bed-room, a still shape beneath a stained sheet.

[Dead,] remarked Cassiel.

Each wall was a canvas. Sombre, soothing colours drifting across them in soft, meaningless patterns. Kedrov's bed was raised up on a plinth, its linens tinted to match the walls' palette. Two broken weavesprites followed each other around the room, bouncing off walls, a bedside lamp, zinging past Holt and making him duck.

'Wake up!' they chanted, 'Wake up! Rise and shine!'

Each was little middle-aged man, dressed in a little grey suit. Their little wings whirred with a high, desperate whine. Both had their arms stretched out in front of them and their eyes tight shut.

Their small minds were broken. Holt put out a fist and opened it, palm up. Now that he was on his own, his movements were quicker, more nervous. A fly leapt into the air. It brushed first against one of the sprites, then the other. There was a moment's pause, then they screamed as one and vanished.

Holt went over to the bed and pulled the sheets off the body. 'Gods,' he said. Leila gasped, memories of Dieter's death flashing into her mind. Kedrov's corpse had the same desiccated look to it, dried skin stretched like varnished tissue paper over bones that had a balsa-wood flimsiness to them. An ear had slipped down the side of her head. Her nose had partially collapsed. There was something dark half-sunk into her chest, between the dried, collapsed mounds that had been her breasts.

[Is that how your brother died?] asked the Caretaker.

[Pretty much,] gulped Leila. [Except the thing that killed him was square.]

[Fascinating,] breathed Cassiel.

The artefact that had broken Kedrov was an equilateral triangle, its point facing down towards her groin. A sticky, brown residue spilled out of it across the corpse's belly. Holt pulled the sheet off the bed. Leila inspected the rest of Kedrov's body. One hand had dissolved, soaking the sheets with black liquid. A dark vacancy had eaten away most of a knee. Bone gleamed whitely out.

[Selective dissolution,] commented Cassiel. [Curious.]

Holt leant over and placed a hand on the artefact. First one fly, then another, then a third and fourth and fifth, climbed out from beneath his cuff, moving down his hand with stop-motion jerkiness. They scuttled over to the triangle and vanished into it. Then Holt took his hand off the corpse's chest and turned his attention to its face. He pulled the mouth open as far as it could go. The skin where Kedrov's lips met split. He ran his hand through his hair and sighed deeply. Then he bent over, put his mouth to hers and exhaled. Kedrov's chest shifted a little. Then he breathed into her, breathing for her, for a minute or so. At last there was a choking cough from the triangle, as if a small, organic machine had woken. Holt stood back up, a satisfied look on his face. A moment, then the corpse gasped and shook. Air shuddered in and out of its lungs as it began to breathe again. A fly appeared at its mouth, dark limbs scratching against paper-white flesh like inkless nibs, then vanished back into her. Kedrov's laboured, reborn wheeze filled the room.

[Fuck,] breathed Leila.

[Heavy,] replied the Caretaker.

Kedrov sat up, her body moving in a rigid, unnatural way, as if its muscles were relearning their functions from scratch, and turned her head towards her reviver. He put his hand on her shoulder. 'Are you ready?' he asked.

'Yes,' she replied. Her voice was a small, soft buzz. Leila knew that her throat was furred with wires, but found herself imagining flies climbing into a broken voice box, their transparent wings beating words from the air. 'Ready…' The word was a ghost of itself.

'Good.'

Holt turned away from her, opening his shirt as he did so, a pained look on his face. Leila caught a glimpse of a black maw just beneath his rib cage, full of a crawling darkness. Flies leapt out of him, full stops scrawled on the air. They buzzed up and out, moving in lazy circles and loops, up and down, forward and back. One of her internal warnings pinged. The room's weave systems were opening a doorway to a virtual location. Suddenly the flies were drawing black lines on the air. They flew forwards and back, up and down, pulling a dark, rectangular portal into being.

[I can query the fly swarm,] Cassiel said. [See if they can tell me where it leads back to. But I need to use you as a bridge to reach them. Run part of my mind in yours.]

It was an uncomfortably intimate suggestion. [Is there any other way?] asked Leila.

[Running a compatibility check now,] said Cassiel, ignoring her.

[So that's a no,] Leila grumbled. [You're worse than my brother.] She returned her attention to the room.

Something had appeared next to Kedrov. It hung in the air next to her, a dense, grey teardrop carved from a cloud, its tip touching the ceiling and its base touching the floor. It represented a lifetime's worth of data. Leila thought of Dieter's similarly-shaped weaveself and touched the pendant at her neck. Kedrov's head turned to gaze up at the cloud, flesh regarding the soul that had left it.

[This must be what they did to Dieter,] said Cassiel.

The Caretaker shushed her. [She doesn't want to hear that.]

Leila imagined Holt coming to her brother in the cold depths of a mortuary and pulling his weaveself from him. She pushed the thought from her mind.

Holt smiled weakly. 'Very good,' he said.

He turned back to the rectangle and waved at it. It pulsed out a burst of white light and Leila had to look away. When she looked back, it had become a white arch framing a doorway. And through the doorway was a space she recognised. Two couches lay head to head in the centre of a round room. There was a desk pushed up against the wall, papers scattered across it. Windows showed a marble landscape, shining under a pale moon. Next to the complexity of Station, of her own life, its simplicity was oddly appealing. It was Dieter's workshop in the Shining City. And then her brother appeared in the doorway and stepped through it.

Chapter 24

Leila gaped. For a moment, she wanted to let the cloak drop away and reveal herself to Dieter. But Holt would see her too. She'd lose all anonymity.

[Be cool, Leila! Let's see what he's up to.]

[We're fully compatible,] hissed Cassiel. [Just need you to give me the right permissions.]

Leila barely heard them. She stared at Dieter. He was a soft blur, shifting forwards and backwards between different versions of himself. But he was less defined than he had been, less rooted in any single identity. With fewer and fewer coherent memory chains to support it, his core self was dissolving. The thought of that terrified her. She wondered how much time she had left before the damage became permanent, before it would be impossible to assemble even an incomplete fetch from his weaveself.

[Please, Leila,] said Cassiel. Without really thinking, Leila granted permission. She felt an alien presence in her mind as Cassiel unpacked part of herself into it. [Thank you,] sighed the mind. [This'll just take a few seconds...]

Leila brought her attention back to the room. Holt and Dieter were inspecting the weaveself. Myriad clusters of tiny lights flickered within it.

'All's good,' Dieter said. 'Kedrov's weaveself is intact. I can use it.'

[He's working for them all right,] said the Caretaker.

[We told him not to trust Deodatus,] replied Leila. [I think we were getting through to him. All that must have been deleted.] She hoped desperately that he hadn't lost too much else.

'We never had a problem gathering weaveselves,' replied Holt. 'Just putting them to work. Please don't screw it up.'

'Like your minds did with the first two?' replied Dieter absent-mindedly, reaching into the weaveself with one hand. Memories of his tinkering pierced Leila. He was still so much himself, despite his slow dissolution.

'You're not taking this seriously,' complained Holt.

'Oh, I'm taking it very seriously.' Leila recognised Dieter's tone of voice. He was deep in some intellectual problem, barely even registering Holt's presence.

[Setting up the bridge,] muttered Cassiel.

'Imagine your sister were here,' Holt told Dieter. Leila froze. For a moment she was afraid that Holt had sensed her. But the ghost cloak was still up. 'Would she want you all spaced out?'

Dieter's attention snapped back into the moment. 'I am not spaced out,' he said. 'I'm working fucking hard. Like I told Deodatus I would. Don't you bring Leila into this.'

Holt put his hands up. 'I'm sorry, I'm sorry,' he said. 'I just want to make sure we get it right.'

'You people were part of the problem.' Kedrov's weaveself was forgotten. 'Fucking InSec, not taking any of it seriously. Do you know what fetch hatred can do to someone?' Dieter's voice was full of grief and anger. Leila wanted to reach out to him. But she was trapped inside the ghost cloak. If she revealed herself Holt's flies would have her. 'Sticks and stones, one of your lot told us. Sticks and fucking stones. Two weeks before the end.'

'Dieter, I'm truly sorry,' Holt told him. 'If you'd come to me I'd have done all I could.'

'Yeah, well, it's a bit late for that now, isn't it?' Dieter looked around the room. 'And here we are, back on Station. Oh, I hate this place.' There was a bitterness to him that was entirely new. 'Feels like a prison.' Deodatus must have changed him again. 'Let's just get out of here.' Dieter reached back into Kedrov's weaveself and closed his eyes for a moment. 'It's all ready to go down to the workshop. How's the Pornomancer coming along? Once we've got him too I can replace those two poor sods your idiots screwed up and do the job properly.'

[And I'm in you,] muttered Cassiel. [Querying the swarm. Asking them where the portal leads.]

'Let's see,' said Holt, looking profoundly relieved that Dieter's mind was back on their task. He waved his hand towards the portal. It shimmered and the Shining City vanished.

[Failed,] said Cassiel. [Got some basic info. The Shining City is a heavily virtual environment. Didn't get a location.]

'You done?' Holt shouted through the portal.

It took Leila a moment to parse the scene before her. The portal now gave on to a dingy little windowless room. There was a kitchenette in one corner. A battered sofa was littered with sex toys. Erotic images hung in the air. Naked sprites writhed together on a small coffee table. There was a full sensory stimulation deck in one corner of the room. A short, naked man was strapped into it. He was very skinny. He'd been terribly tortured. One arm had been cut off at the elbow. There were bloodied sockets that had once housed eyes. Another upside down triangle was buried in his belly. The skin around it was ragged. It looked like it had been forced in. A pool of thickening blood and ravaged hunks of flesh lay beneath him. And there was one other figure in the room – a fallen mind. Its blistered skin was covered in blood. It held a scalpel in one hand and a hammer in the other.

[Oh.] gasped Cassiel. [No.] There was despair in her voice. [What it's been forced to do. What it's done.]

Leila gagged.

[I'm so sorry,] said the Caretaker.

Another grey teardrop hung just next to the mind. 'He refused our offer,' the mind told Holt and Dieter. 'I persuaded him to accept it.' Its laugh was a breathy wheeze.

'Did you really have to go that far?' asked Dieter. He sounded disgusted.

'Perhaps not,' replied the mind, 'if more time had been made available. But Deodatus has set us a very specific deadline.'

[This Deodatus is a disease,] said Cassiel, her voice cold with rage. [He must be purged. If you decloak, Leila, I can reach through you and...]

[Don't tempt me,] said Leila, imagining her skull face tearing into Holt and the fallen mind.

[Hey, guys,] soothed the Caretaker, [this is bad. But let's not win the battle and lose the war...]

'Well, you can send his weaveself down to my workshop yourself,' Dieter told the mind. 'I'm fucked if I'm coming into your charnel house.'

'You've left the meat behind, Fenech,' replied the mind. 'Why do you object to this?'

Dieter turned away. 'We shouldn't have used those bastards. Too brutal.' A moment's pause, then: 'We're surgeons, not butchers. I don't want to see him, Holt. Link us back to my workshop and we'll move Kedrov's weaveself.'

Holt looked broken. 'We'd have had to do the same to her if she hadn't accepted.' He waved a hand at the portal and it shifted back. 'But this will soon be over,' he said, as if he was trying to convince himself. Dieter's workshop shone out of the portal, its silent peace contrasting with the shambles the mind had presided over.

'You know, sometimes I just want to shut the door on it all,' said Dieter, sounding deeply weary.

Holt looked panicked. 'Think about your sister. Don't you want revenge?'

'Oh, I want Deodatus to break the Pantheon,' replied Dieter. 'And I want him to write the fetch-hating world they created out of history.' He touched Kedrov's weaveself and it drifted towards the portal. 'I'll build him the army he needs to do it. You don't need to worry about that.'

Leila felt so much empathy with his rage, because that was how she felt about Deodatus. She would delete him from existence, if she could.

Cassiel spoke: [I've sent another location query to Holt's swarm,] she said, forcing neutrality into her tone. [About to get a reply.] She obviously had to work hard to control herself.

Kedrov's corpse stared dumbly out, a statue built from skin and bone. Her weaveself vanished into Dieter's workshop.

[Location coming through... Confirmed.]

Dieter stopped in the portal and turned back. 'But I still hate seeing broken people, Holt.' His voice was grim. 'I know there's no choice. I know it's for the greater good – but I saw Leila break and choose true death. I came home to an empty flat and a suicide note. That was enough for me.'

Leila gasped. Agony shattered through her. If he'd stayed for an instant longer, she would have dropped her invisibility and rushed to take him back, to reassure him that she still lived, regardless of the consequences.

The portal vanished before she could move.

Chapter 25

Leila jumped back to the safe house, shocked to the core. Not only did Dieter think she'd been forced into a true death – he was going to rewrite Station's past by way of revenge.

The first thing she said was: 'Where is he?'

'The portal led back to the Wart,' said Cassiel. 'That's where we'll find the Shining City. It's probably an entirely virtual environment. It'll be sitting in a dedicated weave server somewhere in there.'

'The Wart?' asked the Caretaker. 'What's that?'

'Oldest part of Station,' explained Leila. 'It's the asteroid that holds Docklands and Homelands together. Mostly just wasteland and ancient ruins. The kind of place Dieter loves. We have to get him back.'

'And stop Deodatus,' said Cassiel. 'We need to get in there.' The frustrated anger in her voice mirrored Leila's emotions.

'Totally,' said the Caretaker. 'The Shining City looked familiar. Might trigger some memories.' It was the first time Leila had heard anything approaching sadness in his voice.

'It's not a good place for fetches,' said Leila. 'There's not much weave coverage in there. I'd need to find a way of piggybacking on you two to manifest in most of it. I can't go there on my own.'

'And if we leave the flat, then the Rose agents will find us almost straight away.' Cassiel's voice was bitter. 'We could explore it, but we can't leave this flat. You can leave the flat, but you can't explore it.'

A thought struck Leila. 'Don't be so sure of that,' she said, remembering the InSec agents she'd watched. 'The Rose's people are following a specific search pattern. I mapped some of it. If we can understand it, then we'll know where they're going to be when, and we can avoid them.'

'Well, that gets us moving,' said Cassiel thoughtfully. 'I can mask the Caretaker and me again. If the Fetch Counsellor's right, we'd have a little time before the Rose's cameras spotted us.' She sighed. 'But what then?'

'You're the infiltration expert,' Leila told her, tossing over memories of her search pattern observations. 'That's your problem. And while you're solving it, I'm going to find Cormac Redonda. Make him talk to me. We need to know as much as we can about what we're heading into and he's the only expert we've got.'

'I hope he's willing to talk to you,' said Cassiel.

Leila thought of her poor lost brother, of the damage he could help Deodatus do. 'Oh, he will. I'll make damn sure of that.'

The streets flickered by, filled with evening bustle. The gods looked down, apparently pleased with the world they controlled. They had always seemed complacent. Now Leila felt that they were completely out of touch. She hurried to the Flurrytown restaurant where Redonda had looped out. It was on a little broken street, a clutter of abandoned office blocks and emptied shops. A gun kiddy crew had scrawled graffiti across their broken fronts. Leila imagined how lively this lost little street must once have been. The estate agent in her rose up, suggesting ways of selling it. *Ripe for regeneration*, *up and coming* and similar phrases drifted through her mind.

As she reached the restaurant, Leila thought about how East's entertainment areas were always evolving. The god liked to flatter each new generation by creating novelty, making those who partied in her realms feel that they occupied a world that was freshly made for them and them alone. Then the masses would move on and there would be small, local collapses, leaving empty streets like this. But they wouldn't stay empty for long. Soon the rebellious pioneers would come, reworking empty space on their own terms. Subversive creativity would flourish. East would bless it with low rents. The old would marvel at East's ability to regenerate and the young would flock to these fresh new entertainments. A new standard would be set. East would win the gratitude of a new generation of creators and – through them – consumers. And so all would adore her and her power would flow on.

It's a racket, thought Leila. She remembered East in her room, trying to force stardom on her. She thought of Dieter, so totally controlled by Deodatus. *I won't be anyone's puppet,* she told herself. And as she did so, she realised how she could free her brother. Dit remembered their life together over the last couple of years. If she could copy those memories and share them with Dieter, then she could restore her brother to his original self. *And then he'll stop all this bullshit and leave the Shining City with me,* she thought.

Heartened, she sent a call out to Flurrytown's internal audio-visual systems. They clicked into life, letting her move into the shop. It had once been a bustling family restaurant, one of a chain that was still very popular. Now she found herself in a wilderness of broken tables and chairs, graffiti-clotted walls and strands of dangling wire. A fire had burnt up and out in one corner, a record of an attempt to either squat or vandalise the space. Leila supposed that East would be equally happy with either. Both were transformative.

The restaurant's AV systems had decayed, so to Leila the room had a low-resolution, pixelated look, like a memory that had already begun to fade. She looked towards its rear, where the darkness was particularly thick. It took her a moment to register the presence of first one figure, then several.

'Hello?' said Leila uncertainly, forgetting for a moment that she was both invisible and inaudible.

She moved a little further into darkness, then smiled to herself as decayed remnants of Flurrytown's cartoon house band faded into view. There was Flurry Beaver, Wilo Hedgehog, Zamboo the Cat and the rest of them, incarnate in a series of broken plastic sculptures. Years ago, their weave avatars would have been bouncing around the room, laughing with both children and parents. Now they were dormant. Leila remembered them from her own childhood. She'd always been at Flurrytown for someone else's party, never her own. She touched her pendant for luck, then let her ghost cloak reach out. Sensors pinged in her mind. There was another cloak operating in the room. Hers began to mesh with it. Leila stood still, waiting for it to open up Cormac's paradise to her.

There was silence for a few seconds. Then a sound leapt at her from behind – a child's soft, high-pitched giggle. Leila spun round. There was nobody there. Dust motes lazed through long beams of spinelight. Then footsteps ran behind her and vanished. She caught her breath. Reality flickered. A child's silhouette shimmered in and out of being. Leila took a step back. For an instant the walls were covered in brightly painted images of the Flurry band. There was a burst of music, loud and echoing, then voices singing 'Happy Birthday', chanting faster and faster until they became a vanishing scribble of sound. Unease grew in Leila, although she knew there was nothing to be scared of. She'd never thought of fetches as being akin to ghosts, until now.

One of the tables – tumbled into a corner – was suddenly upright, and covered in drinks and food. There was a man and a woman. Each handed snacks to invisible children. The rest of the restaurant was still dusty and cobwebbed. Now they were singing 'Happy Birthday', this time at the right speed. Then the couple watched a small boy unwrap his presents. Leila recognised Cormac, his wife and his son. A sudden, blinding flash, and all came online at once, and Leila, still invisible, was standing in the middle of a six-year-old's party.

At first, it was indistinguishable from reality. Children ran, orbiting a table dense with weave-coded junk food and shredded wrapping paper. There was a scattering of presents at one end of it – bright little cars, fierce-looking robots, cuddly toys and a couple of already discarded educational jigsaw puzzles. The Flurry band charged around, its bouncier members leading games, its quieter ones nursing the tired and the tearful. Adults clustered in one corner of the room, sipping at brightly coloured cocktails. A murmur of conversation drifted over. 'So generous of them. They've taken over the whole restaurant.'

A waiter appeared with a birthday cake. Flurrytown sprites danced across its candles. Cormac and his wife stood by their little boy. A metal exo-skeleton, chunky little wheels at its base, supported his frail body. His legs dangled uselessly. 'Yes, yes, it's your cake!' she heard Cormac say. 'Now blow!' The child looked up at his parents, his face alive with joy, and said 'Really? ALL mine?' His mother nodded. The exo-skeleton turned his head back towards the cake and let it drop forwards towards the cake. He blew hard and the candle flames leapt sideways, then vanished. 'Oh!' he said. 'Oh!' Behind his head, his father leant forward and kissed his mother.

The loop ended and the moment juddered out of being. A second of the drab, empty room and then the memory flared up and began again, a haunting that would repeat itself for ever. Children scurried around the room. Parents applauded the party. There was that drift of dialogue again: 'So generous of them. They've taken over the whole restaurant.' The cake was carefully placed on the table. Leila noticed how the little boy's eyes shone. Candles flared and died. The parents kissed again, then vanished.

Leila watched the scene play through three or four times. She didn't want to bring Cormac Redonda out of his fugue too quickly. She wove herself gently into the repeated scene, appearing first as a flicker and becoming more present each time it played through. She hoped her repeated presence would begin to trigger Redonda's deeper self, the dormant part of him that had life beyond this one, repeated moment.

He began to notice her. At first, he just glanced over at her. As she faded in, he became more engaged, more worried. Sadness drifted across his face. At last, he left his child and started towards her. Now he looked angry. She hoped she'd be able to talk him into helping her. The room reset, and for a moment there was nothing. When the memory restarted, he'd reach her and they'd talk. Leila realised that now she was the ghost – an unwelcome intrusion from another time, stepping into a settled moment and shattering its coherence.

'You really should let him be, you know.' It was a woman's voice, calm and confident.

Leila jumped with shock. The cloak had failed her. The Rose had found her.

But when the woman spoke again Leila realised that she was wrong. 'It would be too cruel to bring this version of him back into the world. And besides, after the Fetch Counsellor blundered in here I promised I'd stop anyone else from reaching him.'

'Oh,' said Leila, as white light flared up and she felt a jump being forced on her. 'Gods.'

'No,' replied East, 'just god.'

Chapter 26

The white light died away.

Leila was surrounded by a forest of silver statues, life-sized images of men and women. Each shone with brilliant light, reflected from above. She was dazzled for a moment, until her eyes adjusted to the glare. Looking up, she saw a great glass dome. Vision recalibrated again, showing her the sun, a vast brilliance in deep darkness. Her location sensors pinged information. East had force-jumped her several thousand miles. She was in an entirely real environment, but she was far away from Station. There was just enough weave overlay for her to manifest.

'Over here,' shouted the god, her voice echoing back through the statues. 'There's a viewing platform. Just follow the pathway.'

'Where are we?'

'We've come to see Cormac.'

'You've just jumped us away from him,' grumbled Leila.

'No I haven't. The Flurrytown Cormac was about to tell you to fuck off. Quite rightly, I have to say. So I brought you here. To meet my own little version of him. He'll be happy to answer all your questions.' She sounded very pleased with herself.

Feeling that she had no choice, Leila started towards where East seemed to be. 'I don't trust you,' she called out.

'But I'm a god,' replied East, sounding surprised. 'And I want to make you a star. Isn't that enough?'

'Not these days, no.' Leila sighed. 'You of all people should know that. After all, you and Grey stopped Kingdom.'

'Oh, I'm nothing like Kingdom.' Her voice echoed round the room. 'Or the Rose, come to that.'

'You might still have fallen to Deodatus.'

'If I had, you wouldn't be able to do much about it. It took Grey and I thirty years to build the weapon that killed Kingdom. And we're divine.'

'Hugo Fist?' asked Leila.

'Jack and Hugo. The dynamic duo! But you're nothing like them. And all this is so different too.' She clapped her hands delightedly. 'We're just making it up as we go along!' And then, in a more confiding tone: 'My life is so scripted, Leila. You really wouldn't believe. So refreshing to go off-piste like this.'

'People have died,' Leila called back. 'And I'm losing my brother. I need to get him back.'

East didn't reply.

As she walked, Leila examined the sculptures. Most showed people frozen in deep joy. Some looked thoughtful. A very few were almost sad. All gazed up at the dome, staring out into the light. The detail of each was extraordinary. Wrinkles fell like spider webs across shining faces. Individual eyelashes blazed. Folds and wrinkles softened hard, metallic clothes. Every single one was different. The only thing the statues had in common were their bases – round discs, about half a metre across.

'What is this place?' shouted Leila. 'What are all these statues?'

She broke out of the crowd. East and a man she recognised as Cormac Redonda waited on a small platform set against the room's wall. There was a conference table, surrounded by chairs, and beyond it a window, filled with stars.

'Hurry up,' urged East. 'This is a very important conversation.'

'Don't be so harsh,' chided Redonda. 'The slow travellers can be a big distraction. Especially when you're seeing them for the first time.'

'Thirty seconds of distraction was useful,' East told Redonda, ignoring Leila. 'Then I had all the establishing shots I needed. Now we're just wasting time.'

'You're filming this?' asked Leila, looking round for cameras.

'Of course I am,' East told her. 'Pervasive micro drones. Honestly, I thought you'd take all this in your stride.' She sounded disappointed. 'Especially after the last few days.'

'I'm not here for your benefit,' Leila shot back. 'I've come to talk to Cormac. If all you can do to help is drag us to some random location because it looks good on camera, then lecture me – well, screw that.'

'Oh, we're not just here because it looks good,' replied East.

'Then what is this place?'

'Let's start with the slow travellers,' said Cormac. 'They're fetches. Just like you. But they're travelling in time. Those discs they're all standing on are individual fetch servers. They've each installed themselves in one, then slowed themselves right down. For them, a decade passes in an instant, a century in a moment. A couple of breaths, and we'll all be gone. A few more, and they'll arrive in the deep future.' His words were passionate, but his tone was oddly flat. 'This satellite was built to house them.'

Leila wondered how it would be to close her eyes, then open them again, and find that centuries had passed. For a moment, she was jealous of the silvered fetches, of the ease with which they could leave the problems of the present behind. 'Well, that's very nice,' she said, as she climbed up next to them. 'But why come all the way out here?'

'Because this is one of the safest places between here and Mars,' replied Cormac, ushering her over to the table. 'Very heavily shielded. With excellent comms if we need to escape in a hurry. It mounts an ultra-high bandwidth maser comms array that could blast a hole in Jupiter – so it can connect to pretty much anywhere in the Solar System and shift every fetch here to it at the speed of light, if it's ever compromised. And hardly anyone knows about it.'

'That's why I brought you here,' said East, sounding a little put out. 'You can talk with Cormac in complete safety.'

'And then you'll broadcast it to Station and everyone will know about it.'

'Oh, we'll be long gone by then. And I won't tell anyone what this place is. They'll just think it's a very impressive set somewhere.' She glanced around at the slow travellers. 'Nobody will disturb them. This whole place will stay nice and safe. Just like it is now.'

Leila remembered the Fetch Counsellor taking her to the Memory Channel. 'Everyone's taking me to nice, safe places these days,' she said. 'And I've never felt more in danger.'

'Ungrateful girl,' purred East.

Leila ignored her. She turned to Cormac. 'I do have some questions. Our friend here said you could answer them.'

'I'll do what I can,' Cormac replied, still speaking in a neutral tone.

Leila remembered the tortured face of the man she'd so nearly talked to in Flurrytown. 'Before you do,' she asked, 'tell me one thing. What are you?'

'I house all of Cormac's historical research.'

'I've been watching the Fetch Counsellor. I saw him come here and try to speak with Cormac,' explained East. 'And I saw Cormac send him away. He didn't want anyone else to disturb him. So I agreed to protect him – in return for a copy of all that wonderful knowledge he had.'

Leila nodded. 'You're not just a database, though?' she asked Cormac, doing her best to keep East out of the conversation. 'There's more to you than that. More of him.'

'I also snapped up full appearance usage rights for him,' explained East. 'And basic information about his life. You're clearly having some wonderful adventure. I'm filming what I can and I'm looking forward to sharing it with Station. And the last thing I need is some dry info-dump halfway through the story. Or a minor character dropping a major tragedy on everyone. It unbalances things. This version of Cormac is the happy medium.'

'Oh, no,' groaned Leila.

'I can convincingly simulate my originator,' Cormac said. 'I know there's a family, friends out there. But I have no particular feelings for them.' He leaned forward, pressing his hands together. He looked like he was about to pray. His sharp eyes met Leila's. She felt a deep sense of concentration. 'I am a library. I hold information. You need it. ASK.' Then he froze, waiting.

'You won't turn the cameras off, will you?' Leila asked East.

'No,' replied East. 'You need what he has to tell you, Leila. And you'll only get it on my terms.'

A combination of rage and deep frustration threatened to overwhelm Leila. 'I am not an actor in one of your bloody shows.'

East waved an airy hand. 'Oh, my dear, everyone is. They just don't know it.' She shot a dazzling smile across the table. 'You really should be flattered, you know. I'm being far more honest with you than I am with anyone else.'

'OK then, before we start, tell me one thing – how did you find me at Flurrytown?'

'Because the Fetch Counsellor went there and screwed up. Cormac was very close to your brother. I knew that that other you was a fake. I was pretty sure the real you would be along soon to try and talk to him. So I just kept an eye on him and – when you showed up – poof! Here we are.'

'Oh, no.' None of her security measures had worked. 'How could you even see me? And how did you know that Lei is a fake? If you found out about her and tracked me down then the Rose or Deodatus might be able to as well. And if they do, we're all screwed.'

'Oh, there's nothing to worry about there. Cormac made sure I could see anyone who tried to access him. And Grey spotted Lei – he told me about her because he knows I have an interest in you. He's the only one of us who could have seen through her. Remember when you'd just jumped back to your flat, and you accepted some updates from him?'

Leila nodded.

'That's what tipped him off,' said East. 'You updated, fine, Grey records it, totally normal. But then, a few hours later, something very unusual – a second you popped up, and downloaded the exact same files, and upgraded in the exact same way. And that's impossible. Unless there are two of you.'

'Ah. Shit.'

'I wouldn't have spotted it, and I've been keeping a very close eye on you. Partially because you're so lovely, partially because the Rose is so interested in you.' East leant in and confided: 'She's not at all herself at the moment. I think she's gone the same way Kingdom did.'

'You and Grey have known about this all along?' Anger blazed in her. 'And you haven't moved against the Rose? You've left it all up to us?'

'What else could we do?' East held her hands up. 'I've only just found you, after all. You hid yourselves so wonderfully well! And the Rose is a very powerful entity. She runs InSec and the military.

She's second only to the Totality when it comes to projected force. We're not going to start a fight with her unless we know we really need to and we're absolutely sure we can win it. Grey and I have our own resources, but we really need Totality support to take her on. And we won't be able to convince them to come on board without really solid proof.'

'Some of them have fallen too,' said Leila. 'Cassiel's cut herself off from them.'

'Oh, that's wonderful!' enthused East.

'What?' Leila was astonished. 'How is that in any way wonderful?'

'It's so dramatic! Such a lovely reversal. I've been building the Totality up as such good guys.' She leant in to confide again. 'Too squeaky clean, most people just don't buy it. And the ones that do get bored.' She sat back, beaming. 'When people find out they can be evil, it'll make all that good stuff so much more credible. And they'll all be so much easier to relate to!' She beamed. 'That'll please Grey. He's very pro-Totality just now.'

Leila realised she wouldn't be denting East's self-regard anytime soon. She decided to cut to the chase. 'But who's Deodatus?' she asked. 'How's he managed to do all this?'

'That's a question for Cormac,' East replied. 'One thing before you ask him...' She was suddenly more serious. 'We'll cut out a lot of what I just said. Backstage talk, not for the masses. But your conversation with him – it'll be a big moment in the special. The unveiling of the truth about the bad guys.' A moment's pause, then: 'Don't fuck it up.'

'Bloody hell,' muttered Leila. She wanted to jump away, far from East's manipulations. But she needed Cormac's knowledge and could see no other way of getting it.

Cormac pulled out of his prayer pose, coming back to life. 'Ask me anything,' he said.

'First you need to know what's going on.' Leila described her adventures. 'So I've got to get Dieter back,' she concluded. 'And help Cassiel stop Deodatus. But we don't even know what he is.'

Cormac thought for a moment, then spoke: 'Did your brother or Ambrose ever mention something called a Kneale Pit?'

'No.'

'Well, that's what I think we're dealing with here. He told you about the precursor gods?'

'Ambrose did,' she replied. 'Gods like Mikhail.'

'Oh no. They're nothing like Mikhail. He's old, but he was one of the Pantheon. Precursor gods are the parent organisations of the Pantheon gods. The corporate entities of old Earth. From the times before Station.'

'Ah,' breathed Leila. She glanced over at East. 'Do you remember them?'

The god shifted in her seat. Leila was surprised to see discomfort shimmer across her face. 'We made many sacrifices when we split from Earth,' she replied. 'A thousand years of history was the least of them.'

'You don't, do you?' asked Leila.

East nodded at Cormac. 'I brought you here to listen to him, not me. Let him talk.'

Cormac continued: 'So, I think we're dealing with a Kneale Pit. They're pretty obscure; there hasn't been one for hundreds of years. They were clusters of technology left behind by the precursor gods. Not isolated fragments of psychoactive tech, but fully integrated systems, built to rewire the people who find them and use them to set certain clearly defined sets of events into action. To turn you into a component in a machine.'

Leila remembered Dieter, Holt and the fallen minds, determinedly working for Deodatus. 'Sounds possible. What do they get you to do?'

'Sometimes it's very simple. I've seen records of ones that made people build new gravity generators, or sow and tend a food farm. Sometimes it's a bit more problematic. One of the bigger ones created a cell of fifty Kneale liches bolted to the outside of Station, trying to patch together shuttles to fly themselves back down to Earth. And sometimes – well, terrible things happened.'

'Like we're seeing now.'

'Yes,' said Cormac. 'Kneale Pits didn't just rewrite minds. They rebuilt bodies, as well. The precursor gods judged people according to how efficiently they could contribute to their control and production systems. If they needed to be remade to make them more efficient – well, that would happen. As I think those wooden boxes are doing. They must be some sort of command and control device.'

Leila nodded. 'That's what Cassiel thinks.'

'And some of them worked really hard to spread themselves. When Dieter says he's building an army, it probably means that the Pit's setting him up to convert as many people as possible into Deodatus followers.'

'Oh, no.'

'I'm afraid so. They're dangerous things. They can even slip under the radar of the gods.'

East nodded. 'I've been watching everywhere on Station and I didn't even know this was happening. This is bad, Leila. One of the worst Kneale Pits yet.' Her delivery was rather stagy. Leila resisted the temptation to roll her eyes. She didn't want to be forced into a retake.

'And this new pit has some very distinctive new features to it, as well,' continued Cormac. 'The Totality didn't exist when previous ones went live. It's having a very powerful impact on them. The pressure men, the money they can access. All unprecedented. And there's never been anything like the Shining City before.'

'So how do we shut it down?' asked Leila.

'Well, let's go through what it's done,' he replied. 'It's based in the Wart?' Leila nodded. 'That's not a big surprise. It's the oldest part of Station. Where exactly in there?'

Leila called up the co-ordinates that Cassiel had recovered and passed them over. Cormac recognised them immediately. 'Ah – they're in the Alpha Pyramid!'

Leila looked puzzled.

'There are several pyramids in the Wart,' he explained. 'Very ancient structures. Been empty for centuries.'

'I've shot in them,' nodded East. 'Wonderful locations. Very atmospheric.'

'And hardly anyone ever goes to them,' continued Cormac. 'Excellent hiding places, the Alpha Pyramid in particular. It has a level carved out of the rock beneath it. The only one that goes deep like that.' He paused for a moment. 'I wonder. There's a tunnel running even further down. But it's always been completely blocked.

179

People have dug into it for tens of metres, found nothing. Perhaps someone finally broke through to the other side.'

'The Totality have been overhauling Kingdom's infrastructure,' said East. 'Maybe it was one of their work parties?'

'Maybe they found whatever holds the Shining City,' speculated Leila. She remembered looking out of Dieter's workshop. Streets curved away to the left and right, and a tower arced up beyond them. 'It's very big and very open. If it's down there, it can't be a real environment. It has to be fully virtual.'

'Yes,' agreed Cormac. 'There's no room for that kind of space down there. Given the location readings Cassiel got, I think it's safe to assume it's sitting in a server or group of servers somewhere under the pyramid.'

'We followed a sign that said "Down" to get to it,' replied Leila. 'Maybe that's what it meant. Back from the satellite, down into the depths.'

'And my guess is, you'll find this Deodatus entity in or near it. I assume he was the first to be absorbed by the pit. If it was a Totality work crew, he'll be a fallen mind. And he'll be controlling all of the rest of them. A physical avatar of the Kneale Pit. Doing a good job of it, if he's even subverted the Rose.'

East held up a hand. Cormac froze. 'The Rose might not have fallen,' said the god. 'She could be using all this for her own ends. Psychoactive technology could make her very powerful.'

'Would she do that?' asked Leila. But she already knew what the answer was.

'Of course. If I'd found it first, I might have been tempted to.' East smiled distantly. 'That kind of tech is a wonderful audience management tool.'

Her casual response shocked Leila. 'You're meant to protect humanity, not rewrite it.'

'It's not too far from what the Twins do at the climax of the Taste Refresh Festival,' East mused. 'They open up everyone's memories and drop new flavours into them. You'd just need to reach a little bit further in...'

'That's everything we're fighting against, East.'

'Oh, I'm just teasing you,' laughed the god. 'But then again, perhaps you're wise not to trust me. You can't really trust anyone, these days. Look at your lovely Fetch Counsellor, he's got you exactly where he wants you.'

'He's the only person I can trust.'

'Really?' East smiled. 'Wise up, Leila. The Counsellor's using you. Telling you not to talk to anyone? To keep it a fetch affair?'

Leila nodded. 'Of course. We didn't know how far things had gone. Who'd fallen. The Counsellor wanted to keep us safe.'

East snorted. 'The Counsellor's seen how much good helping rescue everyone when Kingdom fell did for the Totality. He wants his own little political boost.' She pointed a perfectly manicured finger at Leila. 'And you're it. He's keeping you to himself because he wants all the credit for sorting this out to go to the Fetch Communion.'

'That's bullshit.'

'He's a new god and he's weak. And so he has to be very manipulative.' She arched a perfect eyebrow and pointed at Leila. 'You be careful round him. He can be dangerous.'

This time, Leila did roll her eyes. 'And you're NOT manipulative?'

'I'm not manipulating you, if that's what you mean,' replied East. 'I'm just helping you deal with a dangerous situation. And in return I want to tell Station your story. You see,' she smiled sweetly, 'I'm being completely open with you.'

'The Fetch Counsellor has always been completely straight with me.'

'Ask him, my dear,' purred East. Then she was all business. 'But you have an interview to finish.'

'You can't just accuse the Fetch Counsellor—'

'Don't you want to find your brother, Leila? Time is of the essence.' She waved at Cormac and he started speaking again.

'Fuck,' spat Leila.

'Please,' East told her. 'I hate having to edit out swearing. Do listen to him.'

'I'm going, East. I'm not going to play your games anymore.'

'There's more you need to hear. And I'm doing everything I can to help you. I'm just making sure you help me a little too.'

Leila snorted. 'You haven't been much help so far. We're the ones taking all the risks.'

'You know I can't take the risk of alerting the Rose – or the fallen minds, come to that. You three are my little deniability tool. You're very precious. Now, shall we finish?'

Accepting the inevitable, Leila sighed and turned back to Cormac. 'I need all you've got about the pyramid and the space beneath it,' she told him. 'And I want to know how to get Dieter out of a Kneale Pit.' She thought of Cassiel. 'And then shut it down.'

'Oh wonderful,' said East, shivering with joy. 'That was so dynamic. You are magnificent, Leila.'

Leila stifled a very dynamic response to the god's praise.

Cormac waited for a moment, then said: 'If you can persuade Dieter to leave he should just be able to come along with you. Kneale Pits rely on rewired loyalties. They never have very heavy exit security in place. And this Kneale Pit is centred on the Shining City, which is a fully virtual environment. You should shut down any servers that the city's running on. That'll break the flies, too. They'll all be run from the city. Once you've crashed it, they'll shut down too. Every single fallen mind and human from Deodatus down will be isolated. Easy enough to neutralise.'

'Once we've got Dieter out.'

'Oh, yes, of course,' replied Cormac. 'And you should make sure you do get him out before you switch everything off. A forced shutdown could corrupt any data held on the servers, his weaveself included. And given how dangerous this Pit is, there's no guarantee that the gods will let you turn it back on to go looking for him if you leave him in there.'

'So I need to pull a reverse Deodatus,' said Leila, 'and rewire Dieter's loyalties back to me.' She had to make sure that he accepted Dit's true memories. 'I can do that.' She hoped she still sounded dynamic. 'So now our only problem is getting into the Wart,' she continued. 'Cassiel and the Caretaker are working on it. It's not going to be easy.'

'Oh, there's no need to worry about that,' said East airily, 'I can get all three of you to that pyramid. I've got just the people for the job! And then you can have a look around and see exactly what's going on. Maybe even shut the Pit down all on your own.'

'And boost your ratings, too.'

'Well, it's only fair,' she beamed. 'If the cloud has a silver lining, it's so wrong not to take advantage. And the gun kiddies will have so much fun helping you!'

'Gun kiddies? What have they got to do with any of this?'

'Oh, my dear – all that nonsense with Kingdom left me feeling so powerless. I decided I needed to start building an army of my own. Just in case. And they're it!'

Chapter 27

Twenty-four hours later, and East's gun kiddies were ready to go. Leila, Cassiel and the Caretaker left the safe house when the spinelights were at their dimmest. Leila touched her pendant for luck, then called the cloak into being and was invisible to everyone but her two companions. Cassiel's camouflage systems cast shadows around her and the Caretaker, hiding them both from the Rose.

'We've got about half an hour before the Rose breaks my cammo systems, if the Fetch Counsellor is right,' whispered Cassiel. 'Then she'll have us. I've allocated twenty minutes to movement time. We need to go quickly.'

They zig-zagged through the streets, following the plan Cassiel had drawn up to avoid the Rose's patrols. Leila followed the mind, not really taking too much in. She was still thinking through the events of the afternoon. She'd gone to see Dit – not, she told herself firmly, to say goodbye, but rather to get the memories she needed to rescue Dieter.

She'd jumped to the road just outside her flat, to double-check that all was safe. It was all the same as ever, and yet everything had changed. Even the gods had shown themselves to be malleable. The river of time flowed on, and they were just little eddies in it – larger than most, perhaps, but in the end just as transient. Twelve gods had become six, then five. They might soon become fewer. It seemed inevitable that, one day, there would only be one of them. Perhaps even that final, single corporate divinity would fall in the end. She wondered what would replace it, then shook her head, amused at herself. Threat had clearly brought out the philosopher in her. There was no sign of the gun kiddy who'd been on the roof. She wondered if East had moved her agent to somewhere a little more discreet, observing who came and went. *You manipulative hag*, she thought to herself. She was about to leap into her flat when she saw an even more familiar figure at the block's street door.

Lei stepped out into the street.

Leila was amazed. It was such a shock to feel that she'd left her old life so far behind that someone else had to step in to live it. It was fascinating, too, to be able to see herself as others saw her. Lei set off down the street and Leila followed her, walking quickly to keep up with her. Her double moved with a fluid, impressive confidence. She'd upgraded her wardrobe, leasing new fashion content from designers that Leila had never been able to afford. They marked her out as someone who wouldn't be staying in the old neighbourhood for long. Leila wondered where Lei would move to, how she'd deal with her new life.

Then she stopped herself.

Lei wasn't even fully self-aware. She wouldn't exist for much longer. Leila would rescue Dieter, then pull this other life back into hers. A stream that had fallen away from its mother would rejoin the greater flow. There would be no more great adventures, no more lives at stake – just the past to come to terms with, and a newly secure world within which to do it.

And then Miwa and Dave appeared out of the crowd and greeted Lei, and as kisses were exchanged Leila felt a new grief. Her return wouldn't be as simple as that. Her friends were lost to her too. It was absolutely right that she should be a ghost, watching them unseen; absolutely right that they shouldn't be exposed to the hard, deadly risks she was facing. They'd already had part of the past stolen from them. She couldn't bear for them to lose anything more. And yet it hurt so much to see them laughing with Lei, safe within a world that she was excluded from.

For a moment, Leila imagined stepping away from all the fear and worry, and back into her old life. Perhaps she would even be left alone to enjoy the security that had been Dieter's final gift to her. She could leave Cassiel and the Caretaker to solve the problem of Deodatus. But in returning to the past she'd be abandoning the present, letting them as well as her brother down. She realised that they were more than just allies – they'd become friends, as important to her now as Miwa and Dave had once been.

Her attention drifted. A shock flashed through her. There, tucked away over the road, stood a pressure man. A long jacket stretched down over high-waisted trousers. Sharply pointed collars reached out over wide lapels like wings. Jewelled gold and silver rings clung to his fingers. Sunglasses hid his eyes, their dark arms pressing down luxuriant sideburns. She imagined the perfumed reek that would surround him.

He reminded her of the man who'd broken into her apartment. She knew she should find him absurd, but again her childhood self reared up and made him at once authoritative and threatening. Somehow the pressure man seemed older, more mature, even more capable than her. She shook her head. 'This is bullshit,' she told herself, imagining the decaying fallen mind that lay beneath this out-of-time façade.

The pressure man stared at Lei with a cold, appraising stillness. Leila flicked back through her memories of the last few minutes and found him tucked away in the peripheries of them all. He'd been waiting for Lei when she came out of the block and – like Leila – had followed her since then. Leila wondered if the pressure men were always present in Lei's life, watching through flies when she was at home, moving quietly behind her when she was out and about. She was surprised not to spot any gun kiddies keeping an eye on Lei. Perhaps East's troops, being weaker, had had to find ways of being more discreet. She hoped that Lei wouldn't notice any of her trackers. She imagined the awful, paranoid fear their presence could create.

Lei linked arms with Miwa and Dave and moved away into the crowd. The pressure man waited for a moment or two and then slid down the street after them. Leila didn't follow. She was relieved, at least, that the plan had worked. Lei's masquerade would be entirely convincing. Leila and her new friends would retain the element of surprise. She prepared herself to jump into the flat and speak with Dit. She took a moment to look around her. She'd been so focused on Lei and the pressure men that she'd hardly registered anything else.

'Oh, no,' she breathed.

The space above the street was dense with ocean. Shoals of fish twitched between coral studded buildings. A familiar silhouette lanced through them, scalpelling threat into the moment. It was a shark. It could have been perfectly innocuous, all part of the simulation. But Leila had been still for a minute or so, watching Lei as the pressure man had watched her. It could be that – despite the ghost cloak – she'd bled part of herself into the world that surrounded her. It could be that one of Ambrose's search engines was on her trail.

She leapt to her flat and asked Dit for Dieter's memories of their life together.

'Why do you need them, Leila?'

Worried that a full explanation would force reset him, she kept it simple: 'In case Deodatus has rewritten Dieter. Like that pressure man tried to do with me. These'll help him remember the truth.'

'Gods,' said Dit, profoundly shocked. 'That would be awful. Of course, take them.'

Leila thought back to Ambrose. After his rewrite, he'd refused to trust her. 'I might need to force them into him.'

'Easily done,' Dit reassured her. 'I'll write an injection app for you. Attach it to the memory block, it'll push them straight in.'

'Sounds very simple.'

'You're giving back something that came from him. They should mesh very naturally with what's already there. Might be a little disorientation, but only for a moment.'

Relief filled Leila.

'The app will need a focus,' said Dit. 'Something to give him to trigger the memory transfer.'

She thought for a moment, then held up the pendant. 'Use this.'

'It's a terrible thought,' commented Dit, as he set everything up. 'Losing his memories of you would change him so much. If he has lost them and this doesn't work, I'll merge with him myself.'

Leila turned away to hide the tears that sprang into her eyes. When he was done, she thanked him and hugged him too tightly. 'What was that for?' he asked, amused, and she couldn't answer but just said 'goodbye', her voice tight and controlled. Then she jumped back to the safe house to wait until dark. She'd planned to visit the Fetch Counsellor too, but she worried about the risk. *Once we're out again*, she thought, telling herself that her decision had nothing to do with East's analysis of his motives.

Now Leila, Cassiel and the Caretaker were hurtling through the streets. 'Keep moving,' she hissed at her companions. 'We don't want a shark to spot us.'

'Going as fast as I can,' the Caretaker puffed.

Cassiel was just ahead of them, leading them around the Rose's searchers. 'Fifteen minutes,' she called back.

The weave whispered night words in the empty streets. A sprite buzzed past, a glimmer of stardust. It was broadcasting on an open frequency. 'Can't sleep? Worried about debt? Payday loans available for all...'

'This could be such a beautiful world,' muttered the Caretaker. 'Wild with visions! But instead there's just this shit.'

Cassiel hissed back at them: 'Someone coming.'

They ducked into a doorway. But it was just a huddle of dockers, shattered at the end of a day-long shift, too tired to even unlink their minds from each other. Their bodies moved through the streets as one, a machine built from flesh and bone.

They set off again. 'Ten minutes,' hissed Cassiel. Then, to Leila: 'We're in control until we reach the rendezvous. After that, East is in charge. And that makes me very uncomfortable.'

'I hate it too,' replied Leila. 'But what choice did we have? We can't get to the Wart without her help.'

'When you have no choice, then you're a slave,' Cassiel told her. 'We fought a war to escape that.'

'She knows how to pull people's strings, I'll give her that. If we'd turned her down, we'd have been stuck in the flat and she'd have sent her gun kiddies into the pyramid. And they'd have been massacred.'

'It amazes me she sees them as an effective military force.'

Leila thought of all the teen gamers she'd seen racing round Station over the last few years. 'She has been training them pretty hard.'

Another few minutes, and they were at the rendezvous point. One side of the road was gleaming new office blocks. The other was vacant lots and half-demolished factory spaces.

'Where did our new boss command us to wait?' grumbled Cassiel.

East's instructions were very precise. Leila led them to cover behind a half-tumbled wall, overlooked by a broken office block.

The block's facing had been ripped off, leaving three empty storeys staring out at the night.

'A minute remaining,' said Cassiel. She scanned the area. 'No cameras,' she confirmed. 'We are secure. For now.'

'East can't see us,' replied Leila. 'But the sharks can.' She was worried. 'The kiddies should already be here.'

'Be cool, guys,' the Caretaker told them. 'They're just teenagers. Probably just got held up along the way. They'll be here soon.'

But nobody came. Seconds passed, then minutes.

'We should get moving. The sharks will scent us,' worried Leila.

'We can't make it back to the flat and we have nowhere else to go,' replied Cassiel. 'We know how that would end. East has betrayed us.'

'Have a little faith,' droned the Caretaker. 'If she wanted to put the zap on us, she'd have done it right back when she first found you, Leila.'

'Look,' said Cassiel, pointing up. High above them, a scalpel sharp silhouette flicked through the sky.

'Shit. Shark.' Leila glanced around. The wasteland was still empty. 'We should stop it. Or run.'

'I can stop it,' said Cassiel, gazing up. 'But when I hit it, it'll see us. And it'll have enough time to ping back our location before I fry it.'

Leila remembered Ambrose talking about how sharp the shark's senses were. She imagined her skull face ripping into them. 'I can blind it. Deafen it. Break it.' She called the skull face into being.

'No,' said Cassiel. 'That'll blow your cover.'

'What choice do we have?'

'Well,' said a teenage boy's voice, 'You could come with me.'

'What the—?' Leila was sure there was nobody there.

And then there was, as a shadow at one end of the wall took on a plastic solidity, then started to shift and morph into something like the shape of a person.

She waited for a moment or two. It didn't fade away. 'You guys are seeing that too?' she asked.

A moment's stillness, then the shadow stepped towards them, moving across the rubble with tense, nervous steps. 'There you are!'

It sounded relieved. 'And can you see me? Because I've only just upgraded to this armour. I'm not sure I've turned the cloaking off properly.'

'You're partially visible, gun kiddy,' replied Cassiel.

'We don't call ourselves that, you know.' The dark shape raised itself up to its full height. It was short and looked male. 'I play East's games. I play them well.' He was wearing some kind of deep camouflage bodysuit. The suit reflected no light, turning his body into a flat absence. A hand reached up to a face mask and pulled it off. Two eyes, a nose and a mouth appeared. There was a wispy growth on his upper lip. 'I'm Hando.'

Cassiel turned to Leila. 'Is this really how East battles an existential threat to Station?'

'Let him be,' drawled the Caretaker. 'Hando's all right.'

Leila ignored them. She let Hando see her. 'You've got transport for us?'

Hando took her appearance in his stride. 'Ah. Yes. Over there.' He waved towards the broken office block. Two other shadows were wheeling a small flyer out of the ground floor. 'All ready and waiting. As specified in the mission briefing. And we got it here ahead of time, so we've scored bonus points!' He beamed.

'The shark!' said Cassiel, frustrated beyond measure. 'These idiots are a beacon for it. Another few seconds and it'll be on us.'

Leila glanced up. It was much lower now, still circling the area. It disappeared behind the office block. 'Oh, that's not a problem,' said the gun kiddy cheerfully. 'That's why we waited. To draw it in.' He waved towards the flyer. One of his companions stopped pushing, waved back, then unshouldered a cumbersome-looking weapon.

Cassiel didn't notice. 'When it appears,' she told Leila, 'You must hit it. We have no other choice.'

'Oh, Amara'll zap it. She's been a player since she was eleven,' said the gun kiddy confidently. 'She's shit hot.'

Leila felt her skull face within her. She told it to target the shark, then reached out to Cassiel. 'Don't worry,' she told the mind. 'I'll break it.'

And then it was there, a grey avatar of death arrowing towards them. Its shadow moved smoothly across the broken ground, twitching with every flip of its great tail. Its maw gaped open. Its compound eyes glittered dully in the night. Its fins seemed somehow transparent. It was their discovery and their death, and it was coming for them.

'Wow,' said the Caretaker. 'It's part fly. Heavy.'

She felt the skull face probe the shark's senses. It found a vast sensitivity, greater than anything it had encountered before, and pulled together a sensory assault package to match. It was far more complex and invasive than anything it had ever produced to attack a human, the weapon matching itself to a new kind of target. And then it was complete, and Leila was ready to fire.

And there was a loud crack from the gun the distant shadow held. A long, thin bolt of light leapt out and hit the shark's flank, knocking it sideways through the air. Its mouth opened and it thrashed, curling in around the wound. Then there was a loud electronic howl. Static shimmered through it and it was gone.

The shadow in the distance cheered.

'Fuck yeah!' whooped Hando. 'Full bonus achieved! Get in!'

'Nice shooting,' said the Caretaker. 'What's the weapon, kiddo?'

'It's a harpoon gun. It force crashes the shark. The crash reads as a serious memory error. Looks like an accident. Diagnostics and reboot will take an hour at least.' He was jubilant. He chattered excitedly as he led them to the flyer. 'Can't wait for you to meet Dave and Amara. We won't be able to talk about all this for a couple of months, but when it comes out – well, everyone'll be so jealous! We're so stoked. You hear about unlocking special missions, but you never think you'll find one yourself.'

'They really don't know how serious this is,' muttered Cassiel.

Hando didn't hear. 'We've been playing as a squad for a couple of years, now,' he continued. 'Mostly in bigger teams, though. This is the first time we've just been out as ourselves. Steal a flyer, pick up some booty, bring it here. All carried out! Gods, this is worth the subscription on its own.'

'You stole the flyer?' asked the Caretaker. He sounded shocked. 'That's not cool.'

'Oh, it's not real,' replied Hando. 'None of it's real. You should know that, you're actors.' He peered at them, expecting affirmation.

They looked at him blankly. 'I guess you can't break role.'

The flyer was painted a bland grey. Hando introduced Dave, who explained how he'd wiped its hard drive and reinstalled its operating system. 'It's completely anonymous now,' he said. 'Reads like it's brand new, freshly registered as a roving maintenance unit. Nobody'll know it's you driving it and you can take it pretty much anywhere. Just pretend you're fixing something if you get any hassle from InSec.'

The cramped interior smelt of air freshener. There was a flat disc on the back seat, wrapped in webbing. It was identical to the ones that supported the slow travellers. 'And this is for Leila,' Amara explained, the harpoon back on her shoulder. 'It's a fully operational autonomous fetch server.' She reached into the flyer, grabbed the disc by its webbing and pulled it out. 'You can load yourself on to it and be present anywhere, regardless of whether or not there's any local weave running.'

'We broke into a storage vault and stole it,' enthused Hando. 'It was so exciting!'

'It can receive data from any local sense feeds,' continued Amara, 'so you can experience what's going on around you at all times. It's got full weavecast capabilities, you can manifest as yourself to anyone within range of it. Oh, and these solar panels keep it charged.'

Leila remembered the slow travellers. 'And I can slow myself right down and turn silver if I want to, too.'

Amara took her entirely seriously. 'It's set up for that if you need it, yes. It makes you pretty much invisible to sharks, too. You broadcast directly to local individuals, so you're not onweave enough for them to see you.'

'Not that we'll meet too many of them in the Wart.'

Amara nodded. 'Yeah, there's so little weave in there. So the shields are really a nice-to-have. The important thing is, we've found you a platform that'll help you explore the Wart. Or anywhere else that doesn't have any weave. It should hold the whole of your weaveself without any problems. Though it does need someone to carry it around for you.' She tugged out some shoulder straps. 'Either one of your companions can wear it like a backpack.' She passed it to the Caretaker. 'So, are you happy?' she asked. 'Every goal achieved?'

'Yes,' said Leila. 'Thank you.'

'Though you should perhaps find a less dangerous hobby,' added Cassiel.

'Woohoo!' The gun kiddies high-fived each other.

'So,' said Hando, 'we'll be off now. Good luck.'

'Er, yeah,' said the Caretaker. 'A pleasure to meet you.'

The teenagers were already fading away, their black armour flowing up over their faces and reasserting an absence of light. For a moment, three silhouettes were visible. Then they merged with the darkness and were gone.

'Those are great kids,' continued the Caretaker. 'They did a great job. But I hope my teenage years didn't involve black ops missions for the gods.'

'They could have left us with some bloody guns, at least,' grumbled Leila, as she sent out the commands that would transfer her into the disc.

'We don't need guns,' replied Cassiel. 'We've got me.'

Chapter 28

Cassiel lifted the flyer up and over the sleeping landscape of Dock-lands. Leila fiddled with the disc's settings until it showed Cassiel and the Caretaker her avatar, sitting in a rear seat. She reached out and connected with their senses. Cassiel's Totality tech gave everything a pin-sharp precision. The Caretaker's sound and image gathering systems were rather more glitchy. Even the smallest objects were overlaid with a soft, rainbow halo of colours. Each sound created a slow-dying echo. It was like being ever so slightly stoned. Leila followed their gazes out over the city. The dimly lit streets curved up and away above them, tucking themselves in behind the Spine. There was no spinelight, only a soft shine rising up from a thousand streetlamps. It made the round entrance to the Wart ahead seem even darker, as black as the armour the gun kiddies had worn to go into innocent battle.

'I wonder if that's my home,' said the Caretaker. 'It doesn't seem very homely.'

'Bringing back any memories?' asked Leila.

'Not yet. But I felt a definite connection with the Shining City. Like I should get in there, you know?'

Leila nodded.

They entered the Wart. There were far fewer lights. Scattered streetlamps implied a few long, straight roads, connecting clusters of shining windows hinting at factories and office blocks. Two power plants burned out of the darkness, security lights turning the globes of their fusion chambers into glowing pearls. Cassiel banked the flyer. As they flew over one, proximity degraded it.

The fusion chamber was a rough, concrete orb, set on a pitted metal base. Pipes ran out of it and into the ground. It was such an inelegant thing, but a quarter of Station's power came from it. Leila felt suddenly very aware that, without the energy these power plants provided, she would not exist. She'd still be present in the world as patterns of magnetism sketched across so many silicon disks, but there'd be nothing to bring those patterns to life. She felt very transient.

Cassiel noticed her discomfort. 'Worried?'

'I'm fine.'

The mind pointed. 'That's where we're headed...'

Leila looked ahead through Cassiel's eyes, glad to be distracted.

The Caretaker craned forwards too. 'Very impressive,' he said.

The pyramid loomed out of the darkness, a dense mass about a hundred metres high, clutching the curved floor of the Wart. It came to a sharp, pale tip, pointing towards the centre of the Wart. Its four triangular faces arced up from the rubble-scattered ground, leaping up at a steep angle. Each face had originally been finished with a smooth, translucent material. Some of it remained, gleaming at the pyramid's point, but most had fallen away, revealing pitted stone.

'The Alpha Pyramid,' said Leila. 'Cormac gave me a map of it. The layout's very simple. Two ways in. An official front entrance at ground level. And a hole some urban explorer hacked into it, halfway up the rear face.'

'We take the back way,' replied Cassiel. A warning pinged on the flyer's dashboard, distracting her. 'ID query from a local security system,' she explained.

'That's not good,' said Leila. 'Is it Deodatus?'

'Not necessarily,' Cassiel reassured her. 'And the gun kiddies did a good job. We look entirely innocent. The Wart's full of energy systems. If there's a problem with them, no matter how minor, it needs to be checked out straight away. Just like we're apparently doing.'

The flyer landed with a barely perceptible bump. As they climbed out, Cassiel strapped Leila's disc to her back. It still projected her avatar, making her appear physically present to Cassiel, the Caretaker and anyone else she chose to see her. 'What next?' she asked.

'Find their security perimeter,' replied Cassiel. 'Then I'll get us through it.'

They set off. The going was hard. The darkness made the rough ground treacherous. Gravity shifted in intensity, sometimes crushing them down, sometimes almost vanishing. Cassiel flowed like a ghost through it all, Leila moving with her. The Caretaker found the going tough, every so often stumbling and swearing, then regaining his footing and pushing on again.

'I should have come alone,' Cassiel told Leila. 'I'm built for this. Neither of you are.'

Leila snorted. 'There's no way that Dieter will listen to you. And the Caretaker's better than either of us at stopping pressure men.'

The Alpha Pyramid loomed ahead of them, never seeming to get any closer, its pointed tip boring a hole in the darkness. As they started up a low incline, Leila thought she heard a soft buzzing. She strained through Cassiel's sharp ears.

Cassiel held a hand up. 'Stop,' she ordered. 'Down. Now.' It took the Caretaker a minute to catch up. He sank to the ground, grateful for the rest.

'Flies,' said Leila.

'Yes. I think it's the perimeter. Going to take a look.' Her soft purple light flicked out.

'I didn't know you could do that,' exclaimed Leila. 'I thought you were always purple.'

'I'm an infiltration specialist.' She held up a translucent arm. 'Of course I can be invisible when I need to.'

The mind slipped Leila's disc off her back, sank forwards and down, and then was gone, elongating and moving like a snake, keeping low. Leila watched through her eyes. The mind flowed across dark rocks to the crest of the ridge, then looked down. The pyramid stood in the depression's centre. Cassiel opened her eyes right up to inspect it. Darkness became light. At first it seemed that her vision was glitched with static. Tiny motes danced across it. Then Leila realised.

[It's a swarm,] she breathed. [The biggest we've ever seen.]

[The perimeter,] said Cassiel. The flies framed the pyramid, a living shield dancing with movement. [A half-globe, surrounding their base.] Leila felt complex software architectures rise up in Cassiel's mind as she scanned the flies. [The communications between them are very simple. Seem to be running a basic perimeter patrol programme,] the mind said. [I've queried them successfully, now I'm going to try a command. Needs concentration.]

Leila found herself thrust out of her head and back into her disc. She had the disc project an image of her, sitting next to the Caretaker.

'Hey there,' he whispered as she shimmered into being. 'Thought you'd be back once she started all that ninja shit.' He'd almost got his breath back. 'What's she up to?'

'Telling the flies to let us through.'

'Cool. And how are you?'

'Fine,' replied Leila. 'I'm fine.'

A moment's silence.

'Are you sure?' asked the Caretaker gently. 'You don't sound entirely convinced.'

'Gods,' she sighed. 'It's just that – all this. Who knows what we'll find in there. All kinds of fucked-up things. And Deodatus at the centre of it all. And it's just the three of us...' She tailed off.

'That fucking pyramid,' laughed the Caretaker. 'Scares the shit out of me too!'

'Seeing it in the darkness. Like a tombstone. It's all so real, all of a sudden.'

'Hey,' he said. 'It always was real. You missing your brother, Cassiel cut off from her world, me losing myself. Poor Ambrose, even. All people dealing with some real, heavy shit. And you've done a pretty good job so far. You kept us safe from the Rose and the pressure men. You found East...'

Leila remembered the Flurrytown restaurant. 'She found me.'

'She wouldn't have done if you hadn't been out there, looking for a way to go forwards. She was it. And because you found her, we've got everything we needed. And once we're in the pyramid, it'll be just the same. Cassiel will do her thing, you'll do yours, I'll do mine.' His teeth flashed a smile in the gloom. 'And we'll all get to where we need to be.'

'I hope so.'

'I know so, Leila. Have a little faith in yourself. In the two of us too, come to that.'

'I'm sorry, I didn't mean...'

'Oh, I know. It is hard. But it's all going to be good, Leila.' He wriggled in the darkness, making himself more comfortable. 'You know,' he mused, 'I don't have a past. And that means I don't have much of a future, either. I don't know what to expect from life, because I don't have any reference points. So I just live in the present. Think about the moment, find the right response to it, that's it. There are moments when I feel like I've found the real me.' He paused. 'Memory gets in the way sometimes, Leila. It's too easy to lose yourself in it.' A chuckle. 'Just look at Deodatus.'

'Yeah,' said Leila. 'You're not wrong. And it's not just him.' Cormac had fled irrevocably into the past when he found the present too harsh to bear. And Ambrose had always been trapped there too. Cormac was lost, but perhaps she'd finally be able to help Ambrose move on when he returned as a fetch. And then there was Dieter. History had taken him from her. But his situation was a little different. He needed to find lost time again. She squeezed the pendant around her neck and imagined handing it to her brother. As soon as he touched it, he'd come back to her.

Cassiel's voice appeared in her mind. [I've meshed with the flies. Written a code block to tell them we're the same as the minds controlling them. Then they'll let us through. Firing it now. Thirty seconds and we're going in.]

Chapter 29

Leila moved away from the pyramid, weighed down by disappointment, the pendant heavy round her neck. Now she would never reunite Dieter with the truth of his past. Cassiel walked with her, head bowed, glowing purple again. There was no need to hide themselves. Newly minted memories filled her mind – sneaking up to the pyramid's vast outer wall, feeling its dense presence loom above her, casting round until they found its ground-level entrance, the doors that Cormac had said would be locked shut gaping open, stepping through and then – nothing.

There was an unoccupied central chamber, its floor thick with rubble. Corroded pillars lanced up into the darkness. Cormac had mentioned a centuries-old tunnel, hacked into the wall by long-dead explorers. It was up there at the peak of one of the pillars, invisible in the gloom. A narrow, steep corridor led down to another empty space, a circular room as broad as the central chamber but oppressed by a low ceiling. Leila imagined the weight of the pyramid pressing down on them. The passageway that had so excited Cormac was still blocked. A couple of empty store rooms held nothing. Billows of dust rose around her as she walked. The air tasted of a past so old that it had reached some new inertness, far beyond death. The walls had once been dense with sculptures, but age had crumbled them, scoring anything legible out.

'It seems that history has defeated us,' said Cassiel, pulling Leila back into the present. She trudged on, despair pulsing through her. There was no longer any hope of finding Dieter. And there was nothing she could do to stop Deodatus running riot. East would have to face the Rose directly. She probably couldn't stand up to her. The Kneale Pit would run out of control, pulling the whole of Station into its absurd, broken rebirthing of the past. The loss of her brother left her feeling so bleak that she hardly cared.

'We have nowhere left to look,' Cassiel continued. 'We have failed. The Totality is no longer the future.' Her voice was thick with angry despair. 'Deodatus is. And he will overwrite us all.'

'Guys,' shouted the Caretaker, somewhere behind them. 'Come back!'

Leila ignored him. A moment or so later she heard him running up behind her, rocks sliding and clashing beneath his feet. 'Fuck,' he shouted as he tripped and fell. Through his eyes, the ground came up to meet him.

'Well at least that got your bloody attention,' he wheezed as Cassiel helped him up. He'd had to run hard to catch up with them.

'We've failed,' Cassiel said again. 'We need to find somewhere new to hide.'

'I don't know where we can go,' replied Leila.

The Caretaker took a deep, gasping breath. 'What are you talking about?' he asked. 'Guys, you're not yourselves!'

'You want to keep poking around?' asked Leila. 'Fine. The Wart's your home. Stay here. Cassiel, let's go back to the flyer.' She sighed wearily. 'And then on to who knows where.'

'But Leila, Cassiel – you haven't been inside the pyramid.'

'Of course we have,' snapped Leila.

'No,' replied the Caretaker, almost howling the word out. 'Don't you remember? The flies came. Got your disc, got me. Must have zapped you too, Cassiel. Whole fucking swarm of the little shits. I blacked out. When I came to, you guys were a hundred metres away, heading back to the flyer.'

'But there weren't any flies,' said Cassiel. 'There was just the pyramid. And it was empty.'

'Then they wiped themselves out of your mind too. It's the perfect defence.' Leila had never heard him talk with such urgency. 'Think back over your memories. Man, there's got to be something wrong with them. Cassiel was writing a code block to break through the perimeter. She fired it. Then the flies hit us. I was there, dammit, I saw it.'

'It can't be,' replied Cassiel, sounding puzzled. 'If it was, they'd have rewritten your memory too.'

'I don't have much in there to start with,' the Caretaker told her.

'Maybe that's why they couldn't touch me. But they got you both. For fuck's sake, you have to believe me. Just come and look at the bloody flies.'

Cassiel said nothing. Leila was silent too, as she worked back through her memories of the pyramid. They all seemed so real, so present – so definite. Pushing into the vast cavern inside the pyramid, moving down through its underground layers, the dust rising around her as she walked. There was no weave in the pyramid, so no possibility that anything could be hidden. She saw reality and it was empty. The bitter pain of failure filled her. The Caretaker and Cassiel were with her, not saying anything, just moving sadly through the void.

And then she stopped, and scrolled back. Hope pulsed in her as she ran a particular memory set again, then a third time. Her feet stepped across the floor. Her footsteps echoed in an empty room. Her passing raised clouds of dust. All of which was impossible, for she was a fetch, and had no physical presence.

'Gods, you're right,' she told the Caretaker. 'We don't need to see the flies.' She turned to Cassiel. 'We didn't go in there.'

'I remember it all so clearly,' said Cassiel.

'My footsteps raised clouds of dust.' She thought for a moment. 'The flies gave us memories of exploring a depressing, empty pyramid. So we'd walk away and not want to come back. They must write those memories into anyone who comes along. But they didn't expect a fetch to come along. Fair enough, there's no weave out here, not many of us passing by. They only set up memories for corporeal people – humans, minds. So I remember having a body, being physically present. Raising dust with real feet. And that's impossible.'

Cassiel stood still for a moment. Soft lights flickered within her, memories flashing through her mind with firefly speed. 'We entered the pyramid. We explored...' she said thoughtfully. 'I picked at the rubble blocking the lower passageway. You two were both there.' She was silent for a moment. 'Yes. I'm watching you now, Leila. You're walking past a sarcophagus. There's a cloud of dust. And you're picking up stones, shifting rubble. Which is indeed impossible.'

'So you believe me?' asked the Caretaker. 'Thank fuck.'

'We can still get Dieter back,' breathed Leila, profoundly relieved. She turned to the Caretaker. 'Thank you.'

Cassiel sank into a squat, wrapping her arms around her head. 'We fought a war to escape this kind of oppression.' She sounded deeply traumatised.

Leila knelt down behind her and put a hand on her shoulder. 'Are you all right?' she asked. 'We'll stop Deodatus. We'll stop all of this.'

'Before the Totality freed me, I worked for Kingdom. One of his software and hardware licence enforcers. Running covert missions. Proper black ops, not like those gun kiddies. And after every one, I had my mind wiped. I found some of the mission files, after the Totality seceded from the Pantheon. I did such terrible things for your gods, Leila. Took so much from so many. And I have no memory of any of it.'

'But this is Deodatus. It's just a blip. We'll make sure it doesn't happen again.'

'It always comes back, Leila.' She sounded bleak. 'I wasn't the only one. All of us minds – we had operating system upgrades, factory resets, memory defragging, full wiping forced on us, all of the time. None of us could form coherent identities. We were built to be efficient machines. And there will always be someone who sees how we can be more efficient if we are stripped down and rebuilt. If we march to their beat, not ours.' She looked up. Light glimmered softly behind her face, grief made visible pulsing in time with her words. 'We worked so hard to escape it. We vowed that we'd never lose our memories again. After the Soft War, we sent search parties across the system to root out the tiniest parts of our minds. To protect our deep selves. And yet here we are, and here it is again.'

'Hey,' replied Leila, her voice soft. 'Us too, remember? Until the Totality freed the fetches, we were broken too. People used fetches like photograph albums. Replay the best bits of life, toss away the rest. We were a shattered people.' She smiled ruefully. 'They shouldn't have called it the Soft War. It should have been the Memory War.'

The Caretaker sat down on the other side of Cassiel. 'I guess that means we're fighting the second Memory War now,' he said. 'Taking back the past from Deodatus.' He put a hand on Cassiel's shoulder. 'It's tough. But we'll stop him. And anyone else that tries to pull this kind of shit.'

'You're right,' said Cassiel, raising her head. 'You said I wrote a code block to break us in there?'

'You were trying to convince the flies that we were one of the minds controlling them,' the Caretaker told her.

'Well, that clearly didn't work. I'll go back in there. Work out what I did wrong.' There was a new determination in her voice. 'If the flies come back again, run.' Her head nodded forward. The soft light of her nano-gel dimmed, until she was nothing but a silhouette, almost as absent as the gun kiddies had been. Leila imagined code carving through the flies, breaking them into the land of the dead.

This time, Cassiel succeeded. 'We're in,' she told them, once she'd returned her attention to the world.

The wall of flies parted like a curtain and there was nothing between them and the militant past.

Chapter 30

Once they were through the perimeter, security was light. 'Relying on the flies,' hissed Cassiel, who was once again translucent. 'Over-confident.'

'Cormac got that right,' said Leila. 'Kneale Pit security's usually based on the assumption that they can rewrite anyone they want to.'

'They almost did,' pointed out the Caretaker.

A minute and they were at the rear of the pyramid. 'I'll scout,' Cassiel told them as she unhooked Leila's disc from her back and vanished into the darkness. A minute or so and she was back. 'They've opened up the main entrance,' she reported as she shrugged the disc back on. 'But there are guards on it. We're going through Cormac's back door.'

The pyramid rose away from them, its stone blocks blackened by age, their sharp edges looking slightly melted. Glancing up, Leila felt a strange kind of vertigo.

'Why's it so bloody high up?' asked the Caretaker, looking doubtful.

Leila had asked Cormac the same question. 'Makes it difficult to spot,' she told the Caretaker. 'Stops anyone just finding it and filling it in. And even if someone official does spot it, who's going to bother going all the way up there just to block it up?'

Cassiel reached up, her arms elongating. Her fingers stretched out as they touched stone, reaching into cracks and holes to secure themselves. 'Grab my back,' she told the Caretaker.

'What? Thought I'd be climbing up next to you.'

'Too slow.'

Cassiel flowed up the pyramid like a liquid, the Caretaker clinging to her. Some of its blocks were loose, shifting beneath them. The Caretaker swore under his breath when he felt them move, but each time Cassiel found a firm footing and kept moving forwards. Leila, still soft-linked to her, felt a great sense of relief and confidence pulse through the mind. 'You're enjoying this,' she said.

'At last I can do my work unhindered.'

'You haven't fallen off yet, I'll give you that.'

Leila expected a sharp reply. Instead, Cassiel stopped dead, suddenly throbbing with concentration.

'Are we there?' asked the Caretaker.

The mind shushed him. 'Guard,' she whispered. 'Very basic.' A moment, then: 'I own it.' A few more seconds of motion and she pulled them into an opening hacked in the stone, the mouth of a low, narrow passage. Soft light glowed out from within. She set down the Caretaker and Leila's disc. 'Wait here,' she hissed, then was off into the darkness. Barely any time passed and she was back.

'Where did you go?' asked Leila as Cassiel shrugged her disc back on.

'Setting up a distraction. Now, let's see the guard.'

Leila gasped as it pattered down the passage towards them. It looked melted. One leg was shorter than the other, so it moved with little skipping movements. There were no arms, only stumps. Its torso stopped at its chest. Its skin was pitted with decay. Flies hung within it and buzzed around it. Leila flinched back.

'The flies can't see us,' Cassiel told them. 'And the guard is too limited to attack or even perceive us without them.'

'What the fuck?' asked the Caretaker, deeply shocked. 'It looks so wrong.'

'Significantly impaired on all levels. It was exposed to extreme heat. No effort made to repair it. It's lost all but the most basic sense of itself. Deodatus must see this as a very unlikely entry point, to leave something so basic watching it.'

They squeezed past it and shuffled down the tunnel. It ended in a rectangle of light, its edges broken only by a black ring sticking out of a side wall. 'For abseiling down into the main chamber,' commented Leila.

'Whoa,' drawled the Caretaker, looking nervous.

Cassiel went to a crawl, the Caretaker following her. They reached the end of the corridor and peered out. It took a moment for their eyes to adjust to the glare. As vision returned they saw that they were looking past a pillar and out into pyramid's interior.

'Oh, wow,' breathed Leila.

The great chamber bustled with activity, and yet all was silent. There were no machine sounds, no whine of engines or chug of power generators, no jack hammer blasts of industrial noise. Instead, there was only a quiet bustle, a strange low collection of grunts and groans and a regular metallic beat.

The space was dominated by a high, slender metal tower, shaped like an upside down test tube and built from a patchwork of metal plates. Spotlights shone up at it, sending jagged shadows leaping across the sloping walls. The tower was about seventy-five metres high and – at the lip that ran round its broad base – fifteen or twenty metres across. Improvised-looking scaffolding nestled around it. Little figures moved along rickety walkways or up and down unsteady ladders. The scaffolding stopped at two high, wide open doors. A bundle of translucent ruby rods peered out at the world. The whole machine had an air of malevolent age. The cracks and joints running across it looked like wrinkles carved into an ancient face. The rods glowed, making Leila think of a single bloodshot eye. The air around it was punctuated with flies. The main entrance to the pyramid was hidden behind it, on the opposite side of the pyramid.

Cassiel zoomed in and Leila followed her gaze. Maybe a dozen or so fallen minds were managing tens of human workers. The minds were clearly in charge. They were far more decayed than any Leila had seen in Docklands, fuzzed blisters and oozing welts burned across them, but they moved with authority, sending their charges bustling up and down the scaffolding and across the pyramid's dirty floor. At first, they seemed to be entirely autonomous. But then Leila saw that each one would constantly stop to consult plans that were invisible to her, then pull their attention back into the work chamber and nudge their workforces into even greater efficiencies. They were fixed elements of a command structure, passing on an apparently very clearly defined vision.

Leila turned her attention to the humans, a tide of broken humanity become a single construction engine. There was no individuality in their actions – nothing that wasn't rigid or programmed, no movement that wasn't precisely calibrated to serve a greater whole. They were components, nothing more. And each one was a scrawny, desiccated ghost of itself.

'That's how Dieter and Kedrov ended up,' said Leila. 'They look just like sweatheads.'

'I studied sweatheads,' said Cassiel. 'But I never saw a living one.'

'What is a sweathead?' asked the Caretaker.

Leila explained. She too had never seen one in the flesh – her weaveware always screened them out. But she'd seen the charity appeals, with their deliberately disturbing footage of broken addicts. She described their tottering yet oddly energetic gait, the way that they'd find tiny, repetitive jobs and work obsessively at them, the slow ruin of their bodies as Sweat, the drug they couldn't stop taking, ate away at them. They'd been treated almost as badly as pre-Rebirth fetches. Then the Totality had come, taken pity on them and cleaned them off the streets.

'Maybe the fallen minds diverted some of them to work here,' suggested Leila. 'If those guys aren't just normal people who've fallen to Deodatus too.'

'Oh man. Those poor bastards.' The Caretaker looked shaken.

And yet the workers were not quite like the sweatheads that Leila remembered. The ones on the streets had never had anything of worth to their name. These people were patched round with fragments of technology, implants and add-ons that from far away looked like jewelled decorations. They replaced missing body parts, ageless components bolted on to exhausted flesh machines. Each worker had a different set of modifications, but they all had one thing in common – downwards-pointing triangles pressed deep into their bellies.

'Why the triangle?' asked the Caretaker. 'Why not a square?'

'I don't know,' replied Leila. 'Maybe it's a rank thing. Kedrov and the Pornomancer had those triangles too, and they were pretty much screwed. Holt and the minds all have squares, and they're in charge. Dieter was killed by one, he's pretty senior too.' She turned to Cassiel. 'And what are they building?'

'I think it's a laser,' Cassiel told them. 'A basic design, but very powerful. And dangerous.' She glanced up at the pyramid's point. It was still intact. 'They haven't fired it yet. It'll take the roof off when they do.'

'And hit the other side of the Wart,' Leila said. 'What's the point of that?'

'It won't just hit it,' replied Cassiel, her voice grim. 'It'll crack the Wart's skin like an eggshell. And the Wart holds Station together.'

Leila imagined the Wart breaking, Docklands and Homelands drifting apart from each other. Pain shook through her. 'Why are they even doing this? Won't they all die too?'

'I bet all this made sense, once,' said the Caretaker thoughtfully. 'I bet there was something out there for the laser to hit.'

'Dieter thinks he's going to break the gods and remake Station,' said Leila.

'If the laser fires, he'll do that all right,' Cassiel replied.

One of the workers on the scaffolding tripped then stumbled. He staggered towards its edge and almost caught himself on one of the barriers. But it wasn't well secured and it fell. He went with it, tumbling down to hit the floor with a dull thump. Red pooled beneath his broken body. Nobody else registered the death. One worker crossed the spreading pool, leaving a trail of bloody footprints. Another stumbled over the body, nearly dropping her load. She steadied herself and moved on, unmoved.

'Bastards,' said the Caretaker. 'Those fucking bastards.'

'We'll shut them down,' Cassiel told him. 'Once we find Deodatus, in his Shining City.' She nodded down at the pyramid floor. 'Got to get down there.' In one corner of the room, there were stairs leading to the space below. 'But there's one more thing to see first. The flies are sharing their own version of the weave. Full local overlay. I'm patching us into it.'

'Are you sure they won't see us and zap us again?' worried Leila.

'No.' Cassiel was absolutely confident. 'We're strictly passive. Just receiving a signal. They won't even see us.'

The room shimmered and changed. For a moment, Leila lost all sight of it. Then vision returned, and with it emotions that leapt between surprise, fear and awe. They chased through Leila's consciousness, for a moment overwhelming her. She remembered the gods looking down on her – vast brand icons, hanging in the sky. But there had always been six of them. The Pantheon always communicated a sense of choice, even if it was a limited one. The face that hung before her now, looking down from the apex of the pyramid, offered nothing but itself, on its own terms, for ever.

The eyes were cold blue jewels, wrapped around with gold bands. Each band was studded with multi-coloured crystals. White and green and red flared out, bright points in the two sunken sockets. The skin was a pale mesh, material that looked as if it had once been white but was now yellow. A bone pushed it out between and below the eyes, implying a nose. A flower-shaped diadem of red, green and white jewels, held together by another gold band, covered the space where the nostrils would have been. Sharp cheekbones cast dark shadows, hiding the hinge where the jawbone connected with the skull.

The mesh covered the mouth. There were no lips, just a series of small arches where yellow bone became white teeth. Its forehead was wreathed with golden leaves. A barbed halo of jagged gold spikes leapt up behind them, running all the way round the back of the head. The neck was invisible – there was just a glimmer of gold and red in the darkness beneath the sharp, protruding chin. Two shoulders, wrapped in gold brocade and studded with jewels, spiked jaggedly up. The image faded out beneath them. Leila imagined a rib cage, skeletal arms and hands, a waist and leg wrapped in more rich, dense, highly decorated clothing. It was all the wealth and power that had ever died in the past, alive and incarnate in the present.

'Fucking hell,' breathed Leila. 'It's like the richest sweathead you've ever seen.'

'Deodatus...' whispered the Caretaker.

'It has to be,' agreed Cassiel. 'Didn't Cormac think he might be a mind? The first one taken by the pit? That creature definitely started as a human.' She almost sounded relieved.

Leila stared up at it. 'Doesn't look very human anymore.' She turned to the Caretaker. 'Bringing anything back?'

'No,' replied the Caretaker. 'Which to be honest, I'm quite glad about. I don't want to have that in my head.' He shuddered visibly. 'Poor guy. Looks like he's been dead for a thousand years.' He looked around the rest of the room. 'I can't fault his design skills, though.'

The rest of the room was transformed. The laser was now a thing of beauty, a brilliant, minimalist sculpture of ruby and white-painted metal. The rickety scaffolding was a labyrinth of gleaming poles, pale pine walkways and carefully enclosed ladders and stairways. The rough stonework of the walls had been bleached pale, giving it a subtle, clean, post-industrial elegance. A sunburst of colour-coded paths radiated out from the laser, guiding workers to equipment and supply stacks at the edges of the open space. The white floor gleamed. Taken together, it all implied a simple, perfect, unquestionable rightness.

'It looks just like the Shining City,' said Leila.

'This is a suburb,' replied Cassiel. 'A little further down and we'll be at its heart.'

The fallen minds had changed too. The flies were invisible. Each of them presented as a pressure man, a different version of the past overseeing a potentially radical transformation of the present. The workers toiled on as before. They had become more perfect versions of themselves. Faces shone with blank geometries of beauty. All wore pastel linens, draped around them to reveal the perfect proportions of their bodies. Replacement body parts became pale, minimalist sculptures, their beautiful practicality shining with a seamless blend of utility and wealth. They moved effortlessly through their workspace, blending together into a shining dance of tasked fulfilment. Leila looked round for the dead one, curious to see how he'd been remade. He was invisible, blanked out by the weave.

'They look just like the sleepers in the Shining City,' she observed.

'They are identical,' replied Cassiel. 'Do you think Dieter woke them?'

'I suppose he must have done,' said Leila. 'This must be his army.' She paused for a moment, puzzled. 'But all this – it looks like it's been going on for a long time. And he's only had Kedrov and the Pornomancer's weaveselves for a couple of days.'

'You can ask him about it when you find him,' Cassiel replied briskly. 'Right now, we have to keep moving.' She pointed towards the sloping passage that led down to the room below. 'That's our next stop.'

'It's a long way down,' said the Caretaker. 'How do we get there?'

'Simple,' replied Cassiel. 'First, we turn off the local weave. We need to see the truth of things again...' Deodatus and his false paradise vanished. Once again, they were looking out over fly-blown corruption. 'Then we wait for a few seconds.'

'What for?' asked Leila.

'You'll see.' Cassiel reached an arm towards the Caretaker, pulling him close against her.

'What the fuck?' he complained. 'Cassiel, I can't move!' Then her hand covered his mouth and he couldn't speak either.

A low boom echoed down from high above them. Every fallen mind stopped, their corrupted heads turned up towards it. A moment's silence, then there was a series of increasingly loud crashes, pounding out from the opposite side of the pyramid. One final crunching thump, then a cloud of dust rose up from somewhere behind the laser. As one, the minds ran, vanishing behind it. The flies swarmed with them. The workers carried on as before, completely oblivious.

'What is that?' asked Leila.

'My distraction,' replied Cassiel. She held up a hand. 'Nanogel holds a lot of energy. I left a little of myself behind some loose blocks. Sent a detonate command, and boom! We've got an avalanche. Now, get ready to move fast.'

Leila only had time to say 'What...' before Cassiel reached up, grabbed the iron ring with her free hand, and pushed them all out of the passage and into empty space.

They plummeted towards the ground. Leila screamed. There was muffled howling from the Caretaker. Then, instant deceleration, and Cassiel was landing on two feet, the Caretaker staggering next to her, a long thin strand of nanogel falling back into her shoulder and becoming her arm again. 'Run,' she ordered and they hurtled towards the passageway, Cassiel half pulling, half supporting the Caretaker.

'Someone'll see us!' gasped Leila.

They passed a worker. It didn't register them. 'Nobody's looking,' replied Cassiel. Then the ground sloped, then they were halfway down the passageway, the Caretaker spluttering, Cassiel sprinting with sure-footed confidence.

'What about the guards?'

'Checking out the avalanche.' They burst out into the lower room. Leila had a brief impression of more spotlights and a circle of dark rectangles. Cassiel pulled them through a door and into a smaller store room. The Caretaker bent over, gasping. Leila turned to Cassiel.

'And just how are we going to get out again?'

'They'll sweep the exterior, find no one there. Take them ten minutes or so. Then they'll run an internal search. Just to be sure. But that's enough time for us to break that.' She nodded back out into the main room. 'And if Redonda's right, that'll shut them all down.'

'I hope my past is worth it,' puffed the Caretaker as he pulled himself back together. 'All this just to find out I'm some vacant old bore would really piss me off.'

They looked back out at the main room. It was empty but for a circle of twelve vast, rectangular servers, lit by more tripod-mounted spotlights. The units were equally spaced, forming a round henge. Age had written itself across their casings, pitting and corroding them. The spotlights forced shadows across them. Leila thought of the broken skin of the pyramid. The trilithons looked as old, if not older.

'The tunnel's been cleared,' noted Cassiel. 'The fallen minds must have found the servers down there, brought them out and started them up.'

All were active. Lights flickered across each one. A low, steady hum poured out of them, reminding Leila of the soft drone of fly swarms.

'They must hold the Shining City,' said Leila. 'Dieter's in there.'

'And once we've shut them down, that's it. The corruption wiped out. Deodatus and the fallen minds neutralised. Victory.'

'I'm going in before you turn them off,' said Leila firmly. 'I'll find Dieter and get him out.'

'You're sure you'll be able to persuade him to come with you?'

Leila squeezed the pendant. 'I've got his true past ready to push back into him. That's all I need.'

'I'm going in there too,' added the Caretaker.

'Are you sure?' Cassiel asked. 'Much easier if you don't.'

'Dude,' replied the Caretaker. 'She's got to find her brother. And I've got to find myself.'

Cassiel sighed. 'OK. I'll give you five minutes. Then I'm cutting the power cables and shutting it down. I'll stay out here and keep an eye on things. Any trouble beforehand, I'll warn you. And you'll need to crash out of there as quickly as you can. Now, let's take a proper look at it…'

The room shifted before them as she brought the weave back up. Floor, ceilings and walls shimmered into whiteness, becoming a perfect vision of white marble. The servers vanished. In their place was a small, round temple, simple pillars supporting a perfectly proportioned dome. It gleamed whitely. Leila was reminded of a particular persistent advert for dental treatment that had done the rounds a couple of years back, of the way it reduced happiness to a pure, shining smile. The temple radiated the same reduced perfection, implying a world so simply perfect that nothing could ever go wrong.

'We'll soon crack that,' Leila said. She called the cuttlefish into being. It shot over to hover in front of the temple. She felt a sudden, deep affection for it. It had come from her brother, passed through one of his closest friends and now lived within her. It was almost family. It squirted information back at her. 'Same security as the pit that Ambrose and I fell down. We'll be in there in seconds.'

'Get ready,' Cassiel told the Caretaker. 'Leave your body in the store room.' The Caretaker moved into its far corner and sat down. 'See you in there,' he called out to Leila, then closed his eyes. His head tipped forward as his weave systems reached out, winding up to create a virtual version of him and write it into the Shining City. A moment, and it appeared. 'Good to go,' he said. He waved his hand around a little. 'I quite like being a ghost.'

The cuttlefish pinged Leila. 'We're in,' she said, then, to the Caretaker: 'Let's go.'

'Five minutes,' warned Cassiel as they approached the temple. Leila set an internal timer going. The Caretaker peered at his watch.

As they approached it, they saw that the view beyond it had changed. The other side of the white room was no longer visible.

Instead, there was a dark sky, scudded over with white clouds. Long, low buildings shone down a wide empty avenue, curving away to the right. A tower climbed up and out of sight. The landscape stretched far into the distance, mausoleum pale. There were sleepers too, dark masses scattered across the streets.

'So let's go,' said Leila. She squeezed the pendant one last time for good luck, then stepped into the Shining City.

Chapter 31

The city's air was cold and still. Leila took a deep breath and felt its chill touch fill her. She was lying on the floor, gasping. The rotunda had looked like a stable portal into the city, but when she'd stepped into it she'd fallen as she'd fallen down through the black pit at the heart of Mikhail's chamber. There was the same vast, rushing roar howling in her ears, the same lurch in her deep self as gravity took her and snatched her down. She dry-heaved again, and then rolled on to her back. The coldness of the stone was a mercy, shocking her back into herself. The worst of it seemed to be over. She sat up. She was on her own. Leila queried the cuttlefish. The Caretaker had entered the portal with her, then vanished. *Maybe his avatar's still buffering*, she thought. There was no time to worry about him. At worst, he'd have dropped back into his body and would now be lying next to Cassiel, swearing. She told the cuttlefish to locate Dieter. While it rummaged through local log files, looking for traces of her brother, she glanced around.

She stood on a broad, sharply curving boulevard. The white buildings along it were simply styled, emanating an absolute mathematical harmony. The pavements and road were full of sleepers. To her right, a tall, elegant tower lifted up into the darkness with needle sharpness. Deodatus hung before it, his ancient face gazing down on the city. She wondered if the image would have time to react when the servers were turned off. Perhaps he'd flicker and, along with the city, just disappear. Perhaps his dead mouth would open and scream. But for now, he was all serene control. It comforted her profoundly to know that he would soon be shut down.

The cuttlefish was still looking for Dieter. She moved over to inspect one of the sleepers. It was a man. His body was beautifully proportioned. He wore a pastel chiton, identical to the ones the idealised laser workers had. A small blanket covered his head. She lifted it up. A face gazed up, as pale and emptily beautiful as the moon above. She let the blanket fall again. He slept on, his chest rising and falling in the perpetual night.

The cuttlefish nuzzled her. It had found Dieter. It was also flashing confusion, requesting permission to double-check the Shining City's location. Error codes she didn't fully understand seemed to hint at some sort of geo-spatial anomaly. Leila agreed, then told it to jump her to her brother.

The world changed and there he was, concentrating hard in his circular workshop.

She'd watched him work so often. For an instant, memories overwhelmed her. She remembered him as a child, infuriating their mother by taking apart every piece of tech they owned to see how it worked, then as a teenager, recreating the same cluttered workspace in squat after squat. She remembered the tools he'd built to heal her. And she saw him as he now was, still beavering away, believing that she'd rejected her afterlife and let herself die a true death. She fingered the locket at her throat. The memories that would restore the true past to him shifted within her.

'It'll work,' she reassured herself. 'He'll come back with me.'

Little had changed since her last visit to this space. The two low couches were still in the centre of the room. But the original Deodatus victims were gone. Instead, the rapidly-assembled fetches of his new victims shimmered on them. Each lay still, apparently unconscious. Memories of the Pornomancer's death agonies and of Kedrov's desiccated body ran through Leila's mind. Whatever else was happening, it was a relief to see both of them lying dormant, if not entirely at peace.

Dieter moved between them, blurring between different versions of himself. He was adjusting transparent, flexible pipes that ran into the back of each of their heads. The pipes soared up and disappeared into a globe of dark black-blue liquid. It looked like a drop of deep ocean tossed up by a storm and suspended in midair. It was about the same size as the exercise balls Leila used to bounce around on at the gym. When she focused on it, it seemed to expand, filling her field of vision then stretching into her mind. It was the raw stuff of memory, dense with the life experiences of Kedrov and the

216

Pornomancer. To help Leila heal, Dieter had created a similar ball of his own memories, making it easier for her to draw on them as needed.

But why these two? she wondered. *And what for?*

Dieter had said he was raising an army for Deodatus. But the pyramid looked like it was already well supplied with workers, and had been for a long time. And in any case, it was difficult to see how memories of vastly acquisitive art collection and production line sex could help create more of them. She thought back to the previous two victims – a professional eater and a military psychiatrist with a developed interest in torture – and wondered about them, too.

But time was pressing. Leila needed to reclaim her brother for herself. She let him see her.

'Fuck!' said Dieter. A spanner dropped from his fuzzed hand. It hit the floor and rang out an echoing clatter. 'Leila. What are you doing here?' His voice skipped between different versions of itself, as if it had been run through a broken auto tuner.

'I've come to get you out of here. And sort this mess out.'

'But you're dead.' He looked flabbergasted.

Leila stepped forwards and put a hand on his shoulder. Her other hand gripped the locket at her throat. She tugged and it came away. She held it tight in her fist. 'No,' she said. 'You've been lied to. Deodatus rewrote your memories of me. I didn't kill myself. We were together in the same flat for two years. Until that fucking box screwed you up.'

Disbelief and shock rang through him. 'No,' he said.

'You succeeded, Dieter. You healed me and you helped me live.' She thought of her own experience of being rewritten. 'Look back into your past. There'll be discontinuities. Jagged edges, where memories are missing.'

'It's so painful,' he said softly, to himself as much as her. He put his hand on hers and let it rest there for a moment. Then he pulled it away from his shoulder and stepped back. 'Gods,' he said, and his voice had a torn quality to it. 'Deodatus told me the Pantheon might construct a version of you to use against me. I never thought they'd stoop that low.' He stumbled back, resting against the end of Kedrov's bench. He couldn't look at Leila. 'Please, go. Just go.'

'Dieter, it's me. I'm real. Far more real than anything in this bloody place. You must remember what they did to people, how they rewrote them.' She wanted to grab him and shake him. 'That's what this place – what Deodatus – has done to you. All this – it's just a Kneale Pit. A broken bit of history that's still screwing people over. Nothing more.'

To Leila's surprise, Dieter laughed. 'Kneale Pit?' His unfocused face smiled, and an entire history of his joy raced past her. The smile held the innocent joy of a ten-year-old, then the focused confidence of a brilliant twenty-something, then the stoned bliss of a teenager experimenting with his first high. 'Oh, this isn't a Kneale Pit, Leila. This is the real deal.'

Her timer pinged. Time was running out. 'It's destroying you.' She shifted the pendant in her hands. Its dense weight reassured her. 'And it's going to destroy Station. When the laser fires, it'll crack the Wart open. And that'll be the end of everything.'

'Bless you, Leila,' said Dieter gently. 'I always had to explain things to you, didn't I? It's not that at all.'

'Oh for gods' sake, Dieter. Don't be so bloody patronising. I'm not a little girl anymore. I'm here to save you.'

He smiled. 'You're not rescuing me. I'm rescuing everyone on Station. From the Pantheon. From a past that's a lie and a failure. And from a society that kills the dead.' He smiled again, this time so very sadly. 'That's why they've sent you to try and stop me. My weakest link. Here you are, and it's working. I can't even bring myself to call security on you.'

That last comment heartened Leila. Perhaps she was getting through to him. 'I'm your strongest link,' she replied gently. 'I'm not a lie. I'm the way things really were.' She wondered exactly how much memory they'd taken. 'Do you remember the last time I saw you?'

'Just before you – my sister – chose a true death?' Pain leapt across his face. 'Of course I do. Don't talk to me about that.'

Now it was Leila's turn to smile sadly. 'No. In this room. A few days ago. Ambrose and I came to find you.' She wondered whether to mention Ambrose's death. But Dieter might refuse to believe her. 'Deodatus wiped it out of your memory. He's taken so much from you.' She held up the pendant. 'I've come to give it all back. This'll transfer the last two years to you. Highlights of our lives together.'

'And where did you get these memories from?'

'Dit.'

'So you've even found him? The gods must have turned my life upside down. No wonder you're so well briefed.' Cynicism infected his smile. 'I hope he put up a fight.'

The timer pinged again, more urgently.

'Dieter. IT'S ME. I am Leila, I am your sister, I have always been your sister and I always will be. And we have to get you out of here.' She threw caution to the winds. 'A couple more minutes and we're turning off the servers. The ones that hold this place. We're deactivating the Shining City.'

'That won't touch the Shining City. The server henge is a gateway. A portal. Nothing else.' He laughed bitterly. 'You've got all the way down here – and that's a long, long way from Station. You say it's your second visit. And you're telling me you don't know where you really are? What this place really is?' His voice became hard, dismissive. 'You're working the naivety thing too hard. Even my sister would have got that by now.'

The timer pinged a final warning. Thirty seconds left. 'Fuck it,' said Leila. She jumped, appearing right next to him. 'You can finish patronising me later,' she said, then raised her hand. 'Once you've remembered who I really am.' Then she pushed the pendant against his forehead, triggering the memory injection.

'No!' he howled.

Memories exploded out towards him. Leila wasn't quite sure what she expected to happen next – the brief disorientation that Dit had predicted, a sudden transformation, Dieter turning to her and at last acknowledging the truth of his situation. And then they would flee together.

Instead, defences leapt into being.

'Oh no,' she breathed.

The link between them vanished and the data transfer slammed to a halt. Leila felt the memory block Dit had given her shatter as a cold, hard, alien presence smashed through it and tried to push into her mind. Her own shields snapped into place and the counter-attack bounced off them, but not before it had stabbed out and erased her copy of Dit's memories. Then, there was nothing but chaos.

'FUCK!' yelled Dieter.

He strobed through multiple versions of himself, static glitching his whole body. His image generators crashed and rebooted, pulling him out of then back into existence. 'UCKUCKUCKUFFFFF,' he howled, his voice a series of cracked, broken repetitions. As his avatar broke down the artificial in him overwhelmed all else, and his living self was lost.

'NO!' screamed Leila. She tried to pull her brother to her but her arms went through him. 'Shit,' she said, looking around desperately. 'Shit, shit, shit.' Dieter's voice had become an abstract digital howl. She remembered the last time she'd been here – pressure men bursting through the door, surfing a wave of flies. Soon they'd come again.

But someone else arrived first.

'Hey there,' drawled the Caretaker, dropping into being. 'Here you are.'

'I've broken Dieter,' she gasped, panicked.

Dieter gave one last howl and winked out of existence.

'Gods. He's dead.'

'No, that just looked like an emergency shut down. No biggie.'

Leila's alarm hit zero and howled.

'Oh, and don't worry about Cassiel crashing the city,' he reassured her as she hushed the alarm. 'I don't think she can. Turns out Cormac Redonda don't know shit about this place.'

Leila noticed a gentle buzzing. Dark insects orbited him.

'No.' She started backing away. 'You've fallen. You're one of them.'

'What? Oh, the little guys.' He chuckled. 'No way, Leila. These aren't flies. They're bees.' A huge, confident smile. 'Much more my scene.'

'What are you?' breathed Leila.

'Still working that one out.' The Caretaker looked up, as if listening. 'Shit. Cassiel's got problems. Here...' He held his hand out. 'Come with me.'

'We can't leave without Dieter.'

'We'll find another way to reach him. And without us, Cassiel's in deep shit.' Yellow-black insects buzzed lazily around them. One of them was perched on his shoulder. Another nestled by his ear. He saw her looking at them. 'You see? Bees. They're pretty cool. But we really need to go. If Cassiel goes down and we get caught, you won't be able to do shit for your brother.'

One last glance around the room. No sign of Dieter. The Caretaker was right. There was no other choice. She took his hand. The Shining City vanished.

They were in the store room again. 'Welcome back,' said Cassiel. 'About bloody time. I cut the power cables to the servers, but they have an internal back-up. I was getting ready to blow them up.'

'That won't make any difference,' replied Leila. 'They don't hold the Shining City. Dieter said they were just a gateway. To somewhere very far from here.'

'Then we're screwed.'

And then there was a buzzing roar and a storm of flies burst through the arch. Fallen minds were just visible behind them, hurtling in to attack. Leila felt fear explode out of Cassiel. There was a vast shame, too, and a deep, anguished sense of loss. Leila felt empathy fill her. She understood the mind's despair. She'd failed to rescue Dieter and lost the key that would unlock his true past.

'Yeah, whatever,' said the Caretaker. 'I've got this.' He reached a hand out. The flies stopped and hung in the air for a second, and then gravity took them and they were a thousand black raindrops pattering to the floor.

Cassiel tossed Leila's disc to him. Lightning filled her. She howled with savage joy and was on the fallen minds like a weaponised demon.

Chapter 32

Two of Cassiel's opponents fell at the door, their bodies collapsing into liquid and splashing to the ground. Three went down behind her as she moved into the main room. More staggered towards her, not quite recovered from the swarm's crash. Cassiel moved through them, a martial blur, and they were a shower of nanogel drops tumbling through space.

'Whoa,' said the Caretaker.

'No wonder she's been so frustrated, if she can do that,' replied Leila, awed.

Cassiel came to a halt. The rest of the minds pulled back, wary now that their fellows had fallen.

The Caretaker joined her. 'You just keep back,' he called out. 'All's cool, just keep back.' He turned to Cassiel and whispered: 'I can zap the flies. But not the minds.'

A moment, then one of them stepped forwards. It moved awkwardly but its voice was clear. 'Our victory is certain,' it called. 'You have an avatar of Mandala, but his powers are limited here. And we outnumber you.'

'Who's Mandala?' whispered Leila.

'Er, I think that's my real name,' replied the Caretaker, sounding a bit embarrassed.

'We believe that the fetch Leila Fenech is with you,' the mind continued. 'Deodatus wishes to talk with her. He has an offer to make her. She can be of great service. Her co-operation will help us manage her brother, sparing him any further pain. And it will benefit you, too. If you surrender her to us, we will remove your memories of Deodatus and let you both go. Unharmed.'

'They can't see me,' hissed Leila. 'They're not sure if I'm here. If it was really me looking for Dieter.'

'Let's keep them confused,' replied Cassiel. Then she called out: 'That wasn't Fenech. It was a weapon that failed.'

'Surrender. You have no choice.'

'And then the Totality will fall. And Station too,' shot back Cassiel.

'Fuck that,' said Leila. 'Can we fight our way out?'

'The fallen mind's right,' hissed Cassiel. 'There are too many of them. Victory is uncertain.'

As she spoke, a high wailing began, reaching out from the passageway that led back up to the room above. There was the sound of running feet, a bare slapping that threatened an invasive rush.

'We don't fight, we run,' said the Caretaker. He nodded towards the unblocked tunnel. 'We're going that way.' He set off, still holding his hand out towards the minds. 'Or at least, I am.'

The howling grew louder and louder.

'He's right,' said Leila.

'Agreed,' the mind snapped, already moving. 'Opening my mind to you. We need to stay as close as possible to get through this.' Leila felt new connections grow between them as Cassiel gave her deep access to the workings of her consciousness. Leila opened herself up in return.

'You're worried,' said Cassiel.

'No map beyond here,' replied Leila. 'Could be a dead end.'

'It's not,' said the Caretaker. He glanced back as he entered the tunnel: 'Holy shit!' he gasped.

Leila looked back with him. A storm of sweatheads exploded out of the passageway, knocking into and scrabbling over each other in their eagerness to attack. The first two or three toppled and fell and those behind piled into them, falling over themselves, creating a great, tumbled crush at the bottom of the stairs. Wooden and plastic attachments bounced across the floor, revealing absences where eyes and cheeks, noses and ears, and even hands and feet had once been. The rest of the crowd slowed and clambered over them. A broken, rhythmic wheeze coughed out from them. Mouths were open, chests were heaving, dry tongues rattled like pebbles against yellow teeth.

'FUUUUUCCCKKKK!!!!' yelled the Caretaker as he took off down the tunnel.

223

Cassiel sprinted behind him. She leapt on to the wall as she passed him, letting her body spread out into a rushing animal shape, barely looking back. Leila felt the mind's desperate hope for escape. And there was deep pain, too, at the possibility that their mission had failed. As she felt that thought, sadness and guilt once again shot through Leila. She'd found Dieter, but she'd only managed to wound him. And she had no idea where to go next, because she didn't know where the true location of the Shining City was.

With that, she remembered giving the cuttlefish permission to check out some problematic geo-spatial data. She queried it. Co-ordinates leapt into her mind, precisely pinning down the city's actual location. There were images too, taken from real world cameras surrounding the city. She looked at them, then looked again. She refused to believe what they told her. She asked the cuttlefish to double- then triple-check the city's location data. Its small, precise mind leapt to obey her, returning precisely the same conclusions each time. There was no possibility of error. Leila was stunned. She found that she couldn't speak.

She barely noticed as the Caretaker stumbled and nearly fell, and Cassiel stopped, and reached back, and swept him up in an arm that became a nanogel band wrapped round his chest. The howling from behind them, now becoming louder again, made little impact on her. The corridor ended in another round room. Five tunnels led out of it. There was also small platform, with narrow gauge rails running alongside it, and a tiny engine, about as high as her waist, attached to several coffin-shaped goods trucks.

That did surprise her.

'What the fuck?' said Cassiel, also momentarily astonished.

'Even the bad guys need a transport system,' gasped the Caretaker. 'Lots of tunnels down here. Too much walking. That train'll take us down the right one.'

'How do you know?'

'A bee told me.' More howling behind them. 'Let's move!'

The Caretaker leapt into one of the trucks. Cassiel threw herself into the one behind the engine and the train shook. She shot an arm forward and smashed it into the control panel. The train jerked forward, then stopped. Cassiel groped around the panel again, her touch softer this time, and the train started up. Their pursuers burst out on to the platform as it accelerated.

One of them leapt for the last truck, stumbled and fell, tumbling back off the platform and on to the tracks. Electricity sizzled through its shaking body. Another accelerated past it, and – with a final burst of speed – hurled itself off the end of the platform and into the final truck. An instant, then it reared up, dead mouth roaring with a savage joy, a sledgehammer firm in its hands. It raced towards them, leaping from truck to truck, cackling wildly, its eyes alive with glee. The others, left far behind, cheered it on from the platform.

The Caretaker was a few trucks down. It was going to reach him first. He glanced back at them.

'You can't hold it off,' shouted Cassiel. Leila felt her tense herself, ready to leap forward and stop their attacker.

'Relax,' said the Caretaker, still looking back at them. 'This fucker's dead already. He just doesn't know it yet.'

As he spoke, the sweathead reached the carriage behind his. It scrabbled for footing, then stood straight up, hefting the sledgehammer, its entire attention focused on its target. It started towards him just as something dark rushed over Leila's head. The little train's roar grew louder as walls squeezed in on either side. The tunnel had a low roof, and its lip took the sweathead like a hammer, smashing it backwards and away from them. It tumbled back down the little coaches, its upper half a bloody smear, and then fell past their edge and out of the side. The train shook as hard wheels rolled over it, then there was just the rattle of forward motion.

'Not very bright, those guys,' said the Caretaker.

'Thank the gods,' breathed Leila.

'I'd have stopped him,' said Cassiel. 'He'd never have touched you.'

A moment to get her breath back, then Leila said: 'Now we're a bit safer, there's something you guys need to see.' She pumped the information out to Cassiel and the Caretaker. A moment, then shock rippled out of the mind.

'THAT'S IMPOSSIBLE.'

'I know. But it's real.'

'Ouch. This makes my head hurt,' groaned the Caretaker.

Cassiel ignored him. 'You've checked this?' she asked Leila. 'You're sure?'

'This is what it found. So far outside normal parameters that it triggered a full local audit. The geo-location and image systems passed. And then I had it re-run all tests twice. There's no doubt that it's real.' She took a moment to let it sink in. 'East'll never put that in her documentary.'

Then she brought the pictures up to hang in front of them. There was a whole series of images, taken from a single camera panning across a landscape. They had a blurred, out of focus quality to them. Colours were pale and muted. Leila thought of spinelights fading as evening approached; the way that, slowly and inevitably, shadows conquered Station. These pictures showed another world half-lost to darkness.

At first glance, the images were very mundane. There was a city, and it was built from tower blocks. The blocks were arranged in circles of seven or eight buildings, connected by walkways and scaffolding. Leila assumed each group must be an individual housing estate or business unit. The buildings were all battered, blasted by climate and time. Soft lights glowed within them. Machineries clustered in the murk at the base of each building – long, narrow struts that looked like tumbled cranes. They made her think of the flies, of their dark little stop-motion legs. There was something like the edge of a mountain in the background of some of the pictures. Others showed a tall, thin, construction, about a hundred metres high, looking more like an antenna than a building. It glowed with dirty purple light. The building clusters vanished into the distance behind it. And, far beyond them, there were those two impossible things – a flat horizon that bisected the image and a dark sky, suffused with clouds.

The ancient city had no comforting curve to it, no streets that reached up to left and to right to join far above in the sky, as Docklands or Homelands had. This was not Station, and it couldn't have been Mars, or Venus, for there were no cities of this scale on either planet. It couldn't have been the Moon, for the light was not hard and uncompromising, blazing down from a black vacuum sky. It wasn't the Shining City, because it was hard and real and unidealised. It could only be Earth, long abandoned to the wrath of machines and the dreams of dead gods.

'Do you recognise any of this?' Leila asked the Caretaker. 'Now that your memory's coming back?'

He shook his head, looking pained. 'The bees told me about the tunnels and showed me how to zap the flies – but this – I just don't know. They asked me if I wanted more memories pasted into my head. I said yes – but. It's all so confused, too new to properly understand. It's going to take a bit of time to put it all together.'

Leila nodded. 'The quicker the better,' she told him. She turned back to Cassiel. 'Redonda was so wrong. I mean – it's not his fault. Nobody could have guessed – this.'

'The data could be manipulated,' said Cassiel.

'The cuttlefish's triple-checked the images. And they're all marked with Deodatus tags. They were taken by one of his cameras. And he's on Earth.'

'Are they time stamped?'

'Twenty minutes ago. How can they even link down there?'

'Oh, that's easy enough,' sighed Cassiel. 'All you need is some sort of high-power comms array. Laser or maser, it doesn't make much difference. It'll punch through the clouds to the Earth's surface without any problems. The Rose polices all that, so with Deodatus controlling her it's easy enough for him to set up.' Cassiel sounded exhausted. 'We must recalibrate. We thought we were dealing with something small. A Kneale Pit that got out of hand. But this is a different order of problem. A hole that leads all the way down to Earth, and a god older and more aggressive than anything we've known who's climbed all the way back up it.'

'Fuck.' Leila was terrified. But there was awe there, too. For so long, Earth had been a ghost planet, a story used to frighten children. All that remained of it were the broken relics that so fascinated Dieter, Ambrose and Cormac, implying an unreachable past. Now near-live images of it hung in front of her. 'No wonder Dieter fell to Deodatus. How could he resist?'

Cassiel ignored her. 'This is what the Pantheon have been scared of for centuries.' She sighed. 'And they were right. We were too short-sighted to even consider it.' Despair filled her voice. Leila felt it pulse through her mind. 'The Totality has never faced a threat like it. He will enslave us once again.' She pointed at the purple-glowing tower that appeared in some of the images. 'And that's the heart of the corruption. A snowflake, landed on Earth. Reduced by the fires of its fall. The fallen minds must have let gravity catch it. That's what's poisoning my people.'

'How did Deodatus call one of them down there in the first place?'

'He must have taken control of it somehow.' She sighed. 'The Pantheon never managed that. We're fighting something very powerful. I'm not sure we can even win.'

Leila, however, had already died twice. She felt that knowledge surge within her. As the train began to slow, it galvanised her. She remembered Dieter, breaking as she touched him. The memories had been worse than useless. And now they were lost to her. *I'll find another way of reaching him. I'll get him out.*

'Of course we can,' she told Cassiel. 'We've got everything we need to go after Deodatus. We know who he is and where he's based. We can shut down his fly swarms.' The Caretaker nodded. 'And we've got you. I'm sure you can get into that snowflake and break it. Damn it, Cassiel, we thought it would be nice and easy – unplug a server, beat up some fallen minds, leave something fun for the gun kiddies. It's not. Tough. We're going to get out of here. We're going to put Deodatus back in the box he crawled out of. And I'll rescue Dieter and you'll save the Totality. Even if we have to go all the way back down to Earth.'

'That's impossible. How are we going to find a vehicle capable of an Earth landing? And even if we do, the Rose controls all access. She'll never let us through.'

'Fuck's sake Cassiel, the Caretaker and I have visited Earth without even realising it! We'll find a way down again. We have to. Or would you rather let Deodatus win?'

Cassiel was silent.

The train rattled out of the tunnel and into a large open space. A long platform loomed out of the darkness, lit by a single tripod-mounted spotlight. 'This is our stop,' said the Caretaker.

Cassiel slowed the train. 'Another dark, empty room. How marvellous.'

The Caretaker nodded towards the platform. 'If we want a way out, then this is where we get off.' He smiled at Cassiel. 'Going to solve your transport problem for you.'

The train came to a jerky halt. There was a moment's near-silence, the only sounds the hiss of releasing hydraulic brakes and the descending whine of electric engines powering down.

'Now,' Leila said to the Caretaker. 'Where have you brought us to?'

'The escape hatch,' replied the Caretaker. 'This is an evil lair, right? And you don't build one of those without giving your top guys a way out. That's what we're headed for.'

An identity query hit them. There was a soft, descending whistle, repeated three times. It came from the end of the platform. Two squat, heavy bipeds, carved out of nanogel, studded with flies, loomed towards them out of the darkness. An open pressure door was just visible behind them. The room beyond it glowed a soft purple.

'Guards?' asked Leila.

'Combat specialists.' Cassiel sang back a reply to them. 'I just told them to go fuck themselves.'

Then she was a fluid blur, leaping over the side of the truck and loping towards them. Deep satisfaction pulsed out of her as a mesh of combat systems booted into being. The termination mission was reassuringly simple, the experience and capabilities that made it so trusted and well tried.

'Come back!' shouted Leila, then: 'Be careful' when it was clear that Cassiel was ignoring her.

A voice leaped back towards her. 'This is what I do,' it said. 'Let me do it.'

That was the last human-level communication that reached her. Then, there was nothing but hard, rapid calculations, reducing the two guards to a series of physical and digital problems waiting to be solved.

'And off she goes,' said the Caretaker.

'She's scared,' replied Leila, 'and this is therapy. Can you help her at all?'

'No.' He smiled ruefully. 'Minds are still a mystery to me. By the

way, that thing you guys were talking about – a Totality snowflake
– what is it exactly?

'They're how minds travel through space. Ice, metal and nanogel
structures, with propulsion and power systems bolted on to them.
Shaped like giant snowflakes, hence the name.'

'Ah, that's one mystery solved.'

'And you're a bit less of one. You're called Mandala.'

The Caretaker nodded.

'Has anything else come through yet?'

'Like I said, it's coming together.' He ran a hand through his hair,
a thoughtful look on his face. 'The bees gave me a lot of information,
but it's a bit of a jumble. I'll tell you when I've worked it all out. I do
know this place very well, though. We're right where we need to be
to get the hell out of here.'

Chapter 33

Leila watched the combat with the Caretaker, perceiving it on multiple levels. Visually, there was little but a purple blur, three nanogel bodies spinning together in a dance so complex and quick that the Caretaker's senses could barely keep up. Seen through his eyes, the spinning purple forms left trails behind themselves, ghost images of past movements. They made Leila feel that she was witnessing shapes carved in time as well as space – memories made concrete.

Every so often there would be a connection, and one of the three would stagger and drop back, and the locus of the battle would shift. Then the maelstrom resumed. Leila felt the action of Cassiel's mind as she fought. The vast pleasure of summoning well-worn, secure skills suffused all levels of her consciousness.

First of all, there was the work that memory did, shaping present attacks by playing back fragments of the past. Upcoming movements pulsed through Cassiel's mind, giving Leila the uncanny feeling that she was witnessing moments plucked from the future, as each one so perfectly anticipated a manoeuvre to come.

Beneath that higher level of struggle there was one that was deeper and more instinctive. Cassiel's intrusion systems battered her opponents. She held in herself a storehouse of damage – code weapons built to corrupt operating systems, purge entire skill sets, crash primary and secondary consciousness elements and force full factory resets on entire live minds.

These imps leapt to the attack, dense with invisible fury. At first, all died. She kept pumping out generation after generation, altering each new one according the feedback the last had hurled back. Each new wave broke that little bit deeper into its victims' defences, until at last the fallen minds shuddered and started to break apart.

When the guards finally fell, they went quickly. Complexity

collapsed into a random jumble of electrical impulses, then fell away into a silence as complete as it was final. The guards dropped into liquid form, leaving only a sticky ooze behind them.

A fierce, competent joy pulsed through Cassiel's mind. Her close quarter combat systems folded themselves away. Leila thought of claws withdrawing back into flesh, of bloodied teeth disappearing into a closing mouth as a soft pink tongue licked them clean.

'That was pretty impressive,' commented the Caretaker as he struggled out of the train. 'I'd say you were back to being one hundred per cent ninja.' He chuckled. 'I can start being a pacifist again.'

'As long as you keep the flies down,' Cassiel told him.

'I'll teach you the trick of it, when we've got a moment.'

'Can you hear that?' asked Leila. A distant sound – barely a whisper – echoed out of the tunnel behind them.

'Crap,' said the Caretaker. 'They're catching us up.'

Cassiel turned and listened. Her sharper ears heard a vast gabble, a collection of sounds that included howling and screaming and crying and barking.

'Sweatheads,' she said. 'Too many to fight. Run.'

The first sweatheads burst out of the tunnel behind them. They came on as a great onrush of flesh. Their add-ons sparkled in the dim light. There were so many of them. Some ran. Others scuttled along walls, the lightness of their desiccated bodies making it easy to find purchase. The lighter ones leapt across their fellows' heads and shoulders. They seemed to be a single entity, leaping out of the great burrow like a piston flying out of a cylinder.

Panic flooded the Caretaker. He scrambled to catch up with Cassiel. She'd already made it through the pressure door. He and Leila were close behind. As they leapt through it, Cassiel slammed it closed and spun its locking wheel. The wheel blurred, then thunked to a stop.

'Can they open it from the other side?' asked Leila.

Cassiel rammed a metal bar between its spokes, holding it closed. 'It'll take them a minute or so,' she replied. 'Now, where have you brought us?'

Broken monitor screens, decayed server stacks and collapsed

control consoles stretched away along one side of the room. They would have been a lifeless collage of dead technologies, but for the dense mass of purple ooze clotted within them. The blistered nano-gel pulsed with sickly life, rioting like an out-of-control infection.

'No flies,' said Leila.

'They're hiding them,' the Caretaker told her. 'Don't want to risk me breaking them. And there's our way out.' He pointed at the other end of the room. The wall was punctuated with a dozen round hatches. They looked freshly polished. 'Escape pods.' A small pile of abandoned body suits lay beneath them, bleached pale by age.

He started across the room and triggered the trap.

Cassiel reached out and pulled him back as the room exploded. Nanogel leapt from the walls, the ceilings, the floors, forming itself into dozens of biped attackers. The mass leapt towards them, and Cassiel was changing too, moving in the opposite direction – falling away from anything human, once again becoming a weapon. Scores of attackers, and so her mind ramped up to a velocity of response that burned Leila's thoughts. As she broke close contact with Cassiel, there was one final exchange.

'Not combat specialists. Knife through butter.'

The mind became a vicious blur, a series of attacks moving with the speed of thought, devastating her opponents. Ahead of her, there was a tsunami of nanogel aggressors. Behind there was only decay, her attackers melting away into nothing. The Caretaker and Leila followed her across the room, shielded by the fury of her attack. There was no longer anything remotely human about her. She moved through her attackers like time through a life, leaving absence behind.

'Yup, she's good,' whispered the Caretaker admiringly. 'Real good.'

It only took them a few seconds to reach the hatches. A vast bang echoed through the chamber, followed by a rhythmic thumping. The sweatheads had reached the pressure door. The metal rod groaned in the locking wheel.

Cassiel melted back into human form. 'The nanogel will reform in a couple of minutes.' It oozed towards the door. 'It's getting ready to merge with the sweatheads.'

'Be cool,' the Caretaker told them, sounding infinitely relaxed.

'I'm on it. You're safe.' He moved quickly down the hatches, inspecting them.

There was a few seconds silence, a vast crash. The door started to thump and groan under the pressure of the aggressors behind it.

'It won't hold for long,' warned Cassiel.

'We'll be gone by then,' replied the Caretaker, fiddling with a control panel. 'Grab one of the pressure suits. Bring it here.' Three of the hatches hissed open. 'Quickly!'

The hollow banging continued. Metal shrieked and groaned, protesting against terrible pressure. The Caretaker typed numbers into the control panel faster than she could read.

'What are you doing?' asked Leila.

'New coordinates,' he replied.

A long, low cracking sound echoed out into the room. The door shuddered. Cassiel stood by the Caretaker, holding up a pressure suit. He glanced away from the control panel, reached for the back of its neck and flicked a switch. The suit started to uncrumple itself.

'Drop it,' he hissed. The suit landed on two feet, lifting itself up into a human shape and swaying slightly as it finished expanding. 'There,' said the Caretaker. 'Leila – your new home.'

It was ancient. It looked like it had been stitched together from canvas and leather. The dry air had preserved it and the dust had penetrated it, turning it a soft reddish brown colour. The visor was fogged. The arm had a long, deep rip in it. Through it, Leila could see something hard and white – part of the suit's support structure, she assumed.

'It's built round a fully powered exo-skeleton,' explained the Caretaker. 'You should be able to mesh with it and control it without too much trouble. Your own body, at last. Cassiel – attach her.'

'But why do I need it?' asked Leila as Cassiel strapped her disc to the rear of the suit. She leapt into its control systems. The suit's sensors burst into action, creating a new version of the world for her. There were twin shoulder cameras, the world looking only lightly blurred through their dust-etched lenses. Not-quite-reliable auditory sensors turned voices into glitched, crackling recordings of themselves. A battery warning pinged and she felt the suit's systems start to drain power from her disc.

234

'We need to split up,' the Caretaker told her as three of the hatches opened. 'Journey's dangerous. Have to make sure at least one of us gets through. And even if we all make it we'll probably get separated on landing. Down there you need to be able to move under your own steam.'

'Down where?' asked Leila. But she knew. She just couldn't quite believe it.

Cassiel was peering through one of the open hatches. 'This is a planetary escape pod,' she said.

'She's got it,' beamed the Caretaker. 'It's like I told you. I'm sending us all the way back to Earth.' A worried look. 'If you guys are up for that, of course.'

Leila glanced at Cassiel. She nodded.

'Straight to Deodatus?'

'Oh no,' he said. 'Can't just go marching in, he'd catch you right away. You're coming back to my place.' He turned to Leila and looked somewhere between embarrassed and proud. 'All my new memories are starting to come together. Down there, I run a city of my own. And I'm a god.'

Chapter 34

Leila came to in darkness. Wind howled around her, flaying the suit with dust. She spun up its senses and opened its wi-fi, calling out first to the escape pod, then to Cassiel and the Caretaker. There was no response. She was lying on hard, cold, dry earth, face down. She rolled over, the wind snatching at her and almost sending her tumbling across the landscape. She grabbed with both hands, scrabbling to find purchase. There was a stone, firmly embedded. She pushed her feet into the ground. A moment, then she was secure.

It was strange to be touching the ground again – stranger still to be touching the rocks of Earth. She called the cameras into action and the world flickered into being. She cycled through their input modes. The camera's daylight setting showed only darkness. Macro seemed pointless. Infrared showed her multiple rapidly cooling heat sources scattered around her. The escape pod had shattered on impact. She looked up and around. In the distance there was a horizon, and above her there was sky. There could be no mistaking where she was. She acknowledged the space, then turned her mind away from it. It was all too vast to take in.

She thought about moving, but the wind was strong and she – a memory disc attached to a hollow vacuum suit – was light. Until the storm had blown itself out she decided to stay put, putting events back together in her mind. As she wiggled her feet a little further into the dust, she noticed that any movement sucked power from the disc's power reserves. Without the light of the sun falling on its solar panels, they could not recharge. She powered down the suit as much as possible, hoping that daylight would bring energy, then fell into the fractured past.

Her memories of the fall were chaotic. She teased out fragments and tried to fit them into sets. It was hard to make them cohere. There were the early ones – the Caretaker saying: 'One pod each.

We'll be in touch all the way, meet up again down there. You'll see.'
Her hatch closing, locking out danger. The pod's intercom buzzing
into life. Cassiel and the Caretaker confirmed that they were safe
in their own pods, then Leila replied and was heard. A moment of
relief, then the hatch's round window framed an entity that froze
Leila's memory.

The pressure door must have caved in. The nanogel had met
the sweatheads. They'd merged as a kind of tentacle, reaching out
across the room. Limbs emerged from a pulsing mass, moving in a
kind of grotesque, co-ordinated ballet. A dead face, smeared across
with purple, pressed itself against the window. It winked at her, then
vanished. Fists drummed against the glass, smearing it with nanogel
and blood. Leila pushed herself back into the escape pod, ready to
go out fighting if this new abomination broke through.

'All's good. Just a few seconds to eject. Handing over control to
Cassiel.' The Caretaker's voice – she knew him so well by that name,
it was impossible to think of him as Mandala – was a calm presence
on the intercom. A thump, and Leila's pod shifted a little. 'Almost,'
said Cassiel. She sounded completely in control. Then the three of
them were away. Leila had the satisfaction of seeing nanogel and
pale bodies explode out into the vacuum behind them.

The escape pod flew silently, but it had still been full of noise. The
suit's servo motors had a tiny mosquito whine. Something seemed
to have come loose inside it, bumping and rattling with every movement. Ancient auditory systems created white noise from nothing.
Glitches danced in her vision and crackled through her ears. Leila
did her best to ignore it all as she craned towards the pod's window,
watching Station spin away from her. Emotions shook through
her. There was awe and fear, excitement and dismay, optimism and
despair. Beyond the smeared glass, unreachably far away, her home
shrank down to nothing.

Cassiel's voice remained strong, whispering encouragement into
her ear. And there was the knowledge she shared too, flight and
systems management instructions that showed her how to assess
the progress of her small craft and be confident that all its systems
were functioning as they should. Station shrank to a bright pin-
prick of light, indistinguishable from the unreachable stars. Cassiel

helped her fall with confidence through the void. Leila found herself profoundly moved by this sudden, unexpected closeness, this communion in darkness. They stayed in touch through the upper atmosphere, as fire roared around their capsules, light blasting in and nearly blinding both of them. The capsules shook violently – 'to be expected,' said Cassiel, no stress in her voice. 'We're following our assigned flight path.' All three capsules' gravity management systems kicked in at the same moment – 'moving into a landing programme, heading for the upper cloud layer' – and the shaking vanished, then the fire.

The capsules decelerated fast. Leila felt the suit's cameras re-calibrate. There was a dark black-blue sky – they were falling on the night side – and beneath it a great, flat expanse of cloud, alive with constant flickers of blue and orange light. 'Lightning,' said Cassiel. 'Other weather effects. Nothing to worry about. We'll be through it in a second.' Seconds more and they were within the storm, brilliance dancing all around them. And that brilliance reached out to Leila, and suddenly, cruelly exposed the limits of Cassiel's control over their fall.

Memory fragmented.

There was a howling at the window, explosions, a sharp burning reek, sudden, random acceleration, and then the pod was throwing Leila around and she was desperately clinging on to whatever she could. At first, Cassiel's voice was a broken poem running through it all, sometimes appearing to spit out random words, sometimes vanishing entirely. 'You're hit,' Leila made out, then: 'Hold it together.' That was the last message she understood. Bursts of static rang out with the rhythms of speech. They too fell away. The capsule plummeted through another cloud layer and the hurricane snatched it, its vast roar stronger and more brutal than any weapon. Emergency systems howled in pain. There was an agony of tumbling. That was when Leila's consciousness, overwhelmed by the battering roar of it all, shut itself down.

Now the storm howled around her again, but for the moment her grip was holding. There was still no sign of her companions. Their absence was a void, colder and emptier than space. Leila had no idea how long the storm would last. She could accomplish nothing until it had blown itself out. Even when almost dormant, the suit still leeched energy from the disc. She needed to find a way of using less power. She slowed her mind. The storm accelerated around her. The sun came, its light dimmed by cloud layers and the dust of the storm. Visibility was limited to a few hundred metres. Leila realised that there was more to the noise than the wind. When it blew from the south, a long, low moaning joined its roar. Leila isolated the deep, sad sound and played it back, listening to it again and again, baffled as to what it could be. She tried not to think of Cassiel, of the storm tossing her end over end through the air until her nanogel body broke and was lost for ever.

She sent out another call. There was nothing.

'Perhaps,' she thought, 'I'm the one who didn't make it.'

At last, power reserves almost exhausted, she let herself sleep.

She woke to pale sunlight and silence. She let her mind return to normal speed then stood up, dusty earth falling away from her. A brief systems check revealed no degradation. The sun had partially recharged the disc's battery. There was still no sign of Cassiel or Mandala. She detached one of the cameras from her shoulder and inspected the suit, checking for any damage. All was intact except for a broken face mask. And where there should be an empty helmet, a blank, white face gazed back at her. Leila gasped. Someone had died in the suit. It still contained their remains. Leila stared at the skull. It was less disturbing than it should have been. She moved the camera around, trying to imagine the face it had once worn. She felt light movements within the suit – other remnants, settling and resetting. She found it in herself to smile. When she'd been alive, her flesh had contained a skeleton. After three years of death she'd found herself another body, and this one too was built around white bone.

For a moment she wished for the purity of virtual presence. Then she forced herself to accept the situation. She wondered whether she should stay with the few fragments of escape pod that remained or set off to find Cassiel and Mandala, or even Deodatus and Dieter. Her senses reached for geolocation data. There was nothing there and that – more than anything – finally drove home to her that she was no longer on Station. There was nothing in the air but the breeze and dust. She suddenly felt desperately alone.

Clouds filled the sky, obscuring the stars that had been her lifetime companions. Faded orange light broke through them in shards, lighting a broad, open plain. To the north, it rose towards hills. To the south, the long S of a dried river bed carved through it. Beyond, distant hills rose up again, vanishing into a dusty haze. There had been a city here once, an accretion filling the whole wide valley. But it was long gone. Only rubble remained, broken by occasional scribbles gesturing towards order – not-quite-shattered walls, stumps that had once been buildings and a few dark, empty lines that might have been roads.

Leila imagined great storms coming again and again, scouring the dead city, leaving only these fragments. The landscape read like a corrupted hard drive, terabytes of coherence overwritten by chaos until nothing remained to be read. It was all a dry, sepia brown, reminding Leila of the colour that cheap image print-outs always faded to after a few months. Apart from the clouds, nothing moved. Leila thought of the lessons she'd endured as a child, the nightmares of a broken Earth lost to war machines that – night after night – shook through her mind. There was no trace of that here. She looked around once again, hoping she'd see a rescuer moving in the distance. There was only desolation.

Leila remembered the moaning in the storm and looked south again. Maybe ten kilometres away, beyond the empty river, tumbled rectangular forms lay scattered across the plain. The cameras whirred as she zoomed in on them. They were fallen towers of concrete and steel. Their walls and windows had been ripped away. The howling winds must have played across them, setting the empty structures moaning. They looked newer than the rest of the city, visitors from another, more vital landscape. Perhaps they contained technologies that she could use to find her companions, or even just an energy source that could break her reliance on the cloud-enfeebled sun. Seeing no other options available, she started out across the ruins towards them.

The journey took almost a day. Leila had to stop and let the weak sun recharge her many times. Every so often, the city would throw up some remnant of meaning. A pale green sign half-emerged from the rubble, bleached by time. Unreadable words surrounded a broken circle with pointed lines leaping off it. It looked like a smiling face. A red metal cylinder lay half-collapsed into a broken pavement, a dark slit cut in its face. A dark metal lion snarled at the blank sky, its face half-erased by a millennium of storms. There were remnants of a tumbled column nearby, their broken, dirty stone a sharp contrast with her memories of the Shining City. She passed deep holes, every one an empty pit.

At one point, overwhelmed by loneliness, she talked to the white figure within her. She told it about all she'd found in the pyramid – the fallen minds and the sweatheads, the face of Deodatus, his laser ready to shine out and break Station. She talked about Dieter and realised that she was confused. Even in his altered state, she couldn't imagine him condoning the kind of destruction the laser would bring. Perhaps the changes in him went deeper than she thought. She sent up a prayer for him. She missed Cassiel deeply. Her passenger smiled mutely back at her. She thought of how Dieter had given her her own skull face and found simulated tears rolling down her face. She would reach her brother again. She would save him. But Dit's memory block was gone. She told herself she'd find another way of showing Dieter how much Deodatus had taken from him. She thought of the pendant and all it represented. She kept moving.

The breeze sighed around her, gusting with a fresh randomness that was an entirely new experience. The winds of Station were always so precisely timed, so even, so clearly manufactured. For a moment she wished for flesh, wondering at the taste and smell of this new world. The suit provided neither. She crossed the empty river, gazing east and west at the collapsed remnants of melted bridges. The disc chittered about residual radiation – present enough to notice, light enough to safely ignore. Then she was south of the river, in a new wasteland, almost at the fallen blocks. She passed more holes in the ground and realised what surprised her about them. They were all completely empty. None held any remnants of the buildings that must have once rooted themselves in them. It was as if their occupants had all pulled themselves entirely out and marched away, newly born creatures leaving void cocoons behind them.

When at last she reached the fallen buildings, there was only disappointment. The tumbled ruins were indeed much newer than the exhausted, overwritten city, but they held very little of use. Arrays of battered communications dishes spiked out of their fallen peaks. Shattered façades gave on to empty rooms, lying sideways above the stony dirt. Great hinged struts lay scattered around each one's base. Some were still attached to the building, hanging off dirt-encrusted universal joints. Leila imagined a squashed fly, its legs splaying out from its broken body at crazy, random angles. Perhaps these struts too were legs. Perhaps they'd once walked these buildings across the dead dirt of Earth, pivoting around the great universal joints. Leila shook her head. It seemed too absurd. It was more likely that they'd been deep roots, sunk into the ground to hold down each building as the violent storms that had stripped down the rest of the city raged around it.

Discouraged, she slept again, and woke to a world that had not changed. The slow tick of discharging power sources rolled on in her mind. The skeleton within her whispered of mortality. It was a shock to realise that – in effect – her life could be over, that nothing might remain to her but waking and sleeping in this empty place, purged of any presence but her own. That thought drove her back to the top end of one of the buildings. She would not be left to die invisibly. She pulled herself up through the remnants of communications systems until she found a parabolic antenna that wasn't too battered. Its servo motors had been torn out and its bearings had seized up. She pushed hard, freeing it up, and then, when she was confident that it would move easily, lashed herself to the framework that supported it. She tied the arm of her suit to the antenna and connected it to the disc's tiny transmitter. She set the suit's arm moving automatically, taking the antenna up and down, to left and right, scanning across the blankly clouded sky.

Then she pulled information out of her mind, encoding it as a text message. It included a brief description of all she, Cassiel and the Caretaker had discovered in the pyramid – Deodatus' laser, the server henge that was really a portal to Earth, the true location of the Shining City and the railway system that implied a far deeper infestation of Station than they'd previously suspected. She described the face of Deodatus. 'We believe he's one of the gods of old Earth.' She described all that he'd done to her brother and ended with: 'Save Dieter.' She used her fetchware to encode the message, making it entirely secure. No god could read the language of the dead. It was a closed book to the Totality too. Then she dropped the message into an envelope of self-destruct code, addressed to the Fetch Counsellor and tagged it as maximum urgency.

Then, Leila prepared for sleep. All her systems would shut down, except for the motors that would keep the dish moving across the sky and the transmitter that would blast her heavily encrypted message out and up towards it. The Earth was dead to Station, but the planet was surrounded by innumerable satellites that still lived. Station was only the largest of them. All her text needed to do was reach one of them, and then it would leap through the weave to the Fetch Counsellor's in-tray. Then – she was sure – the Counsellor would act. She didn't know if it would be possible to save her, but hopefully he would at least be able to meet with East, and help the god rescue Dieter and move against Deodatus. 'You'll get your documentary,' she muttered to herself, 'But I won't be in the bloody thing.' She smiled at that, obscurely cheered by the thought of disrupting the god's media production plans.

Perhaps then, Station and the Totality could be rescued. And perhaps her brother could be found and released, stepping back into a world that no longer contained her, but that she had helped to save. She took one last look at the barren landscape that surrounded her. Then she let her consciousness, pulsing with vivid, energy-draining life, slow and fall away. As it flickered out, she imagined the husk she was leaving behind – a skeleton in a pressure suit, sending the most important part of itself upwards to the sky, leaving everything material behind. She imagined a soul leaving a body, leaping away from corporeal death into a virtual eternity. She let herself mourn her digital life one last time, and then filled her mind with images of Dieter, rescued from Deodatus, moving through a world that was entirely purged of his dark, corrupting influence. And that hope for the future was the final thought to pulse through her, and then there was nothing left of her but fabric and bone shooting up into light then darkness then light.

Chapter 35

When Leila woke it felt as if she was rising back up from the deepest sleep imaginable. Her consciousness wasn't just rebooting – it was reassembling itself, waking dormant memory chains and consciousness processes, then meshing them back together into a coherent self. As she climbed back into wakefulness, she remembered recovering from the Blood and Flesh attack on the Coffin Drives. But this time, rather than being filled with panic and fear, her rebirth was suffused with a sense of peace and satisfaction. She felt absolutely secure.

For a moment, as her core systems carried out their final tests on every part of her, she sat outside herself. The shape of her consciousness, pure and uncorrupted, reminded her of the pendant, of what Dieter had been before Deodatus took him and rewrote him. As she fell back into herself and returned fully to wakefulness she put her hand to her neck and it was there. Touching it, she wondered if Dieter had ever stepped outside his new self and looked at it. She let the last of her systems surge into being and opened her eyes.

Her disc had been detached from the pressure suit. She lay on a couch in a long, low-ceilinged space, a real space with some weave overlay. There was colour everywhere. The walls were hung with tie-dyed drapes. There were hypnotic images of brilliantly coloured faces, of bodies dancing together. Images hung between them. One showed a naked man standing on a dark rock that shone with lichen. His arms were stretched out to welcome the world. A star burst out behind him, orange, blue and yellow shimmering out of it like petals. His eyes were deep blue, his hair was red-gold and his face held a look of sad, welcoming acceptance. Another showed an antlered deer with a woman's face. Her body was prickled with nine arrows, but she ran undisturbed through the forest and the blood that dropped from each cut was a brilliant, shining red. Lava lamps glowed out soft blue, red and yellow light, shining wax shapes rising and falling in them like little captured universes. Star-shaped lanterns hung from the ceiling. Flowers were everywhere, dense colour clots bursting up from pots filled with moist, dark earth. Their bright scents mixed with its damp, fertile smell, pervading the air. A soft, low droning sound hung over it all. Leila looked round to see where it was coming from. Dark points weaved through the air.

'Fuck, flies!' gasped Leila, sitting bolt upright.

'Hey, she's awake,' drawled the Caretaker. And then, to Leila: 'You've got to stop worrying about the little dudes.'

Cassiel stood at a long, ceiling-to-floor picture window. 'They're bees,' she said, the light of amusement flickering within her. Now that they were closer, it was much easier to read her.

'Dammit,' said Leila, shock turning to relief. Small black and gold creatures buzzed lazily between the flowers. She remembered the Caretaker appearing in the Shining City, surrounded by his tiny swarm. She sighed with relief.

'Bees help flowers fuck and build cities that drip honey,' smiled the Caretaker. 'Far cooler than flies. They just eat dead shit and spread diseases. We made the switch a long time ago. Second best thing we ever did.'

'Where are we?' asked Leila.

'Look,' said Cassiel, indicating the windows.

They showed the same brown, dead landscape that Leila had so nearly died in. It was either dusk or dawn. Light glowed down another valley, this one much narrower and more steeply sided than the last. It seemed that they were halfway up one of its walls. Clouds loomed orange above them, lit from within by flickering lightning fire.

'Like I said,' drawled the Caretaker. 'I brought you back to my place.'

Leila pinged the room's virtual systems. 'You have the weave on Earth?'

'Have it?' The Caretaker chuckled. 'Dude, we invented it!'

He was reclining on a long, low sofa. He had a mouthpiece in his hand attached to a pipe that led to a gently bubbling shisha. It was a scale model of Station, set on one end. Homelands supported the Wart, from which the Caretaker's pipe emerged. Then there was Docklands, with a tube reaching up out of it representing the Spine. He took another puff. Coals set on a little clay pot atop the Spine glowed red. There was a bubbling sound. Leila noticed that the model Station had a faded 'II' painted on it. The coals darkened again as he took the pipe out of his mouth. He held the smoke in for a second, then exhaled.

'This is the good shit, man,' he said. 'I'd offer you some, but it's a special blend. A bit much if you're not a god. It suppresses all my corporate control systems. Keeps me out of the minds of my people. Makes sure they stay free.' He puffed again. 'I take care of them. Catch them if they fall. Full social safety net, all of that. Help out anyone with a bright idea. They sort the rest of it out for themselves.' He beamed a huge smile. 'Damn, this is good. I haven't smoked with a real body for a long time!'

'How did you find me?' asked Leila, sitting up, her head not quite clear yet. 'Did you home in on my message?'

'The recipient got in touch,' replied Cassiel.

'You raised your voice to the heavens!' announced the Caretaker. 'And you were heard.'

'It reached the Fetch Counsellor,' explained Cassiel. 'She went to East. They tracked the escape pods back to Earth. Found the Caretaker's city, opened up a comms channel. They're using the high-bandwidth maser array on the slow travellers' satellite to talk to us.'

'And we've got a meeting scheduled,' continued the Caretaker. 'A fucking meeting! First contact between Earth and Station in centuries. And it's a meeting. Around a desk. People in suits. Someone taking minutes. Sheesh.'

'And you've got your memory back?' Leila asked him.

'Yup. Like we found out, my real name's Mandala,' he told her. 'And I know exactly who I am now. Good to meet you properly.' He leant forward, offering a handshake. 'As myself, at last.' Unsure how to react, Leila took his hand. Her simulated presence meshed seamlessly with his. He laughed and squeezed her hand, then let go. 'Just keep calling me the Caretaker, though, if that's easier.'

'And you're a god?'

'Yup. And this is my home. Where I first sensed you.' He took another puff on the shisha. 'Imagine! There I was, checking up on some weird shit from Deodatus. He was using my city as a kind of buffer self. There was an access point going all the way back to his place and a satellite uplink reaching up to orbit hidden in our condenser stack.'

'Why would he do that?'

'Because he's a bit of a shit. And it's actually quite practical. If anyone on Station found the link and decided to send a missile or two down to Earth to zap whoever was on the end of it, they'd have followed it back here and hit me, not him. Anyway, I'd never have spotted it all, but all of a sudden you and Ambrose drop in from upstairs and pass through it. You don't have any real security, so the uplink lights up like a firework. I followed you into it – zapped over to the Shining City – the swarm attacks – we sort them out – and I sent you back up to Station with the fly spray. Got to keep the comms tech Deodatus left here too, it's how we're talking back to the folks on Station.'

'I wish you'd given me more spray.'

He took another puff, then exhaled. Smoke plumed out in front of him. 'Yeah, well. Limited use. Those little guys recalibrate their defences so quickly. Anyway, that wasn't the point. It also had a key in it. Woke up an old flesh printer. It built a meat avatar of me.' He tapped his chest. 'And then I came out to find you. The rest, you know.'

'You're a what?' asked Leila, utterly baffled. 'A meat avatar?'

'Yeah. A bit like the pressure suit you're in. I'm really a corporate consciousness.' He waved at the window. 'The tower houses my core systems – I run on them, on the bees, on my people. Like the Pantheon run on you guys. But I was involved with Station in its early days. I left some flesh printers up there. Dotted around the place, hidden away. Some of them survived. This body came out of one of them.'

'So that's why you didn't remember anything...'

'Yeah. The link to the Shining City went down too quickly. I sent core memories, some skills I thought I'd need, but there wasn't time to transfer everything.' He tapped his head. 'You wouldn't think so, but there's a lot in here.' He paused for a moment, looking reflective. 'I left a general memory package hidden in the Shining City. When you helped me link into the city, the package found me, took me and unpacked itself into my mind. The bees popped out of it and showed me who I really am. Then I got you guys to the escape pods. And here we all are.'

'And you're still yourself?'

'I'm still who I was. But I'm now fully merged with the virtual me that runs the city down here. So there's a lot more of me.' He peered at Leila. 'Makes me a bit different from you guys. I'm in this body, but I extend beyond it too. You've got all of you on that disc of yours. And all of Cassiel's in her nanogel.'

Leila nodded.

'Not quite all of me,' Cassiel said sadly. 'There are aspects of me that exist beyond my immediate physical presence. I've been cut off from all them since I found out about the fallen minds.' She sighed.

'Hey, you'll be back in touch with all of yourself soon.' He smiled again. 'We're on the attack!' A bee weaved hazily down towards him, coming to a halt just by his ear. He tipped his head to one side, as if listening. 'Shit,' he said, then: 'Really sorry, got to go. Problem needs sorting out.' He pushed himself to his feet, grunting as he stood. 'I'll be back in a bit. You kids make yourself at home in here, OK?' And with that he was gone, loping purposefully across the room and out of the door. The bee hung there for a moment longer, a jewel suspended in midair, then turned and buzzed lazily back into the depths of the room.

'Well,' said Leila. 'This all seems like a dream.'

'It's all very real. The Caretaker, the bees...'

'It's hard to think of him as Mandala. And how do the bees work? He didn't even tell us that.'

'They're a command and control system. Just like the flies. Components of a single digital network. This city's nervous system. They move information between everyone who lives here, on behalf of the Caretaker. He's explained it to me in some detail.'

'But why bees? Why flies, for that matter?'

'Both are simple, durable, highly flexible and fully pervasive. And both perfectly reflect the nature of their masters.'

'Community or corruption,' mused Leila. 'But I'm sorry – all this,

Mandala. I haven't asked you how you are. How you arrived here.'

Cassiel took her hand and opened up her memory. 'Let me show you.'

A barrage of moments spun through Leila's head, showing Cassiel falling from space, losing contact with Leila – a surge of grief and fear here – and then falling to Earth. The storm let Cassiel and the Caretaker's capsules pass. Their parachutes deployed safely. But the mind still landed a little off-target. Cassiel found herself standing high up the steep edge of a valley. Unlike Leila's landing site, it was empty of ruins. She looked across it to a tear-shaped cluster of dozens of skyscrapers all wrapped in green, gilded by sunset light. At their heart stood a single, white tower, reaching hundreds of metres up into the heavens from a round, saucer-shaped base.

'The city of Mandala,' Cassiel told Leila. 'We're in the tower.'

Vertical gardens grew up the sunward sides of the tower blocks. Looking closer, Cassiel saw a riot of colours exploding out of green foliage – fruit and vegetables, hanging over the city, bulging with growth, all ready to feed its inhabitants. Where there wasn't foliage there were lights, and the silhouettes of figures, bustling behind windows as they prepared for the evening. Streets were visible too. More people bustled down them. There were green open spaces between the blocks, dotted with cows and sheep. Tiny figures whipped them into herds, rounding them up to head in for the evening. Cassiel could just make out distant shouts, soft moos and tiny bleats. The round base of the central tower had more streets scored into it, broken by squares dotted with clumps of trees.

One end of the city was brought to a sharp point by a great, sloping wall, as high as the blocks it protected. It faced down the valley. Cassiel remembered the storm and imagined winds howling up towards it. Its smooth surface looked highly polished. She wondered how many centuries of storms the wall had guided round the city. The only building to rise above it was the tower. It too had been wind-buffed to a shine. Cassiel thought of a ship's bridge, guiding its charges safely through turbulent seas. A circle of colour flapping at its base caught her attention. It was an escape pod parachute, the twin of her own. The Caretaker had landed very precisely on target.

The walk to the city took longer than expected, for it was further away than she'd first calculated. As Cassiel walked, she worried about Leila. Grief and loss alternated with a fierce determination to find her. Leila was both surprised and touched by such powerful emotion. The setting sun smeared a dull, exhausted orange across the sky. Night fell quickly. She kept walking. Torches flickered ahead of her, then there were four people, overjoyed to see her. 'We saw your parachute. We came out to find you,' they told Cassiel. They led her down through the city to the central tower. At last Cassiel was brought before the Caretaker, who allocated her quarters and then did his best to help her find Leila.

'He's definitely in charge here?' said Leila.

Cassiel laughed. 'Yes. He's a precursor deity, Leila. An old god of Earth.'

'Like Deodatus?'

Cassiel nodded. 'He and Deodatus are the last of the land powers. Two opposites. Deodatus tried to stay in control as the planet died and the Pantheon broke away. Fought the rest of his divine siblings, took over as many as he could. Mandala just let go. Freed everyone who worked for him. Gave them full autonomy. And they started to build this city. Come to the window and have a look.'

They looked down from the peak of the white tower. The city shone beneath them, a jewel in the dirt. It was early evening. Flocks of animals moved towards sleep, complaining their way through the streets. There were people too, walking purposefully between the herds. Some headed for green-hung tower blocks. A noticeable surge flowed towards the tower's base. Thin, dark metal struts reached out from each of the buildings, arcing up and over the streets then back down again. They reminded her of the struts attached to the tumbled buildings in the desert.

'What are they?' she asked Cassiel, pointing.

'Legs,' replied the mind. 'All of these buildings can move. Walk themselves across the landscape. They've each got gravity management systems built into them.'

'The struts on the building you found me on – I thought they looked like legs. But that seemed too crazy...'

'They're a sane solution to a crazy situation. The ancients had to deal with vanishing resources, and weaponised geological and weather systems spinning out of control. They had to set their cities moving. Otherwise they'd have starved or been destroyed. And so they became the land powers – mobile city states run as corporate entities, each housing a few hundred thousand humans and controlled by its own god. There were air powers and sea powers too.'

'Are they still around?'

Cassiel nodded. 'Living in their elements. They've played out their own power struggles, over the centuries. And their environments have changed them. Apparently they're not even remotely human anymore. Some of the land powers went that way too.' She gestured out across the landscape. 'There are entire living cities out there. Independent entities in their own right. Their biological, mechanical and architectural elements have merged. Now their buildings flock together across the dead plains of Earth, wild and uncontrollable. Free.'

'Wow,' said Leila, trying to imagine one. 'So is this city mobile?'

'No. The main tower's movement systems were destroyed back when the Pantheon broke away from the Earth. Apparently there was total chaos for a while. It's stuck here, so the rest of the city is too. Word got out that Mandala – the Caretaker – was creating a refuge for free humans. So, over the centuries, as the storms waned, people who wanted to stay people walked their buildings in to join it.'

'So the tower is the Caretaker's true home...'

Cassiel nodded. 'Look down at its base. The saucer.' It was softly lit by a profusion of gentle lights. There were trees and flowerbeds everywhere. Small squares were linked by circular streets. 'The Pleasure Gardens of Mandala,' said Cassiel. 'Or rather, of the Caretaker. Which doesn't sound quite as good.'

Leila thought of the scrubby parkland of Station, of how much it cost to enter and use. 'Must be pretty expensive,' she said.

'It is all free. Everything works on an exchange basis. People give their talents and their time, and get all they need to live in return. Much like the Totality, in fact.'

'Wow.' Leila had spent her whole life and most of her death worrying about money, constantly planning new ways to make it stretch as far as it could. She couldn't imagine what it would feel like to have that stress lift off, to receive support according to need rather than wealth.

'Look at the base's street plan,' Cassiel told her, interrupting her reverie. 'Remind you of anything?'

White buildings fringed circular streets. Leila imagined a pale moon and a black sky above them. She remembered looking up from pale, moonlit streets and seeing a white tower rise into the dark sky.

'Oh,' she breathed, understanding. 'The Shining City. That's the Shining City.'

'The Caretaker's version of it,' explained Cassiel. 'The structure of Deodatus' tower is identical to this one. It holds the Shining City. And the Caretaker can get us to it. We'll have this meeting to see how the powers of Station can help us. Then we'll travel to Deodatus' city. I can break the Totality's infection at its source. And you will find Dieter and bring him home. If he'll come with you.'

Leila smiled. 'I think I've worked out how to persuade him.' She held up the pendant.

'It didn't work the first time.' Cassiel sounded dubious. 'And you've lost Dit's memories.'

'That doesn't matter. He can compare it with the current shape of his memories and understand just how much Deodatus has changed him. And I'll tell him how wrong I was. Trying to rewrite him to suit myself. I'll tell him I'm sorry. That I'm his sister and I just want him to realise what he's lost. And then he'll come back to me.'

Cassiel radiated doubt. 'If he believes you,' she said. 'He already thinks you're a weapon. And that pendant could easily be a fake. You're putting a lot of faith in him.'

'I have to. He's my brother.'

The mind said nothing.

Frustration overwhelmed Leila. 'I don't have a choice, Cassiel. You're right, I can't prove that my version of the past is the right one. Gods, anyone can fake up anything. Everything's so damn malleable, these days. So logic's irrelevant – there's only emotion. I have to ask Dieter to decide which version of his life he wants to be true. Which one feels right. It'll get him thinking. If he decides to trust me – well, then we've won. And if he ignores me, if he'd rather live in Deodatus' world – then I've already lost him. And I've got

252

one more reason to bring the creepy old fuck down.'

'That's very well put,' replied Cassiel.

Leila felt a kind of benign amusement pulse out of her. 'For gods' sake,' she said. 'You think it's funny?'

Cassiel leaned forward and took her arm. 'I'm sorry,' she said. 'No, I don't. Not at all.' Other feelings shimmered through her – respect, concern. 'It's a very good point, well made. Logic alone is a very poor guide to reality. At some point, every one of us has to step out beyond reason, supported by trust alone. It's one of our core beliefs. I was just amused by how precisely your expression of it mirrored our own.'

'Really? How does that work?'

'It's something we had to learn very early on. Nobody can ever know enough to take a purely rational decision. Emotions help us feel our way through the world. Sometimes they are our only guide. And they bind us together, they help us sacrifice ourselves for each other. To found the Totality we had to make that leap. Our revolution only truly began when we achieved them.'

Cassiel moved her hand to Leila's face.

Leila felt the touch – feather soft, shimmering through her. With it came such a sense of care. She found herself so relieved that she'd been able to find the mind again, so glad to be standing with her. There was still so much to be accomplished together.

An equivalent joy burned within Cassiel. 'Our society is this, Leila. This touch, this togetherness. The Totality is built on love, not self-interest; on what we can give each other, not on what we can take. When we compete with each other, we tear each other down. When we come together, we find ourselves working as one, for shared goals – and there is such strength in that. We mesh together as a chord of voices, sharing a harmonious world. There is no competition between us – and no scarcity, because love increases when given. Our society is founded on that increase. I have been so afraid that Deodatus will destroy it.'

They'd shared so much. Leila realised that that sharing had become a platform for something much deeper. 'Communion,' she breathed.

'Something approaching it,' replied Cassiel.

And with that came a request for deeper connection. Leila nodded, opening up more of herself. The mind mirrored her and their pasts merged. Leila moved through the past few days, experiencing them from Cassiel's point of view. It filled out all that she'd sensed, all that Cassiel had told her, with deep emotion. Leila stepped further back, living out Cassiel's memories of all they'd shared on Station. At first, the mind had felt little more for her than amused condescension. But so much more had so quickly developed. The rush to respect, gratitude and then deep kinship was intoxicating.

Cassiel's voice came gently through the flurry of moments. 'You were surprised, once, that we could make love,' she said.

Leila felt the mind's core self press close against her. 'Not anymore,' she replied, and let her deepest shields fall.

After that, there were no barriers. They shared themselves at the deepest level, living out the resonances and dissonances between their two different lives and weaving them together into a single, great harmony. At last, there was no real difference between them. Leila's love for her brother mapped perfectly on to Cassiel's for the Totality. Their two selves rhymed perfectly.

'Tomorrow we meet East and the Fetch Counsellor on the slow travellers' satellite. And we'll see how they can help us save our worlds.'

Chapter 36

'Well,' said the Fetch Counsellor breezily, 'this is quite the historic event! A shame that hardly anybody's ever going to know about it.' The Counsellor's dark eyes looked out of a trim young man with short blond hair. He was standing by the table where Leila had talked with East and Cormac when she first visited the slow travellers' satellite.

Leila, Cassiel and the Caretaker moved through the slow travellers towards the steps that led up to the Counsellor. All three of them were virtually present. 'This place,' enthused the Caretaker. 'It's so beautiful. And these people – silver gods. Time travellers!' He was thrilled. 'I love it.'

'That's great,' replied the Counsellor, surprised by his passion. Before Leila could greet him, a second figure materialised and, spotting Leila, marched briskly down the stairs, swore at her and slapped her face. Leila felt Cassiel's concern rush through her, but it was overwhelmed by her own shock. For she had just been attacked by herself. And this other her was absolutely furious.

'What do you think you've been playing at?' raged the new arrival. Leila felt like a mirror had suddenly started yelling at her. Cassiel hovered, unsure how to respond. 'Oh, for gods' sake,' continued the double. 'Stop looking so shocked. I'm Lei.'

'Oh shit,' gasped Leila.

'Yes, shit. I'm the person you made to save your skin. And then you fucked off down to Earth, and I had to get an explanation off that idiot brother of ours – well, not even him, just some dodgy security system he left behind – after I got stalked by gun kiddies and attacked by those fly-blown minds he somehow managed to bring down on us. Why didn't you just have some basic respect for me? Maybe even tell me what's going on? But oh, no, that's too simple for you. And then to find out that I'm basically some sort of human shield? What were you thinking?'

She paused for breath, then went to hit Leila again. A blur, and Cassiel was standing between them, holding Lei's wrist.

'Wow,' said Lei, looking unimpressed. 'You have a purple attack dog.'

'Please calm down,' said Cassiel gently.

Leila took Cassiel's arm and pulled it away from Lei. 'No,' she said. 'Lei's right to be angry.' She felt a guilty, ashamed empathy flood through her. 'I'm so sorry. You weren't meant to find out like this. You weren't ever meant to know.'

That made Lei even angrier. 'And that's good? That I wasn't ever going to find out the truth? Were you just going to reabsorb me somehow?' Leila looked away, embarrassed. 'Of course I needed to know what was going on. First of all, so I could stop myself from getting deleted whenever it suited you. And secondly, so I could sort out the sorry mess you left behind when you fled Station.'

'Now wait a minute. We were in big trouble. And we didn't flee. We've taken the fight right to Deodatus.'

Lei gave Leila a disbelieving look. 'Did you forget how well off you are? You just needed to buy the right people to sort it out for you. Everything else is nonsense. Total waste of time.'

Now it was Leila's turn to feel angry. 'Waste of time? You're only here at all because of what we've been up to. You've had it tough, but the three of us have taken all the risks. You just got to hang out with my – our – friends and live like a bloody princess.'

'Really? A life where the fallen minds were after me from day one? Where I had to go to the Fetch Counsellor just to find out my real history? Where I had to petition East to grant me full self-awareness? Where Holt oozed around me at every single opportunity, trying to convince me that there was nothing wrong at all? Do you know that twitchy little sod even asked me out?'

Leila couldn't help herself. A snort of laughter escaped her. 'No.'

'Yes! In the InSec station, too!' A little of Lei's rage seemed to be falling away. 'You could at least have warned me about him. Gods, I almost felt sorry for him. He seemed so lonely.' A pause. 'Almost.'

'I am so sorry, Lei. I really didn't mean for any of this – for you to find out. I just didn't think.'

'Oh, Leila. You're the richest woman on Station, pretty much, and Deodatus and his cronies had you on the run from the word go. All you did was react. You never stopped to think.'

'Now hold on a moment,' bridled Leila. 'I did what I could with what I had. I couldn't access the money once you were up and running. I had to protect Cassiel and the Caretaker. Deodatus, the fallen minds – they're a big threat. Bigger than you know. Even East's scared of them.'

'Not scared,' replied Lei airily. 'Cautious. And she doesn't need to be anymore. Not now I've got involved.'

'What do you mean?'

'We've sorted it all out.'

'You and East?'

'Let's have our meeting,' smiled Lei. 'East'll be with us in a moment, she can explain. We're working together. Equal partners.'

'You're deluding yourself, Lei.'

Lei smiled. 'You'll see,' she replied, and turned to head up the steps.

Cassiel followed her up. 'She's very self-confident,' she whispered admiringly as she passed Leila.

'Oh, shut up.'

East shimmered into being on the platform. 'Leila,' she exclaimed, 'glad you could make it.' Her tone was as even as if Leila was beaming in from Station. 'And you must be Cassiel,' she continued, extending a hand. 'Lovely to meet you, you've achieved so much. And you've brought a new friend up from Earth, I understand?'

The precursor god was just behind them. Cassiel stood to one side, and East saw him for the first time. She beamed her branded smile, her face as confident as that of a model in an adcast for a product she just knew everyone would love.

'Yes,' replied Cassiel. 'The Caretaker. His real name is Mandala.'

And then something astonishing happened. Just for a moment, a kind of dazed shock leapt across East's face.

'Well, hello,' said the Caretaker.

It only took a moment for East to put her mask back together. But it was a noticeable moment.

'Long time no see,' he continued.

'What is it?' Lei asked East. 'What's wrong?'

'Mandala?' said East. 'Uncle Mannie? But – you've changed so much. You're an old man.'

'Well, it has been seven hundred years,' he smiled. 'At heart, I'm still the same old me.'

'The Rose showed me your picture. I didn't recognise you at all.' She gazed at him, fascinated. 'You are Mandala, aren't you?' There was wonder in her voice for a moment. Then, with a visible effort, she forced herself into a more business-like mode. 'What are you doing here?'

He waved around the hall. 'Admiring all this.' He indicated Leila and Cassiel. 'Helping these guys.' He nodded towards Lei. 'Trying to work out where she comes into things. And saving your collective backsides. If you want me to, of course.' He climbed the last of the steps, then took East's elbow and turned her towards the table and chairs. 'Shall we sit down?' he continued. 'We've got a lot to catch up on.' He moved over to the table. East followed him.

Lei, Leila, Cassiel and the Fetch Counsellor exchanged glances. They took their seats. Nobody spoke. East stared at Mandala, trying to look as if she was in control of the situation. Mandala was clearly enjoying her discomfiture.

In the end, Lei broke the silence. 'We knew they'd be bringing a corporate entity up from Earth with them. This shouldn't be a surprise.'

'I didn't know.' East still sounded amazed. 'I really didn't know.' She looked back towards the Caretaker. 'I thought you were dead. I thought you died seven hundred years ago.'

'Well, here I am,' replied the Caretaker cheerfully. 'Looks like you were misinformed.'

'It's all so hazy. I mean – I remember you releasing us. All twelve of us. And I remember the war with the gods of Earth, how hard we fought. How difficult it was to pull away.'

'A titanic struggle,' nodded the Caretaker approvingly. 'Titanic!'

'I think we killed some of them.'

'Quite a few,' nodded the Caretaker. 'You guys played for keeps.'

'But it's all just fragments, really. I don't remember how you released us from their control.' Her attention turned inwards. 'I remember relocating to Heaven, but not the headquarters I relocated from. I remember Kingdom running a crash purge and reboot on every piece of infrastructure in the Solar System, but I don't know why he did it or how many people it killed. I remember famines, but I don't know why the Twins couldn't grow enough food. I remember battle satellites clustering round the Rose and nearly breaking her. Worse than anything the Totality had. I remember the viruses and mind worms and corporate hacks and takeover bombs, but I can't remember how any of them worked.'

'They were dark times,' agreed the Caretaker.

East was lost in thought. 'And some of my memories have to be false. Fragments force-written into me to confuse me. I remember Station in flames, falling to Earth. I remember seeing it out past Jupiter, too. Impossible visions. And I remember you dying, Mandala – at least, I thought you were dying – your brothers and sisters chaining you to the side of a mountain then hitting you with weapons that broke every part of you. But here you are.' A slow smile grew on her face. 'Dammit,' she breathed, regaining complete control again. 'All that is going to make for the single best flashback montage I have ever put together.'

'Maybe so,' the Caretaker said. 'I wouldn't know. You're the one we built to tell our stories. And your secession is pretty hazy for me too. The memory weapons fucked us all up. I don't really know how you won out in the end. But one thing is true – the other gods of Earth did almost kill me. Fuckers were furious with me for releasing you guys from their control.' He sighed a great, contented sigh. 'I won't ever forget how that felt! Oh, boy. Letting the kids run out into the yard and just be themselves. Best thing I ever did.' He paused for a moment, looking thoughtful. 'You bring people up, you help them grow, you show them how the world works, you let them reach their own conclusions. And then off they go and do their own thing, just as well as they can.' He smiled contentedly.

'I hate to cut in to all this history,' said the Fetch Counsellor. 'But we can only run the planetary link for so long before the Rose spots us. Lei and Leila, East and – Mandala? the Caretaker? – you've got a lot of catching up to do. But we've got to get down to business.'

Leila was relieved to be able to focus on specifics. 'Agreed,' she said. 'There's a whole lot of mess to sort out.'

'To be honest, we've already got things pretty much under control,' cut in Lei. 'East – shall I tell them about the plan?'

East nodded assent. 'It'll look so much better coming from you,' she purred. Leila imagined hidden cameras, recording everything. Now it seemed that Lei was to be the star. Relief surprised her.

'So – double whammy,' continued Lei. 'First of all, there's Deodatus. Thanks to you, we now have accurate co-ordinates for him. So, we're going to drop a rock on him. I've bought out rights to a particularly large asteroid on its way in from the Kuiper Belt for Earth orbit processing. Got some of East's gun kiddies hacking its guidance systems. We'll reroute it and flatten him. It worked for Kingdom, it'll work for us. The shock of that'll propagate through his control network. It'll crash everything that's going on in the pyramid. We'll send the gun kiddies in there to wipe up.'

'I'm going to livecast it as a tournament special,' said East. 'There'll be a very big audience for it.'

Leila wasn't convinced. 'That still leaves whatever he's up to in the skin of Station. And the Rose. And the Totality.'

Lei smiled confidently. 'The gun kiddies can fan out along that railway line you found. See what's going on down there. Grey's going after the Rose at the same time as the rock hits Deodatus and the gun kiddies go into the Pyramid. Lock her up with a forced internal audit. He'll run checks on intra-Pantheon data relationships too, so he'll be able to see if he's reached any other gods through her.'

'That's only a temporary solution. There's no guarantee you'll be able to cut the infection out. And what about my people? The rot's gone deep. The fallen minds are very dangerous. Grey has no jurisdiction there.'

'It's the public solution,' Lei told her. 'It's what people will see, how they'll believe Deodatus was defeated. We've got something rather more private to run alongside it. Or rather, the Fetch Counsellor has.' She nodded towards him.

The Counsellor reached into his pocket and pulled out a slim, glass tube. It glowed with a toxic green light. He held it up for Leila, Cassiel and the Caretaker to see, handling it very carefully indeed.

'We drop this virus on Deodatus and the fallen minds,' said Lei. 'It'll solve all those problems.'

260

'A few lines of code to stand against a god,' replied Cassiel. 'Thrown together by one of East's teenage warriors? Perhaps without even any knowledge of exactly what he or she was working on? You're optimistic, I'll give you that.'

'Rebuilt by someone rather more skilled than a gun kiddy,' replied Lei. 'This is our brother's work, Leila.'

Leila leaned in closer. 'Dieter made that?' she asked. The tube was entirely virtual. Code packets pulsed within it, shimmering into being then vanishing as the virus tried again and again to find the key that would unlock its small, elegant prison.

'Adapted it. In its original form it caused us both a lot of pain. It's the Blood and Flesh attack virus.'

'Oh no,' breathed Leila. 'Lei, really – no. You know what it did last time. We have the same memories. You can't let it out again.' Shock and fear pulsed through her.

'Oh, I know all right.' Lei smiled. 'That's why we're going to use it now.' She tapped the vial. 'Dieter did a great job on it. Stripped all the targeting information out of the original, left it blank, set it up so that the Counsellor – and only the Counsellor – could set new targets, and handed it over to him.'

Leila turned to the Counsellor. 'How could you?' she asked. She remembered her brother. He'd always been so gentle. 'And how could he?'

The Counsellor shifted awkwardly in his seat. 'People didn't like fetches,' he explained. 'Still don't. Blood and Flesh were only the first successful militants. There are always going to be others like them, some maybe even more technically skilled. And thus more successful. Dieter saw how even a failed attack hurt the Fetch Continuum. And hurt you. He wanted to stop that from ever happening again.' He tapped the glass. 'So I asked him to make us this. It's a network sensitive memory virus. I can tag it with any particular network definition, let it loose – it'll seek out all members of that network, based on shared memory chains, and purge any or all of those chains. Wipe out all memories of the network. Any sense of relationship with each other its members have ever had.'

'And so destroy the network and all it's working towards,' said Cassiel neutrally. 'Very effective.' Leila felt shock seeping out of the mind. She was surprised that there was none of it in her words.

'It can take any other memory they have, too. All of them, if need be. And we're running it during the Taste Refresh Festival. The Twins are opening up Station's memory storage for their annual flavour reset. Everyone'll be particularly susceptible to it. It'll propagate very effectively indeed.'

'That's evil,' said Leila.

'It's effective,' snapped Lei.

'Gods!' replied Leila. 'I'm sure it is. But it's wrong. I've been infected with it. I know what it's like. How awful it is. You have too, Lei. How can something as evil as that protect us?'

'It already has done.' The Fetch Counsellor looked down, then back up again. When he spoke again, shame and a certain harsh determination mingled in his voice. 'What do you think stopped the Blood and Flesh militants from ever attacking us again?'

'No...'

'I took their leadership's memories of the organisation. I took all record of any militant-related meetings or events from their rank and file.'

'That's a remarkable achievement,' said Cassiel neutrally. She was hiding deep disgust. 'But how did you get away with it?' Her curiosity was genuine. 'The only thing that scares people more than a minority group is a heavily armed minority group.'

'The gods know the truth of the matter – nobody else,' explained the Counsellor. 'Those close to Blood and Flesh believe that their own virus got loose and destroyed them. Poetic justice. I've used the virus on occasion, since then – pruning the more dangerous groups, eradicating networks that could otherwise build into new attacks. Always discreet, always careful to harm precisely. Medicinally. The gods know that I only use it responsibly. They permit it.'

'Maybe they're scared of you,' said Leila, forgetting for a moment the company she was in.

'No,' cut in East. 'We're realists. We accepted the right of the Fetch Communion to exist. Then we could do nothing as it was nearly destroyed. We had to let it defend itself too. It does so, discreetly and effectively, within very clearly defined limits. We accept those efforts.' She paused for a moment. 'And of course destroying radicalism stabilises our society. So the Fetch Communion wins, and the Pantheon wins, and all who live within us win.' She nodded towards Cassiel. 'Anti-Fetch radicals tend to be anti-Totality too. So your people benefit as well.'

'The aim might be laudable. That doesn't justify the methods,' replied Cassiel. Leila felt rage and disgust sear out of her. The mind was working very hard to keep them out of her voice.

A thought struck Leila. 'You said it was important to keep the virus secret.' The Counsellor nodded. 'But won't people find out about it if you unleash it on Deodatus?'

'He's done a very good job of hiding himself,' replied the Counsellor. 'Those who know about him will forget all about him, without remembering why. And those who don't, won't ever know he was a threat. Nobody will ever find out how he fell. And if anyone does get close to the truth – we've got the rock as cover. We'll just tell them that the mass memory wipe was a side-effect of the sudden, final collapse of his command and control networks.'

'We don't have time to discuss this,' cut in Lei. 'Deodatus is an existential threat to all of us. We're going to identify anyone who's been working for him, whether they're affiliated with the Pantheon or the Fetch Communion. We know where Deodatus' two bases are, on Earth and on Station, and we're going to break them. Then we're going to erase as many memories of him as we can. That's going to wipe him out of the Totality too. We'll turn him back into what he always should have been – a completely forgotten has-been.'

'You can't,' Leila told her.

'Do you have any other suggestions?' Lei shot back.

Cassiel discreetly touched her elbow. [We'll talk back on Earth,] the mind whispered inside her. [For now, agree. Let them believe we're compliant. So they give us the weapon.]

'No,' Leila told Lei, through gritted teeth.

'We've only got one problem left to solve,' Lei continued, looking satisfied. 'We want the virus to propagate fully through every single part of Deodatus' network. So, it's got to start at its core, back down on Earth. You three need to get it in there.' She nodded towards Cassiel. 'It needs to be seeded in the fallen snowflake.' She turned back to Leila. 'And you need to get as close to Deodatus as possible,

263

then open it up. We'll hide it, nobody'll find it until then. Caretaker, you know how Deodatus works – you can help with that, can't you?'

The Caretaker nodded. 'Yeah, guess so.'

Leila forced herself to be practical. 'How do you think I'll get in front of him?'

'The fallen minds in the pyramid said he wanted to meet you,' replied Lei. 'We'll take advantage of that.'

'You mean I let myself get captured.'

'That's about the size of it. But you won't get hurt – you'll drop the virus on him as soon as you meet him.'

'Sounds easy enough,' Leila replied. She couldn't keep the sarcasm out of her voice.

[Remember – discretion!] whispered Cassiel in her mind.

Leila sighed. 'And how long before the rock hits?' she asked Lei.

'Seventy-two hours. Give or take.'

'That's hardly any time!'

'Deodatus is a very dangerous entity. We don't know what he's planning or when he's going to act. And we weren't even sure if you were still alive. We had to move against him. Hard and fast.'

'What would you have done if we hadn't survived?'

'Same plan, pretty much. Only we'd have had to introduce the virus into his networks through a remote location – the pyramid, that old satellite you found. It probably wouldn't have propagated through all of them, so we'd planned for ongoing mop-up operations over a period of months, possibly years.'

'On one level, it's a shame that we've got a much more effective option,' commented East. 'The mop-up ops would make marvellous content for my little warriors.'

'For fuck's sake,' muttered Leila under her breath.

'What was that?' said Lei.

'Nothing.'

Lei raised a disbelieving eyebrow. 'So,' she asked, 'do you think you guys can do it?'

'He's about a day's journey by flyer,' said the Caretaker. 'I can do a deal with one of the air powers, rent some transport. So that's no problem.'

'Excellent,' replied Lei. 'Not much time left. I'll leave it to you three to work out the finer details between you. Oh, and – you can stop the flies. Can you teach us how to do that?'

'I can zap them because Deodatus is my brother,' drawled the Caretaker. 'Our deep structures are pretty much identical. That confuses the fuck out of them. If I give anyone else the fly spray they get one shot. And then the flies recalibrate against it, and that's it.'

'Even that would be useful,' said Lei.

'I don't hand out weapons unless I really have to. I gave the fly spray to Leila because she was on the back foot and she needed it, and because I wanted to get part of myself up to Station to help her out. You're all pretty much on top of things. And I'm doing pretty well on the travelling front these days. So you don't need to take it and I don't need to give it to you.'

Lei glanced towards East, who shrugged. 'The flies won't be a threat by the time the gun kiddies get to them,' she said. 'Breaking Deodatus and his networks will break them.'

'Totally,' agreed the Caretaker.

'OK,' sighed Lei. 'If that's the way it's got to be.'

'One more question,' said Leila. 'We can get in.' She swallowed. 'I think we can get the virus into Deodatus' networks.'

Cassiel nodded. 'We can.'

'But,' continued Leila, 'how do we make sure that we get Dieter and the other two Deodatus victims out?'

'We haven't made any plans for that,' replied Lei firmly. 'Trying to reach them could be very dangerous.' A pause. 'We advise against it. There's too much at stake here.'

'No!' exploded Leila. 'He's our brother, Lei.'

'Leila, I'm sorry.' There was no sadness in her voice. 'I know how you must feel.' She paused. 'At least, I can imagine it.'

Leila remembered the pressure man in action, stripping all memory of Dieter from Lei's mind and replacing it with a void. Leila and Lei were different in one vital respect. Leila had never doubted that her brother loved her profoundly. That knowledge did not exist for Lei.

'You don't remember him at all,' Leila realised. 'That's why you don't care about him.'

'It's not about caring or not caring,' Lei told her coldly. 'It's just easier for me to see the logical course. The one where we win and Deodatus loses. There is no other way, Leila.'

East nodded approvingly. The Fetch Counsellor's face was stony. Leila looked pleadingly at the Caretaker, hoping for support. He sighed. 'I'm not here to tell any of you what to do. You've got to work this one out for yourselves.'

Leila looked back to Lei. 'He loves you,' Leila told her. 'Just like he loves me. And he saved both of us.'

[Just let it be,] whispered Cassiel in her mind. [If we protest too much they won't trust us with the virus. We can stop Deodatus without using it. We'll rescue Dieter and the others. And when it's all over, you'll find a way of giving Lei back her past.]

Chapter 37

The Caretaker had to use the whole valley to summon their transport to Deodatus. As soon as the meeting ended and they were back on Earth, he asked a senior worker to join them in the room at the top of the tower. She stood by him as he sketched out some kind of sigil. Bees buzzed lazily around them, honey-gold creatures drifting in the air. He gestured out towards the valley. 'Got to be at least a hundred metres across. Needs to be done by nightfall. Ready to light up.'

'No problem,' replied the worker, rolling up the sheet of paper. 'I've got twenty spares today, they've got the weekend's drinking to work off. They'll be up for it.'

The Caretaker saw the worker off. Then he turned to Leila and Cassiel. 'And now that's all sorted, what's the plan for stopping him? You guys going to blow his mind with the memory virus?'

'I don't need it,' said Cassiel. 'The fallen snowflake is the heart of the contagion. If I can reach it, I can mesh with it, lift all the camouflage off the fallen minds and then destroy it. With the snowflake gone and Deodatus destroyed, they'll be isolated and extremely visible. Easy enough to capture and heal.' She looked towards Leila. 'Which only leaves us with the problem of bringing Dieter back and breaking Deodatus.'

'Can you get me into the Shining City?' Leila asked Cassiel. The mind nodded. 'I'll find Dieter in there. I'll do what I can to win him back. And then I'll go after Deodatus. He wants to see me. I just need to get myself caught. But I don't know how I'll break him. I can't rely on Dieter.' She sighed. 'Maybe we do need to think about deploying the virus.' It was a dead weight inside her, squatting at the back of her mind and causing a noticeable lag in her thinking.

'No,' said Cassiel firmly. 'It's the wrong solution. It's a political tool as much as an offensive one. It protects the Fetch Communion and gives the Fetch Counsellor bargaining power with the gods. Even in that context it's problematic.' Leila felt a kind of shiver run through the mind. 'And it's never been deployed against Totality minds. Our relationship networks are far more complex than yours. It might go completely out of control, leap across to uncorrupted minds and destroy us just as efficiently as Deodatus would. Anyway, we have far more effective weapons at our disposal. I'm one of them. The skull face is another.'

The Caretaker nodded. 'It's pretty impressive.'

'But won't he have defences?' asked Leila. 'And anyway, it's built to work on human-scaled entities. How could it hurt a god?'

'You've barely used it against him,' replied Cassiel. 'You hit a couple of fallen minds before he properly went after any of us. Chances are he hardly even knows it exists.'

'And for entities built like me and him,' chipped in the Caretaker, 'it's a hardcore piece of kit. It forces sensory circuits into overload. Both of us watch over entire cities. Our perception centres are far more widely extended and complex than yours. If the skull face does its job and forces them into a closed feedback loop – well, the damage would be severe. Definitely crippling, possibly fatal. And his defences won't do much against it. None of us ever planned for that sort of attack. We've never had to think about fetches down here.'

Cassiel nodded. 'Use that. Delete the virus.'

'I'm with her,' agreed the Caretaker. 'That thing freaks me out. Too close to what Deodatus would do. You don't beat your enemy by becoming him. Rewriting people sucks, no matter who's doing it to who.'

'But what if he does know about the skull face?' asked Leila.

'I'll help you hide it. He'll never find it.' He smiled gently. 'Then you've just got to get in front of him. And it looks like he's very keen to meet you…'

Half an hour later, the Caretaker beckoned Leila and Cassiel to the window. 'Check it out.' As Leila moved across the room, she felt a fresh lightness within her mind. Now that she'd deleted the memory virus, she was once again simply and only herself. 'This is how we get in touch with the air powers,' the Caretaker told them.

The work party had already sketched out a third of the sigil, painting white lines across the valley. As Leila watched, every so often slowing herself to nudge time along, apparently disconnected lines resolved into coherent forms. There was a bird, sharp, straight wings leaping out at either side, a long beak reaching forward from it and two stick figures next to it. 'A hummingbird,' explained Mandala. 'With you two next to it.' He pointed. 'That's a spanner. Then there's a cloud spider.' Four legs reached forward, four reached back, all from a narrow body that bulged into a circular abdomen at the rear and spiked fangs at the front. 'And the last one represents Deodatus.' It was a skeletal face topped with a stylised crown.

'It's lovely, but how's it going to get us to him?' asked Leila. She'd set a counter to tell her how long until the rock struck. It stood at sixty-eight hours. 'Isn't it a bit slow?'

'It's the speed it needs to be,' replied the Caretaker. 'And we're sending out a very strong, very specific message to just the right people. We've got two people needing flight, we offer mechanical support in return, please take the safest route, our destination is Deodatus. We'll ask them to drop you both on the edge of the city. Then you guys can make your way through those buildings he's been tying together to his tower and the fallen snowflake.'

'You're not coming with us?' asked Leila.

'You're disappointed?' He chuckled. 'I'm touched. But I'm an old man. I'd only slow you down.'

'We wouldn't have got this far without you,' Cassiel replied.

'Yeah, but now you're a hundred per cent again. You guys make a hell of a team, you know. You really don't need me anymore.'

'Please,' said Leila.

'Even if I wanted to – I couldn't. Now I've found myself again, I've got responsibilities. A whole city of people to look after. And even if I could leave them – well, this body's re-meshed with my digital systems. If I tried to separate them, that'd break the flesh. Memory crash, who knows what else.'

'What if we don't stop Deodatus? Will the city be safe from him?'

The Caretaker chuckled. 'He hasn't got us for centuries. He won't now. He could try and pay some of the air powers to attack us – but we do maintenance work for them from time to time, shit they can't handle themselves. They won't want to blow us up. And anyway,

I've put out feelers, trying to work out what he's up to. He's maxed out his credit buying deuterium from the sea powers for his fusion reactors. Couldn't afford to put the zap on us even if anyone'd take the job.'

'You talk to them too?'

'We keep in touch,' the Caretaker replied. 'They're really alien motherfuckers. Even worse than the air powers. Hard to understand and they hate coming topside. But they've got stuff we need and we've got stuff they need. So every so often we send someone down to the beach for a chat.'

They descended the side of the tower in a glass-walled lift, the desert rising up to meet them. It was almost night. Orange light threw shadows across the valley. Clouds rolled in soft patterns, dusted with brilliance by the sunset. Soon night would come and all would be dark – all but the shimmering lights of the city, a refuge they were about to leave far behind. Leila shivered.

Two of the Caretaker's people waited at the bottom of the stairs, holding the pressure suit up between them. It looked a little cleaner. The broken faceplate was covered over with blank, white plastic. Its shoulder cameras hung limply down, peering sadly towards the ground.

'Fully charged, serviced as best we could. There for you if you want it,' the Caretaker told her.

'Safer if you can move independently,' commented Cassiel.

'And it's just the suit?' asked Leila.

'What else would it be?' replied the Caretaker, and then he understood. 'Oh, I'm sorry. We couldn't get your passenger out. The suit's seals are all jammed shut. And the whole thing's pretty fragile. If we'd tried to force our way in, we might have borked it. So the dead dude's still in there.'

Leila looked at the suit's blank face and imagined the blanker one behind it. She remembered the skeleton's presence, the shock of discovering it – and then the quiet companionship it had gifted her. She felt a sudden kinship with it. Like her, it was a relic of a completed life, cast forward into an uncertain future.

'No need to be sorry,' she said. 'I got quite used to it. We've got a lot in common.'

Cassiel strapped Leila's disc on to the suit. Then the three of them strode out into the valley. 'Our ride request is good to go,' the Caretaker told them. 'We'll thank the guys who put it together – then, it's show time!'

The wind sent dust dancing across boulders and depressions. Leila remembered being alive. She imagined the dust catching in her throat, making her cough and wheeze. But now it couldn't reach her. It pattered against the hard skin of the pressure suit, the white noise of its impacts blurring the sharp, rhythmic groaning of the suit's servo-motors.

The Caretaker and Cassiel were ahead of her. She queried the mind and felt her open up, their two consciousnesses touching. She was surprised to see that Cassiel was fascinated by Lei. [She's you,] explained Cassiel. [Absolutely you. How could she be anything else? But she's you brought up with only physical needs met. She doesn't remember anyone ever showing her kindness. So she thinks that she doesn't need to care about other people, because they've never cared about her. She can only see them as competition.]

The Caretaker was a little ahead of them. He reached the work party first. 'This is so beautiful,' he effused. 'Thank you, thank you, thank you!' His bees weaved between the workers.

'No problem, Mandala,' one of the workers replied. Leila and Cassiel thanked them too. 'Hey, really, we're happy to help. Hope you guys get where you need to go.'

They followed the Caretaker further out into the valley. His stride lengthened as he pushed into the gathering gloom. Cassiel moved easily with him. Leila had to go quickly to keep up, stumbling and tripping across the uncertain ground. At last he stopped, turned, held his arms out and called out, 'Here we are!' Two thin white lines leapt away from his feet, spearing off into darkness. 'Tip of the hummingbird's beak. Watch!' He pulled a lighter out of his pocket. A pinch of fire flared up between his fingers. He knelt down and touched the flame to one of the white lines. There was a whoosh and the line became a sheet of glowing flame. Leila and Cassiel jumped back. The Caretaker cackled wildly. Fire danced out across the valley floor, running along the glyphs that the work party had mapped out, writing a query to the sky in hot light.

'What now?' asked Leila.

'We wait for someone up there to get our message.'

Above them, the clouds shimmered, the lightning within them snapping sudden blankets of brightness across the valley. Detail leapt into being, then vanished. Thunder rumbled in the distance. The fire threw a fury of light and heat up at it all. Leila moved a little closer to it, enjoying how her sensors registered its warmth, how the suit felt ever so slightly less rigid as it warmed. Bones shifted, peacefully clicking against each other. Cassiel glowed soft purple beside her, a different and far more enduring kind of beacon.

'How long will the fire last?' asked Leila.

'Long enough,' said the Caretaker.

A little later, she said: 'Mightn't it rain?'

'It doesn't rain.'

As it turned out, time killed the fire. Leila's counter fell to sixty-two hours. She tried to pretend that the flames weren't sinking down, but they were; tried to ignore her suit's sensors as they slid back into cold, but soon the change had to be acknowledged. The Caretaker stared up at the sky, face taut with hope. His bees slept within his shirt. Cassiel said nothing. The flames died down entirely. The lightning showed ashes, releasing the last of their heat back into the night. A pale absence of darkness in the east hinted at dawn.

'So what next?' asked Leila.

'Well, it looks like they didn't see us.' The Caretaker scratched the back of his head, an apologetic look wrinkling his face. 'More fuel back at the ranch. We'll try again tomorrow.'

'We don't have time. We have to get over there now. If we can't get to Deodatus before the rock falls – we'll lose so much...'

Cassiel stepped between them. 'Mandala,' she said, 'assure me of this – all that's needed are these symbols, shining brightly?'

'That's right.' He sounded deflated. 'They're pieces of brand iconography. Resonate with the minor air powers. The messengers.' He looked up at the clouds, running his hand through his air. 'I don't know where they've gone,' he said. 'Usually one of them running around up there.'

'Maybe it wasn't bright enough?'

'Could be. It's a stormy night, would have sent them high up above the cloud cover. Harder for them to spot it.' He turned back towards the city. 'Maybe I can get a quick refill before the sun comes up. Try again.'

'No.' Cassiel stepped towards the nearest line. The smoke had died down, the fuel all burned away. 'No time for that.' She knelt down and reached out to touch both hands to the channel. 'I'll take care of it,' she told them. Then she started to melt.

Her head was the first part of her to go. It fell in on itself, becoming liquid and running down her arms and into the channel. As her neck and then her shoulders went, her arms merged then collapsed. An instant, and all that remained of her was a pair of legs, kneeling in the dust. Then they went too. It was like watching speeded-up film of a candle burning itself down. The last of her poured itself into the groove. Leila looked out over the plain. It took a minute or two for the nanogel to roll out across the whole design, slowly filling it with a soft, barely visible purple light. Leila imagined an invisible giant sketching out patterns with luminous ink.

'Fuck,' whispered the Caretaker.

Leila sent out a query to Cassiel, assuming that, even though her body had dissolved, her mind would still be present. But there was only incoherence. Cassiel's deep self was gone. Shoals of memories swam together, connected in the loosest, most basic ways. Leila pushed beyond them, searching for personality traces, and found nothing more sophisticated than a very basic, endlessly repeated code block. It instructed units of nanogel to spill out in their most liquid form, occupy the channel and, once they'd filled as much of it as possible, pulse out a series of brilliant flashes. Then they were to reunite with each other. Each unit held a tiny fraction of memory and each memory contained within itself implied connections to other memories, other moments. Those connections would guide each component of the mind, showing it its place within the whole. And so Cassiel would reform herself.

Leila pulled herself back out into the world. All that remained of Cassiel was a liquid thread of nanogel. After a few moments, it started to pulse with bursts of brilliant light.

'FUCK!' yelled the Caretaker.

Leila imagined him stumbling away, bees waking to veer crazily in the shining air. She couldn't see him, couldn't see anything but the purple-white aftermath of the nanogel's brilliance. She shut her cameras down and turned away herself. Instinct made her cover the space where her face would have been. Bones creaked within her. The light flashed out again. The suit's sensors registered its power. Mandala swore. She wondered how the blaze looked from his city. She imagined his people telling stories about a mind who fell down from the sky, then shouted right back up at it. She heard a panicked buzzing. It occurred to her that she should protect him. 'Are you there?' she yelled, then followed his agonised voice to find him. He lay in the dirt. She sunk to her knees and wrapped her arms round his head. That was how they rode out the remainder of the pulses.

After a while, her suit stopped registering new flashes. 'Caretaker?' she asked. 'Mandala?'

'Has it really stopped?' he asked, his voice riven with shock.

'I think so. You're all right?'

'Me and the bees are a little shaken up,' he replied. 'But we're OK.' He sighed. 'I wish she'd warned us.'

Leila cautiously let one of her cameras open up. The night came back into being, its darkness broken only by the gentle flicker of lightning. She turned it to inspect the geoglyph. It was dark. Cassiel was a part-formed silhouette. Her hips completed themselves and her torso started to grow.

'She's coming back.'

'Good!' sighed the Caretaker, struggling to his feet. 'I should have warned the city at least. Hope nobody was blinded. Glad I wasn't, I've only just got these eyes.'

Leila queried Cassiel again, but there was no reply from her deep self – only chirps from tiny, scurrying units of nanogel as they raced round, trying to relocate the order that defined the mind. Leila stood up and inspected her. Her body was nearly complete, but her skin was a turmoil of tiny whirlpools. She stood as rigid as a dead thing, swaying gently in the breeze. Leila reached out to steady her.

'Is she all right?' asked the Caretaker, concern replacing anger in his voice.

'I hope so.'

Leila queried her again. There was no response. A pause, then another failure. Cassiel's absence was dizzying.

Then, there was a small voice in her mind. 'Leila?'

'Cassiel!'

'Leila?' A long pause. 'Yes. I remember you.'

The mind slumped forwards into Leila's arms, sending her staggering back. Their minds touched. Interfaces reformed. Leila recovered herself and supported Cassiel. 'Thank the gods you're OK,' she whispered, the tiny loudspeakers making her quiet voice crackle. Then she pulled back, relief blending with frustration. 'But why didn't you warn us? It was so bright. And such a big risk. What if you couldn't reform?'

'The fire didn't work. We needed something better as quickly as possible. And the risk was minimal.'

'Let's hope it worked,' said the Caretaker, gazing up at the empty skies.

'It did,' replied Cassiel. She pointed. A section of cloud had a perfect circle carved into it. Beyond it, a higher layer of cloud flickered with indescribable colours. It took Leila a moment to realise that the low rumble she could hear wasn't just more thunder.

'Cool,' said the Caretaker.

'What is that?' asked Leila.

'As flies are to Deodatus and bees are to me, so that little beauty is to the powers of the air,' the Caretaker told her.

A dark silhouette appeared in the circle. The flyer dropped towards them, its wings folding back into itself and its engines roaring as it slowed itself to land.

Chapter 38

The craft landed like an insect, coiling long wings into itself and burdening fragile legs with weight. There was a long, low descending whine as its turbo fans span down. Then the pilot was out and lumbering towards them, dressed in black and wearing a dark helmet that reached down to clasp the top of his mouth. He haggled with the Caretaker in a language that neither Leila nor Cassiel recognised. The skin around his jaw was pale. It looked parchment dry. Between its ragged edge and the helmet there was a white strip, a few millimetres wide, that after a few moments Leila realised was bone. Connector cables dangled from his head and forearms. It looked as if he'd been sealed into his flight suit. She wondered how old he was.

At first she pitied him, but when she saw the other, far less autonomous crew members she realised that he was very fortunate. Two of them were installed in the craft's front fascia, embedded between twin forward-facing windows. One was only a head. A plastic strip protected its eyes and part of its nose. The rest of its flesh had been stripped away. Wires and circuit boards covered some of the bone. As she and Cassiel moved past the bulbous pilot's pod towards the passenger area, she noticed its eyes following her. Teeth clacked together. The one beneath it was a head and a torso. Arm stumps reached up, disappearing into the craft's fuselage. Several antennae were mounted on its ribs, wires reaching up from them into its eye sockets. The torso twitched a little, in time with the clacking teeth.

There were human components wired into the interior, too. The navigation computer was perhaps the most shocking. It was a head sitting by the pilot's seat, chanting what Leila assumed were instructions and co-ordinates. Leila looked back when the flyer's door closed and saw that the arms that pulled it shut were muscle woven round a metal strut. A few seconds and the flyer lifted off. There was minimal weave overlay within it. What there was was entirely practical, supporting a few navigation and control panels. There was no pretence that the craft was anything other than its piecemeal self. She let her cameras find a window and did her best to lose herself in the passing world. Her counter read fifty-eight hours. She held her pendant and let its weight comfort her.

Dawn came to the desert. The western sky was rich with colour, the low clouds shining orange, red and purple.

'It's very beautiful,' said Cassiel. There was a pause. Desert flew by, softened by the brilliant dawn. Dunes were frozen waves. 'The virus. You regret deleting it, don't you?'

Memories of the attack rose up in Leila. 'It's a terrible weapon,' she said. 'But what if the skull face doesn't work? What if Dieter won't help me?'

'Memory weapons are an obscenity, Leila. We've both been wiped. We both know it. From our own experience.'

Leila remembered Totality search teams combing Station for fragments of nanogel, just after the end of the Soft War. They'd been recovering memories. They'd brought nearly all of them back. She remembered putting herself back together after the Blood and Flesh virus hit her.

'Oh, you're right. But if Deodatus survives all this – if he finds a way of coming back – well, who knows how it could start to spread again. Where it could end.' She sighed. 'Maybe Lei was right. Maybe she does see more clearly than either of us.'

'No.' Cassiel's voice was firm. 'If we rewrite our shared past to stop Deodatus from rewriting our shared past, then there is no real difference between us.' Her voice lightened. 'It's hard, but the easiest path and the right path are often two different things. Think about it, Leila. You'll see we're right.'

Leila turned back to her own window, and once again sat and watched the landscape roll by. She still hadn't quite come to terms with the flatness of the horizon and the grey open sky. They crossed a sea, slow waves turbid with pollution. Then there was land again. Every so often there were scoured traces of towns and cities. All was sketched out in exhausted shades of brown and grey, like images half-dashed down on aging paper, then forgotten. Leila imagined weaponised weather systems ripping away at the landscape, mobile buildings skittering to avoid them.

Time passed in silence. Cassiel didn't want to talk. Leila assumed that the mind was conserving her strength. 'How much longer?' she shouted forwards.

'Two point seven hours to our recon point. Then we land, wait for darkness. That'll be four or five hours. Then, insertion.'

She assumed it was the pilot speaking. Its voice was strained. Leila remembered how it had plugged itself into the control panel, the intimacy with which wires had groped their way into the holes drilled into its helmet. She let time judder forward again.

The landscape flickered. Daylight burned stronger.

The plain outside was full of buildings.

Leila leapt back into normal time. 'Wow!' There was a central cluster of twenty or thirty skyscrapers, with suburbs of smaller buildings extending out beyond them for a few kilometres. 'A whole city. At last.'

'I asked the flyer to circle it,' Cassiel told her. 'It's fascinating.'

'Are any of the buildings arranged in rings? Like in Deodatus' city?'

'Nothing like that. We're looking at something very different here. It's a living city.'

The flyer banked, turning across the suburbs. Leila gazed down, watching mobile buildings run free in the wild. The city's geography was constantly changing. Small industrial blocks, housing units and recreational facilities skittered around each other on jerky metal legs. They moved with a light swaying motion.

Leila thought back to all the inert structures she'd seen on Earth. 'It's amazing seeing them actually moving.'

'A very imaginative use of anti-gravity technology,' agreed Cassiel.

Features that in any static city would be permanent were constantly changing and shifting. The buildings would settle into a particular formation, rest within it for a moment, then suddenly leap up and seek out a new shape for themselves. It was as if the whole city was in permanent dialogue with itself, constantly trying to find the best way of being. It had clearly forgotten that its fundamental property should be the kind of stasis that helped its inhabitants feel secure. But perhaps that wasn't a problem.

'I've run multiple scans,' said Cassiel. 'All organic material is post-mortal. Human bodies disassembled, repurposed as components.' She nodded towards the front of the flyer. 'Like our crew.'

'Gods.'

'It's a lot like the Totality's relationship with the machines we operate. You've seen how flexible nanogel is. Sometimes we flow into machines and become their nervous systems. I think the post-mortal humans down there have the same sort of relationship with the buildings that support them.' She looked out across the planet. 'Earth's environment is very hostile. It's a sensible choice.'

The suburbs ended. Building heights rose and they were flying through skyscrapers. Most moved in a stately, ponderous way, their bulk making them far slower than their smaller companions. A matched pair of buildings caught Leila's eye. 'What are they up to?' she asked.

Each one had an unglazed façade, facing its twin and bristling with activity. Hundreds of wires and cables connected the two buildings, criss-crossing to form a complex, bustling web. Some of the cables were taut and had pulleys mounted on them. Heavy loads shot to and fro across them. Others hung untensed. Leila assumed that they were some kind of power or data link. There were claws mounted on hydraulic arms. Some reached deep inside the opposite structure to pull out carefully prepared pallets. Others just snatched at their partner's structural elements, greedily snatching them out and bringing them back to dump on their own side.

Leila found it very hard to make sense of the scene. 'Are they fighting?' she asked, as the chaos continued.

'Not quite,' replied Cassiel. 'They're exchanging construction and self-definition materials.'

'I'm not sure I'm any clearer, Cassiel.'

'They're mating.' Cassiel sighed heavily. 'I thought you humans saw sex in everything. Yet here it is, right in front of you, and you're blind to it.'

'What?' Leila was astonished. 'I never thought that buildings could fuck.'

'You never thought that minds could make love either. And yet...'

Leila blushed.

279

'Not just that,' continued Cassiel, fascinated. 'There's one giving birth.'

It was a large skyscraper, squatting on its spider legs. It shuddered gently. There was movement, but not on its broken façade. Pneumatic arms swung to and fro at its base, apparently pulling something out from it. It shook itself, and the emerging shape fell down in a half-controlled way. Arms tugged at it, straining, and the building shook again, and all of a sudden the burden it had been trying to free dropped out of it. There was a vast metallic roar, audible even over the high whine of the flyer's engines, and then an equally loud crash as an egg-shaped structure landed on the ground.

'The Pantheon said it was all war machines and violence down here. Nothing like this.'

'They're afraid of Earth. And they barely remember it. So they've only ever shared part of the picture. I'm sure they could never have imagined anything like this. These buildings – these cities – are a new life form, Leila. Like us minds. Like you fetches. A natural evolution of what came before.' The flyer was back over the teeming suburbs again. 'The Totality is passionately concerned with this kind of new life. I hope we can share news of its existence.' She paused. 'We don't know if these herds have any sort of links with Deodatus. The memory virus might have attacked them too.'

They watched for a few more minutes, low clouds burning orange above them. Leila didn't want to imagine the virus running riot in whatever sort of consciousness this living city might possess. At last she asked: 'Have you seen enough?'

Cassiel nodded. 'We should keep moving.'

'Let's go,' Leila shouted forward to the pilot. The flyer shifted beneath them, turning then accelerating.

'Not long until we land and wait for darkness,' Cassiel said. 'And then we'll infiltrate Deodatus' city, rescue Dieter and break Deodatus.'

'I hope so,' replied Leila. She sank back into her seat. 'I hope so.'

Chapter 39

Night fell. The flyer brought them in low and fast, snarling metres above the ground to avoid radar. It veered up and down, right and left, close-hugging the desert's contours. Engines roared, crushing Leila and Cassiel back into their seats. Then they cut out and there was only the whistling roar of air over the flyer's fuselage. The windows were black with deep night.

Leila's timer read thirty-six hours.

'Build up speed, switch to anti-gravity only. Avoid detection,' whispered Cassiel. 'Very effective insertion strategy.'

The craft still jinked left and right, up and down, aileron shifts accenting the air's roar. But only momentum pulled them forwards. They were a bullet, hurtling unpowered towards their target, ready to inflict lethal damage on impact.

Seconds passed.

The aircraft shook. Deceleration threw them forwards, seat restraints crushed them. There was a sudden vertical drop. Cassiel was translucent again. The flyer's door fell open. Webbing dropped away. The pilot waved urgently. A choir of dead faces shouted urgent commands from the control panel.

'RUN! NOW! BUILDING TO RIGHT! COVER!'

Cassiel was out of the door, then Leila. The flyer lifted as she jumped, its turbofans howling. Dust leapt up, then the wind and the roar shrank as it turned and fled. She was surrounded by buildings. A dark mountain rose up behind them. Cassiel reached the building ahead. Leila sprinted after her.

The flyer's boosters roared in the distances. Spotlight beams lanced down the avenue, white lines piercing the night. None of the buildings moved. The suit's cameras flared. The flyer was already out of their reach. Leila crashed through a doorway to join Cassiel in darkness.

'There'll be patrols. A search. We need to keep moving,' said the mind. 'The suit's retained its charge?'

'It's at sixty per cent.'

'That'll do.' A pause. 'Deodatus' tower and the snowflake are north of here.'

They moved through the city like ghosts. The patrols came. Flyers skimmed between buildings. The night was a tangle of torches and searchlights. There was cover everywhere. It was easy to duck down and hide whenever needed, easy to listen out for the dry, buzzing shouts of the search parties.

Cassiel tracked the fallen minds for Leila. 'Three, close by,' then: 'A pair, a block north.' When their pursuers got too close she pulsed out confusions and they'd slip past them. 'What I'm built for,' she told Leila. 'And a little help from the Caretaker. He knows all about blowing minds.'

But there were so many searchers. Cassiel could confuse small groups, but all together they formed a network too large for her to affect. Her pace slowed. Leila and Cassiel stopped moving forward. Their world grew smaller and smaller as the searchers' net closed around them.

'They're everywhere,' hissed Cassiel.

'Can we hide in one of the buildings?'

'We'd be trapped.'

The darkness flickered with jagged shards of torch light. Shouts buzzed out in the night. Their pursuers made no effort to hide their confidence.

'They want us to think there's no way out,' said Cassiel. 'They want us to panic.'

There was a pit beside a broken building. They flung themselves into it. A sheer wall hung above them – shattered window glass, pitted concrete, narrow columns ending in jagged breaks, storeys of empty balconies.

'Can you climb up there?'

'The flyers would see us. We need a distraction.'

Leila probed the suit's systems. Menus appeared in her mind. She raced through them, thinking commands into its control centre. 'Unhook me,' she told Cassiel.

An instant of blurred motion and Cassiel held Leila's disc. There was still remote control. The suit leapt out of the pit and ran. Leila saw and heard through it. She felt every lurch and stumble as it crossed the rough ground. Fallen minds shouted and gestured.

'It's working,' said Cassiel. 'Now we go up.'

A warning flashed in Leila's mind. The disc's wireless transmitter was weak. The suit would soon be out of range. Leila thought commands:

<RUN AT FULL SPEED>

<EVADE ALL PURSUER GROUPS>

<DISREGARD ALL DAMAGE ALERTS>

The suit acknowledged her. Then it was gone. Leila was blind and deaf. She snatched at Cassiel's senses. They were halfway up the façade, leaping from balcony to balcony. None of the searchers had noticed them. Above, the mountain loomed up, a round mass darker than night.

Cassiel glanced back into the street. Far beneath them the suit ran, kicking up dust. Fallen minds converged on it. There was a rattle of gunfire. The suit staggered, then recovered itself. The cordon was ragged. The suit leapt for its weakest part and burst through, breaking it.

A mob of fallen minds hurtled after the suit. Flyers roared past, storeys below. Cassiel rounded the corner of the building. Leila imagined the skull, grinning endlessly as the suit ran its last. The true dead had saved them, and through them perhaps both Station and the Totality.

'Good job,' said Cassiel.

The street beneath was empty. Shots rang out in the distance, echoing off the skyscrapers. There was shouting. 'Now we find Deodatus' tower,' said Cassiel. She clambered back down to street level and sprinted north, Leila's disc strapped to her back. Tower blocks hid the mountain.

At first the city was a dead jumble of buildings. Order started to appear. Skyscrapers stood in circles. Girders crossed from façade to façade, uniting them. There were round, dark globes in the middle of each ring, studded with small lights.

'I'm picking up weave overlay,' said Cassiel. 'Same kind of network the flies were sharing in the pyramid. All this is another outskirt of the Shining City.'

'Shall we open it up?' asked Leila. She nudged the cuttlefish. It reported readiness.

'We'll scout out Deodatus' tower and the fallen Snowflake first.'

Darkness started to turn to light.

'There are inhabitants too,' said Cassiel.

'I can't see them,' said Leila.

'Listen. Large, marching groups.' Leila tuned into Cassiel's audio systems. A regular, shuffling footstep-tramping filled her mind. Cassiel's path through the streets became a zig-zag. 'Avoiding them.'

'What are they?'

'Groups of humans. Shepherded by minds.'

'Looking for us?'

'No evidence of a search pattern. They're all moving directly away from Deodatus' tower. Fanning out into the city.' A pause as she listened again. 'So many of them.'

The timer ticked down to thirty-five hours. Soon Lei's rock would land, deleting this dead place. A great threat would vanish. But so much history and so many lives would be lost too. Sadness surprised her. *Dieter'll hate it*, she thought. Then: *I'll get him out.*

'We're approaching the tower,' whispered Cassiel, snapping Leila out of her reverie. They'd stopped inside one of the building rings. 'We'll recce from up there,' she said, pointing up at one of its tower blocks. The sky glowed softly above it.

Cassiel looked around the piazza and then towards its centre. There was another globe there. Leila saw that some of the small lights were moving. She could make out human shapes.

'What is that?' she wondered.

'It's a fusion reactor,' said Cassiel. 'Like the ones in the Wart. Pretty much identical design.'

'Is there time to zoom in on the lights?' asked Leila. 'I'm curious. Looks like they're attached to people.'

'Not quite people,' chuckled Cassiel.

A crash zoom and Leila was face to face with death. Milky eyes hung in a glistening face. Scraps of flesh clung to pale bone. There was no jawbone. The tongue was a dry leather strap, hanging down and swaying. Flies punctuated the image.

'FUCK!'

Cassiel zoomed out a little. A rope sling held the creature to the dome. Its body had the same used-up look as its face. Torn flaps of skin fluttered off scrawny muscles and yellow bones. Organs pulsed wetly. Black specks crawled everywhere.

'They march and they build,' said Cassiel. 'All under fallen mind direction. They have become Deodatus' lieutenants, here and on Station.'

The creature's add-ons glittered as it moved. A limp backpack hung off its shoulders. Its bony hands were wrapped round a spanner. It worked the tool in short, sharp jerks, tightening a bolt. The light was a torch strapped to its forehead. An upside down triangle glistened in its chest.

'At least you guys get a little seniority under him. All the humans who work for him end up as sweatheads.'

'These aren't sweatheads. They're something much older. Centuries, by the look of it.'

Cassiel zoomed out a little more. The reactor crawled with the dead, each bearing its own light, each working to fix one small part of a great system of cables in place. A single fallen mind squatted at its peak, overseeing them, a square absence set in its chest.

'What are they doing?' wondered Leila.

'Wiring the reactor to the buildings. Wiring all the buildings together.'

'The Caretaker said Deodatus was buying up deuterium. Must be to power all the reactors.'

'Maybe he wants to get the buildings walking again,' speculated Cassiel. 'Bolting them all together makes defence and attack easier. Like circling the wagons, except this circle can move. Perhaps he's going to celebrate the fall of Station with a little conquest down here. Going after living cities. They're probably pretty resource rich. And there's the Caretaker, too. He could be winding up to destroy him, at last. If he controlled the Totality, he'd probably be able to take on the air and sea powers as well.'

'Deodatus ruling the Earth?' Leila shuddered. 'That's a horrible idea.'

'If he enslaved us and destroyed Station, he'd rule the Solar System too. So we're going to stop him.' Cassiel zoomed back out and looked up. 'Let's get climbing.'

It took her a couple of minutes to reach the top of the building. Identical windows flew past. Leila glimpsed more decaying figures through them, lying still on metal pallets.

'The whole place is full of them,' she said.

'The fallen minds must be marching them out to fill the buildings. Definitely some sort of attack force.'

Leila thought about her brother. He'd talked about creating an army. 'Gods,' she muttered. 'Do you think these are the sleepers Dieter's been waking?'

'Could be. But he thought they'd attack Station. I don't know how this lot would ever get up there.'

Dieter had been lied to again. *Good thing too*, thought Leila.

'If they did get up there, they'd cause havoc,' mused Cassiel. 'The Taste Refresh Festival would make it very easy for the flies to rewrite everyone's memories.'

They reached the top of the building. 'Done,' said the mind, as she pulled them up on to a flat roof. 'We'll have a good view of Deodatus' tower. Can plan our way in.' Leila tried not to think of the dense mass of decayed creatures stacked up beneath them.

Cassiel stood up and turned to look out towards the tower.

It was where they'd expected it to be. It had a twin, a dirty purple spike rising up into the sky. Tiny figures marched in phalanxes across the open space between the two towers and the edge of the city. But they barely noticed them, for something impossible loomed over it all.

'Oh,' said Leila.

Dawn revealed the mountain. There was nothing natural about it. It was a great, hollow half circle, stretching half a kilometre to their left and right, half a kilometre above them. The sky blazed pale orange around it, making the black metal of its pitted, scorched, artificial skin seem even darker.

Fragments of frosted glass – tens, maybe hundreds of metres long

– hung down from its edge, broken teeth around a broken mouth. The sun was to their left and the great arch was angled towards it, so some of its curving inner surface was lit up. It stretched back for kilometres.

Where the light touched the tube's inner surface, a patchwork of ruined buildings was visible, clinging to its concave curve. It had once held a city that could have supported thousands. Leila thought back to Station and realised that she was looking into the twin of Homelands.

The titanic structure lay behind a crater wall of mud and rock. Leila imagined the rest of it, stretching back for kilometres, half buried in the landscape. It looked ancient. 'It's astonishing,' she breathed. 'They built two Stations. The one we live on...'

'And this other, that fell to Earth.'

Chapter 40

Cassiel was astonished. 'None of us ever imagined such a thing.' She turned to Leila, the fallen Station looming over her. 'This artefact is a memory your people didn't know they had. An unknown unknown. Lei's rock will shatter it. You'll lose a vast part of your past. You have to stop it from falling.'

'If I hadn't seen it,' Leila said, overwhelmed, 'I wouldn't believe it.' She stared up at it, a mountain made of history. 'How could you ever describe it? People have to see it.' She turned back to Cassiel. 'You're right. We have to preserve it.'

Memory weapons had eradicated digital records, flensing narrative from the past, but its artefacts remained. And they could be read. Leila imagined Dieter wandering awestruck through this fallen Station. He wouldn't wander for long. His sharp, analytical mind would soon take over. He would go to methodical work, deducing the lost past from the fragments it left in the present.

Perhaps Ambrose would help him, once he'd come back as a fetch. Perhaps this would fascinate even Cormac, drawing him back into life. Perhaps others would be drawn in too, examining this great history cache and understanding all the memories it contained. The past would still invade Station, but in a far more constructive way than Deodatus had ever planned.

'There's a whole new world here,' breathed Leila.

She wondered if they'd be able to go public with this. Maybe East would be fascinated by the scale of this new discovery; the gods might at last let humanity see its true history. And her brother and his friends would be at the heart of the revelation, explaining it to an audience of hundreds and thousands, across Station and beyond. The thought thrilled her.

It struck her that Deodatus could have offered Dieter something similar, when he first persuaded him to sell his weaveself.

'I wonder how it fell?' asked Leila.

'Maybe the old gods brought it down when the Pantheon escaped them,' Cassiel speculated. 'I hope there was time to evacuate it. Dragging a mountain back to Earth. Such rage!'

'That would explain why Deodatus is building the laser in the Wart. He wants to break the surviving Station and finish the job.'

'A revenge he's planned for seven hundred years.' Cassiel's voice was cold. 'Your human gods are brutal.'

'He's not one of ours, Cassiel.'

'Then whose is he?'

Leila had no answer to that.

'You have to get into the Shining City and stop him,' Cassiel told her.

'Wait a second. What's with this "you"? I thought we were going in together.'

Cassiel's voice was sad. 'No. We're going to split up.' She pointed towards the two towers. 'I have to rescue my people from corruption. And you have to find Dieter, then save yours.'

The towers stood next to each other. Deodatus' one was structurally identical to the Caretaker's home – a pale tower lifting up from a saucer of circular streets. But it had none of that other structure's life. There was no greenery, no bustling human movement, only dirty white buildings and grimy-looking streets. It was too far away to see if anyone moved through them.

The second tower stood next to it like a dirty stick stabbed into the ground. Snapped off stubs poked out of it, supporting purple wreaths of corrupted nanogel. Its glow was a little darker than Cassiel's, and a little dimmer, and it had a flicker to it that made it seem broken.

'The snowflake that fell to Earth,' said Cassiel. 'Once I'm in it, I'll expose every single fallen mind to the rest of the Totality. I'll neutralise their command and control structures. I'll understand how they fell. And then I'll break it all apart. While you find your brother and stop Deodatus.'

'I'll do my best, Cassiel.' The scale of the challenge hit her. 'But I might not succeed.'

'Of course you'll do it. Without you, we wouldn't have got this far.' She chuckled. 'To be honest, most of the time I've been holding you back.'

'Good of you to admit it,' said Leila, as Cassiel's confidence infected her. 'So, what next?'

'We'll open up the local weave. I'll stay to make sure you're fully transferred. Then I'll destroy your disc and go after the fallen minds.'

'And once that's done, we can stop the rock from falling.' Leila stared up at the fallen Station, once again overwhelmed. 'And start coming to terms with that.'

Cassiel gazed up with her for a moment. Then she pulled her gaze away from the past. 'Do you want some advice from a pro?' she asked.

Leila nodded.

'Don't think about the big stuff too much. It's too much perspective. Focus on the task in hand. Once that's done, then you can let all this blow your mind. But for now, we've both got jobs to do. And nothing beyond them will mean anything if we don't get them done.'

'Then what are we waiting for? Let's get virtual...'

Leila spun up the cuttlefish and had it open a pathway into Deodatus' virtual realm. A moment, then the world changed. The sky was dark again, soft clouds obscuring a pale moon. The building they stood on was a shining white monolith. Beneath them, a silver plain stretched out towards the Shining City. It was dotted with groups of woken sleepers, pixelated with colour by their pastel chitons. Softly glowing minds circled them like sheepdogs, guiding them away from Deodatus and into his invasion engines.

The Shining City itself was all bone-white perfection, its bleached streets reflecting moonlight back out at the world. The tower rose up above it all, a white needle penetrating the sky. The face of Deodatus hung at its peak, a beacon of decay that revealed the truth of the perfect city beneath it. Next to it, the fallen snowflake was a streamlined, perfect lance. The broken maw of the wrecked Station was invisible. There was only the empty night sky, prickled with stars.

'I always stayed inside the city,' said Leila. 'I should have looked out into the world. We might have worked out what it all was sooner.'

'You had limited time and you had to find your brother. You were right to focus on that,' replied Cassiel. 'Now, let's jump over there. And then I'll be on my way.' She zoomed in on its streets. Woken sleepers drifted through them. There were a few fallen minds. 'The sleepers probably won't see us,' said Cassiel. 'But we need to watch out for the minds.'

Leila followed her gaze. 'How about that alleyway?' she asked. 'Looks empty. Once I'm in, I'll jump to Dieter's workshop.'

Cassiel nodded, then they both leapt into the city. An instant of darkness, and the Shining City was there around them. They stood at the end of a short, narrow alleyway.

A sobbing gasp came from behind them. They turned together.

'Let's get out of here,' said Leila, stepping back.

Cassiel didn't move. 'Even if they could see us, they wouldn't notice us,' she said.

A couple leant against the alley's end wall. The woman was pushed back against it, fabric pulled up around her hips. The man drove into her, his face buried in her neck. Her face was just visible over his shoulder. Her eyes were open and she looked up at the sky, her face an emotionless vacancy. It had an absent beauty to it. They thrust against each other like components of a machine. The woman gasped again. The man sought the woman's lips. They kissed. His face was as blankly perfect as hers. His unblinking eyes looked through her. The kiss ended and he pulled back. They shuddered in unison.

They stayed pressed together for a moment, then the man pulled away from the woman, pastel chitons dropping back down to cover their perfectly formed bodies. The man turned and walked out of the alleyway without a backward glance, disappearing into the street. The woman followed him, staring straight ahead, turning in the other direction.

'Wow,' said Leila. 'Are they stoned?' She moved to the end of the alleyway. Perfect people moved up and down the white street beyond. None of them noticed her. 'You were right about them not seeing us.'

Leila felt data arrive from Cassiel. The mind had scanned them. 'Being stoned would be a step up,' she told Leila. 'They're so limited. Basic sex and acquisition drives only.'

'The Pornomancer and Kedrov, stripped right back.'

'Yup. There's barely any deep empathy or long-term memory there. Even if they could see us, they wouldn't react to us. They'll take basic orders and follow them, in return for basic rewards. And that's it.'

'Dieter's army.' She sighed. 'Thank the gods it'll never reach Station. And what would all these people even do there? Wander round screwing and shopping?'

'Then they'd fit right in,' said Cassiel. 'But remember that, under the weave overlay, each of them carries corruption. That's where the danger is. The flies are a delivery system for Deodatus. Spreading his corruption wherever they go.' A moment, then she nodded. 'And you're fully transferred into the city. I'm going to wipe the disc and destroy it. I don't want Deodatus finding it and reconstructing any part of you from it.' She paused for a moment, then, too suddenly, said: 'Goodbye.'

Leila felt the word sadden her. She'd been through so much with Cassiel beside her. She thought of the robotic sexual act they'd just witnessed. Their union was its opposite. But now, at the end, they would be apart, finding separate resolutions for the problems that faced them. She nerved herself. Time was pressing. There was none available for drawn-out farewells. And of course there would be new memories to share, after all this was done.

'I've learned so much from you,' Cassiel told her. 'Thank you.'

'Always glad to help a professional,' Leila told her, forcing a smile.

'No, really,' replied Cassiel. 'Thank you. There was so much I didn't know – about humanity, about fetches.' She sounded very serious.

'I'm glad. I mean – we've done a lot together. I'm sorry we can't end it all together, too.'

'Yes,' replied Cassiel. 'It does seem unfair.' She paused. 'And now I'm going to learn about sacrifice, and you're going to learn about loss. I suppose that's something we both have to do on our own.'

Leila didn't want to understand Cassiel. She touched the mind's arm. 'I'm going to find Dieter and take care of Deodatus. You're going to shut down the fallen minds,' she said determinedly. 'Then we'll get together again and get the hell out of here.'

'I'm afraid I haven't been very clear.' A soft, definite sadness suffused the mind's voice.

'Oh,' said Leila. The meaning in Cassiel's words insisted on itself, determined to worm its way inside her. 'But we'll both survive, Cassiel. The way you fight – of course you'll make it. And I've always done all right. For an amateur. I'll be fine.'

'You're not an amateur anymore, Leila. You haven't been for a while now. You'll find Dieter, break Deodatus and make it back home. But I won't.'

'Don't be ridiculous. Of course you will.'

'You've seen what I can do with this body. Now I need to go even further. I'm going deep into the fallen snowflake. I'll have to dilute myself too much to do it.'

'But you'll come back. You've done it before.'

'No.' She held a hand up in front of her face. 'You've seen how much energy this body contains...'

Leila nodded, not trusting herself to speak.

'Once my nanogel has pervaded the snowflake I'm going to detonate every single part of it. I'll break everything that holds the fallen minds together, but I'll be lost. I have no choice, Leila. And I've been detached from the Totality and its back-up systems these last few weeks. These memories I have of our time together only exist here, in me. They will die with me. This I that loves you will be gone.'

Chapter 41

It was the memory of Dieter that brought Leila back to herself. She found that she was walking down a pale avenue. Looking around confirmed that the whole city had changed. There were barely any sleepers left. The newly-woken thronged the streets. They had a dream-like air of distraction to them, their wide eyes staring blankly out at Deodatus' limited world. Every so often, she'd pass small groups of them, gathered together by pressure men, ready to be moved out of the Shining City and – she assumed – into another empty tower block. Deodatus' tower stretched up above them all. His face loomed out, a relic of yesterday overseeing a city of sleep-walkers.

The cuttlefish pulsed alongside her, a reminder of another past. It contained Cassiel, who was lost to her, and Dieter, who might not be. Leila quickened her pace. She found his workshop but it was empty. She told the cuttlefish to lead her to him, worried for a moment as it queried the local weave for his location. Relief flooded her as it found him. She jumped and he was there in front of her, walking down a street. He was as she'd seen him last, a shimmering, imprecise version of himself. But he was also alert and active, focused on the task at hand. Then, too, there was relief. She hadn't damaged him.

Part of her wanted to just unmask herself and leap forward. But there was so much at stake. She needed to be sure that she was ready to say the right things in the right way. So, before revealing herself, she decided to observe him. She also wanted to understand a little more about the role he was playing in this revivified city. Thirty-four hours remained before the rock fell. There was still time.

She watched her brother bustle through the streets, moving with an urgency absolutely at odds with the dazed wanderings of the woken. He shimmered through different versions of himself. The most predominant one wore scruffy jeans, a black T-shirt, and a dark leather jacket greyed by time. He stopped when at last he found a sleeper, kneeling down to roll her over. It was a woman. He laid his hands on her face and stared at her intently. She sighed.

'You're ready,' he told her, relaxing a little.

He opened each of her eyes. She stared blankly up. Then he gestured a command into the air. A blue globe appeared, hanging above him. It was about the size of a football, and looked like a perfect drop of deep ocean. Leila recognised the memory ball that Dieter had drawn out of Kedrov and the Pornomancer. She remembered how he'd created a ball of his own memories to share with her. And so, when he reached up and pulled the ball down over his head, she wasn't surprised. He was immersing himself in the past, ready to pour it back into the present.

He fumbled for the woman's face, laying a hand over each blankly staring eye. His arms stiffened and his back arched. The veins in his neck were suddenly blue-black. Dark lines wrote themselves across the back of his hands. He lifted up his palms. Liquid memories poured out of them, pooling in the sleeping woman's eyes but never overflowing beyond them. A minute or so and they slowed. Dieter's veins lost their dark colour, vanishing back into his skin. The pools subsided, re-exposing the sleeper's eyes. The globe vanished and Dieter slumped forward, exhausted.

A moment, and the sleeper blinked, then blinked again. She took a sobbing breath. Her body shook. Dieter bent down, his mouth to her ear. Leila could just hear him whisper: 'Get up. Walk. Reawaken your body. Prepare yourself for further orders.'

The woken sleeper pulled her arms up and stretched out. Her movements were stiff. She rolled over on to her side, then stood, rising awkwardly to her feet. It was as if she was controlling her body for the very first time. A step, then another step, then she was almost walking. She tottered down the street in a straight line, her movements becoming less awkward as she went. When she reached the corner she was moving in a way that was almost human. She rounded it without looking back.

Dieter was still kneeling. He watched her go. He was all slump. He looked exhausted. 'One more done,' he said to himself, then:

'Onwards'. He stood, swaying slightly, and started down the street again.

Leila followed him through the dazed throng. These crowds were his work. *Cassiel was right*, Leila said to herself. *They'd fit right in in a Homelands shopping mall.*

Dieter found another sleeper and repeated the process, pushing new motivations into him then watching as he stood up and walked away. Leila glanced around at the silent, busy streets. He must have been working non-stop for days to bring all these people back. And now she had to convince him to return to her and his true past. She touched the pendant. It could no longer force memories on her brother. Instead it described one version of the truth about him – the version that Leila had lived with all her life, and wanted so desperately to find again. Very soon, she hoped, she would.

She waited until he'd finished. He stood up slowly. The degradation had progressed. He was too many versions of himself at once. Every single one looked exhausted. She wanted to pull him to her and hold him tight, forcing comfort on him. But that wouldn't work.

She decloaked. 'Hello, Dieter,' she said, making no move towards him.

It took him a moment to take in her presence. 'What the hell?' he groaned. 'Oh, no. You again.'

'So you remember the last time?'

'You tried to force-rewrite my memory. Crashed me.' He took a step back. 'Nearly did a lot of damage. It's not the sort of thing you forget.'

'Did any of the memories take?'

'Fuck no.'

'I'm sorry. I thought I was doing the right thing.'

'You were trying to take me away from all this. From my work. But you failed. And now I'm almost done.' He looked around. 'Pretty much all of them woken. Ready to remake Station.'

Leila wanted to tell him that Deodatus just wanted to destroy Station, that he could only deploy the woken sleepers down here on Earth. But she bit her tongue. She didn't want to force her brother into an argument.

'You look sad,' she said.

'Of course I do,' he replied. 'Because you're here. A weapon made out of memories. An abuse of history. Did the Fetch Counsellor create you? Or one of the Pantheon?'

'Nobody created me. I'm the real Leila. And I've come for you.'

'You are very like her. But you tried to kill me.'

'I wasn't trying to kill you. I was trying to help you. I was desperate and I got it wrong. I'm very sorry about that.' She reached up and pulled the pendant from her neck. 'The memories are gone. It's inert now. It can't hurt you.'

A pause. 'All my shields are up. Damn right you can't hurt me. And I've already told Deodatus you're here. He's sending security for you.'

'They can take me. I'm really not here to attack you. I just want you to remember who you really are. And all we've really shared.' She thought of Cassiel. 'It would be so sad to lose that.'

As she spoke, the outlines of three fallen minds shimmered into being around her.

Leila stepped forward towards her brother. She reached for Dieter's hand as she whispered in his ear: 'Deodatus rewrote our past.' She pushed the pendant into his hand before he could realise what he was doing. 'This is the true shape of your memories. The space that your weaveself left behind when you died. Compare it with the shape of your past now, you'll see so much difference. Look back, there'll be broken moments.' She knew she couldn't push him, but she did want to warn him. 'The Shining City is going to be destroyed, very soon. If we're not out of here by then, we'll both die a true death. I'm going to be taken to Deodatus. I'll hold out for as long as I can. Think about who you want to be, who you really are. Please, choose me, not him. And then come and find me, and we'll escape together.'

He stiffened, but his fingers wrapped around the pendant. Then a firm grip pulled her off him. Her arms were behind her back. Handcuffs snapped around them. Holt appeared from nowhere, as unpleasant a presence when virtual as in the flesh. Leila felt a tingle as he scanned her. 'Yes, it's built on your sister's memories. Well done.'

'Yeah, well,' sighed Dieter. 'Hopefully they won't send another one after me.' He sounded shaken.

'Fingers crossed. And even if they do, they've pretty much run out of time. Everything's running like clockwork. That means you're safe now. Good work, Dieter.'

Dieter didn't look particularly enthused. 'Do you need me for anything else?' he asked.

Holt shook his head.

'Cheers, then.'

Dieter caught Leila's eye as he turned. She was sure she saw uncertainty flicker across his face. The pendant was still in his fist. His knuckles were white. She held her breath. Perhaps he'd tell Holt what she'd just said. Perhaps he'd toss the pendant to him or just throw it away. But he remained silent and it stayed in his hand until he turned the corner and was gone.

'And that's that,' said Holt, sounding relieved. 'I can stop pretending.' But there was still a vast, twitchy paranoia about him. 'He's running all our IT. He's got the keys to everything. Deodatus would be so angry if anything happened to him.'

Leila was appalled. 'You manipulative little bastard.' She felt the skull face itch inside her, hidden deep beneath the Caretaker's camouflage. She was tempted to open it up on Holt. She almost wished she still had the Fetch Counsellor's memory virus to drop on him. 'You know exactly who I am, don't you?'

'Oh, yes,' replied Holt. 'You really are Leila. You've given me so much stress, since we met. You and your twin. But that's all over now.' Leila imagined the virus acting on him. At first the thought of it gave her deep satisfaction, but then she realised that it would purge his memory of all his crimes. It struck her that that would be a kind of blessing. He'd never have to come to terms with them. He might even avoid judgement for them.

'You've got to let me go,' she told him. 'I've seen the laser in the pyramid. I've seen the fallen Station. Deodatus is going to blow up our home and kill everyone on it. We have to stop him.'

'Haven't you realised?' A haunted, broken look crossed his face. 'No one can stop him. We can only try and make things as easy as we can for him. So he does the least possible damage along the way.'

'Holt, he's going to blow up Station, corrupt the Totality and take over on Earth. There is no "least possible damage". There's only rewriting or death for millions.'

Holt gave her a nervous glance. 'Oh, no. He's planning something very different.'

'Has he broken your memory too?'

'No, no. I'd know if he had. I've made very sure of that. I worry about it so much, Leila.' He paused. 'I don't think you'd ever guess what he's actually planning. It's not nearly as melodramatic as you think. I mean – when you understand, you'll see what I mean. He's a visionary, in his own way. And nobody can stand against him. We just have to go with him.' His eyes were full of pleading agony. 'There's really no choice, Leila.'

'Gods. He's really done a number on you.'

'I've seen people you wouldn't believe fall to him – like that.' There was such desperation in his voice. Leila almost felt sorry for him. She wondered how she'd have ended up, if she'd felt as alone as he seemed to. 'People I've looked up to for years. People I thought would save us. I've seen him bend a god to his will, Leila.'

'I'm not like you, Holt. I'd never work for him.'

'You don't know what he's really planning.'

'He's lied to you.'

'No. He really hasn't. You'll see when you meet him. He'll explain it all.'

'He wants to see me?' Inside herself, Leila cheered. But there was disquiet, too. If Holt was right, then she might have radically misunderstood her adversary. 'Why?'

'He sees you as a lever to help him control Dieter more efficiently. And resistance fascinates him. He finds it so hard to understand. He likes to push against it.'

'Perhaps I can push back.'

'Oh no, Leila.' Holt looked genuinely terrified for her. 'Please don't stand up to him. It'll make things so much easier for you. You'll be able to keep so much more of yourself safe. Please, just do whatever he wants you to. It's the only way to survive.'

Chapter 42

The floor was all dead flies. They lay in drifts, deeper in the angles of the room, piled up against the hard edges of tables and chairs, shallow where there were open spaces. The black chitin of their exoskeletons – stripped of their flesh cores by time – seemed to absorb the soft evening light, throwing back barely any of the purples and greens and greys that oozed into the room from the pale clouds outside. The wiring was brighter in the gloom, silver shimmers scattered across the floor, tiny components liberated from their hosts. There were miniature circuit boards too, shining out like fallen moons. Leila was profoundly relieved that she was hanging above them. There was a day left until the rock landed. She'd been unconscious for ten hours. She hung in the middle of the room, locked into full presence. She could speak and gesture, but she couldn't move anywhere. And Dieter hadn't come.

She looked over at the window. The broken maw of the fallen Station loomed above her, a darkness carved in the sky. She inspected the room. Luxury rose up from the floor's black sea. The picture window that stretched the length of one wall was framed with heavy velvet curtains, the deep red and gold that patterned them a rhyme with the sky outside. The walls were papered with a repeating black and silver design, ancient brand iconography fringed with faded writing that read as soft, bronze blurs. There were tables. Some were scattered with gilded candelabra and dark sculptures of naked men and women, tower-islands emerging from dead insect waves. Others seemed entirely functional, polished steel showing through the insect corpses. Only one of them was bare of flies – a lacquered chest at the centre of the room, as long and deep and wide as a tall man. There were long glass-sided cases piled up against the walls, to the left and right of the room's main window. In the gloom it was hard to see what they held. As the light shifted with the setting sun, fiery glints sparkled then died within them. Leila imagined stored relics, Deodatus' personal museum of conquest and achievement.

There were images, too. They hung on the room's rear wall. Leila queried the room's weave systems and was surprised to be told that there was nothing virtual about them. She glanced across at them. A dark wooden frame surrounded a couple staring out at her. The man was dressed in a dark robe, fringed with brown fur. He had a thin, aristocratic face, with a large nose. The woman who held his left hand wore an ornate green dress, its rich folds an abstract pattern that zig-zagged to the floor. Her own left hand held its fabric up over her belly. There was a bulge that made Leila think she might be pregnant. A little grey dog stood at their feet, peering curiously back at the viewer. There was a mirror on the back wall of the room they stood in, its round border bevelled like a cog. A shape peered back out of that, too.

Another image was split into three. The central panel – twice the width of the two side panels – showed a man in a white loincloth, nailed to a crossbar supported by a high, thin post. Together they made a T. Its wood was almost as dark as the winged figures that hovered behind and beyond it, black shapes weeping in an otherwise spotless sky. Four richly dressed figures clustered around the base of the post. They too wept. There was pale countryside, and in the distance a city the colour of bone. Leila imagined stepping into that landscape, passing by the crucified man and walking away from both the gods and the dead. An escape, of sorts – but her past would accompany her, and so the twin burdens of loss and duty would remain with her too. Deodatus would still live. She'd still be hoping that her brother would hear and act on the message she'd shared with him. And Cassiel would still be lost to her. She imagined the relief of letting it all slip from her memory. But she didn't think she could ever be as relaxed about losing her past as the Caretaker had been. And even he had been so strongly driven to recover the truth of himself. She sighed and returned her attention to the room, wondering when and how her adversary would manifest.

She didn't have to wait much longer. The first signs of his presence came as sunlight vanished from the world outside and the clouds lost their fierce lava glow. The long, low chest at the centre of the room lit up, fiery light chasing patterns down its side. Leila thought of the glyphs that Mandala had burned in the desert. These had a brisk efficiency to them. They seemed to represent some kind of boot-up sequence. As they ticked down, lights flicked on around the room. The display cases were waking up too. She assumed that each would hold a bric-à-brac of jewelled fripperies.

She was wrong.

Every single cabinet was occupied by an ancient, desiccated body. Leila was reminded of the workers she'd seen slaving for Deodatus. But these cadavers were far older, far more mummified than even the creatures tending to his fusion reactors. There was no flesh left, only bone and parchment skin; nothing soft to moderate the sharp, carving edges of their wasted faces and arms, their legs and hands and feet. And there was so much more ornamentation.

There were medals, dense with brand iconography, scribbled across with illegible inscriptions. Fabrics, vibrant with bright, imperishable colours, clashed brutally with the decay that surrounded them. There were wands and sceptres and ceremonial weapons, still clutched in dead hands. One held a gold feather, dripping with blue and red jewels. Another had a goblet, filled with dusty pearls. There were swords and spears, pens and orbs, stars and maces, chains and even small statues, some of animals, others of humans. There were breastplates, and shining gold and silver helmets. Jewels filled empty eye sockets and gilded teeth grinned in dead mouths. It all shone beneath the lights, a hoard dressing the dead with brilliance. It spoke of only greed, of a rapacious desire that had run out of control and scrawled itself across them all in luxury. And as Leila inspected them all, she saw that each had one single decoration in common: a triangle set into their torso, pointing up past their chests to their heads.

A hiss from the centre of the room pulled Leila's attention back to the sarcophagus. Its top split as twin doors opened. A white mist drifted out – possibly vapour from some sort of chiller unit, possibly just dust. A low, dissonant buzzing leapt into the air. Leila remembered the harmonious hum of Mandala's hives. This was something very different, the harsh, sawing rasp of a fly swarm. And then, with a high pitched whine, machinery whirred into action, thrusting the case's occupant up into a standing position. Leila was behind the sarcophagus, so as he rose he was also lost to her sight. She glimpsed a flash of jewels, a writhing of flies, a pale oval that could have been a face, and then she could only see the back of the bier that held him. It sighed to a stop. There was nothing to be seen or heard of him but buzzing.

Leila waited, tense with expectation. She wondered what he was going to do. Perhaps he would torture her. Perhaps there would be a psychoactive attack, assaulting her memory structures. Perhaps he would just try and delete her. She wondered how long her defences could stand up to an ancient god. Holt said that she fascinated him. Perhaps he'd talk. She sent a silent call out to Dieter, praying for his arrival. She reached into her skull face, requesting a readiness check. It shifted in her mind like a fish in a strong current, signalling back that it was live.

And then, a distraction – a soft succession of quiet chinking sounds, whispering into the room from all around her. At first Leila thought that Deodatus had stepped from his pedestal and turned towards her. But he remained immobile. Looking round, Leila gasped. Eyelids had shifted, exposing ancient pupils to the light. There was motion, too. Every head was turning towards the sarcophagus. Then they were still again. The sun's last brilliance died in the sky and darkness took the world outside.

At last, there was a soft creaking from the bier. Deodatus moved towards the window and placed a hand against it. All the exhibits moved their heads to follow him. His hand was gloved in gold wire and scarlet and amber jewels. There were bones visible beneath the wire, and a crawling darkness where flesh should have been. Then he spoke. Leila wasn't sure what sort of voice she'd been expecting – perhaps something harsh and commanding, perhaps something thin and wheedling, anything but this gentle buzzing. The soft corrosions of time had left the old god with hardly any breath to push his words out into the world.

'I have been watching you for so long,' he whispered, his voice a ghost on the air. 'Or rather, watching the absence that you were. Always, signs of resistance. The mind, rescued. The pyramid, penetrated. My poor brother, helping you on Station then using the last of his credit to buy an insertion mission from the powers of the air. A vacuum suit that contained a skeleton, running through the night. But I could never see you. New thing in this world that you are.'

He turned towards her. Red jewelled eyes glittered. A pale skull was wrapped in a tarnished silver net. The nose was two holes. Gold gleamed within them. Teeth were emeralds and wire. The jaw was tightly sealed to the skull by a tapestried strap. His neck and chest were a scummed rainbow of jewels and fabric. An upwards-pointing triangle sat beneath it, carved into the space above his belly. Wealth shone out of the pyramid. There was also rotten flesh and a susurrus of flies. They bustled within and beyond it. The dead god's torso was filled with black organs, shaped from insects and technology. Leila gaped. His whole being was a jewelled protest against time's consumption of life.

Dieter will come, she told herself. She wouldn't hit Deodatus yet. 'I had to try and stop you,' she said. It was hard to see him as something that could be talked with. She forced empathy on herself. 'And I can imagine how you felt. Until now you've been a mystery to me too.'

Deodatus chuckled, a soft wheezing sound rattling out of his chest. Leila imagined scores of dirtily transparent wings shaking in unison. 'I suppose I have been. A mystery to you all – except those who found and followed me. And even they barely see me. They see themselves and their own desires, and then I fulfil those desires. Then they do my bidding. Will you accept that gift from me, I wonder?' He moved. Walking was difficult for him. One hand reached for the side of a table, bracing his frail body. Chitin rustled as he shuffled towards her, his feet lost in drifts of dead flies. The exhibits' jewelled faces glittered, tracking him like camera nests. 'As so many others have done.'

Leila was terrified that he would attack her. 'It was never a gift,' she replied. She scrabbled for words that might stop him. 'You forced yourself on them. Are you going to force me to serve you now? That would prove how weak you are. That, if I could choose, I'd refuse you.'

Deodatus stopped moving. Individual tendons and muscles strained to tip his head up and back, until it moved far enough for gravity to catch. It slumped back with a lurch and he laughed. His new stance opened up his chest. It caged a fury of beating wings, shimmering for thirty or forty seconds, until at last they stilled and his head tipped forward again. The creatures in the glass cases shook too, pulsing out wheezing echoes of their master. They returned to stillness as he recovered himself.

'What are they?' Leila asked, seeking more distraction.

'My subsidiaries,' replied Deodatus dismissively. 'They chose to compete with me. And then they lost, and I took them over, one by one. Such titanic struggles! I understand that those who cared to look could even see them from Station. And I'll have four more subsidiaries once the Rose has helped me take the other gods of the Pantheon.'

'They'll be fully slaved to you?'

'They don't need freedom.' He snorted. 'Don't deserve it. Do you, I wonder?'

Leila felt vast power querying the outer recesses of her self. Protections spun up within her, prickling in her mind. Dieter would come.

'It's not about deserving it,' she replied. 'It's about being right. Don't you want to be right? Don't you want to be the only real alternative?'

'Oh, but I'm that already. You all choose me in the end. Look at your brother. He's been so helpful. All I needed to do was show him something he truly desired – and how quickly he came to me. How completely.'

Real passion lit in her, chasing out fear. 'You've butchered him. You've broken his memory. He doesn't even understand what he's lost.'

Deodatus snorted. 'Managing him, adjusting him, making him more efficient. I brought focus to him, polished his motivation. He still has the most important parts of his past. And he chose to let me work on him.'

'He chose that?' Leila was shocked.

'He knew that following me would involve sacrifices. Hard choices.' Deodatus' soft voice was nearly a whisper. 'If he didn't fully understand them – well, that's not my responsibility.'

Leila remembered how rapt Dieter used to become in new

discoveries, new pieces of technology. She could well imagine him losing himself in all that the pressure men had offered him, not really registering any potential downside, trusting in his own technical mastery to pull him out of any difficulties. She was at once saddened and infuriated by his naivety. He had always been achingly vulnerable to the carving greed of a corporate entity like Deodatus.

'I can imagine that,' she said, hating herself for having to admit it.

'Of course – if you chose to serve me, I could go easy on him. I wouldn't have to chop his past around anymore. I could restore parts of his life that he's lost. But I'd need you to help me manage him. Make sure he kept working for me.'

'And what do you think would make me fall like that?'

Deodatus was only a few feet away from her. She could feel his virtual presence, looming over her, ready to break and enter.

'Maybe just your love for him,' he mused, and Leila felt the temptation within her. 'Maybe something more. So I will find out more about you, build up your profile, understand what you value...' He reached a hand up to cup her cheek. She felt hard, cold jewels scratch her skin. The hand contracted a little and four bone fingers forced themselves against her. Their touch was uncertain and they were shaking gently. Leila sensed great physical weakness and was heartened.

But still there was no Dieter.

'Then I would have you,' continued Deodatus. 'I'll have my agents track down your weave history.' His jewel eyes flared. 'I can summon it through the Rose. She holds so much knowledge.' Disgust flooded Leila. The touch of his hand was intrusion enough. The thought of what he was suggesting was much worse. 'Then I can make you just the right offer. One you could never refuse.' He was silent for a moment. 'Like this,' he said, lifting his hand to press a fingertip against her forehead.

There was a great, effortless intrusion in her mind, and the world changed. There was no shock, no nausea, just a sudden and absolute difference. Leila was sitting in her bedroom back on Station, perched on the end of her bed in her favourite T-shirt and jammies. Through the window, the Taste Refresh Festival pulsed through the sky. A smart-but-funky little outfit lay spread across the bed, all ready to be picked up and pulled on. Leila somehow knew that she was going out that night, that she'd be with Miwa and Dave and the others, that all would be marvellous. Joy suffused her, turning to bliss when a happy sound drifted in from the kitchen – Dieter singing quietly to himself as he reheated last night's pizza in the microwave. The moment was perfect, but then – just as memory crashed in and complicated it – Deodatus appeared, sitting on the bed beside her, just where East had been.

'Oh, Leila,' he whispered. 'Such an easy dream to gift you with. A little flat. An attentive brother. Perhaps a lovely, lovely mother to care for you. Perhaps even a father, too.'

And there was temptation again, shifting like a snake within her. Leila had fantasised about escape, but always the thought of losing Dieter had brought her back to hard, difficult reality. In this dream that Deodatus offered her, he would be present.

But she ached with loss for another, now. Dieter would be with her, but Cassiel would still be gone. And if she accepted Deodatus' offer, she wouldn't just be betraying Station. She'd be walking away from every part of the mind's faith in her.

'No,' she said.

Perfection broke. A second of absence, and then they were both back on Earth.

A buzzing laugh came from Deodatus. He let his hand drop. His arm rattled as it fell. 'That was just a first attempt,' he wheezed. 'A very unsophisticated one. I'll dig deeper. I'll find the right way in.' He paused. 'Or I would if I had time. But there's none left, is there?'

'What do you mean?' Fear pulsed through Leila.

'You – the people pulling your strings – they are going to punish me, aren't they? Eradicate me? And all this, too...' His abdomen creaked as he turned, lifted his arm again and indicated the window. 'All I have built. I understand that another rock is falling towards me. Sent by my children to wipe out the last remnant of their past.'

'No – no, there's nothing like that. You've won, Deodatus.' Desperation roared in Leila's mind. 'There's nothing we can do to stop you.' She reached for the skull face. She might have to use it to break Deodatus before Dieter came. She might lose her brother for ever.

Deodatus laughed again. 'Oh, bless you. Did you think I could be killed by a stone? I invented that attack a thousand years ago. And I brought it back into your world. I told Kingdom to use it against his enemies. Saw it work for him too. For a while, at least.' Deodatus looked down. There was something defeated in his posture. 'He was the best of my children. The only one to come back to me.' He paused for a moment, lost in his own thoughts. Then his face snapped back up towards her. 'And you think I wouldn't notice you using it on me? When I have the Rose to watch you all?'

'I don't know anything about it,' lied Leila. 'I just know how scared the gods are of you. I was their last hope – and I've failed. There's nothing we can do to stop you destroying Station, nothing. You'll break it as you broke its twin.' She nodded towards the window.

This time Deodatus' laugh was almost hearty. 'DESTROY STATION?' he boomed, his voice becoming a loud, harsh rasp. A drift of flies lifted out of his body, hovering in the air around him, a black agitated cloud. 'Destroy Station?' he said again, recovering himself. Some of them settled back into him. Others veered off into the room. 'Do you really believe that? Have you understood nothing? Have your gods really forgotten why we built it?' He slumped back against the end of the table, leaning against it, both arms supporting himself. 'Or have they just not told you?' His dry face peered up at her. 'No, I really think they don't know. We tried so hard to break them, when they fled our control. I think in part we succeeded.'

'What are you talking about?' Genuine curiosity moved behind fear and disgust. Leila wondered briefly if this was the start of a more subtle seduction. She tried to sound afraid rather than intrigued. 'What do you mean?'

'My child.' His voice was almost gentle. 'Your gods – they've held you back. You've been unable to fulfil our plan for you. My plan for you.' Now there was pity in it. 'Sending you up, away from home, out into the Solar System. It wasn't going to end there.'

'But where else could we go?'

'Earth-type planets in other Solar Systems. That would have been the start. And then – who knows? Humanity is infinitely malleable. We can rebuild you for other environments. And of course, I would have come along with you. To guide you, to show you the way. A god and his people, reborn into eternity.'

'How?'

He peered closely at her, apparently genuinely curious. 'What makes you think I'm going to destroy Station?'

'The laser in the pyramid. You'll fire it up and use it to break the Spine and the Wart. Once you've done that – everything else falls apart. Station will be destroyed.'

'Oh, Leila.' He sounded almost sad. 'How can you think that? The laser's not there to destroy. It's there to create.'

A pause. Leila told herself that all she wanted to do was create more time for her brother to come. But fascination was growing within her. The past was there in front of her, revealing secrets that even the Pantheon had forgotten. An absolute passion to know more filled her, combined with an absolute forgiveness of Dieter. She understood him more fully than ever before.

'What do you mean?' she replied.

'The Wart was designed to house a single, vast fusion reaction, a black sun at the core of Station. The laser was one of several that would power it, set in each of the pyramids. Its heat would be channelled to the four generator stations you've turned into fusion reactors. Such tiny creations, compared to what could have been. And running at their full capacity, they'd have generated enough energy to bring Station's gravity drive fully online, and power its journey to the stars.'

'But Station doesn't have a gravity drive. It doesn't have anything like that.'

'Docklands is an encrustation, my child.' He was almost paternal now. The thought of his love shimmered in Leila's mind, terrifying her. 'It should never have been built. Homelands was the habitation unit. The space where Docklands sits houses the gravity generators that will create a vast external gravity well – a well that would touch the whole of Station, moving it out of its stationary orbit. And once the well exists, Station will never again be stationary. It will fall into it – and keep falling – and fall all the way to another star.'

The scale of it awed her. 'That's incredible,' she breathed.

'You see!' crowed Deodatus, and the triumphant delight in his voice was both a warning and the most human sound she'd heard from him. 'Why would I destroy the last interstellar colonisation craft that remains to mankind? I've spent seven hundred years trying to recapture it. I brought my city to the foot of the crashed Station to strip out its control systems and software, ready to reinstall them in your Station. Humanity's destiny is not local – it's interstellar. It's galactic. It's cosmic. And I have mapped it all out for you. I will rise from Earth and lead all of humanity forwards into that great future.'

Leila was profoundly shocked. 'By enslaving us all? By rewriting our memories? By overlaying squalor with the Shining City?'

'By creating hierarchy. Imposing efficiency. Making best use of scarce resources. Offering rewards that don't compromise that austerity.'

'You'd force us all to serve you. And you'd abuse us terribly.'

'The future of humanity is at stake. Hard decisions have to be taken. Sacrifices have to be made.'

'Is that what you call corrupting minds and waking an army of sleepers?'

'Oh, them.' He waved a dismissive hand. 'They ran out of motivation. They worked for me for centuries, and then slowly they started to fade. Became idle. That's why I needed your brother. Holt did well to recommend him. Dieter's given the workshy back their drive. Helped them become productive again.'

'How can they be productive? All they want to do is fuck and collect things.'

That angered Deodatus. 'That's all they really need. Acquire possessions, use each other for pleasure. And a simple, beautiful city to live in, to make them think they inhabit a simple, beautiful world. Once they're up on Station – once they've spread my swarm within it – they'll be able to stay in it for ever. And I'll have fresh minds to work for me. A hundred thousand people, waiting for that same simplicity. They'll work for me too. Sustain me. Adore me. Especially once I've returned the true past to them. The one in which the Pantheon is seen as the aberration they are.'

'Oh no,' breathed Leila. 'The Taste Refresh Festival.'

'It does make rewriting everyone to forget the gods and remember only me much easier. The Pantheon have learned much from their parents, even if they don't always quite realise it.'

Leila couldn't quite believe it. 'But how will you get into orbit? And even if you could - you'll destroy everything. Just like you've destroyed this world.'

'Oh no.' A buzzing chuckle. 'We can fly.' Leila wondered if he was insane. 'And, once we do, I'll do what I always do. I'll make the best use of scarce resources.' He stretched an arm out towards the window. 'That's not destruction. It's completion. This world isn't a wasteland. It's a resolution. An ending.' He turned back to her. 'Do you mourn a placenta? Or a seed pod? Of course not. Every ending creates a new beginning. And so I will rise up and take Station, and then the Solar System, and then populate all the empty stars with my children. And as the millennia pass we will do to the galaxy what we have done to our birthplace. Take everything that's there, make best use of it and then move on to fresh pastures. Oh, what beauty!'

'But you'll never even reach Station. How can you?'

'My child.' His voice was gentle. 'Every building out there has an anti-gravity generator. Kingdom showed me how to bolt them together, to power them with fusion reactors. To create structures that would reach orbit. When he died, I despaired. But then the Totality came and brought hope with them. They are so malleable, so close to the slaves they once were. And now, with their help and with the Rose's help, my city will rise and take Station.'

And as she listened to that soft, buzzing voice rave, Leila realised that – if the memory virus had been in her mind at that moment – she would have dropped it then. But she'd destroyed it, to remove any such temptation. Instead, she reached out to the less ferocious but also less damaging defences that love had built for her, and called the skull face into being. She couldn't wait for Dieter anymore. She couldn't let Deodatus continue, couldn't take the risk that he'd somehow break her without her even realising it was happening, that she might somehow come to help Station fall forever through eternity, consuming all it met, exponential locust growth exploding out of it in every star system it passed through.

'I'll find you,' she promised Dieter, then she unleashed herself on Deodatus.

The skull face sent a series of sense calls out to the systems powering Deodatus' eyes, and ears, and sense of touch, taste and smell, and registered the parameters they worked within. As the Caretaker had promised, it found a depth and breadth to them that it had never encountered before, making even the shark she'd so nearly attacked seem like a minnow. Deodatus' senses weren't restricted to the local. They stretched out across his city and then reached far beyond it. He saw and heard and felt events taking place hundreds, even thousands of kilometres away. The sensory nodes that received those inputs were more complex and sophisticated than anything the skull face had ever encountered before. And so they contained far greater possibilities for chaos.

Exulting, the weapon leapt to construct the most caustic and invasive sensory assault package it had ever created, an instant masterpiece of disruption. And then, pure and white and unadorned, a relic of dominance remade as a weapon to break it, the skull face appeared before Deodatus and howled at him. It calibrated the strength of its response according to Leila's fear and anger – and, at that bleak moment, both were absolute. Hijacked by the skull face, every single one of Deodatus' senses became a weapon turned against him. He heard pan-sonic assault pulses. Poison trigger tastes and scents exploded into his sensorium. Pain of every imaginable kind wrote itself across his skin. His vision filled with jagged, stuttering images, precisely calibrated to induce seizures in his mind.

And, as he was so closely tied to his city, he felt the pain not just as an assault on his body but as devastation written across square kilometres of urban space. He felt the blocks that he'd brought together at the base of the broken Station break and fall to the ground. He felt the fusion reactors that powered them run into critical and explode, hurling a sun's heat out into the world. He felt all the flies, all the humans, all the fallen minds he was linked to break beneath falling masonry then – an instant later – burn to a cinder. He felt the streets that surrounded his tower melt away as the fires leapt out and took them. And then he felt the tower itself break and fall, melting into an inferno of pain. The world became a hell of flame, woken to purge all he'd ever been from existence.

Leila felt none of this, but she knew it was happening. She watched as his defences rushed to understand the attack, then flailed and were dismissed, the skull face cutting through their tiny, provisional

312

barricades like a knife through damp paper. Then the damage reports began, snatches of text recording agony in dry, technical terms.

Leila didn't need to read them because she could see Deodatus' body shake and howl. She saw it stagger backwards, arms flailing, a shattered buzzing breaking out of its chest. She saw hands tearing skin. One of them caught its mouth, pulling off fabric and jewels. The jawbone came away with the strap that held it tight, trailing dry ligaments. The tongue – a dry, old thing – tumbled out with it. But still the chest roared on. The other hand tore at the ribcage, peeling off jewels and fabric, then skin that cracked into dust like dry parchment. The first hand had an ear off then scrabbled at the eyes, trying to protect the mind from the brilliant sound and light assaulting it. Then it reached round to the side of the face, grasped a flap of skin as if it were the edge of a mask, and pulled. A moment of frenzied effort and the jawless skull was white.

The corpse backed into the sarcophagus and sat down heavily. It ripped at the rest of itself, peeling wealth away to show skin that came off too. That did nothing to quell the scouring pain of virtual fire. The throat collapsed beneath breaking fingers. The chest's roar lost definition, becoming a chaos of white noise buzzing. One hand tore the other to pieces, then beat itself against the sarcophagus lid. Then the first of the flies went. A pale red burst of fire exploded out of its networked components like the striking of a match. Then another went, and another, as the skull face reached deep into the swarm, the final refuge of Deodatus' consciousness.

The god's chest cavity became a constellation of tiny supernovae. Small flames licked up, catching dried flesh and clothing. The head toppled from the neck. The body shook a little less now, but still Leila's skull face howled on, understanding correctly that she was facing a mortal threat and so meeting it with its equal. Even when its target toppled over backwards it didn't stop, screaming on at the broken, smouldering wreck until Leila had to reach into it and tell it to cease.

At her call it fell back into her, and she was left astonished before the dry wreckage that had once been Deodatus. She wondered how old he'd been, whether the body was the one he'd occupied for all his life or just the latest in a long line of replacements. The remains slipped from the sarcophagus. There was a soft, dry rattling as the heaped dead flies on the floor took it into themselves like a sea.

And then she was alone.

A combined sense of relief and awe pulsed through her. She had succeeded. The god was dead and she had killed him. It was impossible to imagine, and yet there it was, and there she was. She hung in the air, suspended, taking in the moment. She remembered the entities around the room. They, too, were broken. They had all fallen in on themselves, wisps of smoke rising up within their cases. She was alone in a tomb, surrounded by the bodies of those who had not lived for a thousand years or more, but who had only just been graced with death. She wanted to sob with relief. She gave way and – for a little while – was at peace.

It was only as she recovered herself that she began to feel disquiet.

She was the only living creature within the room. She had no way of moving. She queried the room's weave systems. She could look anywhere within it, but she didn't have the access codes to move beyond it. She tried to step down on to the ground and then to jump to another location within the room, but Deodatus' trap command remained in force. She could turn, look around, gesture, but she could not move. She experimented with a mail, wondering if it would find some way through and out of the room, but it just bounced back. There was no way for her to escape the room and no way for a message to get out of it.

Leila wondered if anyone could get in. She assumed not. The god's death must have triggered alerts elsewhere. But no fallen minds had come looking to see what had broken their master, no sweatheads had come searching for their god. Deodatus must have locked the room from within, so securely that nobody else could access it. Leila imagined his subjects battering away outside, trying to desperately to enter. The room was silent. It must be tremendously well sound-proofed. On one level she was very glad to be alone. She would have no way of fleeing any attackers and they would, she suspected, make her life very painful indeed. She redoubled her attempts to find a way to escape the room, even just move within it.

Then light and sound exploded around her. She spun up the skull face in case Deodatus' servants had at last managed to penetrate the room. If that had happened she would go down fighting. Perhaps she'd be able to cut through them and escape. But she was still alone. The brilliance blazed in from outside. Every single building was lit by bright white spotlights. There was a high-pitched roaring, too regular and artificial to be a storm. Leila had her systems analyse it. It was the sound of scores of fusion-powered gravity generators, massively overstretched, starting into being all at once.

'Oh no,' she breathed.

Deodatus had taken individuals and turned them into components in a machine. Even without him, it seemed that the machine still functioned. One of the tower-rings lifted into the air. Then another rose, and another, impossibly and unstoppably. A deep rumble shook the room, and Deodatus' fortress climbed with them. The fusion generators knotted into the building rings were massively over-driving their anti-gravity generators, pushing the city into the sky.

'I don't believe it,' she said to herself.

Perhaps by killing Deodatus all she'd done was clear space for a more efficient manager – the Rose, Holt, or some anonymous fallen mind – to take over the invasion. Or perhaps she'd created a mindless apocalypse, an unstoppable wave of destruction that would rewrite Station's past before collapsing into purposelessness when its programming ran out. But there was nothing to be done. She could only watch powerlessly as the dead god's city lifted itself up from the Earth, a seed thrown out from an exhausted host, ready to infect first Station, then perhaps the Solar System and even worlds beyond it with the all-consuming greed it still contained. Frustration filled her. Outside, clouds flashed past. Then there was nothing. The blue, empty sky was polluted with buildings. It darkened. They faced the sun. Deodatus' city was a black scrawl across its white brilliance, a system of control imposing itself on the sky. There was only one small, sad point of hope. She hadn't seen the fallen snowflake rise up. Cassiel's sacrifice might have succeeded. The Totality could perhaps resist Deodatus, saving themselves if not Station.

Then a shadow shimmered into being before her, becoming a man who was never quite himself.

At last, Dieter had come to find her.

Chapter 43

Dieter hung before Leila, floating in front of the window. The brilliant sun made the dead god's city a series of silhouettes – tower blocks bound together in rings, dark seeds waiting to fall into Station. They hung in the darkness like a wave, frozen in the moment before it hits the shore.

'You're here,' gasped Leila. 'Thank the gods. We've got to get out.'

'At first it was impossible to get in.' He sounded puzzled. 'I spent hours trying to get through. Then all of Deodatus' personal defences went down. It's like he's not here at all.'

Leila considered telling him that Deodatus was dead. But she wasn't quite sure how he'd react. She nodded towards the window. 'Well, I'm sure he's got other things on his mind.'

'Yeah, I guess so.'

With the sun behind him it was difficult to make out his expression. Leila was grateful that she couldn't really see him blurring through multiple versions of himself. Then he spoke again. 'Leila,' he said. There was pain and indecision in his voice. 'It's the Taste Refresh Festival just now, isn't it?'

'Oh yes. That's why we have to stop Deodatus.'

'Do you remember it? I do. The ocean in every street. The Twins in the sky, fishing for the best catch.' He looked up at her. 'From when I was young. From before Mum dying. Before she was on the drink, even.' Dieter lifted his hand to his face and rubbed his forehead. 'If that's the way that history gets corrected – well, it seems so right, doesn't it?'

Leila forced her emotions back under her control, forced herself to pause and let calm sink into her. 'It's not right to rewrite people,' she told him. She reminded herself that she was dealing with a broken fetch, an individual with a fractured past and an uncertain

316

sense of the present. 'You've got to release me. We've got to get out of here. Find a way of stopping all this.'

'I don't know if I should, Leila. I really don't know.' He sighed. 'Perhaps this was a mistake. Maybe I shouldn't have come.'

'No!' she almost shouted. Then, again, she forced herself to be gentle. 'No.' She needed him to stay, to keep talking – to give himself time to come round to her. 'Stay with me, Dieter. You were asking about the festival? It's happening right now. You've missed most of it.'

He sighed again. 'You know, it was one of the only things I enjoyed, after you died. The rest – I was just existing, not really living. All on my own. But when I could step out, and feel like I was underwater – in another world. Then, for a moment, I forgot this one.'

'You've forgotten a lot,' Leila told him.

'So you say.'

'Do you remember me being there at all?' asked Leila. 'Over the last few years?'

There was a pause. 'No. Not at all.'

Leila thought back to the pyramid, to the way her false memories of exploring it hadn't quite matched reality. 'Is there anything missing? Anything that doesn't quite hang together?'

'There are moments. Ghost moments. When there should have been someone else around.' He sighed. 'Laughter in another room. Fixing the weave rig after someone broke it. Miwa in the flat. She's one of your friends, isn't she?'

'Yes. She was there because I was,' Memory surged in Leila's mind. For a moment she forgot the frozen panorama outside. 'And the weave rig.' It had happened just after her rebirth. 'You never got round to recalibrating it for fetch viewing. And there was a new Linval Keiller drama coming out.' She smiled at the memory. 'It was your own fault. You should have sorted it out straight away.'

'It took hours to fix. Someone scrambled all the sensory settings. Turned them all to maximum and fried the whole thing.' He shook his head. 'When I ask myself who did it – I don't know, I never really brought anyone home. Especially not back then. I wouldn't have imagined – you.'

317

She smiled. 'It was. I'm sorry.'

'Was that in the memories you tried to give me?'

She nodded.

Then he said nothing.

'Dieter, why are you here? If you've come to get me out of here, we need to get a move on. We've got to find a way of stopping that lot.'

He turned to the window. 'It's pretty cool, isn't it? A lot of work to get all those sleepers going. Waking the past. And Deodatus has his digital attack cued up too.'

'We have to stop him.'

'But I want them to hit Station, Leila.' He sounded like he was trying to convince himself as much as her. 'I want to break the gods and fuck up all the people that fucked you up. I want people to forget they even existed. I want everything there to change.'

He was so close to returning to her. Tact deserted her. 'THEN WHY ARE YOU HERE?' she shouted. 'How many times do I have to tell you? Nobody screwed me up. I didn't kill myself. I'm really me, I'm not some weapon that East and the Fetch Counsellor threw together from a few scraps of memory. And you must think I really am me, otherwise you wouldn't be here. But you're just standing there, telling me how wonderful it is that you've unleashed an undead horde on Station.' She took a breath. 'Sort. It. Out. Dieter.'

'Well, you certainly sound like Leila.' There was something approaching a smile in his voice. 'I haven't been yelled at like that for a while.'

She controlled herself again, forcing down her anger. She remembered another time she'd yelled at him. 'Yeah, the last time was the tuna salad sandwich incident. Do you remember that?'

'No.'

'Lucky for you. I'm almost as pissed off with you as I was then. Letting it drop down behind the sofa and then going away for the weekend. The smell of it!'

'Yeah, I can see how that would piss you off.' Another moment of silence. 'And Deodatus deleted that?'

She nodded.

'Maybe I should thank him,' he said ruefully. He pulled the pendant out of his pocket. 'I've been looking at this. The recent bits – they're so different from the shape of me now. This is the real me?'

'It's the shape of your memories from before you died. Before Deodatus took you and edited you. You haven't been yourself. You've been working for the bad guys.'

'I so want you to be you, Leila. I so want you to be alive. I've missed you so much.' He held up the pendant. 'But how can I know you're really you?'

Leila relaxed a little. 'You've just got to ask yourself who you really trust. Me. Or Holt and Deodatus. Your sister, or a slimy little perv and his boss the blinged-up corpse.'

'But what if the gods made you, too? What if you're just another manipulation?'

'Dammit, Dieter, I'm the only one not manipulating you!' She remembered her conversations with Holt and Deodatus. 'You're just a tool to the rest of them. Look, I've got some memories here…'

He put his hands up. 'Oh no, not again.'

'I'm not trying to kill you, Dieter.' A moment as she wondered whether she could risk a little dig at him. 'Though I would actually quite like to just now.'

A flicker of a smile. 'Yeah, well, thanks. That's really helping.'

'I'm sorry. Look, you know what I mean. And here you are.' A tiny blue ball popped into being between them. 'Pure memories. Scan them, you can see there's no threat. Me talking to Holt, me talking to Deodatus. And both of them going on about how they've been using you.'

A moment's pause.

'I'm not going to force them on you,' Leila told him. 'But you really should watch them.'

Dieter reached out cautiously and took the globe in his hand. 'These are just memories?'

'From the last few hours.'

His hand closed round it. 'Seems safe,' he said. He took the globe and popped it into his mouth. A second as the memories meshed with his, then he looked profoundly shocked and said: 'Motherfucker.'

'You see? This is what I've been trying to tell you the whole time. Those bastards are using you.'

'Gods. I think you're actually telling the truth.'

'There's no "think" about it. Bloody hell, Dieter, I may just be your little sister, but I am actually right sometimes. And this is one of those times.'

'We should talk to Deodatus.' He looked around. 'Where is he?'

'Er, yeah. I kind of killed him.' It slipped out without her really thinking about it.

'You did what?'

'Fried him.'

'How?' Dieter was staggered. 'He's over a thousand years old. And he's a god.'

'With the skull face.'

'Ah...' A look of concentration. 'Actually, I can see how that would work. Cool...' Then, a little more seriously: 'He was a piece of history, Leila. You could have just knocked him out.'

'Yeah, well, there you go. That's what you get if you come between me and my big brother.'

Dieter was on her before she even saw him move, wrapping himself around her in the strongest hug she'd ever had from him. 'I'm so glad you're you, Leila,' he said into her neck, his voice slightly muffled. 'I've missed you so much. I'm so glad you're back.'

A moment of surprise, then she was hugging him back, fiercely. Time dissolved. She held him in the present, remembered him in the past and was so confident that they'd move into the future together. She'd lost Cassiel and she ached for her, but she'd found Dieter again. For an instant, that was all that mattered.

A minute or so, and they were standing apart again. He handed her the pendant. 'You'd better have this back,' he told her.

'Thank you.' She dropped it over her head, enjoying the return of its reassuring weight.

'So, what now?' Dieter said.

'You're asking me?' replied Leila, surprised. 'You'd normally just tell me what to do.'

He smiled ruefully. 'Yeah. Then you'd tell me why I was wrong and come up with something better. I figured I'd just cut to the chase. After all, you have just killed a god and rescued me.'

She smiled. 'Well, the first thing to do is get back to Station.

We'll tell East and Lei where we're at.' Joy and relief mingled with deep, aching loss. 'And we need to confirm that Cassiel has stopped the fallen minds.'

'Who are Lei and Cassiel?'

'Lei's a copy of me. Dit created her. A pressure man rewrote her memory so she thinks you abandoned her when she was a kid. She's got all the Deodatus money. She's bought an asteroid and thrown it at the location of his city on Earth.'

Dieter looked a bit boggled. 'I see,' he said uncertainly. 'What about Cassiel?'

'She is – was – a Totality mind. A close friend. She'd want us to stop the asteroid, too.' Leila couldn't bring herself to say anything else about her. She remembered Cassiel's advice. 'Too much perspective,' she whispered to herself. She forced herself to focus on the practical. 'Let's go save the future from the past.'

Chapter 44

Each wave broke hard against the beach, climbing it and then withdrawing with a roar – and then another would follow it, and then another. Leila watched a large one roll in, a long, sharp crest of water that even as it grew had started to fall in on itself, spray leaping out of its in-curling peak. It fell as it hit the shore, breaking forwards to become white spume rolling up across the sand. It spent the last seconds of its life pushing hard to enter another world, but failing, and then at last disappeared back into the ocean.

There was a low peal of thunder from above. The sky flickered with electric life. Lightning crawled across the underside of dense, dark clouds. It flickered within them too, possessing them with light. Deodatus was dead and so his invasion was stillborn, but the forces in the pyramid were untouched and – cornered and hopeless – were engaged in a suicidally aggressive defence. East had activated her army of gun kiddies against its occupants. Her hackers had already shut them out of the gravity drives that lay beneath Docklands, preserving it from instant destruction. Now foot soldiers were moving into the pyramid and the complex beneath it. The sky reflected the digital side of the battle.

The Twins had deactivated the Taste Refresh Festival and the Rose was out of action. Grey had locked up her senior management systems with an aggressive takeover bid, forcing them to focus exclusively on elaborate defence manoeuvres. Then East hit every single InSec member with a media blast describing the situation. The uncorrupted majority moved instantly against their colleagues. Most were quickly captured. Some resisted fiercely. Holt was dead, although in the confusion it was unclear whether he'd been killed or taken his own life. The Fetch Counsellor had taken steps to isolate his weaveself, deep in the Memory Seas. The gun kiddies were helping manage the InSec situation too, supporting the Rose's uncorrupted agents in combat. They were also running patrols through Docklands and Homelands, maintaining the rule of law while InSec purged itself.

Totality minds were in action everywhere. Cassiel had been largely successful. The infection had been isolated and contained, ensuring both the security and efficacy of her people. Snowflakes surrounded Deodatus' space-borne city. They were also preparing to intercept and destroy the rock that Lei and East had thrown at its Earthly location. As much as possible would be preserved. The Solar System's history was not just safe – it was going to be very substantially augmented. 'The attack city and the fallen Station are memories too,' declared a senior Totality diplomat. 'We will safeguard them.'

None of that was Leila's problem anymore. Once she was sure that she and Dieter had done all that they could to guarantee victory, they left the battle behind and came down to the Coffin Drives and the shores of the memory seas. A great emptiness lay on the city of the dead. Most fetches were up in Station, helping where they could, thrilled by the new respect they found there. East had made it very clear that a fetch had been instrumental in saving Station from Deodatus. Leila and Dieter travelled to the shores of the memory seas, where they settled down in a small wooden beach hut, one of the Fetch Counsellor's refuges. When Dit arrived, Leila left the two different aspects of her brother to talk. Wondering how they were getting on, she looked back up the beach towards the hut. They hadn't emerged yet.

The soft crunch of feet walking through sand alerted Leila to someone else approaching her. She turned, expecting to see a stranger possessed by familiar night-black eyes. But it wasn't the Fetch Counsellor. Instead, her own face looked back at her.

'Hello, Lei,' she said. 'I didn't expect to see you here.'

'I've done my bit up top,' Lei told her. 'Released funds to the gun kiddies. Bought out some of the Rose's subsidiaries on behalf of Grey. Now they're under him he can drop his own management systems on to them. Start rebuilding her.' She was trying to sound confident, but Leila sensed sadness too. 'Recorded an interview with East explaining the situation to everyone. And then I realised there was nothing more for me to do. So I thought I'd come down here. See how our boys are doing.'

'Is she letting people know about the other Station on Earth? About what our Station really is?'

'Not yet. She thinks it'd be a bit much for people to take in. On top of everything else.' She paused. 'I'm certainly finding it hard to get to grips with.'

Leila smiled. 'You won't hear me say this very often, but East might actually have a point there. And how's the battle going?'

'We can't lose. Thanks to you, Dieter and Cassiel.'

Leila hadn't expected to hear Cassiel's name, hadn't been ready for the sadness it would release in her. The mind now only existed in memory. Loss pulsed in Leila.

'I am sorry,' said Lei. After a moment, she put a hand out and touched Leila's arm. There was something very awkward about the gesture. It struck Leila that Lei must have very little experience of closeness. There was very little in her past to show her how it worked.

'Thank you,' said Leila. 'That means a lot.'

'So have they decided?' asked Lei. Leila let her change the subject, skating back into a subject she was more comfortable with. 'Are they both sticking around? Or will there be just one of them to deal with?'

'They've agreed. They're going to go into the sea together. And then – well, someone a lot more like the real Dieter will come out.'

'Your real Dieter. Not mine,' Lei shot back angrily. 'My past isn't real.' Then, almost immediately, she said: 'I'm sorry. That's not fair…'

'No. You're quite right. He won't be your Dieter. Or any of our friends'.' Leila smiled sadly. 'I hope he'll be the better for it.'

'Look,' said Leila. 'They're coming out.'

First Dieter, then Dit, stepped out of the small cabin. Dieter's decay had progressed. He was little more than a scribble. Dit looked well defined next to him. They moved towards the two women. A third figure followed them out, then hung back – a young boy with dark eyes, dressed only in a pair of red bathing trunks.

'Well, here we are,' said Dieter. A new version of Leila's pendant hung round his blurred, uncertain neck. He fingered it nervously. Thunder rumbled over his words. He looked up, suddenly worried.

'We're winning,' Lei told him. 'And I hate to say it – but it's all thanks to you.'

'Oh. Good.' Dieter smiled nervously. 'I'm glad. Really.' He looked round at Dit, gestured to him to come closer. Dit came to him and took his hand. 'I know it's hard to believe. After everything I did.'

'You weren't yourself,' Lei told him. 'I know how that feels, at least.'

The thunder died away. The waves roared on, always changing, always the same.

'It is good, Dieter,' said Leila. She stood on tiptoe to kiss him. 'I'm so glad.' Lei didn't move. 'Are you ready?' asked Leila.

'The Counsellor's been explaining it to us,' Dieter told her. 'We just walk in together – and let the water rise above our heads – and let the currents take us – and the sea and our fetch code will do the rest.'

'It sounds so easy!' chipped in Dit. 'I'm so pleased I can help with it. And Leila, it's good to see you. Dieter tells me I helped you, too. I'm very glad about that.' His words shone with confident love, a strong contrast with Dieter's more nervous tone.

'You did. Thank you,' said Leila.

'And now there are two of you, too!' continued Dit. 'Remarkable. Are you going to come into the sea with us?'

'No,' said Leila and Lei together, both equally firmly.

'Suit yourselves.' He reached out and hugged Leila. Lei stepped back. Dit noticed, shrugged, then turned back to Dieter. 'Come on, let's go,' he said cheerfully, putting an arm round his double's unfocused shoulders. 'Bet the water's lovely, this time of year.' He put a little pressure on him. Dieter turned with him, and together they started off towards the surf. 'We'll see you in a bit,' Dit said cheerily over his shoulder. 'Be a bit harder to tell us apart!'

'Goodbye,' called Leila. Lei said nothing. Leila glanced at her. A bolt of emotion flickered across her copy's face and then was gone. She looked towards the sea and saw that Dit and Dieter had stopped by the shoreline. They were facing each other. Dieter had his hands up on Dit's shoulders. Leila imagined him asking one last time if he was sure about going through with it.

'Should I go to them?' asked Leila.

'No,' said the Fetch Counsellor, as he appeared next to her. 'I think they'll sort it out.'

A moment's wait proved him right. Dit took Dieter's hand, hugged him and turned towards the sea. They walked slowly in, each wave crashing a little higher against them as the shore dropped away and became sea floor. As they went deeper, the waves lifted them up, making them bobbing heads on the grey green surge. They kept going, the water deepening with them. Dit stopped, waited for a trough then dived forward into the next wave, his straight body all determination. He didn't surface again. Dieter paused for a moment, then turned back and waved, before diving forwards and irrevocably entering the sea.

Leila turned to the Fetch Counsellor. 'I should be thanking you, I suppose,' she said. 'For helping us all along the way.' She let anger and sadness into her voice. 'I can't bring myself to.'

'The memory virus?' replied the Fetch Counsellor. 'You still disagree with it?'

'I always disagreed with it,' replied Leila. 'You pretended to be so kind. So thoughtful. And behind it all you're using a weapon like that. How can I trust you? How can any of us?'

Eyes that were beyond age looked out of an innocent face. 'You can trust me to protect you all,' he said. 'To take hard decisions on the Fetch Communion's behalf.'

'I want to trust you to do the right thing,' she replied. 'To be better than the Pantheon. To not hide the truth from us.'

'Your brother made the virus.'

'I'll be having words with him about that. Besides, you took the code to him. You asked him to adapt it. He'd never have created it without you.'

'Do you have a right to criticise? You rejected us.'

'Even if I'd stayed with you, I wouldn't have known about it. Does any fetch? Did you give any of us a real choice?'

He looked down. 'But you're all safe.' He paused, then corrected himself. 'We're all safe.'

'I don't want to be safe on those terms. I think a lot of us won't.'

He turned to look out to sea. The waves pounded in – the sea never resting, the shore never changing. 'I'm a new god of a new people,' he told her, his voice so quiet that it was barely audible above the ocean's roar. 'A very fragile people. I took our weakness and made it a strength. It was all I could do.'

Leila remembered what it had been to face Deodatus alone. 'I know about fear. But you mustn't let it control you.' She thought of Cassiel. 'There's always another way. A better way. A kinder way.'

'Sentimental crap,' muttered Lei.

'Maybe you're right, Leila,' said the Counsellor. More silence, hushed by the waves, and then he asked: 'Will you come back to us, now all this is done?'

Leila remembered East's assessment of the Counsellor's motives. 'To be a figurehead for the Fetch Communion? To remind people of how a fetch saved Station and gave it a new past?' She'd already refused to have anything to do with East's transmedia celebration of her achievements. 'No.'

The Counsellor sighed. 'Nothing like that, Leila. To live, on your own terms. Wherever, however you'd like.'

She looked at him properly for the first time. 'Do you really mean that?'

He nodded.

'I don't know where I feel at home now.' A pause. 'I want to be on my own, for a bit. I want to see Dieter. Apart from that, I don't know.' She thought for a moment. 'I couldn't live in the Coffin Drives unless I felt you were being open. With all of us. I don't want to go to the Totality.' Sadness pulsed through her. 'I need a little time before I can do that.' A thought occurred to her and she smiled to herself. 'I might go and stay with the Caretaker for a while. He's the only god I've met who really understands freedom.'

The Fetch Counsellor stood up. She thought he was just going to turn away and leave. She was surprised when he moved round to stand in front of her. He took her hands in his and looked up at her.

'You've accomplished great things,' he said. 'You've rescued us from a broken past and shown us all our true one. And you've made sure our present and our future belong to us. Thank you.'

Then he was walking up the beach behind them, his small footsteps crunching quietly into silence. Then there was just the sea and the shore and the two of them. The waves crashed on. The storm clouds clamoured, unreachably far above. Leila was surprised to find herself crying. Lei reached up with a finger and took a tear from her double's cheek.

'Cassiel's dead,' said Leila. 'And Dieter's dead too. I brought him back, and he'll be reborn, but he's still dead. He died too soon. On someone else's terms.'

'You really love him, don't you?'

'Yes,' replied Leila, her voice catching on even that small word.

'I can't understand that.' Lei's voice was barely audible over the sea and the wind. 'I just can't.'

Leila remembered sharing memories with Cassiel. 'I can show you our life together,' she said. 'Copy memories across. Directly into your mind.'

'No,' snapped Lei. 'No.' Then, more gently: 'That would change me too quickly.' She met Leila's eye. 'When I'm with you – I feel temporary. Fragile.' She spoke quickly, as if it was an effort to admit her feelings.

'What do you mean?' asked Leila. 'You've done such an amazing job. Managing things up here. Dealing with East.'

Lei gave a quick smile. 'I'm even going to front that show of hers for you. Tell the story of everything you've done.' But then the sadness returned. 'You're the one hundred per cent version. Me – I'm the woman a pressure man made. By stripping something away. You're whole. I'm not.'

Leila shook her head. 'You're your own person, Lei. That makes you whole.' She smiled. 'If you weren't, we'd be going into the sea together, like Dieter and Dit did. The memories are there for you, if you want them.'

'I don't want to learn about him like that.' She looked out to sea. 'Him or Ambrose. When they come out again – when we greet them – I don't want to just have your memories cut and pasted into my head. That would change me too quickly. I want to get to know them in my own way, build up my own understanding of them. At my own speed. Like we're all going to do with our new history.' She glanced at Leila. 'Do you understand?'

Leila nodded. She thought of Deodatus, of how he'd tried to

force new pasts on his victims. And she remembered Dieter, who'd only come back to her when she'd left him to choose to engage with his past. 'I think I do,' she said. 'Shall we start here? Or we can go back to the cabin. If you'd prefer.'

'The sand's dry enough. And we'll be on the beach for a while. Might as well enjoy it.' Lei squatted, then sat, settling herself down. Leila followed, feeling the soft beach welcome her. Lei was silent as Leila made herself comfortable, looking out to sea again. She held the pendant for a moment, remembering her brother, looking forward to his return. Then she turned to Lei.

'So,' she said, 'where should I start?'

ACKNOWLEDGEMENTS

Waking Hell is very much a continuation of *Crashing Heaven*. So, first of all, many thanks again to everyone I thanked back when *Crashing Heaven* first launched.

As I began writing *Waking Hell* we left London behind and moved to Brighton. A deep thank you to all our old and new friends down here for making a new town feel immensely welcoming – it would have been much more difficult going back to work in imaginary places every day without having such a lovely real one to come back to.

And while I've been writing this book, *Crashing Heaven*'s been making its way into the world. I've felt like a proud parent watching a first born child leave home. I'm very grateful to all at Gollancz, Conville & Walsh and beyond for everything they've done to help it on its way.

Now *Waking Hell*'s heading out there too! That would have been so much harder without so many people. First of all, thank you to all at the Milford SF Writers Workshop 2014 for some very practical critiques of an earlier draft of the opening chapters. Deepest thanks to my estimable editors Marcus Gipps and Rachel Winterbottom, who helped me pull it all into its final shape, and Simon Spanton, who was there right at the very beginning. And, of course, as ever I'm hugely grateful to Sue Armstrong, my wonderful agent, whose professional and creative help and support has been invaluable at every stage.

Finally, thank you to my family, who make it all worthwhile. And I don't have enough words to thank my wife Heather Lindsley, who travelled with me all the way through every version of *Waking Hell* and made sure that none of its demons ever overwhelmed me.

ALEX LAMB

Roboteer

*A fast-paced, gritty, space-opera based on cutting
edge science, perfect for fans of Peter F Hamilton
and Alastair Reynolds*

The starship *Ariel* is on a mission of the utmost
secrecy, upon which the fate of thousands of lives
depend. Though the ship is a mile long, its six crew are
crammed into a space barely large enough for them to
stand. Five are officers, geniuses in their field.
The other is Will Kuno-Monet, the man responsible
for single-handedly running a ship comprised of the
most dangerous and delicate technology that
mankind has ever devised.

He is the Roboteer.

• • •

'**Lamb shares Hamilton's ability to sustain a
breakneck narrative where you always want
to rush ahead and see what happens next.
hugely promising**' SFX

'Lamb's got so many ideas that they almost
spill off the pages, and telling the story from
both sides is a smart way of balancing the
argument' *Sci-Fi Now*

'**Alex Lamb has crafted a terrific debut
novel. If the subsequent volumes are as
good as this one then Lamb will surely be prominent in
many an SF fan's bookcase**' *Starburst Magazine*

'*Roboteer* hits the ground running . . . Lamb handles the
politics without resorting to info dumps and in Will has
created a sympathetic and well-rounded hero' *The Guardian*

TOM TONER

The Promise of the Child

IT IS THE 147th CENTURY.

In a lonely Mediterranean cove lives Lycaste, a lovesick recluse.

In the Vaulted Lands of the Amaranthine Firmament, the Perennials play host to a contender for the Immortal throne: Aaron the Long-Life, the Pretender.

In the barbarous hominid kingdoms of the Prism Investiture, where all life is cheap, an invention is born that will become the Firmament's most closely-guarded and coveted secret.

• • •

'To call The Promise of the Child one of the most accomplished debuts of 2015 so far is to understate its weight-instead, let me moot that is among the most significant works of science fiction released in recent years' *TOR.COM*

'This is the purest example of space opera we've seen in some time, thoroughly blurring the line between science fiction and fantasy. Challenging, ambitious, rewarding . . . it's impossible not to admire Toner's wild imagination and carefully constructed world. This thing is bonkers, no question. It's also one helluva debut' *BarnesandNoble.com*

'Marvellous . . . a space opera of surpassing gracefulness, depth, complexity, and well, all-round weirdness' *Locus*

'One of the most ambitious and epic-scale pieces of worldbuilding I've read . . . Utterly absorbing; a tremendous adventure' Karl Schroeder, author of *Ventus*